W9-AMB-245

ns Dry

Black Caucus o   015 Honor Book for Fiction

O, The Oprah Magazine 10 Titles to Pick Up Now

Booklist Starred Review

"A sweeping epic that spans generations and cultures, encompassing a woman's love for a man and a mother's love for her children. It's also a love letter to Trinidad. . . . The narrative draws readers into the characters' love, grit, and determination." —*The Baltimore Sun*

"Marcia's story, told lovingly in this, Francis-Sharma's debut novel, is as universally touching as it is original." —*The New York Times*

"A savory, sensuous, and seductive debut novel steeped in the full and pungent flavor of life on the island." —*Elle*

"Haunting, emotion-laden scenes are rich with secrets and revelations. There is much to discover about this family and its matriarch. And there is much to discover about her homeland and its residents. But, most of all, there is much to discover about secrets that require sacrifice and the fight for survival. Lauren Francis-Sharma's talent shines with this rich, solid debut. Book club recommend." —*USA Today*

"A remarkably accomplished first-time novelist . . . Francis-Sharma's spellbinding, intimately detailed, psychologically lush, and suspenseful tale of racial and sexual trauma, hard work, love, and family devotion makes personal the injustice people endured in the years leading up to the civil rights movement in both multicultural Trinidad and segregated America." —*Booklist* (starred review)

"You'll hear the calypso music in this vivid debut about a spirited seamstress and devoted mother with a family secret." —*People*

"A saga ripe with heartbreak and joy . . . Francis-Sharma delivers a rich and satisfying debut on the ties of family, love, and culture."

—*Kirkus Reviews*

"Love dominates every aspect of this debut novel. . . . But Francis-Sharma's greatest strength is the way she brings to life her family's native Trinidad, an island 'rich with calypso and carnival.'"

—*More*

"Francis-Sharma's debut draws you in, and the feelings it evokes stay with you long after you put it down."

—*Bookreporter*

"Infused with the sounds, scents, and spells of Trinidad, this debut novel is an artfully spun love story, a multilayered coming-of-age tale, a treatise on devotion, ambition, survival, and a mother's love. Read it, weep—and rejoice."

—*Family Circle*

"This expansive first novel opens in Trinidad in 1943, when a fiery sixteen-year-old becomes involved with a seductive but unreliable police officer; their relationship sets off a chain of events that brings a family's dirty laundry into public view."

—*O, The Oprah Magazine*

"Lauren Francis-Sharma turns the family drama on its ear with this lush, elegant epic. The writer, a former attorney, can at last rest her briefcase—she has presented all the evidence she is a voice that should be around for some time."

—*Essence*

"Francis-Sharma's breathtaking debut . . . is as stunning as the art-work on the cover. She creates a heroine in Garcia that readers will root for—and remember fondly. This story of one woman's journey of womanhood and discernment is not to be missed."

—*The Network Journal*

"Francis-Sharma is blasting onto the literary scene with an exquisitely written story set in 1940s Trinidad. You can almost smell the salt water around the main character, sixteen-year-old Marcia, as she struggles to get by as a seamstress and caretaker to two children. . . . The author's incredible talents make her more than one to watch. She's one to find." —*Juicy*

"The thin threads of the little [Francis-Sharma] knew of her grand-mother's life [are] woven into *'Til the Well Runs Dry*. . . . The calypso music that echoed through her grandmother's apartment and the tra-ditional Caribbean food and drink, such as sorrel and roast bake, a flatbread dripping with butter, that her grandmother often made . . . But beneath all of that Carnival flair and celebration are stories and sometimes secrets. . . . The notes she receives from other West Indi-ans who have read her book include messages such as 'My mother didn't tell us either.'" —*The Washington Post*

"Francis-Sharma tells the story of a young Trinidadian woman who finds love in an unlikely suitor. As the couple goes through courtship and eventually enters a serious relationship, secrets are unveiled and transgressions arise, all working to sever their seemingly unbreakable tie." —*Ebony* (Spring Must-Reads: Editor's Picks)

"A multigenerational saga that has already earned loads of acclaim for its heartfelt, poetic approach to storytelling. Focusing on the life and love of Marcia Garcia, a sixteen-year-old girl living in a village in north Trinidad, the story weaves a complicated tale that should leave readers wanting more." —*Upscale*

"In her historically fictional world-crafting, U.S.-based Trinidadian Lauren Francis-Sharma shows how commendably she can straddle a pastiche of emotional felicity and societally induced fissures. . . . Following in the tradition of novels that seek to carve identity niches amid a tumult of shifting values, strange continents, and uncertain fortunes, Francis-Sharma's players assail daunting odds, torn between states of hope and despair, of home and uncomfortable exile."

—*Caribbean Beat*

"Stretching all the way from a tiny seaside village in Trinidad to the shores of America, this multigenerational saga blends issues of class, race, and gender with notions of love, deception, and the power of decision."

—*Uptown*

"An irresistible read . . . Francis-Sharma proves herself a gifted storyteller."

—*Bustle*

"The islands are calling you this summer. . . . Because author Lauren Francis-Sharma (herself the child of Trinidadian immigrants) writes with her characters' natural patois, we get a definite sense of place and time for this story. After a while, it can seem almost as if you actually hear their voices, which makes them come alive. . . . The perfect getaway read, even if you don't really go anywhere but in your mind."

—*The Philadelphia Tribune*

"A richly woven tale about family, love, and sacrifice . . . Francis-Sharma deftly tells this story with grace and confidence. . . . A thought-provoking novel that would make for a good book club selection."

—*Clutch*

"Lawyer turned author Lauren Francis-Sharma bursts through the curtains, making a stunning debut with a page-turner, flavored with everything that makes a Caribbean 'cook-up' the tasty concoction that leaves you wanting for more. . . . This book takes you on a roller-coaster ride from the north coast of Trinidad to the Maryland suburbs, Flatbush Avenue in Brooklyn all the way to Manhattan's east side. . . . You can taste the food that is being cooked, you can smell the greenery of the lush tropical setting. . . . Lauren leaves you on the edge of your seat at the turn of every page." —*Profiles 98*

"From a New York City–born daughter of Trinidadian immigrants, a debut novel set on the latter island. Francis-Sharma's story begins in a seaside village in the north of Trinidad in 1943, where sixteen-year-old smart-aleck seamstress Marcia Garcia is raising two small boys and hiding a secret. Everything changes when the boys disappear, she meets a young cop, and they fall madly in love. Along the way she moves to New York, encountering new risks and rewards." —*New York Post* (This Week's Must-Read Books)

"Like the best poetry, it has all the high notes: a beautiful girl, a spell that leads to love and death, and a terrible secret—in language pierced with the cries and colors of the West Indies. But this is not just a story; it's the author's retelling of her own origins. Sweet, brutal, and unsparing, this is Lauren Francis-Sharma's first book, yet she commands the page." —Jacquelyn Mitchard, author of the #1 *New York Times* bestseller *The Deep End of the Ocean*

"A story of love, loss, and triumph set in a world of secrets and moral consequence. Like the obeah woman in her story, Lauren Francis-Sharma has cast a spell that refuses to release me. I won't forget this story or the voice of this wonderful new writer any time soon." —Brunonia Barry, author of the *New York Times* bestseller *The Lace Reader*

"[A] sparkling debut . . . The story was inspired by Francis-Sharma's desire to know more about her family's roots in Trinidad, and their immigration to New York; she effectively evokes that longing to belong, to live a good life, both in the tiny villages in sunny, colorful Trinidad, and in the bustling yet impersonal cacophony of New York." —*Historical Novel Society*

"I devoured *'Til the Well Runs Dry* in three short nights. I couldn't wait to get back to the stories and the characters who I almost didn't want to be fiction, because I cared so much about their ever-after. I found Lauren Francis-Sharma's world, so familiar to me, a place with hidden corners hiding deep secrets I couldn't wait to unravel and then to have my breath pause as they revealed themselves in ways I couldn't imagine. Her story might be about a girl from Blanchisseuse, but above that it is an extraordinary story about a misunderstood girl who knows how to stand her ground."

—Victoria Brown, author of *Minding Ben*

"With an intense voice, Lauren Francis-Sharma draws us into old Trinidad, weaving a classic immigrant's tale, punctuated with the heady scents and rhythms of a bygone time, carrying us to the new world."   —Cheryl Lu-Lien Tan, author of *A Tiger in the Kitchen*

"Lauren Francis-Sharma's debut novel, *'Til the Well Runs Dry*, illuminates a complex and beautiful Trinidad. . . . At the heart of *'Til the Well Runs Dry* is Marcia Garcia's delightful, eccentric story of several decades, several children, much resilience, many secrets, romance, and harrowing immigration. In *'Til the Well Runs Dry*, Lauren Francis-Sharma has gone looking for her own personal history and has written as well an important narrative celebrating the African and South Asian people who created Caribbean culture."

—Breena Clarke, bestselling author of
River, Cross My Heart and *Angels Make Their Hope Here*

"Lauren Francis-Sharma has expertly stitched a vibrant, kaleidoscopic garment, rich with mother-love, spiced curry, frenzied passion, bitter teas, and obeah magic. Its scent slips under your skin, is breathed into your lungs, until, in a rush of blood, it reaches your heart. I was gently guided, then yanked into the lush, dangerous world of old Trinidad, turning and spinning—crashing through doorways, con-

fronted by sinister lies, bone-crushing loss, opulence, poverty, despair, and ultimately triumph. Taken through the salt air and red roads of Blanchisseuse to New York streets—being surprised again and again—*'Til the Well Runs Dry* reveals delicately woven yet explosive truths that, in understanding, allow us to see the world differently."   —Cynthia Bond, author of the
New York Times bestselling novel *Ruby*

"A first novel, yes. But balanced with experiences, imagery, and characters that linger on the flesh. Eyes. In the heart. And as I read the last paragraph and closed the book, I knew that I had experienced an amazing journey of light. Thank you my dear sister for this wonderful book."   —Sonia Sanchez, poet and writer

"Lauren Francis-Sharma is a true storyteller. *'Til the Well Runs Dry* burns through its telling like the best gossip, but has the controlled mystery of a fairy tale. This narrative is surprising, winding, and always gratifying."   —Tiphanie Yanique, author of
Land of Love and Drowning

"Lauren Francis-Sharma takes us to the island of Trinidad, the 'land of the hummingbird,' in a story that feels like a song, with a chorus of voices across generations, revealing a culture as vibrant and enriching as it is overlooked by those on the mainland."
—Henry Louis Gates, Jr., Alphonse Fletcher
University Professor, Harvard University

"I was swept away by this thunderous, witty, and deeply soulful novel about family, Trinidad, secrets, porch sitters, dirt roads, and passion. And so satisfying, like the first time I read my aunt's novel, *Their Eyes Were Watching God*."   —Lucy Anne Hurston

'Til the Well Runs Dry

a novel

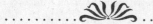

Lauren Francis-Sharma

PICADOR   HENRY HOLT AND COMPANY   NEW YORK

'TIL THE WELL RUNS DRY. Copyright © 2014 by Lauren Francis-Sharma. All rights reserved. Printed in the United States of America. For information, address Picador, 175 Fifth Avenue, New York, N.Y. 10010.

www.picadorusa.com
www.twitter.com/picadorusa • www.facebook.com/picadorusa
picadorbookroom.tumblr.com

Picador® is a U.S. registered trademark and is used by Henry Holt and Company under license from Pan Books Limited.

For book club information, please visit www.facebook.com/picadorbookclub or e-mail marketing@picadorusa.com.

Designed by Kelly S. Too

The Library of Congress has cataloged the Henry Holt hardcover edition as follows:

Francis-Sharma, Lauren.
    'Til the well runs dry : a novel / Lauren Francis-Sharma.—First edition.
        p. cm.
    ISBN 978-0-8050-9803-7 (hardcover)
    ISBN 978-0-8050-9804-4 (e-book)
    1. Women—Trinidad and Tobago—Trinidad—Fiction.   2. Families—Trinidad and Tobago—Trinidad—Fiction.   3. Trinidad and Tobago—Trinidad—Fiction.
    I. Title.
    PS3606.R3658T55 2014
    813'.6—dc23

                                                                2013021371

Picador Paperback ISBN 978-1-250-07467-6

Our books may be purchased in bulk for promotional, educational, or business use. Please contact your local bookseller or the Macmillan Corporate and Premium Sales Department at (800) 221-7945, extension 5442, or by e-mail at MacmillanSpecialMarkets@macmillan.com.

First published by Henry Holt and Company, LLC

First Picador Edition: September 2015

10   9   8   7   6   5   4   3   2   1

For Sage and Ava, together, my heart and my soul.

And for Jane DeGannes. This is my tribute to you.

Our hearts break not
Though they are ever broken,
A froth of laughter
Tops our sea of sorrows

Light flickers on horizons;
Our souls like sunflowers
Turn toward the dawning:
Our hope begins its orisons.

—Eric Merton Roach,
"The Flowering Rock"

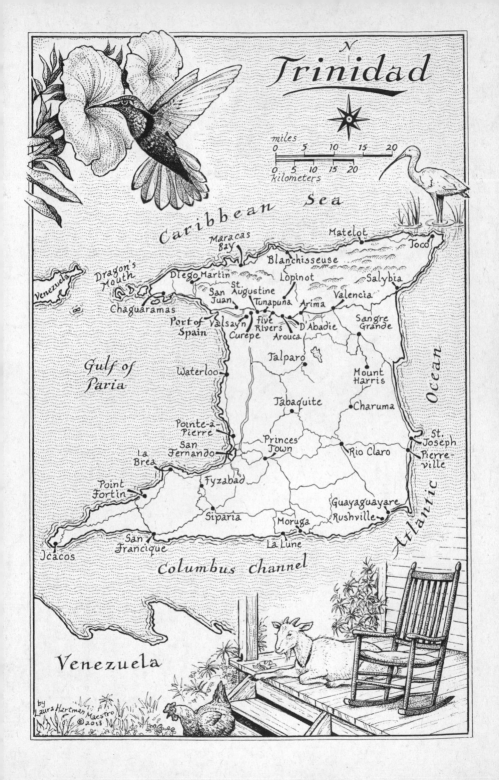

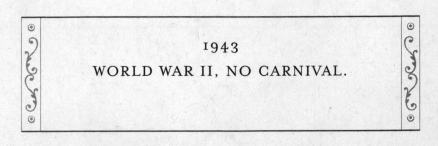

1943
WORLD WAR II, NO CARNIVAL.

Chapter 1

MARCIA GARCIA

The cardboard box trembled. The panicked squeals from inside it grew louder as I hurried through the overgrown grass.

The school day was half over. Children were noisily filling the road across from me, unbuttoning their stifling uniforms in the heat of the lunch hour, scrambling home. I'd long ago stopped wondering what they thought of me. I didn't want to feel the pang of loss for that old, simpler life.

I crouched to peek inside the box.

A wild opossum, a *manicou*, clawed at the corners. For an amateur hunter, a manicou was a big prize—a delicacy that could stretch for days—but distaste for finishing the job held me back.

"Can't be lucky if you's a coward," my mother had always said.

Over at the right side of the yard, under the purpleheart tree, the boys were digging rusty spoons into the hot earth, hoping the bitter mounds of caked black dirt they piled onto their warped utensils would magically turn into warm slices of coconut bread. They hadn't noticed me yet, off to the left, watching our dinner plan its escape.

I ran to the underside of the house, finding the hammer my father had used to repair the base of my mother's sewing table before she died and long before the neighbors sent him away from the village. Returning to the trap, I steeled myself and reached inside.

Breathe. Breathe.

I snatched the manicou's small furry neck. Its rigid body thrashed across the damp floor of the box, its slanty, black, rat-like eyes looked up at me, wide and frantic. The manicou's pulse quickened against my fingertips. It was putting up an honorable fight. But it could change nothing about its fate. The same was true of me.

I wouldn't look into the darkened box again. Instead, I squeezed its coarse fur and its next layer of squishy flesh, harder and harder, pushing its flailing body down into the peeling bottom of the box. I slid out the hammer I had wedged between my thighs and with half-closed eyes, I smashed its skull over and over until, finally, the throbbing between my shaking, bloodied fingers came to an end.

The boys sat side by side on the cool slab floor. I spooned the boiled manicou from the pot and scraped away the spiky fur with the knife I'd sharpened on a yard stone. The slightness of its body in my palms made me feel sickly. I swallowed thick bile before making a delicate cut down the middle of the manicou's spine, pulling back its slick skin to expose the soft, pink-grey meat.

The boys moved onto their knees and watched through eager brown eyes as I sliced the meat into inch-wide strips, layering it with seasonings. Lemon juice, salt, black pepper, fresh chunks of garlic, onion. I lifted the bowl to their noses, letting them smell the flavors seeping into the meat before I tossed the tender, sticky pieces with my fingers. I never tired of seeing their awe at my performing the simplest tasks. I loved them for being with me when there was no one else left.

I nudged them aside and relit the coal pot. The shimmery flames smacked the pot's rusty bottom. The boys drooled. I passed my shirt over their mouths and tried to shoo them away, but they refused. The sugar melted into the hot oil, turning silvery black. I slid the damp cuts into the searing pot. The smoke swallowed us. The coconut milk whitened the pieces, offering a promising sizzle.

My plan that afternoon was to feed the boys early and get them to my neighbor, Carol Ann, so I could leave on time for my appointment with Mrs. Duncan in Tunapuna. I wanted to avoid the after-school ruckus and the judgmental eyes. But it took a few hours for the tough meat to soften and stew, and then the boys took their time, massaging each bite between their small teeth.

"Eat up," I said.

I wiped their faces, cleaned their ears, then set aside slivers for each of the next four days. Rice, bread, cassava, breadfruit—any one of those would accompany the leftover meat and gravy quite nicely.

I hurried the boys to Carol Ann's, where they both pressed their backs against her door and began to cry.

"Come. Let her go," Carol Ann said, yanking at their shirtsleeves.

Being a seamstress required house calls. And living way out in Blanchisseuse, where roads were often blocked by landslides, for weeks or even months, I could never be sure when I would make it back. Carol Ann, a client whose taste didn't match her budget, had been kind enough, on occasion, to mind them for me, though I long suspected by the way she chewed the inside of her cheek that she'd rather repay her debt to me any other way.

In Tunapuna, I delivered four drop-waist dresses before arriving at the top of Mrs. Duncan's road. Although Mrs. Duncan had been my mother's most loyal customer and likely wouldn't have cared that I was ten minutes late, I despised the tardiness. I was sixteen years old. It was difficult getting customers to trust me. Sticking to my word, keeping my mother's past clients happy, kept food on the table.

I walked briskly with the sun disappearing behind a sky half-full of dust-colored clouds. I smiled at two ladies who stood near the road chatting with metal spoons in their hands. The thick scents of their aromatic foods boiling outside in heavy pots reminded me that I hadn't eaten enough.

I tapped on Mrs. Duncan's door. I had scrubbed my fingers with vinegar and lemon juice before leaving home, but as they gripped Mrs. Duncan's dress box, I could still smell the musky manicou fur.

"Eh, who knockin' the door?" came the deep bass voice of Inspector Duncan, Mrs. Duncan's husband.

I could hear Mrs. Duncan sucking her teeth for a long *cheups*. "Take two steps and open the door, David."

"Boy, you smart to stay to yourself," Inspector Duncan joked to someone. "Get married and from the day you bring she home, you only gettin' lip."

Thunderous footfalls grew close. I wiped thumb-size drops of rain from my face. I had to get out of Tunapuna within the hour or I wouldn't make it back to Blanchisseuse in a rainstorm without flapping all the day's money at some taxi driver who'd complain that "Nobody in dey right mind would leave Blanchisseuse one day and expect to go back de same day."

Inspector Duncan finally opened the door, gulping the last of what smelled like a spicy puncheon rum. "Good afternoon." His hands were each the length of a newborn baby. His face sank into pillowy, purple-black, shiny skin that covered a head the size of a small boulder.

"Good afternoon," I said.

I smiled but could say nothing else. My face had reddened at the sight of the East Indian man sitting on the floral-printed couch, cradling a glass, staring at me.

He was quite handsome, I'll admit. But he was old. Probably twenty-two or twenty-three. His skin, a deep-fried, golden brown and smooth like velvet pile. The outline of his lips like a bow tie. His nose, downward sloping and strong, with a black mole at its tip. His midnight-black shoes shone like marble, and his shirt, lightly starched, caressed his small muscular frame.

I tried to release his gaze, but his large, dark eyes attached themselves to me. Eyes like a black, hot night. Eyes that made me want to crawl into something small and cool and shadowy.

"Jennifer!" Inspector Duncan called. "The young lady . . . uh . . . Ma-Marcia . . . is here with your dress. Come back in here!"

Mrs. Duncan shrieked with delight, wiping her hands on a red and white cotton apron I'd given her as a gift. When she smiled, her cheeks grew into small, firm circles. "Oh, my dressmaker! Come, chile." She sweetly scooted her husband aside. "Don't mind them two old fellas. They don't teach manners in the police force."

Again, I tried to shake off the Indian fella's gaze. Staring straight at him and making sure not to be detected by the Duncans, I rolled my eyes to the top of my head.

"Good afternoon, Mrs. Duncan," I said, patting her hand.

"This chile is always so polite," she said.

The fitting took only fifteen minutes, but by the time we returned to the parlor, Inspector Duncan's patience with his wife had worn thin. "Jennifer?" he said, with a hard cheups. "Where's the food? We're hungry."

I was pretty certain their conversation would wind up in a fight. I mumbled, "Good night," closing the door behind me. The Indian fella sat, huddled in his corner seat, watching me leave.

If I had any luck I'd catch the last bus and make it back to Blanchisseuse before midnight. If I didn't, I would have to beg Mrs. Duncan to let me stay the night and run off early the next morning so as not to leave Carol Ann in a pinch past lunchtime.

It was raining harder. I scrambled toward the bus stop where a quiet crowd had already gathered. Footsteps crunched on the gravel behind me. I heard someone say "Hello," breathlessly, at my back. I didn't bother to turn around.

"Sorry," the voice said, moving closer. "I said 'hello.'"

Finally, I turned. The Indian fella from the Duncans' couch. Had he left before Mrs. Duncan's dinner was served?

"Hello." The wetness on my bare arms left me so chilly, even my voice shook.

"We just met at the Duncan house up the street there," he said.

The bulging, bright headlights of the bus caught my attention. I didn't have time for that fella's gibberish. "We didn't meet," I said.

The bus forced its way through new puddles, and I squeezed between two skinny fellas in the middle of the line. Tapping my wet sandals against the muddied walk, I climbed the steps, positioned myself in the first empty seat I could find, and never once looked back.

FAROUK KARAM

I wasn't sure why I wanted to see that gal. She was saucy. Saucy women were too much of a headache for me. Actually, women, saucy or not, were too much of a headache for me. In my twenty-three years, I hadn't yet met a gal who coulda kept my interest longer than three weeks. I didn't think she would be any different, but the fun was in the hunt, eh?

My dinner at Inspector Duncan's house had marked the first evening of my monthlong holiday. I'd hoped to take a quick trip to Tobago, but my money wasn't feeling right, so I decided to just lime with a few fellas on the weekends, head out for a couple of days to Maracas Bay, and perhaps go down south to visit some old school friends in Princes Town. You know, enjoy myself. How I ended up way north in Blanchisseuse was beyond me. A cousin I had met maybe twice lived in Blanchisseuse-proper. My thought was, if I found that gal and wanted to spend a little time with her, I could stay with my cousin for maybe a week, swim and fish in Marianne Bay, talk to the gal a bit, and then head back into town.

I knew it wouldn't be the most luxurious way to spend my holiday. People in Blanchisseuse were still dragging their bare heels along hot dirt roads, growing their own produce, and sweating to keep their one or two underfed fowls from straying into a greedy neighbor's yard. The pace would be slow. But for a city boy like me, an easygoing place like Blanchisseuse could be a good change.

During my school years I had learned that when the captain of the British surveying engineers sailed around Trinidad in 1797, he came to a settlement at the mouth of a river. A place the Spaniards had called *Madamas* after the women who washed their families' clothes there. A place the French settlers had translated to *Blanchisseuse*, meaning "washer-woman." It was this place, this Blanchisseuse, that the British captain had described as "lush and beautiful."

I had only been twice before, but what I most remembered about Blanchisseuse was the quiet. At the end of the main road where the spring bridge arched over the Marianne River had to be the quietest place on earth. I could sit on that bridge six hours a day and not hear one other human sound except my own breath rattling over the trickling water and my own feet tapping in rhythm to the rustling of a million trees. And when that river detoured into some thick woodlands I'd probably never see, my imagination had no choice but to roam wild and free with it.

In Blanchisseuse, people could live simple lives. While mothers scrubbed tattered clothes and gossiped alongside friends, children played on steep, rugged cliffs, dove into frigid, fresh water, and laughed by the riverside, half-naked, for long afternoons.

Me showing up there asking the neighbors questions and trying to learn that gal's routine naturally upset some things. People in Blanchisseuse didn't want to be bothered by outsiders. But there was something else. I had been a policeman for years, and there was something about the way those neighbors were holding back words that didn't set well.

By the way her house sat at an angle, it was difficult from the road to tell how far it stretched behind the front door. It didn't seem like much. Crooked and unsteady on its legs, it wasn't any wider than two outhouses squeezed together. Close to the porch steps, heaps of black-brown dirt were piled to one side, with no sign of grass ever having grown there. There were no fruit-bearing trees in the yard, which was almost impossible in Trinidad, and wild bamboo stalks, seemingly misplaced, sat in a patch of tall grass covering the only window on the left side of the house.

The one noteworthy plant remaining was a brawny purpleheart tree to the right of the porch, where I was standing when she opened the front door.

Her jaw stiffened and her eyebrows seemed to collapse when she saw me. She had been ready to collect water, not a man, her face seemed to say.

"Good morning," I said.

Two old-timers, a man and a woman, slowed to eavesdrop while she walked down the rocky slope toward the road.

She was as beautiful as I remembered. She wore a loose, yellow cotton, sleeveless dress that tickled her knees. Her brown hair had a golden shimmer and was pulled into a neat, thick bubble, tucked above her broad shoulders. Her *bamsee* was like a perfectly round melon, and she had the slightest bandy-leg, that soft bow between her thighs, which made me long to know her better.

But she strode right past me, her two empty buckets swinging alongside her.

"Girl, a man does show up to greet you in the mornin' and you have nutting to say?" I scrambled to catch up with her.

She held her head high and her knuckles paled from the tight grip on the handles. She was a strong walker, with an even stronger will not to speak to me. But I hadn't gone all the way into the bush to have some gal pass me by. I trotted patiently behind her until I got it into my head to tug at her elbow.

It was just a small tug.

"Don't touch me, nah-man!"

"What's wrong with you?" I said, pulling back.

"What's wrong with me?" Her pace slowed. "You come to my home uninvited. Have some respect, nah."

"Respect? Whatya t'ink this is? I just wanta talk."

She walked downhill toward a red-painted standpipe. I was taking two steps for her every one. The cool, daybreak breeze suddenly changed into wind gusts, causing strands of her well-groomed hair to dance. "You doesn't know who I live here with. You doesn't know if I have a man or a husband."

"I know you live alone." I jogged backward in front of her. I wanted to see her reaction. She shook her head in disgust.

"You don't know me," she said.

"That's why I'm here."

"Maybe I don't wanta be known."

"I hear that too," I said. "You don't wanta talk to nobody. You livin' like a crazy ole lady and you're a young gal. A young, beautiful woman."

A squat fella with egg whites in his moustache shuffled toward us.

"Don't pretend like you know me 'cause you shook some neighborhood tree and got a li'l rotten fruit." She politely nodded to the fella. He impolitely ignored her.

"Everybody's a stranger to you, gal? Even the neighbors?" I said. "If so, that's a problem."

"Whose problem?" She slammed her buckets down. "Lookin' like it's your problem since you was the one holdin' up my tree this mornin'."

I laughed but she turned away. The person who'd been at the standpipe ahead of her had left the faucet open. She slipped off her sandals and stepped into the deep pool of standing grey water.

After filling her buckets, she steadied herself and began carrying them back up the steep slope. She handled them heartily, like a strapping man. It was clear my assistance wasn't needed.

"May I?" I tapped her hand. Boy, that gal had skin like silk. Forget silk. Like butter. It looked downright tasty, too.

"Nah-man." She pulled away.

I was relieved. I wasn't sure I could carry those damn buckets. Yet, for some reason, I offered a second time.

That time she stopped, set the buckets down, threw up her hands.

I wobbled. It'd been years since I'd carried much of anything, and though it required prayer, I finally arrived at her door.

"T'ank you," she said, giggling at the multiple puddles I left on the small porch. "Good day."

She took hold of her door, which barely fit in its frame, and shut it closed. I heard the sound, unusual in Blanchisseuse, of a metal latch being hooked.

I showed up the next day, and the next. I waited each early morning by the thick-canopied purpleheart tree, watching the neighbors glare while they tried, under the cover of the maroon sky, to empty pots of urine into their fruit-bearing yards, too tired or too lazy to take the long walks to their latrines. I showed no judgment. I was excited to see Marcia, excited to see the expression on her lovely face when she realized I hadn't yet given up.

On the twelfth morning when she opened the door, I thought I saw a smile. "It's alright if you show me you happy to see me."

"Happy to see you?" Her eyes flashed with mischief. "I want you to make me happy by not being here one mornin'."

"Don't worry. You not gettin' that kind of happiness anytime soon," I said. "I extended my stay at my cousin's."

She puckered her lips and handed me her buckets. Progress indeed!

The maroon gave way to a pale blue and the sun settled easily into the morning. The jersey vest I was wearing had yet to stick to my chest, though Marcia moved at her usual rapid pace.

"Last we were speaking, you were telling me about your books. How much you love them."

"When my mudda's fadda died, he left land for his son in Sangre Grande and here in Blanchisseuse. To his daughter, he left his books," she said. "Fair, wouldn't you say?"

"Now you have the books?"

"I would've rather the land."

"But with an education, the land will come, right?"

"Oh yeah?" she said. "God ain't makin' no more land. Land is opportunity. Many educated people in Trinidad does be livin' like me. It's always about opportunity. Not about what you know from some books. Them books ain't real life. Even the English them people use don't sound like how people does sound."

The road was empty that morning, except for two sleek cockerels who had taken their squabble into the muddied street. Marcia scooted around them as we made our way to the standpipe.

"So, what about your studies?"

"I not talking about my studies," she mumbled. "That part of my life is over."

"You wanted to finish? What happened?"

"I does have t'ings to take care of during the day." She pulled a browning purple petal from an orchid and ripped it in half. "There's war, the government is rationing food, sendin' the good t'ings to British soldiers. I can't even barter for a few fish when the boats come in; everybody's keeping their food in tight fists. Sittin' in a room full of li'l chil'ren wasn't helping me do nutting."

"How much t'ings could you have to do? It's only you to mind from day to day."

"Listen," she said. "You always prying information. Let we talk about you, nah."

"Nutting much to say," I said.

Marcia controlled the faucet while I held the buckets.

"Why you feel like you does have to carry both buckets by yourself?" she asked.

"Because that's what a man does do."

"Who says?"

"I say."

"But I'm stronger than you." She said it with a straight face. "What sense does it make for you to struggle up and down the road when it's easier for me?"

"Eh-eh? You stronger than me?" I was embarrassed she would think so. "What makes you t'ink you stronger than me?"

She brushed loose strands of her brown hair away from her face. "Look at the way you does be wobbling across the road, spilling half the water before we even make it to my yard. You keep this up, I gointa have to bring t'ree buckets just to hold what you spillin' with your two."

I laughed hard and spilled half the contents of her buckets.

"You see!" She smiled. "That's what I mean!"

I was beginning to love her.

When we arrived at her front porch, I set the buckets down. I knew the rules by that time: no further than the door and we'd see each other the next day.

"I brought you somet'ing," I said.

She seemed both excited and anxious.

I wiped sweat off my face, then pulled a small, round sapodilla from my pocket. It was no bigger than the heel of a baby's foot. "I found this li'l tree way up in the bush with my cousin yesterday afternoon. It does be sweet sweet sweet. Taste it."

She took the sapodilla, but her eyes fell as if she'd been chastised. "I was wondering what that big t'ing was in the side of your pants," she said.

"Oh . . . you was wondering, eh? How come you just didn't ask? I would've pulled it out to show you."

She blushed and flipped it over in her hand. "T'ank you," she said. "I'll take it inside and have it a bit later."

"Can you take a bite now? I wanta know that you like it."

She twisted her mouth in contemplation, then pulled back the thick, soft, brown skin with her two thumbs. She bit into its flesh with her sparkling white front teeth. Juice ran down her chin like pink raindrops.

"You like?"

Her eyes were closed. She carefully, quietly, chewed its insides. "It's very nice." She wiped her chin with one finger. "T'ank you for the t'ought."

She walked inside her home and closed the door.

Heading back to my cousin's that morning, I could think of nothing else but Marcia Garcia. She filled my afternoons and my nighttimes. The way she did this, the way she did that, her buttery skin, her aloofness, her walk, her smile. All of it, all of her, attacked my mind in such a way that I found it difficult to do everything . . . anything. Even on the last day of my holiday, when I said goodbye to her almost-sad face, expecting never to see her again, I just couldn't shake her.

Tunapuna was where I lived and patrolled. I knew everything that happened there. The good and, more importantly, the bad.

On Freeling Street is where any person searching could've found a woman people called "Tanty Gertrude." Her reputation preceded her within a certain crowd who dabbled in the "darker arts." Though *obeah* was never spoken of too loudly and absolutely never in large crowds, it was present in nearly every village, on nearly every road in Trinidad. A traditional gift passed down from generation to generation, obeah offered its devotees both hope and fear.

Over the years I had asked plenty of people what Tanty Gertrude had done for them. Some would say. Others would not. But there was always talk. Talk of men with certain inadequacies who'd come at nightfall hoping Tanty Gertrude could make them feel like real men. Talk of women who'd suffered through unspeakable moments, unraveling years of secrets at Tanty Gertrude's table, begging for justice in a man's world. I had seen the lot of them, leaving her home with their bits of paper rolled up in cucumbers, their stomachs rubbed down with smelly oils, their hands caressing dirty glass jars filled with stale juices and herbs. And after every debate with a recent convert, I left the conversations feeling skeptical and more than a little guilty for even being interested. I would remember the sermons of my father, a Hindu pandit, and his warnings that obeah was for people who didn't understand that there was only one master.

But women and religion had always been two separate things in my head. And that gal in Blanchisseuse—that Marcia Garcia—was on my mind every second of every day. I would've done just about anything to get past her front door.

"You finally comin' to see me, eh?" Tanty Gertrude said, as I approached her white wooden gate.

Her clapboard house sat apart from the other houses. It was across from a wide sandbox tree the government had decided not to chop when they paved the road. Hers was a small, comfortable-looking home, with a scrubbed-clean door and a quaint rocker on the blue front porch. I stood back for a moment and watched her sitting there, waiting for me to respond. I had patrolled that road for years, so it wasn't my first time seeing the woman, but something about her had always both repelled and fascinated me, and that day was no different.

Perhaps it was her smoky-black, flawless skin, or the odd way her watery blue eyes seemed to pierce my chest. Maybe it was the two olive-size keloids dangling behind her earlobes like cocoons, or the flat, oval mole on her cheek. I honestly don't know why I stayed there when I felt such an intense urge to turn and run.

"I just passin' by to make sure you makin' out alright," I said. "Some young fellas out here causin' trouble. Your daughter inside?"

Tanty Gertrude smiled. Her nearly empty mouth was like a dark cavern. Her white hair, big and bushy, crowned her full face like a misshapen fluffy cloud. She glanced back at the round-bellied little girl, who stood just inside the doorway, as if to say "Where else would she be?" Then Tanty Gertrude seemed to nod off to sleep.

I was three days thinking about every minute I'd spent with Marcia before I approached Tanty Gertrude's gate again.

"What you does do in this house?" I asked. She was again seated on her sun-weathered rocking chair. The yard fowl clucked. One white goat lay chewing a ball of brown paper alongside her.

I guessed by the way she pushed her rocker with the force of a young boy that Tanty Gertrude was not yet sixty years old, but her tottering speech and stooped posture could've easily placed her into her late seventies. Either way, I couldn't wrap my head around the small girl from the doorway being her daughter.

"Me? I takin' a rest," she said. "My big son bring me some goat and after it get a li'l cooler, I gointa cook it up nice nice nice. I ain't like most Trinidadians, you know. I does truly like goat. And it's a nice nice boy I have who remembers what his mudda like."

The poor goat alongside her probably didn't think her boy was so "nice nice."

"What I'm askin' is what can you do for *me*?" I said.

Her cracked feet, which looked like they'd been rolled in powder, stopped their jerky movements. Her second toe, the longest, was pointing right at me.

I thought she would say something. I thought she would invite me inside, sit me down, and show me her secret ways. Instead, she pushed her rugged heels into the floorboards and rocked again. After several minutes, I heard her say, "Nutting atall."

I was vexed. I left her yard, promising myself I'd never go back. But after my morning papers were filed at the station, there I was again.

"Tanty Gertrude," I said, after properly greeting her. "I t'ink I need your help."

She was on her porch drinking a tall glass of light-brown ginger beer. "Ooh boy, you shoulda come before now." She dunked her middle and index fingers into the tall glass and tapped the sugary drink to her perspiring forehead. "That curry goat was the best batch I cook-up in a long, long time. My udda son, the next one, he come and take the rest of the pot. He bring me big sweet sweet mangoes. Good boys I have. That boy know his mammy does love sweet sweet mangoes. He bring up some nice ripe *zabocas*, too. You wanta mango?"

"Uh . . . no . . . t'ank you," I said. "I comin' to see if you can help me with somet'ing."

Tanty Gertrude pushed her large body up from her rocker. "You don't need nutting from me." With glass in hand, she straightened her red-striped housedress and walked inside.

The next weekend I was off from work. On Friday morning, I paid a taxi more than a few shillings to take me to Blanchisseuse.

"Man, you crazy or what?" the taxi driver lectured. "Your eyes *must* be burnin'! You payin' this kinda money to go way into de bush for some gal? You mad? I not goin' more than t'ree miles to find nobody! You're a good-lookin' fella, too. What you does need a country gal livin' behin' God back to rub against for? You can't get no nice Indian girl in Tunapuna to make some *anchar* and some *dhal puri* for you? You spendin' up your money on some red red, country, bookie gal?" He pushed the money I had paid him up front into his shirt pocket. "If I can't pass on de road, I keepin' de money and turnin' right around, you hear? I not goin' up to Blanchisseuse to dead in no pool of mud. Dem hills lookin' to bury me. I'll drop you right back here in Arima, but I keepin' de money. We a'right with that?"

I met Marcia Garcia at her house early Saturday morning. Her beauty hadn't diminished in quite the way my patience had.

"But wait, nah," I said, when we arrived back at her front door. I set the two pails down. I could tell she had long been expecting that

moment. "I come way up here to carry your buckets and you not invi-
tin' me inside? How I can learn about you, if you don't spend some
time with me? If you doesn't tell me about yourself?"

"Whatya wanta know?" she said.

"You know what I wanta know. I wanta know *you*. And havin' the
door shut in my face at a quarter past six in the mornin' ain't gettin'
me there."

Her mind seemed somewhere else.

"Whatya hiding inside that house, anyway?" I said.

Her pupils moved with my finger. "I ain't livin' in darkness. I not
hiding a t'ing." She shifted her weight from left to right, a small fidget,
but for me, a telltale sign.

"Well, maybe not, but for sure, somet'ing in there is livin' in darkness," I said. "What's inside?"

She reached for the pails, as if she would take them and leave me
with no answer, then suddenly she seemed to decide I wasn't worth
lying to. "My two li'l bruddas does live with me," she said. "Two sick
chil'ren I have behind them doors."

"Sick? What kinda sick?"

"Nobody does know." She shrugged. "In the blood, they say. Makes
them slow."

"You alone takin' care of them?"

She pursed her lips. "My fadda left after Ma died. So . . . yes, I
does do it."

I wished I had never asked.

During those mornings we had spent walking together, I had
allowed myself to wonder what a future with her would look like.
Now that I knew she wasn't alone in the world, the picture in my
head was a troubling mess.

"Alright." I avoided her eyes. "I'll come and see you tomorrow
before I go back."

I left, but because I was an impatient man, at midday I found
myself across the road from her home, hidden behind a clump of

black sage bushes. Across from the purpleheart, and just past the dirt pile, two small boys sat next to an extra-wide chicken-wire coop with its door swung open. They dug deep holes into the ground with spoons. Marcia Garcia walked back and forth from the house, throwing water from a grey pitcher onto their piles of dirt while they flung muddy bombs at the hem of her dress.

I was desperate for her not to catch me watching, but I was taken in by the sight of them. She was giggling hysterically and the children, thin-boned and lacking the sparkle of normal young boys, each had a glow. A faint glow of happiness, it seemed, because *she* was there.

I left Blanchisseuse that afternoon totally upset. It was childish not to knock on her door, childish not to say goodbye, but I had never in all my years felt the way that I did when I was with that gal. I had been in and out of women's kitchens, closets, bedrooms—you name it—and none were more than a minor distraction during a slow workweek. Until I met Marcia, I never felt I could make a life, have children, or introduce any woman to my difficult and judgmental family.

What was I supposed to do with some young gal from the bush with two boys to take care of? Two boys who could make her smile in a way I didn't know was inside of her. What was I supposed to do with a gal who already had a story, one beginning and ending with two people who weren't me?

Monday morning I carried with me a moist paper bag of fresh goat meat and a small basket filled with fragrant mangoes, two near-ripe avocados, and three thick-skinned plantains.

I inched closer to Tanty Gertrude than ever before. "Mornin'," I said. She didn't acknowledge me. She was in her rocker picking out her plaits with a metal fine-tooth comb. She smelled of bake and of saltfish stewed in tomatoes and chopped onions.

"Look what I bring for you. Some goat, zaboca, and mangoes I picked myself, with a rod. And some plantains, too." I pushed the blood-wet meat bag and the full basket into her lap. "You gointa talk to me now?"

Tanty Gertrude sighed. "I can't."

"I didn't even tell you what I need."

"When any man come, it's either for power, money, or a woman. No udda reasons." She set my gifts on the floorboard. "I know a big shot like you not comin' here for money and for power. It's only one t'ing left. And you don't need me for that."

"How you does know what I don't need you for?"

"A good-lookin' boy like you?" She sucked on her one remaining tooth and shook the stiffness from her raised arms. "Any woman who does say no to you does have a good reason and it got nutting to do with you, you hear? She just not ready or somet'ing just not right with she."

I knelt and unknotted the cloth covering the mangoes and the avocados. "Look at these big zabocas. Slip this between your dirty clothes and they'll be ready by tomorrow. You can have a nice slice with that goat you like to cook-up. Save me a li'l taste, eh?"

Tanty Gertrude smiled. It was the kind of smile I wouldn't want to remember when I closed my eyes at night. "Too bad I don't have a big daughter who could make you a good wife." She winked. "The li'l one in there, Nicole, will take a while to get ripe."

"I can bring more fruit when you want," I said.

"That's not how my business does work, boy. The Indian man might do business like this, but I does work when I wanta work. When I don't wanta work, I does sit here and drink my tea. No goat, mango, or ripe zabocas gointa change that," she said.

I stomped off her porch without another word. Who the hell did she think she was talking to? I wasn't begging some old crazy lady who believed she was God to do anything for me. It was bad enough I had knocked on her door. Worse that I showed up with bribes. I knew all the "goat this" and "mango that" the first time we'd spoken was her letting me know what she wanted before she did what *I* wanted. She'd stop at nothing to drain every last red cent from me before I walked away with a drop of cheap lavender oil potion stirred up in her greasy, goat-laden coal pot. Enough was enough. I was through going all the way to Blanchisseuse to carry Marcia Garcia's heavy buckets. I was through kissing that old lady's behind and watching her perch on her porch like the damn mother of the King of England. I was through with it all. If Marcia Garcia was going to wind up in my arms, it would be *she* choosing me.

Chapter 2

MARCIA GARCIA

He told me he would come and say goodbye, but he never showed up. I was embarrassed that I wanted to search for him, but when I found his cousin at the back of his vertical-board house, he didn't seem at all surprised to see me.

He tipped his ax over his narrow shoulder. He was much older than Farouk, looking more like an Amerindian than an East Indian, and not nearly as handsome. "How come we never met before?" he wanted to know.

"I don't know." I had seen *him* many times.

"You livin' just up the road there?" He stepped closer. "What's your family name?"

I offered the name—my father's name—that wouldn't pique his interest. "Garcia."

He stared as if there were a million more questions he would ask.

"Is Farouk here?" I said, quickly.

He swung the ax into the fresh stump between us. "My louse of a cousin, Farouk? These last two visits were the only times I remember meetin' him. Then I wake up this mornin' and he gone. Left behind some of his t'ings, too. Not a proper goodbye, a proper t'ank-you, or nutting." He cheupsed. "I t'ought you would come. You musta scared him off pretty good."

"Me?"

"Yeah, the fella took a real likin' to you." He looked me over like I was a shaved-ice cone on a hot day. "And I does see why."

I woke up the boys. I felt silly going to the police station, but I had convinced myself something must've been wrong for Farouk to have left both his cousin and me without a goodbye. The boys zigzagged across the winding road, clapping to the rhymes I sang while we dodged fast-pedaling cyclists turning blind corners.

Blanchisseuse wasn't a big ward and was not known for crime. I passed the one-story station nearly every day. The only thing that ever changed there was the fresh coat of paint added each year for King George VI's birthday.

The doors and jalousie windows were open. The stiff air inside had layers to it. The boys and me were three of only four people there, the fourth being Rap-Tap, the drunken father of a family of eight who lived off the main road. By the expression on the face of the policeman reading a comic book, it was clear we were less desired than Rap-Tap, who was in a woman's cotton housecoat, snoring on the wooden bench.

"I lookin' for an Indian fella," I said to the officer seated behind the tall front desk.

He was square-shouldered with an inch-wide gap snuggled between his two front teeth. "You wanta be more specific?" His voice sounded like thick branches cracking on kneecaps.

"An Indian fella who does work as a policeman in . . ."

Gawd. I didn't know Farouk's district assignment.

"Farouk is his name," I continued. "He's Indian and about this tall." I reached over my head three inches. "He has a full full chest and real swagger. Black hair, scar over his right eye, straight top teet', Indian fella's nose with a mole just so." I pointed to the tip of my nose, hoping I didn't look as ridiculous as I felt.

The boys had scooted off the bench. They were kneeling on the floor, gathering dry leaves.

"Can't help you." The officer stared into his comic book. "You just described t'ree-quarters of the Indian fellas in Trinidad."

"Then find me someone who can help," I said. "Not many Indians on the force."

The officer's eyes flipped up. His forehead creased. Over my left shoulder, he watched the boys stick the crunchy tree leaves into Rap-Tap's ears. I moved toward the bench, pulled them by their wrists. The officer slumped over when I returned. "What you need, chile?"

"I need to find Farouk." Then I remembered. "He's friends with an Inspector Duncan who lives in Tunapuna. Inspector Duncan's wife's name is Jennifer. Jennifer Duncan. She used to be a DeGannes, I t'ink."

The officer frowned. Then all of a sudden his face brightened. "Oh . . . Duncan from Tunapuna?" The twins began to whine. I let go of their wrists, leaning toward the officer with greedy anticipation. They moved toward the open door. "Duncan from Tunapuna—" The officer chuckled. "Duncan from Tunapuna does be in Tunapuna."

I fell back onto my heels. "Oooh boy. You funny *and* funny-lookin'. That is a real talent."

"Move on, Miss Lady," he said.

I took the boys on my next work trip out of Blanchisseuse. I dressed them in white-collared shirts and grey slacks, squeezed too-small shoes onto their feet, and landed at the house of my mother's old friend, Aunty Marilyn, who lived a little past Cleaver Road in D'Abadie.

Aunty Marilyn had been my mother's closest friend. After my mother—who was French and Portuguese, with a splash of Negro—refused to obey her parents and married my father, a half-Negro, half-Spanish fella, she was turned away by her family. Aunty Marilyn, my mother told me, had been the only person in all of Blanchisseuse who remained a close ally.

"Marcia?" She looked from me to the boys and back again.

I held one twin's hand in each of mine. "You said if I ever needed a place to stay I should stop by."

"That was almost t'ree years ago, chile." She flicked her fingernails against each other, leaning into the door's threshold. Her skin was more cratered than I remembered. I had caught her before she had had time to prepare herself for the day. "I have two more chil'ren now, and after my brudda died I had to take his in, too. I doesn't have space for not even anudda cockroach."

I nudged the boys closer to her. She looked down into their tired eyes, their faces unwashed from the day's travels. "Aunty Marilyn, it's only for a few nights. I not movin' in," I said.

She squeezed her bottom lip between her fingertips. "Your uncle does ever come up to see you?"

I shook my head.

"Alright." She hurriedly pulled us inside. "It's no problem. I wished I coulda prepared betta for allyuh, but I not gointa turn my back on your mudda's only livin' chile, eh." Then she placed one foot back outside and peeped at her neighbors' homes.

The next day I left the boys with Aunty Marilyn, her six children, and her four nephews, three of whom had been crippled by polio. I delivered two dresses, measured for four more, and got three new clients. After I was done with work, I found my way to the Tunapuna police station.

A long line of people were waiting to be seen. Some had tossed themselves across the shallow benches in the waiting area. Others leaned into walls, fanning their bosoms and chests with cotton hats.

I stood at the end of the line, happy for a few moments to myself. After nearly forty minutes, the desk officer, wearing a large pair of brown-framed glasses and an unintimidating frown, called me up. "Yes?" He jotted notes from the woman who had been in line before me. Someone had stolen her only pair of shoes from outside her front door. She had cried while she spoke to him; her baby-soft heels had grown blacker on the dusty concrete floor.

"I'm lookin' for an Indian—"

Suddenly, over the top of the officer's greying hair, I spotted him.

"Farouk!" My delight was obvious and I'm not sure I cared. "I found him," I said to the officer. "I found who I was comin' for."

Farouk gestured for me to wait. I watched him glide through the congested desk area, surrounded by the sounds of a snapping typewriter and heavy male chuckles. Oh Gaaawwwddd, he was a handsome man. Rugged, but not too much so. Tender-faced, but not too much so. His fingers were unblemished and gentle-looking, yet thick and firm. His gait, like a dance.

Boy, I loved him. I knew it at that moment. I was relieved to see him walking amongst the living, walking directly toward me.

"Everyt'ing alright?" He stroked the bottom of my chin, as if he had expected a visit from me just that day, just that minute.

The fear I had experienced waiting for him, believing he might've been dead, rose up into my chest, transforming itself into one piercing slap right across his smooth, brown cheek.

There was a collective *hiss* the second after my hand connected with his face.

"You couldn't even say goodbye?" I said. "Here I am t'inking you in a ditch somewhere in Blanchisseuse, and you here?" I pushed the strap of my bag up onto my shoulder. "And you askin' me if 'everyt'ing alright,' like I'd be here if everyt'ing was alright?"

The onlookers strained to hear what would happen next. I had nothing left to say. I expected never to see Farouk again.

Except . . . he showed up the next morning at Aunty Marilyn's house in D'Abadie.

I had walked out onto the plank of wood at the front of her home, hoping to get some quiet from the chaos on the other side of Aunty's door, and Farouk was standing in the yard.

"What you want?" he said.

The crisp white of his shirt, long and loose over his waist, against the dark red bark of Aunty Marilyn's "naked boy" tree, made him look like a fallen angel.

"Eh-eh." I folded my arms high across my chest. "How you find me?"

"In your wildest, biggest fantasy," he said, moving closer, "what you want?"

He was trying. And I wanted him to try.

I rubbed the tired from my eyes and kicked up dust from the plank. "I want freedom," I said. Freedom was all I had ever wanted, and my life, caring for two sick boys, would never deliver it.

"Maybe we can find it togedda." He held out a paper bag filled with aromatic tea leaves. His voice lowered, almost into a whisper. "This is for you to take back. A nice tea I got from a lady I know. Tastes real good. Drink it every day and t'ink about me, alright? I'll come and see you when I get a few days off."

The air was thick the night the boys disappeared.

With the money I had collected earlier in the week, I bought groceries and put together a tasty fish broth: kingfish head, a splash of coconut milk, sweet onions, ground provisions, carrots. I picked through the boys' bowls for small bones that might've been hiding under the chunks of cassava and plantains. They slurped and smacked their lips against the tender carrots. I'd hoped the broth would soothe them, but by the time I got them to Carol Ann's, they were even more agitated than usual. They screamed out as I walked uphill. I could hear Carol Ann reprimanding them. Part of me wanted to run back. The other part of me knew to leave, or I would miss the bus that would get me to Uncle Linton's before sundown.

• • •

When Aunty Cecilia, his wife, sent the letter asking me to design her a dress for the Governor's Ball, I knew I would have to stay there overnight. Going to Sangre Grande, seventy-five miles from home, wasn't something I would normally have done for a job. But saying no to Uncle Linton, his wife, and the occasional money left under my fruit bowl didn't feel like an option.

Except for the photographs in the newspapers, I hadn't seen Uncle Linton since right after my father left. He came to the house with cotton socks for the boys. It was then that he had made it clear I was never to even think about him again.

"Hello, Marcia." Uncle Linton's wife greeted me with a tight-lipped peck. I had seen her only four times in the many years she and Uncle Linton had been married. The first time, at their wedding, I was only six years old. In her stylish white gown, I thought of her as a beautiful princess. The second and third times were when each of her children was born. My mother, who was already sick by then, had taken us to visit, but the beautiful princess bride had turned into a royal witch, refusing to allow her precious babies near her husband's high-country nieces. The fourth time was the day of my mother's funeral. She hadn't come back to our home with Uncle Linton after we put Ma into the ground. The heat had been too much for her, Uncle Linton had said.

"Your uncle went down south for a few days," she said now. "He had business to attend to. I t'ought it'd be a good time to have you come. How you doin'?"

"Good, t'ank you, Aunty Cecilia." I hated the way it felt to have to call her "Aunty," but my mother hadn't raised me to be the kind of young woman that would even *think* to call her otherwise.

We walked down the narrow corridor, the walls filled with pictures of Uncle Linton greeting important officials. "Money does really follow money," I thought. Uncle Linton and Aunty Cecilia's house had at least two new additions. Rooms, once cozy, now opened into other rooms through double doors.

"You know the governor is having his annual ball?" Aunty Cecilia pushed aside her bangs, then opened a door at the end of the corridor. "It's a big night for our family."

Her bed was the largest I'd ever seen. Soft-white mosquito netting hung like a silk web over it. On either side, a wooden step next to a pair of brown leather slippers. White sheets with a high sheen were adorned with tiny white pillows. Each square had embroidered blue roses pressed into its middle.

"Let me tell you a story, nah." Aunty Cecilia opened her dressing room door, reaching for the lamp. "I stopped by my lady to make an appointment for my hair." I wondered if by "hair" she meant her wig or the neglected mop that sat underneath it. "There was a lady there who heard me talking about the ball. She insisted I call on a young gal who she said could make me a gown 'right out of Hollywood.' She wrote the name and the address on a slip of paper. You wouldn't believe when I opened that paper later in the day, it was your name right there. 'Eh-eh,' I t'ought. When I came home and asked Linton if I should reach out to you, he tole me he knew you were very talented but he'd also heard you were quite unreliable."

Aunty Cecilia reached for a pair of red high-heeled shoes. "You does promise somebody on a Tuesday, your uncle said, and they does get their clothes on the last Tuesday of the t'ird mont' coming," she continued. "So I bringin' you here because you're my husband's niece, and I gointa pay you nicely for your work. But you betta not come in here and play any silly li'l girl games, you hear?" She wedged her feet into the shoes and disrobed, baring a flat belly and clean, bright white underpants. Her skin shone like new steel. She smelled like tangerines.

I took her measurements, draping the black silk she had chosen across her chest and bottom, making sure to *chook* her with the pins when I could. As I folded the fabric to take back with me and while she adjusted her itty-bitty breasts, we heard his voice.

"Cecilia!"

She wrapped herself in a puffy white robe and perched on one of the wooden steps, waiting for Uncle Linton's entrance. I knelt, packing up my sewing kit, hoping she wouldn't see my eyes.

Uncle Linton rounded the corner. He wore a dark-blue pinstripe suit. His face was somber, bordering on angry. "How are the boys?" he said.

I thought my heart would rip through my blouse. I nodded and managed to say goodbye, already knowing that Aunty Cecilia's invitation to stay the night had been revoked.

I ran to catch the last bus to D'Abadie. I would have to beg Aunty Marilyn to let me stay, as there were no more buses leaving for Blanchisseuse. If I left her place early the next morning I would be home by late afternoon, if not earlier, with plenty of time to put the boys down for a nap. They'd be waiting for me to carry them into our house. I would light the kerosene lamp and leave it burning through the evening to scare off the bloodsucking, Euro-African "Sucouya" witch— the old hag who, according to Trinidad lore, sucked the blood of children at night and turned them into animals before the cock crowed.

But there was an accident on the road from Arima and the sun was long gone when I got to Carol Ann's house to find nearly everyone in Blanchisseuse gathered there—everyone, except the boys.

"What's happenin' here?" I pushed past two women standing in the doorway, holding thick-thighed babies on their hips.

Carol Ann looked up from her chair, her husband's belly touching her shoulder. "I'm really sorry."

The mumbling amongst the neighbors behind me grew louder. I couldn't make out their muffled words. "What happened?"

"Yesterday, I put them outside to play," she said. "You know how they don't like to be inside. They were antsy. So I put them out for a few minutes." Carol Ann looked up at her husband, hoping, it seemed, that he would finish for her. "Back in your yard. That's where they does like to play. In that li'l cage you have there."

She clasped her hands, hunching her shoulders, her eyes filling with tears. "And then . . . I had my eye on them, until . . . I looked away for just a few minutes. Believe me, Marcia, I does always take good care of them chil'ren . . . and I only looked away for a few minutes while I swept the floor here . . . and when I looked to see if they was alright . . ." She snapped her middle finger against her thumb.

My heart pounded in my ears. My breath was quick, shallow. "What you saying?"

She shook her head from side to side over and over, then fixed-up her face to cry again. "Them two boys disappeared. We called the police to investigate, but it was too dark to see anyt'ing good. But we were out most of today."

I squinted as if it would make her words clearer. "It was too dark? What time did you put them outside, if it was too dark by the time they disappeared?" I spoke through tight teeth. "You sent them how many feet away, by themselves?"

The neighbors made a square around us, hoping, it seemed, to reach me before things got out of hand.

"There was some light." Carol Ann scooted back into the chair, planting her elbows into its arms. "It was only a few minutes that I wasn't looking."

I turned my back before she had finished speaking. The square opened and I sprinted into the deep Blanchisseuse darkness to search for those boys.

The next morning, each man, woman, and child who could walk joined me in my search. Every hole, tree, latrine, stretch of river bank and seashore was covered by human voices, hands, feet. We searched for four days, our lungs scarred from the bellows. By the fifth day, everyone except me and Farouk (he had arrived on the second day), had given up hope.

"They gone," the neighbors whispered.

"Chil'ren don't just disappear!" I argued.

I had the same nagging feeling I got when I lost something and couldn't remember where I put it last. I kept walking the road in deepening shades of blackness, trying and trying and trying to remember, afraid to stop. Afraid to go inside to meet a childless silence.

Farouk, who had practically seen it all, was baffled too. "Chil'ren jump off cliffs, eat poisonous herbs, chil'ren, on rare occasion, even leave on their own. But two t'ree-year old boys disappearing without a trace is unt'inkable."

On the seventh day, I could no longer get out of bed. My head thumped, my joints felt like dry-season flames. I was congested from nights of sobbing. Every other breath was a deep sigh launching up my chest, then straight down to my toes.

Nothing felt normal. I had no purpose. No eggs to collect because there was no one to eat them; no water to fetch because there was no one to bathe in it; no sun to let in because there was no one who needed to see the light of day.

Nothing comforted me. Not even God. I had long ago stopped attending Mass. The hard eyes of former friends had been too much to bear. I wondered, as the pain numbed into nothingness, could He have taken those boys as retribution?

But worse was the other thought. The thought that swept over me each time I saw the chicken coop, the mounds of dirt in the yard: how much the twins had begged for me not to go, and how relieved I had been to board that bus for one day of freedom.

FAROUK KARAM

I don't remember who came to tell me. I had been the second officer to arrive at the station that morning when a woman tugged on my uniform shirt and said I needed to be in Blanchisseuse.

If I could've sprouted wings, it wouldn't have been fast enough.

I went to Marcia's house and nudged open the door, thinking she may have been asleep. As I'd imagined, it was dark inside but tidy. White dishes were washed, drying on a blue dishtowel. A black pot rested on a coal grate. Her kitchen table, pushed against a wall just below the front window, smelled of the Dettol she'd used to sanitize it. Next to the table was a Singer treadle sewing machine on a wooden base with four misaligned drawers overflowing with fabric.

And the books. Her inheritance. Everywhere. Spines faced outward, piled to six feet, pushed against the cool walls. More books than I'd ever seen in one home.

I didn't peek inside the one remaining room. The bedroom, I supposed, hidden behind a heavy blue curtain hanging from a wood rod.

I had gone to Blanchisseuse believing my presence could help Marcia feel better, but when I laid eyes on her, I was convinced that maybe not even God had that power. I felt so sorry for her. I had seen many people gripped by tragic losses, I had seen many people grieve. This time felt different.

"You have to eat," I told her after she'd combed the overgrown hills for five long days.

She let me feed her morsels of white bread and cheese. She laid her head across her splayed arms, and I stroked her dry-curled hair, hoping to make her sleep. Only a few minutes passed before she lifted her head again. I could see she was trying to convince herself to go back outside.

"Stay in for a li'l while," I said. But she couldn't sit for long. We dusted and cleaned, leaving the boys' belongings untouched. When she passed by their tiny folded shirts and their pressed khaki-colored pants, her hands trembled.

I saw her every weekend I wasn't working. I wanted to mend her so we could get on with our life together. I washed and combed her thick hair. I helped her dress in the morning. I made her tea, kissed her cheeks, and a few hours later I would make her another cup and give her another kiss.

"T'ank you" was all she ever said. For months.

She sat, never sewing, mostly staring at piled dirt in the yard through the open door. There was never any change in her until one Friday evening when I arrived to see she had a visitor.

"Good evening," I said to the man whose large head was bent next to hers.

"Good evening." He was a long-legged man, in his late fifties, with a well-groomed grey beard lying flat against fair skin. The brightness of his brown eyes battled the hard lines etched into his forehead. It took a few moments to recognize him—the Chief Economist in the Office of the Colonial Secretary. There were wealthy, powerful people in Trinidad who would have given an arm for a few moments of that man's time. Why was he here? Was it a government publicity stunt because of the boys' disappearance? No. No one except folks in Blanchisseuse knew about those boys.

None of it made sense. But the look of indifference on the chief's face showed that my presence wasn't as surprising to him as his was to me. Marcia didn't look up at me and the chief didn't rise to shake my hand. Instead, he dropped his head back down, next to hers, and dried the tears, which had fallen onto her pleated dress. He pushed his knees against her chair, his large hand covering both of hers, his soft-spoken words, undetectable to me, traveling across the three inches separating his mouth from her ear. The sting of watching her with him was indescribable.

Finally, tortured enough, I began to leave. The abrupt scrape of her chair legs against the pitted floor was like my heart's cry. After months of near silence, Marcia spoke. "This is my uncle."

The chief's face reddened. Her uncle? How could a man of his stature allow his sixteen-year-old niece to quit her studies, fend for herself, and raise two boys alone in near squalor?

I stepped onto the porch and lit a cigarette.

The sun was dipping behind the horizon when Linton Beatrice left Marcia's house. He cleared his throat on the top porch step.

With the sweetness of the cigarette lingering on my tongue, I watched the chief stroll to his wide, polished black motorcar. His blue suit perfectly tailored, his European shoes barely worn, his silk tie in a Windsor knot. He was in his Sunday best on a Friday night. He had driven all the way to Blanchisseuse to visit his grieving niece without his wife and children?

The sweeping branches of a plum tree brushed the roof of his motorcar. The chief started his engine and wiped his face with a folded handkerchief. He began to drive away, then glanced back to see if Marcia was watching him go.

I had done that every time I left that house too.

That night, I tenderly pressed my way into Marcia. Somehow she knew I needed her to take what I offered. She let me hold her grieving body in my arms, her soft breasts collapsing into me. Slowly, I pulled back from our embrace, unbuttoning her pink cotton sundress, letting it fall to the floor around her weary feet, lessening the weight, I hoped, which hung on her shoulders. I touched her face, her hair, her neck, trying to give her back a little life, trying to make her feel she was still needed, still loved, and could still love.

"I love you, Marcia Garcia." I kissed her full, sweet lips. "I love you, Marcia Garcia." I kissed her body with the thirst of a man who needed to know he was wanted. "I love you, Marcia Garcia."

After some seconds, some minutes, some hours, she kissed me back.

1945
WWII NOT QUITE OVER.
NO CARNIVAL, AGAIN.

Chapter 3

MARCIA GARCIA

Twelve months to the day after the boys disappeared, Patricia "Patsy" Karam was born. It had been a dark and heavy pregnancy. I bled throughout the months, while thoughts of the boys swelled my aching heart.

The night Patsy was conceived, the night of Uncle Linton's visit, Farouk asked me to marry him. We hadn't planned to have a child before the wedding, but when we learned of it we made the best of things.

"You happy?" He kissed the top of my head and stroked my hair. "I am."

How could I tell him that though I wanted to be happy, I didn't feel as if I would really ever be again?

We agreed to keep the pregnancy a secret until Farouk could discuss it with his family. Time passed and his promises of telling them tomorrow became next week and then the week after next. An investigation that took too long, his parents' travels, and my refusal to press him on the issue, soon turned a secret pregnancy into a secret child.

Yet Patsy brought a new light into Farouk's eyes. The way he stared at her face, the way he held her little body against his chest, the way he kissed her toes, the way he loved her and loved me even more than before, because I had given her to him, was wondrous.

Six months after she was born, while we sat at the shallow end of the river scooping out the soft, white jelly of two green-skinned coconuts, I told Farouk it was time. "Let me talk to my mudda this week," he said. "Then, we'll go together next week."

We would leave Patsy with Aunty Marilyn for the few hours we were to be with his parents. "They'll see her next time," he had said. Our plan, after the evening with his mother and father, was to spend a few weeks together in Tunapuna until Patsy and I returned to Blanchisseuse.

When I arrived in D'Abadie, Aunty Marilyn greeted me coolly. "How come I just now hearin' you had a baby?" she said.

"Aunty Marilyn, between my work, the loss of them boys, and this baby, I didn't t'ink to send word."

"Funny how you t'ink of me when you down here and need somet'ing, eh?"

I took my verbal licks, then handed bubbly Patsy over. Aunty Marilyn cooed. "The fadda Indian?" she said, smoothing Patsy's thick curls. "He the one who gave you them red tea leaves you drank last time you were here?"

"Yes," I said.

"Eh-eh." She lifted her chin toward the road. "Speak of the devil."

Farouk opened the wooden gate. We were running late. I kissed Patsy and headed toward him, forgetting for many years how Aunty Marilyn's question had made the hairs on my arms stand up.

In Valsayn, Farouk's mother met us at the door. A sweet kiss for her son. A warm, reserved smile for me.

She was plump, with splices of yellow gold between small teeth. She wore a green and gold silk sari that left a wedge of thick brown belly poking out from the bottom of her well-constructed sari blouse. Her gold bangles clanged with the sway of her arms, and each of her chubby fingers was dressed in no fewer than two gold rings. Her short nails were polished in bright red paint, and her black, heavy-stranded hair, textured much like Farouk's, was cut just below her shoulders. She smelled of honey-scented perfume.

The Karam home was pleasant. It had plenty of windows, two or three on each side. The walls, a bright peach, had faded to a pale pink in the kitchen. Across the parlor, sitting atop three wooden shelves, were well-preserved black-and-white photographs of the Karam children. Four boys in all. Farouk, the smallest, had the thickest hair, the deepest, darkest eyes, the face that seemed aware that the picture would tell something of him. I wondered while I stared into Farouk's childhood image if our future children would carry his features more than Patsy. Only Patsy's big, dark eyes and long eyelashes let on that her father was Indian, while she otherwise had the fair skin and round face of a Garcia.

"He was a beautiful baby, eh?" his mother called out. She made her way out of her kitchen and sat across from me in the parlor. Farouk hovered a yard or so away, pacing, as if ready to leave. "Farouk was telling me you does make nice nice clothes, eh?"

I'll give his mother credit. She was trying hard not to stare. Trying hard not to judge me for my simple blue dress, my well-worn white sandals. But those knife-'n'-fork Indians couldn't help themselves. "My son knows nice t'ings when he sees it. He has the very best taste." She sweetly glanced at Farouk, who was taking a seat next to her, across from me. She looked down at my handbag and pressed her hands together, expectantly. "So let's see what you have."

Before I had an opportunity to show confusion, Farouk spoke up. "Ma, I wanted you two to meet first. She didn't bring anyt'ing this time."

"Oh." She shrugged and rose from her plastic-covered couch. Farouk began to fidget with a Hindu lunar calendar on the coffee table.

"Is the food ready?" he said to her backside.

"I have to make a few more roti for you, and then I'm done. Your fadda's in the room, reading. He doesn't move his nose away from them books," she said. "Go and see if you can get him to come out."

Farouk moved toward the corridor leading to the bedrooms. I followed his mother into the kitchen. "You need any help?"

My offer seemed to surprise her. "Uh, no, t'ank you."

The Karam house smelled of fresh *aloo* and roti. The lingering spiciness in the air suggested that, unlike other Indians, they cooked curries inside. I liked the mixture of odors. It promised a hearty and delicious dinner.

"You staying to eat or is Farouk droppin' you to meet the bus?" she said.

I wasn't sure if that was an invitation for dinner or an invitation to leave. "Yes, t'ank you, I t'ink I'm staying," I said. "I could never make it to Blanchisseuse tonight."

Her face moved a bit closer to mine. The cherry-red lipstick had faded, leaving two thin lines of color on the outer edges of her lips. Her lime-green eye shadow and black mascara were painted heavy around her eyes. Her left eye trembled. "Blanchisseuse?"

"Yes," I said. "That's where I does live, despite Farouk's nagging me about moving."

She walked back to her counter, popping the dough balls between her palms. They sounded like cracking blocks of ice. "You does come all the way from Blanchisseuse to Tunapuna to fit Farouk for clothes?" She slapped the dough onto her floured counter, rolling it out with the pin, pushing it down with her red-tipped fingers. The click-click of the handles was comforting, though things between she and I were beginning to feel less so.

"I don't make clothes for Farouk, but I do travel for my customers," I said. "Nowadays, though, I can't get out so much, so Farouk comes up when he can."

"Sorry?"

"All that walkin' you does have to do when you going on the bus from Blanchisseuse to Tunapuna. That chile can't take them kinda travels in that heat too often," I said.

She yanked her hands from the brown wooden pin handles and wiped the gooey white crumbs across her sari. "What chile?"

My mouth was still partially opened when Farouk's mother brushed past me. Her pudgy body jiggled down the hall, her bangles singing their song of outrage.

Hers was the first voice, screaming bloody murder from the back room.

Then I heard the father. His speech, softer, but filled with ire.

And then, there was Farouk's. Small like a child's, different from the voice I loved, as if the length and narrowness of the hallway between us had shrunk it.

They began to talk on top of one another. The walls in the parlor shook. The family pictures, so perfect and orderly before, now crooked and unstable. I sat for what seemed like hours, listening to Farouk explain me in, explain me out, explain me and Patsy, somehow, to his parents.

I couldn't tell by their words if they were most angry about Patsy and me existing or about our failure to exist until that night. Either way, their greatest wish seemed to make us nonexistent again. I could hear this, as they shouted at one another and even still I sat like a fool, waiting for them to find me quietly seated in their parlor.

I'll admit a small part of me expected them to return, calmed from their talk, and embrace me. I was a good girl. A good woman. I loved Farouk. I hoped against hope they would see these things. And if they couldn't, I hoped Farouk would walk out, defiant, with his chest puffy, and lead me by the hand.

Instead, three faces, red and glowing with rage, met me in the parlor. Farouk's mother's hair a sweaty and unruly thatch, her eyes burning into my flesh. Farouk's father, a tall man, though not handsome, stood behind his wife and son. He didn't look at me. Maybe he was too upset. Maybe I was too insignificant.

"Come go." Farouk touched my back, his head hanging toward the floor.

"You t'ink you leaving with *dat*?" his mother screamed behind us. "Is dat what you t'ink you doin'?"

Farouk pushed my shoulder blades harder, hurrying me to the door. I wanted to walk slower, to remain dignified. "Come go," he said, with urgency in his fingertips.

His father, the pandit, followed behind. He seemed not to know what to do, which was clearly not the case for Farouk's mother.

"Miss Lady." She flung herself before the door. Tears had dried, leaving grey streaks along her chubby cheeks. "You know how badly you messed up my boy's life?"

I locked my shoulders. "I don't believe I messed up your son's life atall."

What had Farouk told them about me that would've resulted in such furor? Why had I never before seen the small, cowering boy inside him?

"Nah, of course you don't," she said. "You does smell like the bush, look like the bush, my son's spendin' days and nights in the bush t'inkin' life's gointa be alright if he can just have a li'l rub-up, make some babies, and bring allyuh down here, hopin' we not gointa smell you. But a cockroach got no right at a fowl party." Her dry, doughy hands were firmly planted on her squarish hips. "And you, Miss Lady, are the cockroach, and I spit on you!"

Then, right on the bridge of my nose, she did exactly that.

It was three months before I saw Farouk's face again. The days were long, the nights even longer. Then one morning, he was standing against that damn purpleheart tree, holding another small bag of tea leaves.

"I'm so, so sorry," he said. "Can I see Patsy?"

With my two pails of water I began to walk inside. "See her quick."

I had strapped Patsy to a chair, a cotton belt around her waist, while I had hurriedly fetched the day's water. Farouk untied the knot. "Hello, Patsy," he whispered. He raised her into the air, then placed her two wiry legs on the floor to see if she would stand. She took off! Though Patsy was ecstatic that someone else was delighted by her early walking routine, I couldn't tell if she remembered her father or not.

"Gawd, you got big," he said.

He reached out to take her slender hand, pulling her to him. He kissed her forehead and held back tears, which only angered me more. Where were the tears the night you chose your parents over your own child? What a shame it must be to be a man and not be able to live like one.

Farouk stayed for a few days and took care of Patsy while I worked. He slept on the bare floor by the kitchen table. Those were quiet days, they almost felt right. They almost felt normal again. Normal, right up until I stared at him too long or too hard. Normal, right up until I allowed myself to think about what he had done. Or what he had not done. There were moments I would look at him with Patsy and get an urge to smash him up.

"Can we talk?" he finally said.

He had just put Patsy down for a nap. I had moved from the Singer and was hand-stitching bullion knot roses, seated on a kitchen chair. I didn't raise my head from the needle and thread. "Speak your mind."

"I don't know how to make this up to you. I didn't come 'cause I was afraid you wouldn't let me in."

"You stop comin' to see your chile because you afraid of me?" I snorted, and chewed the inside of my lip.

"I know it's not right. I was frightened you wouldn't let me see her. That you wouldn't even let me near the door."

My needle bent. I tried to straighten it against my thigh. It bent in the other direction. "At least you would've tried," I said.

"I didn't wanta just try. I wanta be with you and Patsy. I want us to be togedda, never mind my family."

I searched my wooden sewing box. "Never mind your family?" I said. "You, the man who took me to your mudda's house and made me out to be your damn seamstress? What kind of nonsense is that? All you doin' here is bumpin' your gums."

I threaded the new needle. "You know how disgusted I am by you?" I continued. "You does know how hurt I was that you denied me, let your mudda spit on me, and then put me on a bus by myself to go and fetch our chile?"

He lowered his whole head. "I know. I know."

"You know? I lost them two boys and I never t'ought I would breathe again," I said. "But you was here with me. And then we had Patsy. I t'ought we had a life we was plannin'."

"Everybody *but* the family knew about us. Everybody."

"Your commanding officer? Your barber? Who cares about them people?"

Farouk rose from the table and walked to the coal pot, where he had put water to boil. He dropped my favorite tea leaves into a cup of hot water and stirred three spoonfuls of sugar around and around, making the sweet clanging sound of metal against enamel.

"Come and have some tea with me," he said. "I don't wanta fight." He strained out the leaves and placed the steamy cup before me. "I'm here because I love you."

"I don't want no tea," I said. "Take it back to the lady who does sell it to you."

He squeezed my shoulder, pushing the cup closer. I stared into its reddish pool. It smelled delightful. Fruity. The right remedy for a long day.

"Let we be togedda, eh? Come and give it anudda try."

"Nah-man."

"I really love you, my *chou-cou-lounks*." The corners of his bow-tie mouth rose to meet his cheeks. He placed one knee on the hard, cool floor.

"You callin' me your sweetheart?" I stopped sewing. "I can't be your sweetheart if you can't choose me, Farouk."

I picked up my needle again, forcing myself to avoid his big, dark eyes.

"I did. I have. I comin' here to tell you that I tole my family you're gointa be my wife. They tole me never to come back and I haven't seen them, not once since the night we were there togedda. I swear."

I pushed and pulled that needle a hundred more times until he dragged my hand into his. I tried not to look into his hopeful eyes. I really did. But when he pushed up my chin, I couldn't not look.

Then, we drank tea.

1946

"DAILY MAIL REPORT"

BY ATTILA THE HUN

Chapter 4

FAROUK KARAM

Marcia worked on her wedding gown while the fruits for the wedding black-cake soaked in rum.

I was there, in Blanchisseuse, every minute I could manage, but I wanted nothing more than to move Marcia and Patsy away from there. To begin at a place where she didn't have to remember those boys, where I didn't have to remember the shame of my mother's house. No, I didn't know everything a man should know about his woman. I didn't ask many questions. Like most people, I thought we would get to it—that nothing much mattered except beginning our new life together.

"Marcia, when you gointa finish that dress?" I asked one Sunday afternoon. I was leaving for Arima in an hour.

"I'll be done next week."

"You said that last week."

"Then you should know it's give or take a week," she said, smiling.

"Most young ladies would be dying to get married and would just as well put on a paper bag. What's this need to get fancied up for a ten-minute ceremony?"

She stopped sewing and set her palms on her thighs. "I know you t'ink I should be happy just to be getting married. A poor gal like me, marryin' a pretty, coolie boy like yourself. But my dream was to have friends and family there. We won't have that," she said. "All I have is this dress."

"And me."

Her face softened. "Yes. You and Patsy."

I reached down and took her hand.

"I'm also a seamstress. If I can't look proper at my own wedding, how I gointa make somebody wanta buy their wedding dress from me?"

"Okay, okay, okay, now that's a winnin' argument. You coulda saved that udda dreams and feelings nonsense."

"Oh, feelings aren't important to Farouk Karam? The same fella who come knockin' on my door, talkin' about 'Oh, Marcia, I does love you so much. Oh, Marcia, take me back. Oh, Marcia, drink some tea with me.' Feelings nonsense does mean nutting to that fella, eh?" She lightly punched me on the arm and we laughed.

Laughing was something I did with Marcia. Something I hadn't had with anyone else. When I was with her I felt everything, as if I had been flipped inside out. I felt Trinidad: the rhythm of its language, the rhythm of its music, the breeze between the hills, the warmth of its sun. When I was with Marcia, I felt joy. "Come, let's take Patsy and go do it now." I pulled at her arm. "Let's get married right now, and we'll plan a nice party after. Then you can wear your dress."

"Farouk, you're a fool." She pulled her arm away, though her eyes danced. "A quick quick marriage does have teet', you know?"

"I mean it. Let we go."

That afternoon we packed up Patsy and went to my place in Tunapuna. The next day, we were married by a part-time Methodist preacher on a lunch break from his part-time factory job at the sugarcane mill. Marcia giggled like a schoolgirl and we kissed until our lips burned. Then we signed a few papers, making it official.

Afterward, at my place, I finally convinced Marcia to stay for good. I knew she had always believed the boys would find their way back to her in Blanchisseuse. But I wanted us to have a fresh start.

"It's nice here, right?" I said.

We were eating my favorite curry crab and dumpling. I'd prepared it especially for her, for my new wife. "I'll miss Blanchisseuse," she said.

"We'll keep the house and you can go back sometimes. I just want my family here with me." I rubbed her shoulders. "I'll come up on Friday and help you pack. Alright?" She kissed her finger then put it to my lips.

Marcia and Patsy went back to Blanchisseuse the next day. I worked long shifts the rest of the week, throwing myself into work so as not to think too much. I hadn't wanted to tell Marcia that I too had dreamt of my family and friends there to share our day. I hadn't wanted to tell her that I had felt the loss of not having a blessed three-day Hindu ceremony, with people coming from all over the countryside to celebrate, and eating so much curry it'd be pouring out of their ears. I couldn't tell her. But I couldn't continue to lie to myself.

When I arrived to Valsayn, my parents behaved as if they'd been expecting me. I kissed my mother on the cheek. She gripped my shoulders and began to sob. Indian mothers had the victim market cornered. I didn't take her on too much.

"We've been trying to reach you. We left many notes for you at the station," my father said. He had always let my mother handle the affairs of the children. Him leading the conversation threw me off. "Have a seat." He pointed to the couch in the parlor, where I'd once sat across from Marcia.

"I was on holiday, plannin' my wedding." I wasn't quite ready to tell them the rest.

"Yes, we heard about your plans. We're very sad about it," he said.

"There's no reason for sadness. She's the mudda of my chile. Your grandchile. This is what I want."

My mother, seated next to me, fiddled with her bangles. They were like a flock of agitated birds on her wrists.

"You're a very intelligent boy," my father said. "But you always had poor judgment when it came to the company you like to keep. You should realize by now that we have your best interest in mind." My father sat with his elbows angled, his fingers pressed into the chair's arms. "And we're telling you that tying yourself up with this girl is the worst decision you could ever make."

My father always spoke softly, so even when I wanted to be angry with him it was difficult.

"It is not," I said.

"Those who don't hear, gointa have to feel," my mother said.

My father glanced over at her as if to remind her of some agreement they'd struck. He scooted to the edge of his armchair. "Farouk, you don't understand what kind of gal this is."

"She's lovely. She's a wonderful mudda. She does work hard. She's everyt'ing allyuh tole me to look for. She may not be a Hindu or even a Muslim girl, but she does respect me. She respects everybody. That's more important than marryin' a girl who does show up at the *mandir* every week but doesn't give two bloody shakes about how to live like a decent human being."

My mother massaged the loose folds of her sari. "You're hurting us. We can't sleep. We can't eat. Look how skinny I does look now?"

I didn't notice any difference in her roundness.

"I'm happy," I said. "There's nutting allyuh can do to change my mind." It had been a mistake to go there.

"Farouk, listen to your fadda," my mother said.

"I came here lookin' to receive allyuh's blessing, but allyuh too bloody judgmental." I stood up. My father pinched the bridge of his nose and rose to his feet. I moved toward the front door. "I have no need to listen to allyuh again."

They trailed me only by a few inches. "She's not who you t'ink she is," my father said.

"I'm leaving."

Then I heard my father utter words cobbled together specifically to break me: "Them two li'l boys—the twin boys who disappeared? They were hers. By she own fadda."

I turned to face them. My mother moved behind my father, holding her stomach. The veins in my father's neck swelled. "What? Them boys were her bruddas. Her bruddas!"

My mother smushed her tears with open palms. "They weren't her bruddas! She's a liar!"

My father stepped back and gripped her shoulders from behind. "Her mudda died a whole two years before them boys was ever born," he said. "They couldn't be her mudda's chil'ren."

"Nah," I said. "No."

"There were all kindsa t'ings happenin' in that house that nobody in Blanchisseuse does wanta talk about. Then one day, your lady friend up and leaves Blanchisseuse, and some mont's later, she comes back home with two babies."

"You buyin' the fight without all the facts," I said. "You have the story wrong."

"Then what's the story?" My father asked the question with such confidence it unnerved me.

Suddenly, I was a child standing in front of them.

"Somet'ing was wrong with them babies, right? Did you ever see them?" he said.

My parents moved in for the kill.

"It's because she own fadda gave them to her," my mother said. "The fadda's blood made them chil'ren sick. And she lived with him until the neighbors made him leave. *They* sent him away. Not she. And they say that when he left, she cried. Cried in the streets. You t'ink a girl who was raped by she own fadda gointa cry when somebody finally make him go away?" My mother stared at me like I was a fool. "She loved him like a husband, they say. Like a husband!"

I held onto the doorknob, hoping it would bear my weight. It wasn't that I didn't know there were secrets. She was a private gal. But this? It couldn't be.

I left Valsayn and walked the streets of that island for days. I didn't sleep. I ate ears and ears of black-kernel roast corn from sleepy-eyed street vendors, wondering how I could dare to ask Marcia the question, wondering what I would do if it all turned out to be true.

MARCIA GARCIA

Farouk didn't come on Friday. I waited five days, then on Wednesday, I went to the Tunapuna police station with Patsy in my arms. No one had seen him. I rang the bell in Valsayn, while Patsy played beneath the Karam front window. Not once did the curtains part.

On Friday I said goodbye to Aunty Marilyn, who had been letting us stay with her, and began to make my way back to Blanchisseuse.

It was a long day of travel. Patsy was tired of walking, tired of hearing me sigh, tired of not having a comfortable place to rest. Her wailing grew with each step closer to home. It was past dusk. I was pointing out the shadowed form of the purpleheart tree, her daddy's favorite spot, when the outline of something struck us both.

"Farouk? That's you?"

He was sitting open-legged on the front porch. "Where you been?" he said.

"All over Trinidad lookin' for you." Patsy quieted, coiling her neck, struggling to connect the darkness with the voice she had grown accustomed to hearing. I moved closer, but Farouk was still sitting.

"Whya lookin' for me?"

"What kinda craziness you talkin'? You tell me you were comin' here last Friday. I t'inking you dead. *My* Farouk wouldn't leave us right after we get married. *My* Farouk must be layin' in a ditch some-where," I said.

"*Your* Farouk?" I could see his face now, his blanched color. He wiped the wetness from his cheeks.

"What's the matter?" I asked. "What's happenin' here, love?"

"I should be askin' you that, *love*," he said. "What *has* been goin' on here?"

He had heard something. Gossip in Trinidad was like a wild, deadly virus. It could take your life. "I don't know what you talkin' about." My heart began to pound. He stood, pushing his weight into the post of the porch, his back like an arc. I tried to move by him, but he blocked the steps. "Look, I need to get Patsy inside. She's tired and hungry."

"She can wait until we're done," he said.

Patsy wailed on cue. "Let we go and put her down."

There were shadows across his flaky face. His saggy brown pants bunched on top of his shoes, as if he had forgotten his belt. His usual crisp shirt was wrinkled and ripe. "I wanta talk now," he said. "If you try and put her down before we have a chance to speak, you may never see her again."

He knew threatening my child was a good way to get me started. "Eh-eh? You goin' mad or what?"

"Nah-man, I not mad," he said. "I curious."

"Go and ask your *chupid* questions." I didn't know what he'd heard or how much of it was the truth, but I was getting annoyed. I was con-vincing myself that I didn't care.

"How come you never tole me your mudda was dead long before them boys was ever born?"

I should've been prepared for that question, but I wasn't.

"You have no answer?"

I jiggled Patsy up and down, hoping I could calm the both of us.

"Maybe the reason you didn't tell me was because them boys really belonged to you, eh?"

I stopped jiggling.

"And they was your fadda's sons, too, right?"

I had been afraid every day since meeting Farouk that he would've heard that story. And each day that had passed, right up until Patsy was born, I was surprised not to be confronted by him. But after Patsy, after we had started to build a life together, for some reason, I grew easy with the idea that he might never hear it. I allowed myself to believe that even *that* story couldn't destroy us. "You have it wrong," I said.

"Come and sit down right here with Patsy and set me straight, Marcia. Please, please, set me straight." He plopped himself back down, slapping his hand hard against the wooden slats of the porch.

I swear a large part of me wanted to do what he asked. Wanted to sit next to him, with my head on his chest, my hand in his, and tell him everything. But how? I hadn't even allowed myself to think of it. Of all the horrible things that had taken place after Ma died. How would I begin? Where would it end? Farouk was literally asking me to do the impossible.

"Did they make your fadda leave? Is it true they made him leave Blanchisseuse?" His eyes pleaded for the answer to be no.

I held Patsy firmer against my chest. She was quiet, almost motionless. Her empty belly growled. I gave her my finger to suck and massaged her warm gums with it.

"Is it true?" he said again, his voice louder.

"Yes," I said. "That's true."

He shook his head. "How could they force a fadda to leave if there was no wrongdoing? No man would agree to leave his chile if he didn't do anyt'ing wrong."

I watched him weave his pieces together, knowing that in the end he would have one large colorful piece of scrap.

"Oh Gawd, Marcia. Talk to me, eh? Tell me anyt'ing that will make my mind stop gointa these terrible places."

Farouk couldn't understand that my story wasn't just my story. I couldn't risk anyone knowing all of it, not even Farouk. Especially not Farouk. I said, "If you really love me, you won't ask me about this again."

He stood up. He was within inches of my face, his breath like warm milky froth. "Then it must be true," he said. "My mind can't create anudda story to take the place of this one if you don't help me."

I wanted to reach out to him, take him into my arms. But the air had grown too thick, too heavy, too stifling. And I was too scared, too powerless, too ashamed to try and stop what was happening.

"You know how much I wanta take my hands and shake you?" His tone was deep, subdued, as if only the words lay between my neck and his fingers. "I can't believe you did this to me."

"You have to trust me. It's not as you t'ink."

"What part, Marcia?" One last bit of hope dripped from his tongue. "The part about the boys not really being your bruddas? Just tell me that. Tell me, yes or no," he said. "Were them two boys your bruddas?"

I knew I would always remember the moment I lost him.

"No," I said.

He struck the wooden post. The house shook. His fists in rigid balls, he said, "I can't believe I stayed in this nasty place. You been lying to me every day since we met. Every single bloody day."

I had never seen him like that—angry, disgusted, broken. I knew even if I told him a story, even if I could tell him *the* story, he would never trust me again.

"You lucky I don't rip that girl from your arms," he said, wiping the wetness from his face. "I gointa take pity on you and leave you with my chile . . . because that's the only t'ing you'll ever have from me. Ever."

1954
"STEEL BAND CLASH"
BY BLAKIE

Chapter 5

MARCIA GARCIA

Farouk was mostly right. The only things worth mentioning I ever got from him were his children: Patsy, Jacqueline, Wesley, and the one I was expecting eight years after he left.

By the quiet life I lived many would say I grieved Farouk from the very moment he left Blanchisseuse. But I would never say that. Grief is losing your mother as a young child; grief is watching your sister die an unnecessary death; grief is losing two little boys on a dark, hot night and never being able to look at another without feeling wounded; grief is *not* having your heart broken by a man. I refused to think of losing Farouk as grief. Yet in those eight years of living without him, I was never the same as I had been that one year with him.

Each night he came, I would let him in. I wanted each time to be the time he changed his mind. I wanted each child to be the child to make him come back. But Farouk never really came back. And while big in the belly with our last child, I began to suspect that even if Farouk wanted to come back, he could no longer do so.

I was strolling through the Curepe marketplace with the children, sniffing spicy cucumbers, groping bags of dried sorrel. The marketplace was not yet crowded. Mounds of fruits and vegetables in wooden crates were still firm, fresh, displaying a rainbow of crisp, bright colors. The sprigs of herbs and dry spices were fragrant. Sellers called out for me to be their first sale of the day while the children, at my rear, bargained prices with them.

Patsy was nine. She was a pretty girl, with new white teeth. Her body remained babyish but her mind moved with haste. Always arguing with Farouk, because she was so much like him, Patsy was a fast-talker and cheeky. She was also a fighter, like a poison-arrow-throwing Carib: The world wouldn't pounce on Patsy without her pouncing back.

Jacqueline, born two years after Patsy and a year to the day after Farouk and I were married, looked like Farouk, walked like me, and behaved like no other child I knew. She was nosy, bright (the smartest in her class), loving (especially toward that father of hers), but also terribly shy. At times she could hardly speak without withdrawing into herself.

Wesley, our boy, was five. He wasn't as sharp as the other two. He walked, spoke, and even drank, slowly. I babied him because I felt he needed it. I realized, probably too late, that I might have done him a disservice.

Whether we tired of one another or not, the four of us, together, made a family. I was always reminded of this fact while at the market on Saturday mornings.

"Patsy, take Wesley and go buy some fresh ginger," I said.

She held out her hand. She had recently begun filing her nails. They were square and buffed to a shine.

"What happened to the change you got back from buyin' the breadfruit?"

She and Wesley opened their mouths, revealing bright pink coconut shavings.

"You spent all that money on sugar cake?"

I wanted to be angry, but they were laughing too hard.

"Eh-eh, you betta sell off them rotten teet' inside them two big heads of yours and get me my ginger." I reached into my brassiere for another dollar. My business had grown and Farouk was generous. My trips to the market were no longer filled with anguish. "Pick up a sugar cake for Jacqueline, but no more sweets for you two, alright?"

Patsy and Wesley ran to the far side of the marketplace, while Jacqueline and I continued to rummage through the okra and dasheen bush, searching for the freshest of the bunch to add to the Sunday callaloo.

"Are you Marcia Garcia?" There was a prune-skinned lady with piercing blue eyes standing next to a crate of onions. The blue, contrasting with the blackness of her skin, made her seem otherworldly.

"I am." I had no reason to question how she knew me. My reputation for being an excellent seamstress was beginning to spread wide and far.

"Oh boooyyy, what a treat it is to finally meet you." She smiled, her mouth empty, except for one tilted tooth at the bottom.

As I readied questions about what item of clothing I could make for her, there was a tap on my shoulder. Claire Clarke, one of my long-time clients, stood behind me. Claire had a pressed and put-together look, the look of a woman who had time to care for herself. She had hands soft like powder, a flat, unmarked belly—features that had long ago left me.

"Good morning, Marcia." Claire fidgeted with her silver bangles. Her perfume was like a bouquet of fresh lilacs.

I realized I hadn't put a brush to my hair.

"Hello there, Jacqueline," Claire said, offering Jacqueline a warm smile.

Although Claire had a reputation for being a "debauched" woman, Jacqueline had, on many occasions, delivered Claire's dresses and had nothing but nice things to say about her. "Hello, Miss Claire," Jacqueline said. "I like your dress. It's lookin' real real pretty on you."

How many words had fallen from Jacqueline's lips! "It's one your mammy made for her, Jacqueline. Of course it looks nice," I said.

"Speaking of dresses— Oh, sorry to interrupt, my dear," Claire said to the old woman who had been waiting and watching. "I need to bend Marcia's ear for just a moment."

The woman said, "Sure," but glared at Claire as if she had heard all the rumors.

"I know," I said to Claire. "I owe you t'ree dresses and before this baby comes, I'll have Jacqueline bring them."

"When does that mean? This week or next?"

"This week, Claire. I'll have Jacqueline bring them in a few days, alright?"

"I really need them to wear for this comin' weekend."

"You'll have them."

Turning back to the old lady was a relief. But only temporarily. "Sorry," I said to her. "And you are?"

The old lady watched Claire leave before speaking again. "In Tunapuna where I live, they does call me Tanty Gertrude."

She seemed to expect me to know of her. "Tunapuna is a big place."

"Freeling Street," she said proudly.

"Well, it's nice to meet you." I thought she would ask about the price of some blouse or skirt she wanted, but she seemed to be waiting for me to say something. I wasn't interested in small talk. I started to leave, when Wesley and Patsy came back holding out the bag of ginger and offering me the change.

"Oh, these must be Farouk's udda chil'ren?" she said. "That boy look just like he fadda."

Wesley looked nothing like Farouk.

"What's your name?" she asked Wesley.

"Wethley," he said, sucking his thumb.

"Eh-ch, Farouk didn't give the boy a proper Muslim name?" She frowned.

Farouk wasn't Muslim.

"Come, chil'ren." I tried to scoot past Jacqueline, who was standing in front of me, but the growing marketplace crowd hemmed
me in.

"And you, li'l one?" the old lady continued. "What's your name
again?"

"Jackie," she said, behind her hand.

"And no Hindu names for the girls?" She arched her back, thrust-
ing her chest forward. "That's how they does do it in the Karam fam-
ily, you know. The boys does have Muslim names, the girls does carry
Hindu first names. You know that, right?" she said, seeming to know
I did not. "Farouk's fadda's great-great-grandfadda was one of them
first indentured Indians in Trinidad. Straight off the first ship—the
Fatel Razack. He was a li'l Hindu boy when he came off the boat.
After the plantation owners gave him his papers he married into a
Muslim family and took the wife's father's name. She gave him six
sons and four girls. They gave each boy a Muslim name to honor the
wife's fadda and each girl a Hindu name because he remained a
Hindu."

I couldn't hide my surprise. "How you does know Farouk?"

"Oh, you don't know?" she said. "He used to patrol my street. We
spent many many days togedda. But you come and see me. We can
have a cup of tea and I'll tell you all about how I really know him."
She winked. "Alright?"

The four of us watched her leave and meet up, in the distance, with a
woman about twenty years old, dark like her and striking. I sensed that
the young woman's absence during my talk with the old lady had been
intentional, for when she narrowed in on me and the children, with the
same blue-colored eyes as the older woman, it was with pure rage.

The memory of the old lady quickly faded. I had my business to manage, children to care for, and a baby on the way. Farouk had recently
moved us from Arima to Curepe and there was still some settling in

to be done. It wasn't until the morning the baby made her entrance that I was reminded of that morning at the market.

Usually, at the end of my pregnancies, Farouk visited two or three times a day. He had been present for the births of each of the other children. Though we weren't together anymore, each birth seemed to mean something to him. I didn't completely understand it, but I much appreciated it.

However, the week our fourth baby was due we saw him only once and for only a brief, strange visit.

"Allyuh does want too much!" he had screamed at the children when they asked what he had brought for them. He had shooed them away. "Allyuh ungrateful, just like your mudda!"

I got angry then and told him to leave. I never expected he wouldn't return later that day or the next. When I went into labor, I told Patsy to fetch Aunty Baba, my midwife, and I sent Jacqueline to go and find her father.

Aunty Baba took awhile to come. By the time she did, it felt like that child would burst out any second. "Get your mind here," Aunty Baba yelled at me.

When Jacqueline came back, I was hot, irritable, unable to bear down hard enough to push the baby out. "Where's your fadda?"

"He said he not comin'."

"Huh?"

"He said he not comin'," Jacqueline said, chewing the *he* and the *not.*

"Chile, whatya sayin'?" I was panting. The weight of each breath felt enormous.

"I found him, but Daddy said he not comin'!" Her arms were stiff across her body.

"Your fadda not gointa miss the birt' of his own chile. You tell him what's happenin' here?"

"Yes, Mammy."

"Well, I'm asking you what he said. Whya makin' me pull your teet' for answers while I'm here trying to birt' this baby?"

Jacqueline dropped her shoulders. "Remember the old black black lady from the market?" she said. "When I found Daddy he was with that gal the lady had been with. The one with them same funny-lookin' eyes." Her forehead floated toward the ceiling and she held her hands behind her. "When I tell Daddy to come, he got up to leave, but the girl said somet'ing in his ear and he sat straight back down. Then he tole me to tell you he not comin'."

Before I could say another word, the baby began to writhe; she felt as if she would tear straight through my flesh.

Aunty Baba sent Jacqueline out of the room.

"Whya does waste alla that time with that man, Marcia?" Aunty Baba pushed apart my knees.

"I want him here for his chil'ren."

"You wouldn't need him to be with his chil'ren if you didn't keep havin' his chil'ren." Her thumbs felt large and firm against me. "The man is not nice to you. You're a smart woman. You already know this."

I closed my eyes and lifted myself onto my elbows. I needed more air. "I don't know anyt'ing, Aunty Baba. I don't have a second to stop and t'ink about how I does feel or t'ink about what the best t'ing to do is."

She slid another cloth beneath me. "You can make time for that. You need to make time for that."

Those were Aunty Baba's last words before the baby, Yvonne, crowned. I bore down, pushed, gripped, yelled. Within minutes, Yvonne was out, howling and wet, much like her mother.

Inside my head felt grey, like rolling mountain fog. After Aunty Baba promised that Yvonne seemed healthy, I drifted into sleep.

"Daddy's here," Patsy whispered a while later. She rubbed petroleum jelly on my parched lips and set a water cup on the jiggly side table next to my head.

I wiped the sleepiness from my eyes and smoothed the edges of my hair. I knew he would come. At the heart of it, he was a good man. A man who loved his family. A man who didn't want to disappoint me. I didn't know where Jacqueline had gotten that nonsense about him not coming. I was going to give her a piece of my mind when I got myself together.

"Tell him to come in," I said. How slowly the children seemed to be moving that day.

Patsy pulled the blanket up to my chin, patting the fold against my collarbone. "He said he not comin' in."

I fixed my eyes on her, but I could hear Farouk, in the other room, yelling at Wesley. Aunty Baba, who had been seated quietly with Yvonne, rose from the chair across from me, placing the baby in my arms. "I comin' right back." She glided out, her sizable frame barely making a sound.

I strained to hear Aunty Baba's exchange with Farouk. *Chupid-stupid. Pompous. Ignorant. Betta go.* I was too tired to make sense of any of it.

A few minutes later, Farouk walked into my bedroom, brazen, strutting like an old peacock. "Whatya callin' me here for?" he said.

Aunty Baba had drawn the window curtains so that I could rest. The room was dim, shadowy. By his tone, I wasn't quite sure it was Farouk standing there.

"What you screamin' at that boy for?"

"You raisin' a house fulla gals, that's why."

"You're too much of a *saga boy* to come and spend time with the chile. How he gointa learn to be a man without his fadda?"

Farouk cheupsed and shook his hand. "I always hearin' that nonsense from you women. Allyuh and your damn excuses for not raisin' ya boys like real men. If you don't treat him like a li'l woman, he wouldn't behave like one."

Farouk's suit vest was tied snug around his waist, like a dress sash. He wore a pair of too-short pants some untrained tailor had sewn for him. He didn't look like himself. He didn't sound like himself. "You losin' your mind or what?"

"Woman, I have t'ings to do. You wanta keep havin' babies, that's your business."

I hurt for that sweet child in my arms. A baby with a head full of slick, straight black hair and kissable, soft lips, who had a jackass for a father. It was a terrible plight I had heaped upon her.

"Go and leave, Farouk. You're a damn *salope*," I said.

I realized that Patsy was there watching. I didn't have the good sense to tell her to leave.

"You havin' babies with nobody to take care of them, and you callin' me disgusting?"

"Leave before I raise up myself from this bed and kill you."

Farouk's grin pushed me past sanity.

"Damn bastard!" I hoisted myself, picked up the water cup next to me, and threw it. It knocked him on the forehead, then crashed to the floor. The dripping water made his muffed hair a mess of slick black bangs.

Farouk wiped his head. He pointed his left index finger at baby Yvonne, his right index finger at Patsy, who was wet-faced but not because she had been splashed by water, and said, "I'm not the real bastard here."

Yvonne was three weeks old when I called Jacqueline into my room. She was holding a black cloth doll I had made with brown buttons for eyes and grey yarn for hair. "Where is Patsy and Wesley?"

"Patsy went fishing with Daddy. Wesley's out runnin' with that boy and his big brudda from down the road."

"The big big one? Byron? Go and ask him to keep an eye on Wesley for me. Tell him we'll be back in a few hours," I said. "Then come back and help me get this baby dressed."

When the three of us stepped off the bus in Tunapuna, the sun was bearing down on my head. Before we left home I had put a white lace bonnet to cover Yvonne's soft crown and forced Jacqueline into a pale pink sun hat. She loosened the bow beneath her chin. "Where we goin', Mammy?" she said.

"Eh-eh, don't ask me that, nah." I drew light circles in the middle of Yvonne's back to soothe her belly from the bouncy bus ride. "When we get there, you stay quiet and take the baby if I need you to, alright?"

"Yes, Mammy."

Funny thing about Jacqueline was that when she was by herself, when she didn't think anybody else could hear her, she was full of words. Full of voice. She couldn't stop herself from talking. But when she was near other people, especially near me, she was meek, almost scared.

We stood at the side of the road watching the bus move away. I didn't know whether to turn right or left. A woman no taller than Jacqueline walked toward us. She held a thin-strapped striped bag and the hand of a small, beautiful, ebony-skinned child.

"Good day," I said.

"Good afternoon." Her pitch was deep and layered, like a portly woman's.

"I lookin' for a Tanty Gertrude. She does live around here?"

The woman took one step back. Her head, in a bright red scarf, shook, almost violently. "Me? Don't ask me dat. I don't know nutting about dat kinda t'ing."

She tightened her grip around the child's delicate-looking hand and hurried away.

I glanced down at Jacqueline, raising my eyebrows in confusion. Jacqueline shrugged. It was the first time I'd giggled in months.

With Yvonne settled into my shoulder, we walked east, toward a flock of boys and girls playing netball in the street.

"Tanty Gertrude?" I said.

They pointed down the road. "The blue porch by the big tree in the road," one of the girls said. "You gointa make trouble?"

I told her I was not and patted her fine-woven hot plaits. She stared longingly at Jacqueline. "You wanta play?" Jacqueline knew what my answer would be; the corners of her mouth fell and she shook her head at the girl.

There was nothing unusual about Tanty Gertrude's house. A few lime trees in the front, one big hen clucking away on the porch. The top half of the white door was open.

I shooed away the hen and knocked on the bottom half just before Yvonne began to whine.

"Come in," a voice called out.

"Tanty Gertrude?" I said. "Good afternoon."

"I said come in," the voice called again.

I patted Yvonne's back, but her cry ripened into a wail. I sat down on an old rocker, offering her my breast. She sucked for a few moments before falling back asleep.

I didn't knock a second time.

Tanty Gertrude was seated at a table wearing a white cotton dress with two-inch wide pleats from the neckline down. There were red candles lit around her. Her elbows were planted into a blue and beige polka-dot tablecloth. "You finally come," she said.

"You were expectin' me?"

"I gave you an invitation."

"That didn't mean I was gointa come."

Her kitchen appeared clean, but smelled of soured meat. Something deep inside urged me to push back from that table and run, but I was too prideful.

"I made it so you would come," she said.

"What you mean by that?" I pressed Yvonne's belly deeper into my chest.

"Come and sit with the baby, here." She pointed to a white stick-back chair across from her. "Leave the big one by the door."

I signaled to Jacqueline to obey, wondering what it was about Jacqueline that made the old lady want to keep her at a distance.

"Tea?" she offered.

When offered tea one must always say yes or risk offending the host. I agreed to a cup. She rose from the table with strong legs and returned with a grey clay pitcher. "This is my special tea." She placed a full cup before me.

I took a small sip and, though my three teaspoons of sugar were missing, the taste was all too familiar. I had had that tea a million times. I pushed the cup away. "Farouk gives me this tea."

"I know," she said.

Jacqueline was staring out the door, watching the children play. I could hear the laughing screams of the girls. I must have been out of my mind to have brought her and Yvonne into that situation.

"You gave it to him to give to me?" I asked.

"He come here askin' for it."

Over the years, Farouk had brought me steady, frequent tinfoil packets of tea. He said it was one thing he knew I liked and he always wanted me to have it.

"From the first days he carried your water in Blanchisseuse," she continued. "You knew that, right?" I touched Yvonne's fingers. They were warm, moist. "Your mind changed so quickly about him."

"Lady, I was a chile. How could I know my mind might've been changin' because somebody was playing tricks with it?"

She wagged her index finger, as if I had called her out of her name. "Nah-man, no tricks," she said. "I don't play games."

I moved Yvonne belly-down onto my lap. Her head was now beneath the tabletop, her face cushy against my thigh. "Even without you, even without this, I woulda loved Farouk."

She cheupsed.

"Well, no matter," I said. "In the long run, you failed. We not togedda."

"You're as togedda as you need to be."

I leaned over the table toward her, careful not to startle Yvonne, careful not to raise my voice. "You does make it the way you see fit?"

She grinned.

"This is what you wanta show me?" I said. "Am I supposed to feel bad that Farouk loved me so much he came to you? That doesn't make me feel bad. Not one bit." I pushed the chair back and gently placed Yvonne over my shoulder again. Her breaths were deep and sweet by my ear.

The old woman looked up into my face, her blue eyes cloudy. "You came here for somet'ing."

I hated that she thought she knew me. "I came here to find out why the man I knew as well as I know my own self no longer behaves like the man he once was. But now I understand." I looked back at Jacqueline. She was no longer peering outside. Her confused eyes met mine. She wanted to come to me, but my firm stare told her to stay put. I turned back to the old lady. "You might be in control of him, but you not in control of me."

"You got too much pride, gal," she said. "You does like to beat your own drum and dance. I tell Farouk from the beginning, t'ings couldn't work out with a gal like you."

Just then, I felt I had real belly. "Listen, Miss Lady." I tucked her chair beneath her too-long tablecloth. "Stay away from me and stay away from my chil'ren. You can keep that lousy man and do what you does need to do with him and this obeah, this devil t'ing you messin' with. But if you come near my chil'ren again, I'll finish you off."

Though I didn't go to church anymore, I was a woman who still held out hope that there could be something powerful, something good in the world. I wouldn't stay in that house any longer. But when I took my first two steps to leave, my chest tightened. My breath seemed too far ahead. My knees buckled. The drop to the floor was like a long, slow, terrifying dream. Clutching Yvonne, hoping her head wouldn't smash against the floor, we landed with a forceful clunk, my breasts cushioning her fall. She howled. It was her cry that kept my mind alert.

"Mammy!" Jacqueline screamed from the door. "Mammy!" I prayed she wouldn't try to help me, but I couldn't tell her to run. My eyes, my mouth, open and burning, were static.

Then Yvonne began the slow slide onto the floorboards. Tears poured into my hair.

"Mammy, I have her!" I heard Jacqueline's frantic shuffle, felt the rush of hot air from the opened door.

I had no physical energy left to fight whatever was happening, but my mind was like an anxious kingfish, pushing its way through resistant currents, swimming back to Blanchisseuse, before my mother lay dying, before my father had become a bitter and frightened man. I remembered my sister Ginny. Her open and lovely face, happy and radiant like it was before she became a sad girl. I lay wondering, with much sorrow, what would become of my children. Would Farouk do right by them? I thought of the many things I should've told them, taught them.

Behind my thoughts I could hear the old lady. Removing the teacup from the table. Blowing the wicks of the candles. Licking a wet, sugary spoon dry. Her footsteps grew close. She knelt beside me, smelling of incense and wax.

"I *can* control you," she said into my ear. "Stay away from Farouk. He's with my daughter now. No more chil'ren. No more money. No more nutting you gointa get from him. And if you mess with what's mine, I gointa take the rest of them chil'ren of yours, and make you feel the t'ings you felt when them udda two disappeared."

She kicked me deep in the ribs with a sharp foot. I winced at the thick toenails digging into my side, until I realized pain meant my body was awakening.

I moved slowly, carefully. My hand to my face. I couldn't stop blinking. I wiped drool that had dripped to my chin. My breath returned, steady, certain, and I could hear the old lady crossing the kitchen again. My children needed their mother. I crawled toward the door, waiting for the strength to rise. I knelt. I put one leg before the other, again and again, until I stumbled onto the blue porch.

"Jacqueline? Yvonne?"

No pink.

The crowd of children hovered. "At least this one's alive," a girl said.

Was she talking about Jacqueline? Yvonne? Had I fallen straight into the old woman's trap and caused my children harm?

"Jacqueline!" My vocal cords were tight, defiant. "Jacqueline. Where are you?"

The children's eyes widened. I pushed past a boy in a navy blue shirt, clearing my view down the road. No pink. What could've happened to them? How long had I been in that woman's house?

"Jacqueline!" I leaned over at the waist. "Jac-que-line!" The horror in my voice frightened even me.

Then, as if in a dream, the sweetest sound. "Mammy, I'm over here! Mammy!"

The pink hat fell. Jacqueline ran to me from behind the fat-trunk tree perched in the middle of that road. Her pigtails leapt around her shoulders as she tried to soothe a whiny Yvonne with gentle bounces. She guided me off the porch. "You alright?" she said.

"Yes. I'm alright because you're here." I held on to her strong, slender arm. "You mustn't ever speak of this day to anyone. Not even to me, you hear?"

I thought Mammy was strong and fearless. She wasn't supposed to fall. She wasn't supposed to cry. Especially not because of Daddy.

That day at the blue-eyed lady's house, Mammy became small, almost as small as me. I was ashamed of how I felt about her and I never talked about that day to anyone, except Patsy.

"Patsy, what's obeah?" I said, a few days later.

"Whya askin' me that stupid question for?"

"Just askin'."

"Tell me why and I'll give you an answer."

Patsy, like Daddy, had a quickness about her that made most people around her feel slow. She often said she wanted to be a policewoman, but Daddy had told her many times over that he didn't think it was a good idea. He encouraged her to set her sights on teaching. But Patsy didn't want to listen. She knew she would've been a good policewoman. She was smart and strong, with thick arms and powerful legs. She was two and a half inches taller than any girl her age and could take down most ten-year-old boys with one hit to the face.

Sometimes I wanted to be exactly like her; other times, I despised her.

"Mammy took me to a lady's house and they was talking about it," I said.

Patsy was reading on the bottom porch step. We were both supposed to be shucking corn, but I had lost a bet that I could pelt a rock further. Patsy figured if Mammy caught her not working, she could easily use reading as the excuse. She placed her index finger on her page. "What lady?"

"Remember the lady talking to Mammy at the market before Yvonne was born?"

"The one with the scary eyes?"

"Yeah, her." I was excited Patsy seemed interested in what I was saying.

"So?"

Suddenly, I felt silly. I had mostly been watching the children play outside. I hadn't listened to every word between Mammy and the lady. But if I didn't tell Patsy something, she wouldn't pay attention to me anymore. "I t'ink they were talking about Mammy using obeah to make Daddy love her."

Patsy's eyes grew big and tall. "Mammy does do obeah?"

"Yep."

"She's so chupid." Patsy stared into her book. "Daddy doesn't wanta be boddered with her or with us. Mammy should take the money Daddy gives her and let him go."

Patsy was beginning to be angry with Daddy almost all the time, but that was the day I saw she thought less of Mammy, too. And she didn't seem ashamed of it.

"I t'ink Daddy probably loves us," I said. "But he doesn't love Mammy. The lady tole her that."

Of course, I couldn't tell Patsy everything. I couldn't tell her how Mammy had cried on the floor, and how when I ran with Yvonne to the tree, the old lady's daughter, the one I had seen with Daddy the day Yvonne was born, had tried to snatch Yvonne from my arms. I couldn't tell Patsy how, when the daughter realized I wasn't going to let Yvonne go, she had cursed Yvonne and plucked her on the top of her head, so hard, with her nasty fingers, that Yvonne had started to scream. I couldn't tell Patsy because I was afraid she would tell Mammy. But I wanted to. I wanted Patsy to know about all I had seen. I needed her to explain it to me.

"You betta not go to school tomorrow talking that nonsense or the Sistas will have your head," Patsy said.

Patsy's lip curled to one side and she closed her book. The clouds over us were thinned out like pieces of yarn. The sun was high, but the day wasn't too hot. "How come you does be with Mammy when she does alla them t'ings?" Patsy asked.

"Weren't you with Daddy?"

"Never showed up." Daddy had sworn he would take Patsy fishing that day. Patsy's bottom lip drooped. "I'm sick of him."

"He probably got busy," I said.

"Too busy for his own chile? Mammy's bad enough with her sewing, with Yvonne, with Wesley, and now with her obeah." She dug her heel into the black soil where we had planted carrots the year before. They had been small and yellow and bland. "I'm done with the both of them."

I was sure Patsy didn't mean it. As angry as we all could make one another, I didn't think any of us could ever turn our backs for good.

FAROUK KARAM

Aunty Baba heard the exchange between me and Marcia the day Yvonne was born. Before I left the house she brought Yvonne to me.

"Take this chile in your hand before you never see her again," she said.

My clothes were wet. "I don't wanta hold her. Look at what that woman did to me."

"Look at what you did to yourself." She pushed Yvonne into my damp arms. "You lucky if you ever see any of them chil'ren again. Marcia will take a lot, but if she find out what you doin', she'll never forgive you."

Aunty Baba looked me right in the eye and said, "Very few secrets does go to the grave."

Not seeing the children was harder than I had expected. But having to deal with the angry mother of your children can make any man stay away. I couldn't stand to hear all the rubbish, get all the grief, deal with all the damn commotion that came with talking to that woman. At work nearly every day, I saw dead bodies, handled grieving families, racked my brain on the who-done-it question, and believe it or not, dealing with Marcia was harder than all that. Sometimes, it was easier to not show up.

It had been almost four weeks when I made up my mind to go and see them. It was a murky-sky Friday and I left a witness interview early, hoping to spend a little time with the children, then meet up later with fellas from work.

When I got to Curepe, children were home from school, running the streets. Grown-ups were arriving after work with groceries in hand. Aunties and grandmothers who'd been watching babies since dawn were washing them up for dinner. Every home in Curepe showed signs of life, except Marcia Garcia's house.

"Where allyuh?" I said, softly, at her locked door.

At the back of the house, I patted clammy garments on the line. I peeked through the window, but long, gathered drapes blocked my view. "Marcia's damn fancy curtains," I cursed.

I walked back to the front and knocked harder. I wanted to hold that new baby and I show up to find nothing but a piece of lumber staring at me?

Whenever Marcia and the children left the house, they never closed it up like that. I pounded the teal-painted paneled wood. "Open the damn door!"

Marcia hadn't given me a key. I paid the damn rent, but I had no key. Craziness. "What if somet'ing's wrong inside there?" I had said. "What if I can't get in to help allyuh?"

"If, if, if," she had mocked me. "If shit was sugar, Farouk, farmers wouldn't plant cane, eh? *If* you t'ink we dead inside, I'm sure you'll find a way in besides gently turnin' the key."

I was jiggling the doorknob with outraged fingers when the next-door neighbor came outside and stood on her porch. She glared. Damn nosy people. "I'm the fadda!" I said.

She stared as if I'd told her I was St. Nicholas, then said, "If every fadda show up makin' noise like you, the whola Trinidad would be up all night and day."

I gave her a long cheups and this time with open palms, I slapped Marcia's door. "Open up!"

And that's when the flower-printed curtain moved. A soft sway of two red roses.

"I can see you, Jackie! Open the damn door! It's your fadda here. You see me?" I wasn't sure it was Jackie, but if she *was* inside, I knew she'd be the first to break. "Jackie! Do you hear me? Open the blasted door!"

The neighbor stepped into the road. Her hands met her hips. Her headful of cane-rows shook-shook-shook, until another neighbor came over to ask her what was happening.

I couldn't give a damn about those stupid women, but Marcia—if I knew Marcia—she'd do anything to keep attention away from her door. If she saw those two ladies in the middle of the road looking at her house, she wouldn't hold out much longer.

Within the minute, the lock turned. Marcia, her breasts bountiful with milk and her back bowed, opened the door.

Gawd. The second I laid eyes on her, I grew hard. Though we'd been together plenty, I hadn't wanted her that badly in a long time. I had no idea why that urge hit me, but the feeling was raw and uncontrollable, and feeling it made me angrier.

She licked her full pink lips. "Go away, Farouk."

"Whatya mean, 'go away'?" I heard my voice, softer than I expected it to be. I couldn't keep my eyes off her chest.

"I have the chil'ren inside and I tole them you're never to set foot in my house again."

The white jersey vest she wore with no brassiere underneath was mine. She was wearing *my* shirt and keeping me from *my* house. "Your house? Your house? I pay for this house."

"You can't control me again." She stretched her arms over her head, in an oval. "I know everyt'ing. I know what you did to me. With the boys. Everyt'ing. I know who you really is."

"Woman, what kinda craziness you talkin'?"

Marcia leaned back into the house. "Take Yvonne and go out back. I'll be there soon," she said to the children. She stood with her hip pressed into the doorframe. "Just go, nah." She cheupsed. "Go start anudda life with that woman and she crazy daughter."

Blasted Tanty Gertrude. My head was hot with worry. "It's not what you t'ink it is," I said, with such desperation I surprised myself.

"Oh no? I remember you not believing me once when I said that." She stepped onto the porch. Small milk dots stained my shirt. "The woman bring me to she house and try to kill me, and it's not what I t'ink it is?"

"What? That's madness."

Her voice dropped to a raspy whisper. "Threatening to kill our chil'ren if I don't leave you alone. Tellin' me sh-she killed them boys because you asked her to. And you wanta tell me *it's not what I t'ink it is?*"

I leaned back against the porch rail. She cupped her breasts with both hands and pushed them up in such a way that I thought I'd literally die if I couldn't have them again. She needed to nurse. She wouldn't let me in and she wouldn't stay out much longer. "I never had anyt'ing anyt'ing to do with them boys going missing and you know that. Let me come in and explain the rest."

"All them years, I couldn't understand why I couldn't let you go," she said. "Why you wouldn't let me go. Why so many t'ings . . ." She sighed. "None of it was real? Was it all made up by some obeah woman you gave away your soul to?"

"Nah-man, no." For some reason just the thought of Marcia leaving me for good was shaking me to my core.

"You're such a fool." She cheupsed again. "Your life hasn't been real atall. She's been controlling you the whole time."

Marcia wasn't that angry, which bothered me all the more. She seemed disappointed. Disappointed that the man in front of her wasn't the man she believed me to be.

"T'ink what we coulda been togedda if you hadn't done all that rubbish. I really t'ought you understood me betta." Tears, which I hadn't expected, bubbled up from her big, tea-colored eyes.

"Let me explain myself. Let me at least talk to the chil'ren."

"Don't come here again." She took one step back toward the door. "I not gointa tell them everyt'ing and I can't keep you from them outsida this house, but your dirtiness is not welcome in here. I trying to raise good and decent chil'ren. Whatya t'ink all that shitty karma you now have gointa do to them?" She pointed her finger at my eye. "The son of a pandit lying in bed with the obeah lady's daughter!"

"She tell you that?"

"She tell me everyt'ing."

I held out my hands in a plea. A gesture I'd seen criminals perform more times than I could count. "The chil'ren don't deserve to have us broken like this. We do a good job of keeping t'ings togedda for them."

She stared past me. "You destroyed them t'ree chil'ren." She wiped her last tear. "You've broken their hearts over and over. And their mudda's, too. If you cared about them, you'd remember that the sins of the parents does fall unto the child. And God don't sleep."

1958

"PAY AS YOU EARN"

BY THE MIGHTY SPARROW

Chapter 6

MARCIA GARCIA

"Eh-eh, what's happening here?" I asked Farouk.

For four years, he had come around for and with the children, sometimes sparingly and sometimes not sparingly enough. He left money for school, would drop by to talk over some issue or another while I hung clothes on the line, but in those four years, though we never officially divorced, I had never let Farouk back inside my house.

Then, one chirrupy day, he breezes by with a truck and two men. "I have a surprise," he said.

I placed myself before the door, my arms crossing my chest. "I don't want no surprises. I've had more surprises than any woman can take from a fella named Farouk Karam."

Farouk muttered something to the two stocky men, who then scurried back to the truck. "Don't ruin it, Marcia. Come, move aside."

The children, hearing us at the front, squeezed past me, making their way onto the porch.

"Daddy, you got a promotion?" Jacqueline said, sitting down on the top step.

For just a moment, I saw a flash of the same humiliated boy I had seen when Farouk took me to meet his parents. Jacqueline, who was only eleven years old, couldn't have known that her father, who had a reputation for being quite a good corporal, was long overdue for another stripe.

"A nice commendation is all," he said.

Over the next half hour, as the men began to remove something big and heavy from the truck, I watched Yvonne, Wesley, and Jacqueline, loving Farouk despite the cloud of disappointment that hung over them. Patsy's face, on the other hand, alternated between the slightest expressions of pleasure, sadness, pain.

"Patsy, come here," I called out.

I gently spun her around. "Let's go and wash you up."

In the rear of the house, I helped Patsy wash out the blood from her dress. It had only been a few months since she had started to bleed. I handed her another piece of terrycloth to put inside a fresh pair of underpants.

"Maybe your fadda should ask what we need instead of bringing what he does want," I said. "I see them sanitary belts down in Port-of-Spain and can't figure out who does have money for them t'ings. The woman in the store tole me they have some that when you finish using it, you just toss it in the trash and go and buy more."

Patsy moved slowly, putting on a clean black dress I had chosen. "Your belly hurtin'?" I touched her face. "After your fadda finishes with this craziness, go and lay yourself down. Mammy will make you tea and boil you up some dhal and *caraili*. The caraili's bitterness does be good for the pain."

"T'ank you, Mammy," she said.

"You bleed heavy like your mudda, so take special care, alright? If you feel the flow getting heavy, go and change your cloth. Leave it just so in this bucket. Mammy will get it later."

She dropped her eyes as if she wanted to say something else. "One girl at school tole me this means I can have a baby."

I cheupsed long and hard, hoping the sound would cover my panic. "Yes, you can make a baby if you foolish enough to let some boy come that close to you, but I know you betta than that." I wrung out her dress, hoping to avoid another question.

"Mammy?" Her eyes moved from left to right. "What if I wanta have a baby?"

My nose flared. She was taking in every moment of my reaction, wondering how far she could push me. I moved into the yard, hanging her dress on the twine nailed from my lime tree to my mango tree. "You're my chile. Don't be like them chupid gals in school. You need to study them books. Don't you wanta be a teacher?"

"A policewoman," she said.

"Only one in a million girls are picked to be a policewoman. You have to have real connections for that."

"Daddy is on the force."

I could hear the other children and Farouk laughing out front. "Even if he knew the right people, he wouldn't help you, because he t'inks it's too dangerous," I said. "And he's right. Teaching is a betta choice for a smart girl like you."

Her hand floated to her hip. "But that's not what I want."

"Two seconds ago, you wanted a baby." I was trying not to lose patience. "You can't know what you want at your age. Focus on your studies—on passing the Common Entrance exam. That will keep your future open, Patsy."

We walked back to the front. The two fellas had finished carrying the whatever-it-was inside and had set it in the middle of my floor.

Farouk glanced at Wesley, who made a drum roll with his tongue. Farouk pulled off the cloth cover with one swish. "It's a Primus kerosene stove." He spread his arms wide, palms to the ceiling. "I t'ought it'd be nice for allyuh to have." He took a deep breath and patted the stove, as if reassuring himself, in my silence, that it had been the right decision. "We can set it up where you like."

The stove was a yard in width and as tall as Wesley. It had a square door on its front with a silver-colored horizontal handle I could pull down to slide in a well-shaped loaf of dough to be buttered within an hour. There were four burners on top. One for my pot of callaloo, one for my pot of lentils, one for my pot of stewed chicken, and the other for my pot of rice.

"Oh Lord, I gointa need more pots!" I clapped my hands in delight. Farouk and the children roared with laughter. I couldn't take my eyes off that black beauty. Nobody had ever before given me anything meant to make my life easier.

I cooked that evening—thick cuts of meat, heavy sauces, light pastries. The house smelled the way I thought a Parisian bistro might. We had six sturdy chairs (two of them borrowed); Farouk, with Jacqueline and Yvonne on one end, and Wesley, Patsy, and me on the other. Together, we ate.

FAROUK KARAM

The decomposed man who washed up on the banks of the Caura River had been a father to six small children. He left behind a grieving wife and two heartbroken sisters. He had last been seen arguing over a poker hand in St. Augustine with Derrick Rogers, a fella well known for distributing large quantities of marijuana across Port-of-Spain and possibly into British Guiana and northern Venezuela.

I had promised the children I would take them out for a few hours the very afternoon I collected the last bit of testimony from the witnesses in the case.

"I'm just gointa take a quick trip to St. Augustine and get a feel for the Rogers fella," I said to Duncan, not long after the lunch hour.

"Wait here. Rogers isn't a fella to go and see alone."

"But it's a quick chat," I said.

Duncan set down his forage cap and pulled me aside. "That fella's into some real craziness." His tone was severe. "Cocaine, prostitution, and some kinda business where they set up women to work for free in America."

"For free?"

"Some fellas working for him gets them women to believe they goin' for good jobs. The white people up there does pay these fellas and nobody hears from these women again," he said. "Rogers is a vicious fella. Inspector Marlock from Arouca wants in on the interrogation. You'll go with him."

I gave Duncan a questioning eye—Inspector Marlock, himself, had a reputation for being vicious.

"Keep your eye out for Marlock, too," he added.

I waited more than two hours for Inspector Marlock to arrive. By that time, the only chance I had of making my set time with the children was to get out of the questioning altogether.

"Inspector Marlock." I trailed behind him. "I was hoping to have finished our questioning by now. I have plans with my family."

He brushed lint from the side of his right trouser leg. "So?"

"So, sir, perhaps we can visit Rogers tomorrow? I can meet you early."

Marlock was a short man with distinct Chinese eyes. He was well known for his skilled politicking and his intimidation tactics, and though his rank wasn't yet equal to his importance, he was now a major player in the force. He had been put in charge of the new narcotics division. "You want me to change plans because you need to go see family?" He snickered and turned his back. "You betta t'ink twice before you approach me with nonsense, Corporal. Your family's not more important than this job."

He tossed the keys over the wet hood. I drove us to St. Augustine, with only the pitter-patter of raindrops between us, thinking the entire ride how Marcia was going to have my head for disappointing those children again.

When we arrived at the locked gate of a large white house, a woman with wide hips and high cheekbones walked down a lengthy stretch of concrete steps to meet us. She asked what we needed with Rogers.

"You his wife?" Marlock asked. "If not, open up and go about your business."

Rogers, with a long forehead and nostrils that widened when he inhaled, met us at the door. Despite the rain, he insisted we speak to him on a narrow, outdoor platform. In all my years as a policeman, I'd never had anyone refuse to let me come in during questioning, but it didn't seem to bother Marlock, who chatted with Rogers about cigars, liquor, diamond and gold prospecting in British Guiana, along with whatever else came to Marlock's mind. When I finally squeezed in a question about the dead floater, Rogers threw open his reddened eyes at Marlock, as if speaking to me was too far beneath him. "I hardly knew the fella," he said.

Marlock thanked him and hurried me down the steps. "Lay off Rogers. I'm building a big big case against him and I don't need him doing time on some li'l nobody drug user."

"There's no evidence the dead fella was using anyt'ing," I said. "He's got a family, some chil'ren who care about findin' the person responsible for this."

"So?"

"So, if Rogers is involved, we probably need to question him betta than what just happened up there," I said. "Don't we, sir?"

Marlock stopped, rubbing his tongue along his teeth. "No, *we* do not. It'll work out betta for alla us this way," he said. "Big promotions coming up, Karam. You could use a good word from somebody with more weight than your friend Duncan."

I'd be lying if I said I never thought of Mammy and Daddy being together. I daydreamed about it plenty more than I wanted to admit. And some days that hope, which had a habit of chewing up my insides, seemed more promising than other days.

I was tapping crunchy, caked mud from my shoes, imagining Mammy and Daddy smiling at one another, when Miss Edith, the lady who lived across from us, called out, "Allyuh not havin' a party for your fadda?"

"A party? For what?"

"Eh-eh, you didn't hear the announcements on the radio? Your fadda a big-time sergeant. Ambition chokin' he now." She laughed and walked back into her house.

I ran inside to find Mammy. She was at her machine, stitching white-petal flowers at the bottom of a long, blue, fishtailed dress. "Chile, you ain't seeing I'm working?" she said.

Friday was Mammy's sacred workday. It wasn't smart for God Himself to yell out to Mammy on a Friday.

"Mammy, Miss Edith just tell me Daddy made sergeant."

"Good for him," she said, with a needle pinched between her lips.

When Daddy had brought the stove she had been skinnin' up her teeth then; making jokes, cooking food, singing all night like some kinda *mou-mou*. Now, I was telling her good news about him and she hardly showed interest?

"We have to do somet'ing for him," I said.

She waved me off. "Do what you does have to. But not while I'm workin'."

I gathered up Patsy, Wesley, and Yvonne into the bedroom. Even Patsy, who was almost thirteen and didn't seem to care much for anything anymore, agreed we should have Daddy come for dinner.

The next morning, the tip of the orange ball of sun was just peaking when I sent Wesley to tell Daddy to be at our house at exactly six o'clock that night.

Mammy was at the table with her morning tea, staring out the front window with a book in her lap.

"Mammy, you gointa bake the cake for Daddy?"

She looked at me almost without focusing. "What you sayin?"

"For Daddy's party," I said. "A cake?"

"Eh-eh, who tell allyuh you can have a party for your fadda?"

Patsy, Yvonne, and me rolled the dough for the roti and boiled the white rice and cassava. Mammy, returning from her room, watched us for a moment. "When allyuh gointa give me some space to put this cake togedda?" She half-smiled and tapped her toes, forcing herself, it seemed, into a good mood. "Go and put on the music, Yvonne."

Before we knew it, six o'clock was on top of us. We had all bathed, put on nice dresses and fixed our hair. Neither Daddy nor Wesley had shown his face.

Mammy turned off the radio. The smell of cake and spicy curry blended in the silent air. "Nobody's comin' here tonight," Mammy finally said.

We had begun to dish out our dinner when we heard footsteps on the porch.

"This a funeral or a party?" Daddy rubbed his hands together, and I ran into his arms. He was wearing a silky black shirt with black pants, and smelled like woods and cinnamon. Wesley stood behind him, looking sheepish. "Hello, Marcia." Daddy was still patting the top of my head. Mammy nodded. He walked to the open pot and sniffed the food. "Let's eat," he said. Then, he saw the cake. The white icing letters spelling "Congratulations."

His face reddened. "This means a lot to me," he said.

At dinner, Daddy praised me and teased Mammy. "Jackie, you cooked this strimp betta than your mudda. Her strimp does be small and hard and you does have to pull the li'l buggers out your teet' with such force, sometimes you ain't sure it's the strimps or a piece of your toot' you does be chewing."

"You lucky you got teet' left," Mammy said cheerfully, putting up her right fist.

After dinner, the Mighty Sparrow's "Pay as You Earn" got us on our feet. Wesley, pretending to be Sparrow, pressed a cucumber to his chin. Mammy wined her hips around and down, while Daddy held her waist and threw back his head, laughing hard. Patsy, who used to love to dance with Daddy, only watched while the rest of us carried on. By the end of the night, I could think of nothing but sleep.

But tired meant little to Mammy. She didn't want her "stove lookin' a mess in the morning," so we cleaned. Afterward, Mammy told us to "go and rest yourselves" and she walked Daddy to the door.

The four of us huddled in the dark hallway.

"T'ank you," Daddy said to Mammy.

"Not me," she said. "Your li'l *pickneys* did this for you."

"Even Patsy?" Daddy grinned, but there was a bit of sadness behind it.

"She helped, though she should've been studying," Mammy said.

Patsy inched to the front of our circle. "At that age, girls can be a li'l down. She'll snap out of it."

They began to stare at each other like two small children trying to figure out if they wanted to play or to fight. Then Daddy reached for Mammy's fingers.

"Good night, Farouk." She pulled her hand away and cleared her throat. She looked toward the back of the house. She knew we were there. "And congratulations again," she said. "You got what you always wanted, eh?"

"Nah." Daddy pulled her into him and tucked his arms under hers. She didn't push him away. "No, I didn't."

In air still filled with the odor of blown-out candlewicks, Daddy leaned into Mammy and kissed her softly and quite beautifully.

I had never seen Mammy and Daddy kiss, and I had never been as happy as I was when his lips touched hers.

Monday was Daddy's day off from work. After we arrived home from school, Mammy packed us up and put us on a minibus to Tunapuna.

It was a new beginning and the excitement was overwhelming. Fresh air from the open windows blew onto our faces. Mammy cracked jokes on the bumpy bus ride, making us promise to behave, while she behaved the silliest of us all.

She had demanded that we dress in our newest and best clothes: Wesley wore a white button-down shirt and tan pants; Yvonne, a pink, frilly dress; Patsy was in a yellow halter-top number; and I wore a long, grey skirt with a pink, flowered shirt.

Mammy too wore a never-before-seen, straight-lined, periwinkle-blue dress with white high heels.

Walking from the stop to Daddy's house, we were quite the smart-looking family.

"When your fadda opens the door, Jacqueline, make sure you tell

him coming to see him was your idea." Mammy was nervous, but she
also seemed delighted.

I thought about how when Daddy moved into our house, we would
have more time with him. We would see him in the mornings, maybe
sip from his teacup. We would see him for supper, which Mammy
would have ready when he walked through the door. Maybe he would
help us with homework and pay for piano lessons, since he'd have more
money with only one house to keep up.

We passed a field where I had seen boys playing football once when
I visited Daddy, and I wondered what Mammy would say to him.
"Hello, Farouk," she might say. "I'd like for us to get married and be
togedda forever." If she had asked me, I was sure I could've come up
with something more romantic, but of course, Mammy wasn't the
type to ask for help.

We made the left onto Daddy's road and walked halfway toward his
house before Mammy slowed. "Isn't that your fadda's house?" Her head
was cocked to the side, her left hand ironing the fabric of her dress.

I didn't know if Mammy had ever visited Daddy. When she asked,
I just thought she didn't know which house belonged to him. "It's the
one with the yellow door," I said. The five of us stood in the middle of
the road and looked toward the house with the yellow door. Daddy,
not seeing us, held the door open and hugged a woman whose face
was blocked by a tall, potted tree. A baby *palmiste* tree Mammy had
pulled from our yard for him.

"Who's that?" Wesley said.

Yes, who in the bloody hell is that? was exactly what the rest of us
wanted to scream out to Daddy before he closed the door on our
future.

Mammy nudged our backs with sharp fingers. She seemed to not
want Daddy, his neighbors, or his woman, to see us in the middle of
the road, all fancied up with no place to go . . . and with nobody who
wanted us.

1961

"ROYAL JAIL"

BY THE MIGHTY SPARROW

Chapter 7

FAROUK KARAM

The circumstances under which I received my promotion bothered me a great deal. But I turned out to be a damn good sergeant. After kissing Marcia the night of my party, I had hoped to have the same success in my family life. I thought she and I could make something new out of the old.

But when I went to Curepe the next week, she told me not to set foot back in that house again.

"Crazy woman!" I screamed at the unbending door between us.

I was embarrassed. Every damn time I turned around, Marcia was changing her mind. So, I pulled back. Got myself a little break. Of course, I saw the children . . . once a month or so. Occasionally, I'd ask one of the bigger ones to bring Yvonne to see me in Tunapuna. But mostly I saw Jackie. She liked to be alone with me. And I liked spending time with her. During many of her visits we cooked, prepping food on two wicker chairs I'd put in my front yard.

"You ever wonder why Mammy won't let you come see us at the house anymore?" she asked one day, as we peeled potatoes.

"T'ree years is too long to be t'inking of why your mudda does anyt'ing." I took Jackie's potatoes and added them to my bowl.

"Don't you wanta see us more often?"

"What I want has never made a difference to your mudda."

"She shoulda tell you we saw you with a woman." Her words were cutting, as if she'd been sharpening the blade every day for three years. She watched my hands harden around the edge of the scratched tin bowl; she dug her heel into the blades of grass underfoot. "The week after you kissed Mammy in the house, you held open the door and kissed some udda woman." Jackie motioned with her arms to show me how I had invited trouble that day.

"That's why allyuh wasn't speakin' to me?"

She took her schoolbooks out of her bag while I carried the bowl of browning potatoes into the kitchen. I watched her through the door, the potatoes sweating in the pot behind me. I had wanted a nice, easy meal with my daughter. Now, it felt like a battle. A battle she had come prepared for, when I didn't even know there was a war.

It was the end of our meal before either of us spoke again. She said, "Daddy, you should spend more time with Wesley." She was mashing the last of her curry potatoes with the back of her spoon.

"Bring Yvonne next time you come," I said.

"I didn't say Yvonne. I said Wesley."

I wasn't going to let Jackie tell me how I would spend my time with her. "What's going on with Patsy now that she failed her exam?"

Jacqueline dropped her spoon against the plate. "She can't even stand to be in the same room as you, so why do you care?"

"Chil'ren should be seen and not heard, you ever hear that?"

"Every time I'm with you, I does hear it." She stacked my empty plate on top of hers. The plates rattled. "You only say that when you don't like what I'm saying."

I helped put her schoolbooks in her bag, and walked her to the door.

"Wesley's been running with the wrong boys."

"Well, at least he's not in the house with your mudda sewing pretty dresses."

"He loves to sew. And he's good at it." She rubbed her thumb along the strap of her bag.

"He's not even making men's clothes." I opened the door. "No boy of mine should be in the house sewing."

"In Europe and even in America, some men sew."

"We're in Trinidad. Real boys don't sew dresses here."

She clutched her bag to her side. "You'd rather see him smoking cigarettes, running like he's crazy, and not treating his sistas properly? He's rude, Daddy. Rude."

"He's being a boy." We walked down the steps toward the gate. "Boys go t'rough rough times like this."

She took one step out of the gate before stopping again. "I know you t'ink running me out the door means this conversation is over," she said, reaching for my neck and kissing me on the cheek, "but I won't stop bringing these t'ings up until you right them."

I turned from her. "You don't get to talk to your fadda like he's a chile."

"I'm not," she said, standing behind me. "I know that I'm the chile. I'm *your* chile."

MARCIA GARCIA

I hadn't seen Uncle Linton since the day he showed up in Blanchis-seuse to offer sympathies about the boys. As before, his wife, Aunty Cecilia, wrote the note asking that I come to Sangre Grande.

When I arrived, yardmen in green jumpers were working the vast lawn. They were cleaning, painting, pulling weeds, preparing the house for some grand occasion, it seemed. They worked at an easy, island pace they could maintain throughout the toasty afternoon, a pace that could turn a three-day job into a five-day one.

Uncle Linton's house had fallen into a bit of disrepair. The yellow stucco exterior was stained with grey watermarks, three window shutters dangled from their black upper tips, and the two-story, wrap-around porch, chipped and dented, appeared as if it would cave in on the top of my head.

I rang the bell.

"Good day, Aunty Cecilia." I reached out to give the required kiss on her tight cheek, but she pulled back.

The sun had weathered her skin. It now resembled icing on a novice cook's homemade cake, droopy and swirly. The wig was there, as glossy as ever. This time with streaks of red dye, like a Carnival hairpiece. Her face powder, which had left a bit of caramel color on the collar of her button-down tan dress, was several shades lighter than her complexion. Her eye shadow, applied heavily under sharply arched brows, was a too-blue royal.

"I read your note," I said. "You need an outfit for your grandchile?"

She moved aside, closing the door behind me. "*He* wants to see you. I don't need anyt'ing from you, dear."

I followed her through the house, past the bedroom where Uncle Linton had found me the last time, into his office. He stood at the window, his broad back to the door, giving instructions to one of the gardeners. "Eh-eh, you know the difference between a flower and a weed?"

Hearing his voice made my stomach plunge.

When he finally met his desk again, he was startled to find his wife and me standing there. "Oh . . . well, good day." He pulled up his slacks with hefty, thick-fingered hands and rubbed the skin on his neck downward.

Uncle Linton had been a relatively thin man, but, by his now-full face and round belly, life had gotten quite sweet. His hair was grey, frizzy, thinning at the front. He had brushed it flat, as only a man proud of his semi-straight-hair heritage would do. His prominent nose was less narrow, a tad longer. His real teeth, which had been overcrowded at the bottom, had been replaced by super-white, custom-made dentures.

His eyes, however, remained the same. A reserved yet dazzling grey-brown he used to stare me down.

"Cecilia, you can go now." He didn't look at his wife when he spoke. I realized that life with him had probably always been like that for her.

He pointed to a black leather chair with rectangular metal legs that must've been imported. "Have a seat."

I placed my bag and sewing kit beneath the chair. I hadn't noticed Aunty Cecilia still lurking in the doorway until he waved her out again. He walked to the door. "Excuse her." The lock echoed.

I listened to his footsteps, gripping the arms of the chair until he faced me again from behind his desk.

"You wondering why I called you here, eh?" He leaned his weight into the palm of his left hand. He wasn't wearing his wedding band. Maybe his fingers had gotten too fat.

"Somet'ing funny?" he asked.

I was smirking? "No . . . no." My voice cracked.

He stared a moment longer. "You know your uncle is the head of the Trinidad Federation Party, right?" He pointed to himself as if I needed direction. "And as the head of the party, I'll become Prime Minister if we win against the PNM, which we'll do."

Uncle Linton seemed quite sure of himself, which was strange since most people had already concluded that there was no way the Trinidad Federation Party could win against Dr. Eric Williams's People's National Movement Party. Dr. Eric Williams was a genuine hero. Barring death or the second coming of Christ, nobody would win against him.

"What do you t'ink about that?" he asked, taking his seat.

"What do I t'ink about you wanting to be Prime Minister?" I wasn't accustomed to him asking my opinion on anything. "I t'ink you're too old."

"Ha-ha," he said, tightly. "With age comes wisdom, no?"

"And death."

"You're a lot like your mudda," he said. "You remember her?" He sighed and sipped something from a white mug that teetered on the edge of the desk. "She was a good gal." He lost his words for a moment. "The best part of my life was with her. I miss her every day."

Uncle Linton wanted me to think of my mother, but all I could think of was him and what he had done to us. After Ma died, Daddy's legs had slowed to a stop. We were starving. Me and Ginny were boiling bark, stealing runaway chickens. Then Daddy sent word to Uncle Linton. We needed help.

"Listen, we mustn't spend too much time reminiscing. I have plenty to do." He searched his papers, rearranging them, shuffling them again. "You need to leave Trinidad," he said. "And soon." He pushed himself up and leaned over his massive wooden desk. "And for good."

Why could I think of nothing to say?

"It's the only way I can be sure that everyt'ing I need to be in order for the election, will be."

Finally, my mind and mouth met again. "Whatya saying?"

"You know what I mean, girl."

I was thirty-four years old with four children, and he was still calling me "girl"? "No, I don't."

"I made a few mistakes, but I did a lot to help you. You owe me." He rubbed his hands together. They sounded as if they'd been dipped in chalk. "I'll give you a good start wherever you wanta go. America. England. Let's not make this difficult."

I swallowed hard, willing myself to speak. "I have chil'ren. Chil'ren born here in Trinidad."

"What are they doing with their lives?" He squeezed himself back into the chair behind his desk and picked up a cracked fountain pen, twirling it. "The oldest one failed her Common Entrance. The next will probably fail too. The boy hasn't shown promise. And the baby . . . if you really love her, you'll give her a betta life in a country with more opportunities."

"Wonderful t'ing for the next Prime Minister to say." He leaned back. The leather rumbled. "And please don't bad-mout' my chil'ren." My nails slipped from the metal arm of his chair. "You know nutting about my chil'ren. They'll be just fine."

"Not if you stay. I'll make sure of that." His fat fingers waddled their way down the front of his shirt. He fiddled with the plastic buttons along his heavy cotton stitch. "When t'ings or people get in my way, I find a way to move them along. You understand?"

I did not understand.

He raised his eyebrows. "You t'ink I was gointa let two li'l retarded chil'ren get in the way of my life?"

He slapped his feet up onto his desk. "I was givin' you a chance at a life, too," he said. "They wasn't your chil'ren. Your sista died and left you with too big a burden. It wasn't right to have you lookin' after them for the rest of your life."

I was beginning to understand. I rose, stood behind my seat, but what I really wanted was to crawl over his desk and claw his eyes out.

He yawned.

"You're a rapist *and* a murderer?"

I had finally said it.

Out loud.

After almost a lifetime.

He slammed his feet back onto the blue and black shag rug beneath his desk, grabbing the handles of the windows, winding them shut. "There's workers all over this house. Hush your mout'!"

Uncle Linton had always wanted people to hush because he had plenty to hide. He had been ashamed of his family, ashamed of everything about his roots except for the land inheritance that helped to make him a rich man. My mother told me that from the moment he left Blanchisseuse with the village *patois* dripping from his tongue, he had been determined not to return. When she had begged him to visit, he would send her something pretty and expensive, but he never came back until the day of her funeral.

And then he was angry.

Angry at my father, the Negro, who had taken away his baby sister and kept her living in the bush. So, he made Daddy pay by taking his daughters and making him listen from outside on a broken porch.

"Hush?" I said.

He walked to my side of his desk. "You will. You always been a smart gal." He held one hand open, close to my face.

"The last t'ing Ginny asked me to do was to mind them boys as if they were my own."

He smoothed the front of his shirt, then pulled up the waist of his pants, over his stomach. His voice was even, calm. "You have a bad mind, chile. You forget I'm your family? I'm trying to protect you."

I needed to leave. Nothing good would come if I stayed there longer. Yet, walking out, saying no to him, felt so hard—impossible.

"What about that husband of yours?" he said.

I picked up my bag and sewing kit from the floor. "I don't have a husband."

"Oh right, right," he said. "Well, him leaving you was probably best. He'll turn out to be a no-good man. I'm sure of it."

Hearing Uncle Linton mention Farouk took me to a place I didn't want to be. Uncle Linton had been the reason Farouk left me. My lies shielding Uncle Linton's lies.

"We talked a long time ago about the kinds of t'ings that could happen if alla this ever got out." Uncle Linton's eyes, driven downward by gravity, grew large, pensive, excited as if we had finally arrived at where he wanted this to go. "Does he know of my connection with them boys?"

From the moment I met Farouk, I knew if he knew the truth about my family, he would never have allowed it to rest. There would've been questions about my willingness. Questions about Ginny's willingness. Questions Farouk would've asked until the dead was unearthed, until hell was raised, until Farouk was satisfied. God only knows where he would've taken it. I wouldn't have had a moment's peace. I could never have told Farouk. Uncle Linton was worried about someone who should've been the least of his worries. The uneasiness in his eyes . . . I had only ever dreamt of seeing Uncle Linton in such a place.

I stretched out my smirk long enough to make him wonder. "You t'ink it's just you and me, alone, sharing your dirty li'l secret?"

Uncle Linton seemed to be concentrating on keeping himself under control. He pulled at his shirt collar as if he needed air. Then he walked back to the other side of his desk and watched the gardeners. "You t'ink about my offer," he said. "And send a note. I don't want people seeing you coming here again."

I pounded the door.

"Aunty Marilyn, please open up."

She must have seen me walking down the road. There was no reason for a door to be locked in D'Abadie in the middle of the afternoon.

I tossed myself against it and waited. My head ached, my hair felt itchy from the perspiration, my feet were swelling from a black pair of too-tight shoes. But I had nowhere else to go. No one to help me figure it all out.

"I can hear them chil'ren inside. I know somebody's in there with them. Please open the door." Chocolate fingerprints, splashes of fruit, streaks of mud. There was life on the other side of that door. A life Aunty Marilyn had not wanted me to be a part of.

Her dismissal had been abrupt. After Jacqueline was born I had taken her and Patsy to visit, and Aunty Marilyn had shouted from behind the closed door that I was never to come back. She had drawn her curtains. Curtains I had made for her. She left me crying in her yard with two babies, cooking in the hot sun.

"Aunty Marilyn?" I made my voice softer, gentler, less panicked. "You were my mudda's best friend. The one person I could always turn to. Why did you turn me away?"

There was silence on the other side. As if someone had muted the crying children. I stood, wondering if it was time to return home, when a hand snatched my blouse.

I fell to the floor, barely pulling my foot in before the door slammed shut.

Standing over me was Aunty Marilyn. She couldn't have been

much more than fifty years old but was looking more like seventy-five, with penciled-in eyebrows and slack cheeks. "Girl, you got no sense?" She whispered in the way people do when they want to scream but know they shouldn't.

"I needed to talk to you." I pulled myself up from the floor.

"I tell you many many years ago not to come back here." The thinness of her frame surprised me. "I have chil'ren and plenty plenty grandchil'ren, you hear? I don't need no trouble. You was always trouble." She shook her head in disgust.

"I didn't mean to be." The lightness in my voice carried me back twenty years. "I t'ink I know why you didn't want me back, but I need to hear it from you."

She peered at me with compassion and suspicion. "You lookin' more and more like your mudda in your ole years."

I knew that was true. Sometimes my reflection in a mirror shocked me. I looked like my mother. I also looked like Uncle Linton.

"Come," she said. "But you need to leave in five minutes and you betta not mention ever comin' here to nobody, you hear? No-body."

She poured me a cup of warm lime water, then offered me a seat on a wooden stool with a yellow bird painted on its leg.

"What happened that bring you here?" she asked. "That Indian man break your heart or somet'ing?"

"That happened years ago," I said. "No more heart to break."

"I seen that coming. Pretty-face Indian boys's nutting but trouble." She drummed her fingers on the narrow table between us. "I askin' ya what happened that bring you here? Your time here is runnin' runnin' runnin'," she said.

"I just came from Sangre Grande."

Her bottom lip loosened. Her eyes shrank. "So it is him?"

"He tole me to be careful. To watch my chil'ren," I said.

She rocked herself back and forth on her stool, her toes gripping the right-front leg. "Then, you betta."

"You know somet'ing? Tell me."

She took a sip of her lime water and stuck out her tongue. She reached for a shaker of salt, pouring a pinchful into her cup, then licked her fingers. "He tell me the same t'ing back then. Never to let you back here or my chil'ren wouldn't be safe." She threw a pinch into my cup and licked her fingers again. "I felt truly sorry. I loved your mudda. But I love my chil'ren. You understand?"

I understood. I really did.

"That man is a real *bad john*," she continued. "I grew up with him and your mudda, and he always been bad. Your chupid mudda loved him, but he got an evil mind. Just when you t'ink he's fed up and done with you, he does have anudda blow waitin'."

"Did he do somet'ing to you?"

She cheupsed long and hard. "I ain't stirring up no trouble with the past. I don't need the past knockin' on my door," she said. "Knowing him, he's got somebody watching this place right now."

I took a sip of the salty water. The taste was horrible. "What would you do?"

She walked to her back door and threw out her water into the dirt. She glanced around her yard. "First, you need to calm yourself before you get home." She held up her index finger and pressed it upward. "Try not to let them chil'ren feel how scared you is," she said. "Make sure you does lock your doors. Keep a light burning when allyuh sleeping. Make sure your li'l ones—you have more, right?"

How much Aunty Marilyn would've enjoyed my children.

"Don't let them li'l ones run the street too much without somebody watchin' them," she continued, holding up four fingers. "And mostly, you must pray to Gawd, chile. Pray to Gawd that He'll take that man away from your life. Because as long as your uncle is alive and walkin' this eart', you gointa have to protect everybody and anybody you love. You never know who he'll go after first."

FAROUK KARAM

I wasn't at the station ten minutes before I heard his voice at the door behind me.

"Beatrice isn't a crook," Marlock said, getting louder. The constable he was arguing with hadn't respected Marlock enough to quiet himself and bow out of the conversation. "You listening to Eric Williams? A man who does call himself a doctor but can't write no prescriptions?"

"Not many people in the world is as smart as Dr. Eric Williams," the constable said, walking beside Marlock. "University of Woodford Square?"

I kept busy at my paperwork, managing to avoid him until he punched my shoulder. "Karam, you're coming with me." Duncan had suffered a mild stroke. Marlock was covering for him until he recovered. "Our friend's acting up." He slapped the motorcar key into my hand. "We'll go and pay him a nice visit, eh?"

We arrived at Derrick Rogers's house in the early afternoon. We waited for almost an hour in an uncomfortable silence before Marlock exited the motorcar.

There was a new gate: nine feet tall, white metal, sharp teeth sprawling across the top. And there were three new guards: the first, a stout black fella with gold splices between his teeth; the second, a slim Indian fella, with bumpy skin and a handlebar moustache; and the third, a severe-looking Spanish one, who patrolled the back and sides of the house.

The black fella opened the gate.

"Rogers!" Marlock wiped sweat from his forehead and flicked it onto the stucco wall before opening the door. "I don't wanta have to crawl over this place to find you!"

The house was larger than it seemed from the outside. It was fully decorated, broom-swept, organized. The floors were a silver-green marble, the walls a sharp white.

"Can I get my pants on, Inspector Marlock?" Rogers, wearing only long underpants and a green button-down shirt, walked through a door on the left. Wiry, hardened, he had pointy fingernails and scraggly facial hair. He smelled like sulfur.

"You knew I was coming," Marlock said. "Don't make me wait long."

Rogers took another puff of a cigarette that matched the color of his skin. A few minutes later, he returned, holding two glasses of Old Oak rum. He held up a glass to me. "You want?"

"We ain't comin' to have a lime," Marlock said to Rogers. "You lookin' too *sawatee* nowadays. Too flashy." Marlock rested his arms across his belly. "There's an election coming up, if you hadn't noticed. Eric Williams has plans to send the Brits back to England if he wins, and what them Brits want the most is to show people that ever since Williams has been Chief Minister, crime's been up."

"And if the top-brass Brits get sent home, somebody like you has to replace them, right?" Rogers downed the contents of both glasses and set them on a walnut-colored console table. "You planning on makin' life hard for me, Inspector?"

"You needn't worry about what I'm doing," Marlock said.

The shock on my face should have been impossible to miss. But neither Marlock nor Rogers seemed to notice.

Rogers pointed to me. "And who is this?"

"Eh-eh. You don't remember Karam? Your man that showed up floatin' in the river? This fine fella made sure the fingers weren't pointing at you." Marlock slapped me on the back. "Well, Karam is my new horse. The fella who'll be collecting my change from now on. So make nice with him."

I watched Marlock, but he didn't take his eyes off Rogers, who was pulling another slim brown cigarette from his front shirt pocket. "Next time, let me know when you bringin' in somebody new."

"Next time, let *me* know when you runnin' around this island showing my money," Marlock said.

Rogers pushed and pulled and pushed and pulled the cigarette between his long, veiny fingers.

"If you have so much, we might have to work out a li'l bonus," Marlock added. He took two steps toward the console table and lifted one of the empty glasses. He flipped it over. Two drops of sugary rum browned the marble. He rolled the glass back over and set it down on the table again.

He signaled to me that it was time to go.

"I have moves to make," Marlock said, as we walked downhill toward the motorcar. He watched his black shoes dig into pea-size rocks. "Can't be seen here again. And I know you does have moves you wanta make. You have a woman and chil'ren to take care of, right? The best way to do that is t'rough me. You rub my belly and I gointa scratch your back."

MARCIA GARCIA

I had moved the stacks and stacks of books away from the uneven walls. Half of them rested on layers of fabric. The other half, spines downward, lay on the warm floor. Book after book, I searched for those loose pages my mother's father, my grandfather, had stuck inside a back cover. As a child, I had flipped through that book and asked my mother about the sheets. "Some British magazine my fadda liked to read," she had said. "He'd rip out the articles he liked and put the magazine back in the white man's house he was workin' in."

Which book, though?

Jacqueline, Wesley, and Yvonne came in then, smelling like fresh, wet grass. "Mammy?" Jacqueline's hand covered her damp forehead. "We just need to get somet'ing from the room. Can I pass?"

I watched her dip her toes into the few spaces of bare floor remaining. My children knew the rules: Don't misuse the books, don't mark in them, and you must read them all.

"Jacqueline! Wesley! Yvonne! Come!"

The three of them pressed their backsides against the wall as if the books threatened to crawl up their legs.

"Allyuh read almost alla these, right?" I said. "I lookin' for some loose sheets, like from a magazine, that were tucked into the back of one of these books."

"I never saw them," Jacqueline said. Yvonne shook her head.

"Alright. Go on outside and don't come back until I call allyuh in, you hear?" My last hope was Patsy. She was working the evening shift at a bakery. She'd been offered the job after I had spoken to the shop owner about what a bright girl she was.

Yvonne and Jacqueline left the house but Wesley was still there, staring at the floor, his mind in some faraway place.

"Don't feel bad," I said. "You have time to read them. We'll read some togedda soon, alright?"

"Stroker stick," he said.

That boy was always talking nonsense. "Chile, go on outta here with your sistas." I flipped to the back of Hardy's *Tess of the D'Urbervilles*.

"Stroker stick," he said again, one hand resting on the doorknob.

"Wesley! Leave, chile. Mammy is busy."

"The pages were about sticks. Sticks in Stroker," he said. "I read those pages. I liked them. They were in . . . Stroker."

"Stroker? Stoker?" I asked. "*Dracula*?"

I pushed books on top of books and at the bottom of the third-to-last stack, close to the chair where Wesley slept, I found Bram Stoker's *Dracula*, and at the back of it, folded in eighths, the yellow-tinted pages.

I scrambled over and grabbed Wesley's chubby face. I kissed him. "God, you're like a li'l quiet genius."

He ran outside, jumping from the top step of the porch to meet his sisters.

"Don't go far!" I yelled.

"How a Man May Defend Himself Against Every Form of Attack." When I had read the article as a child, the words had meant nothing. Back then, it was just fun to look at the pictures and read about the crazy man in England, Barton-Wright, who wrote pieces in *Pearson's Magazine* teaching people how to fight.

I had four faded articles. The papers were crispy, fragile, the black letters nearly invisible on the outer edges. I read them through dinner. Jacqueline had cooked macaroni pie. I read them through bath time. Jacqueline made sure everyone was soaped and oiled. I read them through bedtime. Yvonne fell asleep with the light, bright and yellow, in her face.

I soaked in those words, reading them over and over, convinced that the lives of my children depended upon them.

The next morning I called the children into the kitchen. Faces hadn't been washed, hair hadn't been combed. "I want allyuh back home this afternoon right after school," I said. "And, Patsy, straight home after work, you hear? We have to work on somet'ing."

"Lessons on sewing again?" Patsy said.

"No. But don't t'ink that me and you is t'rough with that. All you girls in this house will learn to sew."

Wesley had been the only child to show any interest in the work that kept us eating. He liked to be at my side, watching and learning the trade my mother had passed on to me from her mother. He was beginning to understand that sewing was not only a tool, it was sustenance, it was an art.

That morning, after the children left, instead of sewing, I practiced what I would teach them. I moved parts of my body I hadn't ever moved. I walked the streets of Curepe searching for five long, thick tree branches, dragging them back to the house, smoothing the jagged edges with a sharp knife.

By early afternoon I was ready. When the children arrived, I told them to change into comfortable clothes.

"We gointa do cali-cali-stenics?" Wesley asked.

"We're gointa learn the t'ings in the Stoker book," I said.

Wesley chopped the air with pressed fingers and kicked his right foot with pointed toes.

"Alright, alright," I said. "We have two rules before we start. The first is that I don't want no complainin'. You hear? The second is that from here on out, I don't want allyuh runnin' the streets without somebody knowing where you going."

"I'm sixteen," Patsy said. She was looking out the window, as if she could see the place she wanted to be at that moment.

"Well, Trinidad is changing," I said. "I need allyuh to make sure somebody in this family knows where you are at all times. And nobody should leave Yvonne by herself, even if you t'ink she's a big seven-year-old who can be left alone. Jacqueline, you're to watch her like a hawk."

My words surprised the children, particularly Patsy, who until that moment had had the most freedom of all of us. I had worked hard to give my children a normal life. To make them feel like I was a normal mother. It had taken me years to learn to push down the protective urges whenever I couldn't see the tops of their heads or hear their voices in the yard. And now I had to undo it all.

"Alright, we're gointa learn somet'ing called the art of self-defense. Or Bartitsu."

"You joking?" Patsy folded her arms across her chest.

She could see on my face I wasn't joking.

I lined them in a row. "If somebody is attacking you, the t'ree t'ings you must try and do is, one: Disturb their balance. Two: Surprise them before they have a chance to get back their balance. And t'ree: Strain their neck, shoulder, elbow, wrist, back, or ankle, so they can't resist you. Let me show you some moves."

We spent the afternoon and well into the evening in the yard. I showed each of them how to snatch ankles, pull shoulder blades, twist wrists, strike ears, swipe legs, and bloody a nose by smashing it with the back of their heads.

That night, I went to sleep smiling, thinking about my children kicking Uncle Linton's behind.

FAROUK KARAM

I woke drenched in a hot, dense sweat. Snakes. Up into my nostrils, into the crevices of my body. Trinidad was full of snakes and there was hardly a soul in the country who hadn't stared one in the eye, but dreaming about them was altogether different. An omen.

I met Tanty Gertrude on her porch. She was eating from a green bowl cupped in the palm of her right hand.

"If you comin' here to see Nicole, she wants nutting atall to do with you."

"I comin' to see you," I said.

"When you takin' up with Nicole, you have no time for the ole lady. When you not takin' up with Nicole, you hurtin' my daughter's feelings."

I couldn't tell her that Nicole was nothing but warmth on a chilly night.

"Cat got your tongue?" She stirred inside the bowl, clanging the spoon along its sides. "You was never too busy for your ex-wife, or whatever you call she."

"Let's not talk about Marcia."

"Eh-eh. Why not?"

"You know why not."

She cheupsed. "You should be t'anking me for bringing she here and talking some sense into her."

I sat on her top step, unable to avoid the sight of her muscular legs. "Look, let we discuss somet'ing else or I gointa leave here angry and I don't want that." I was embarrassed I'd never confronted Tanty Gertrude on what she'd done to Marcia. It'd been seven years and I had never once mentioned it.

"Angry for what?" She pushed her neck back. Her knees clamped. "I give you everyt'ing you ever asked, didn't I?"

"You shoulda left well enough alone."

"Eh-eh," she said. "I tell you long long time ago I wasn't gointa let you run my daughter like a whore. You had no time for her because you always too damn worried about your ex-wife and her chil'ren."

"They're my chil'ren! I does have to worry about them."

"Yes, true," she said, softly, sniffing the contents of her bowl. "But you worryin' too much about the mudda. You comin' back here after anudda baby and anudda, hoping I can make it right. Nutting atall about that does be right."

I rubbed my hands together. They'd been dry and cold since I woke with snakes in my head. "Look, I not here to talk about Marcia," I said. "I dreamin' about serpents and all sortsa craziness. And somet'ing not feeling right at work."

"It's not right," she said, almost too quickly.

"What's going on?"

"Plenty treachery." She shoved a spoonful of creamy oats into her empty mouth. Her gums echoed like popping rubber. "Don't trust nobody. No-body."

"How you can do my job and not trust somebody?"

"Well, if that's how you does feel, sleep with one eye open. There's plenty plenty people who wanta do wrong by you. And you've been protected up 'til now."

"By you?"

"Of course." She smiled.

I hated when she smiled.

"Let me make some tea." She began to raise herself from the rocker.

"None for me, please."

"You sure?" She sat down again and rested her bowl in a dimple in the floorboard. There were no more chickens. Her goat was long eaten. The quiet could almost be mistaken for peace. "Alright, then give me somet'ing to hold."

I stood and unlocked my gold wristwatch. I placed it into the lined palm of her hand. She pushed it back at me, like it was on fire. "This not yours," she said.

I examined the back of its face. I had forgotten that it was my father's watch. He had given it to me when I'd first become a policeman.

I reached into my pocket again. There were a few coins and one other thing I'd never shown to anyone, except Marcia. I twirled it between my fingers before placing it on the arm of Tanty Gertrude's rocking chair.

Her face soured. "This?" she said.

I had worn my gold wedding band only a few days, but I had carried it in my pocket every day for nearly fifteen years.

"You see what I mean?" She held the ring up. It glimmered like new. "I didn't do my job well enough. You does be still holdin' on to that woman."

She closed her eyes and shut my ring in her fingers. A few moments later, her eyes flapped open. She shoved the ring back into my hand. "You in too deep for me to help you now." She shook her head. "But you gointa come out alive," she said. "And alive, in this case, is a good t'ing."

"What about the chil'ren? They gointa be alright? And Marcia?"

Tanty Gertrude picked up her bowl and walked into her house.

Two weeks to the day after we visited Rogers, Marlock gave me instructions.

"Carry a dark-colored bag with a sturdy handle," he said. "Blend in and nobody'll notice you. It's Carnival time."

"I have plenty of work to do here, Inspector."

Marlock leaned over the desk. "You work for me," he said, quietly. "It's Carnival. Let's have a good time."

During Carnival, the country was electric. House lamps were lit, streetlights were aglow, even the stars pushed through clouds to fill the night skies. Music-filled cars passed through the roads, radio dee-jays announced new tunes, bands practiced for the Road March and Monarch competitions. Family members and tourists were arriving from all over the world with money to spend. There were roti to fry, curry to simmer, rice to cook-up, pepper sauce to blend, coconut to grind, green mangoes to spice, sugarcane to cut, and callaloo to swiz-zle. The whole mind of the country was on the sweet goodness of drinks, food, music, and skin-rubbing.

That night, when I approached Rogers's open gate, the three guards from my previous visit were spruced-up, smelling like cheap Ameri-can cologne, and more interested in monitoring breasts than in the comings and goings of any one man.

Holding a bottle of Old Oak, I walked inside.

Calypso seemed to pour from the walls. The sweet rhythm of a nice nice party was taking place and if I hadn't been so paranoid, I might've enjoyed being there. There were plenty women. Three for each fella, it seemed. Big-breasted women with nipples barely cov-ered. Big-bottomed women with no panty lines. Tall women sit-ting on short men. Short women sitting on tall men. Light, dark, pretty, young, not-so-old, ugly, and lovely. There was talking, danc-ing, laughing, teasing, loving, grinding. It was a party, the likes of which I hadn't seen in awhile. Yet, all I felt was a heaviness in my chest.

I searched the darkened front room. No Rogers.

I walked to the rear of the house. Splotchy shadow-figures threat-ened me from every corner. Down the main hallway were three closed doors. The passageway continued around a bend and from what I'd seen from outside, I knew at least one room was there.

I came to the first door. There were soft movements on the other side, like the sounds of a painter's brushstrokes. No voices. I calmed my breathing, plastered a confused expression on my face, and slowly opened the door.

The room was covered in mirrors. There was a maple coffee table flanked by two black couches. On the couch to the right sat two half-naked, semiconscious women. On the couch to the left, two men, posted on the edge, their heads bent over the table. "Who you want?" one of them said, clearing phlegm from his throat. White powder smothered his nose.

"Sorry, chief," I said. "I lookin' for Rogers."

"Down the hall." Their heads dropped back toward the table, as if choreographed.

Although I was a policeman I'd never seen cocaine. Seeing it made me more nervous than I ever thought I could be. I searched the corridor again, hoping not to run into Rogers before I had a chance to inspect the second room. I pressed my ear against the door. Silence. I nudged it. Small white paper bags of a heavy-scented marijuana lined the floor. I gently closed the door and moved on.

The hallway was dark until the third door flew open.

A heavyset fella walked into the corridor with a slim, square-shouldered girl. She couldn't have been older than fifteen. There was still baby in her face. He slipped cash into her hand and closed her fingers around it. "Make sure you back in forty minutes." He smacked her bottom. "If he try anyt'ing more, come and let me know, you hear?"

Her frightened gasp made him notice me.

I softened my brow, walking closer to the fella. *Relax.*

"Whoya want?" His voice was thick and stiff like new leather shoes. His skinny legs seemed unable, unwilling, to hold the heavy bulge of his belly. A black bushy beard covered most of his face.

"Rogers," I said. "He in there?"

He pried open the door. "Derrick! A coolie boy here for you."

Rogers never replied.

"He in there or what?" I said.

The big fella ground his teeth, pushing the door open wider. "Derrick, I sendin' him in!"

Most warm-blooded men would have been excited by the sight: unclothed couples draped about each other like tossed toys. But I wanted to get the blasted evening done and over with. Rogers dropped his hands from a woman's bottom. "Eh-eh, what you doin' here?"

I lifted the bag in the air. "Donations."

"Anwar!" he yelled out to the big fella. "Have this chap wait outside!"

Anwar cocked his eye as if it was the first time he'd seen me. I dropped the bag to the floor, before Anwar shut the door.

Rogers strolled out, bare-chested, pissed off. He dragged the limp bag behind him, leading me to a room on the other side of the bend. The room I hadn't inspected.

I began to perspire. He pulled out a key and unlocked the door.

If the door was locked, it was likely the money room. If it was the money room, there were likely things in there to protect the money. "I gointa wait here," I said.

Rogers looked at me like he wouldn't have given me any other choice, which both irritated and relieved me. I waited. Waited for the unexpected. Waited for the one thing that could upend everything.

When Rogers returned, he shoved the full bag into my chest. "Go on," he said.

I started to back away. I'd decided I wouldn't turn my backside to either Rogers or the big fella until I reached the bend in the corridor. I stared at them until there was enough distance between us. "How long you been here?" Rogers shouted.

My answer to an all-too-late question was lost in the beating currents of calypso.

• • •

At two o'clock in the morning I met Marlock in a bar off St. John's Road. During Carnival most places with a bottle behind their counters didn't close until the sun rose, but the crowd there was already winding down.

Marlock snatched the bag from my arms and shoved it under his table. "Have a seat," he said. "You wanta drink?"

"Nah."

"Come have a drink." By his glassy-eyed appearance, Marlock had had plenty already. He yelled out to the barman to bring us two rum-'n'-Cokes. We waited in silence. The silence always made me uncomfortable, and he knew it.

"How'd it go?" he asked.

"No problems."

He raised his glass toward me, as if I needed to be congratulated. I lifted the small tumbler between my fingers. The damn drink was warm like day-old piss.

"You stay there long?"

I pushed the glass into the middle of the table. "Long enough."

"He does t'row a good fête, eh?"

"Seems like it."

"He slip you any extra?"

"What?"

"Rogers. He slip you a li'l change?"

"Me? I ain't takin' nutting from him." I regretted the words the moment they came out of my mouth.

Marlock swallowed the last of his drink. He raised his glass to the barman for another. "Oh yeah, Mistah Big Shot," he said. "One brudda a doctor. The next brudda, a banker. Udda brudda, a big-time jeweler. Fadda, a man of the cloth, eh? I hear your connections does serve you well. Moving up the ranks pretty fast for a so-so investigator. I guess everybody does do what they have to do, right?" He crunched on ice from the glass the bartender had set down. "How'd you like them pretty gals Rogers had there?" He nudged my drink back toward me. "Oh yeah, I hear you're a one-woman man." He snickered. "A wife and four chil'ren, right?" His tilted eyes peered over his tilted glass. "Oooohhhh yeah, yeah, that's right. I hear she kicked you out. You takin' up with some obeah lady's daughter. I hear she's as rough as the mudda."

I glared at him and finally spoke. "Rough can be good, no?"

"Depends on who's roughin' you up. Or if the person being roughed up is somebody you love." He grinned. "Not so good when you can't see it coming and you can't do nutting to stop it." He extended his small, wet hand toward me for a solid shake. "Keep doin' whatya doin', Karam. Everyt'ing and every *somebody* gointa be alright."

Chapter 8

JACQUELINE KARAM

July 1498. Columbus sails on behalf of Spain. Goes through Dragon Mouth into Caribbean Sea and lands on island north of Venezuela. Twenty-four Amerindians in a canoe. Well-proportioned. Graceful. Heads bound with colorful cotton scarves. Peaceful Arawaks or warlike Caribs? Attempted colonization of island by Spaniards. Amerindians enslaved. Amerindians revolt. "Arena Massacre." Spaniards fail in colonization efforts. All of Europe knows.

The limes were damp from the night's rain. The branches hung low and heavy. The limes glistened. I massaged their smooth, firm rinds before pulling them. I heaped them in the bowl I carried.

1618, cocoa discovered. Slaves needed. Africans brought to Trinidad. Spaniards need white management on the island. French planters need land. Spain offers land to French and free Negroes, but leaves island unprotected. Great Britain captures Trinidad in 1797.

The gate creaked. Daddy was in the front yard by the road. I should've known something was up—he hardly ever came to see us.

"What you doing here?" I said, slightly annoyed that the first moment I'd had in days to study, I was again being interrupted.

He kissed me on the top of my head. "Not even a 'hello'?"

"Sorry. Hello, Daddy," I said, adjusting the bowl of limes in my arms. "I'm just going over my notes in my head." *After Haiti revolts and with pressure from abolitionists, Trinidad becomes a model British slave colony.*

"How allyuh keepin'? Your mammy inside?"

"Deliverin' somet'ing in Sangre Grande." I closed my eyes, trying hard not to lose my thoughts. *The Brits want Trinidad to be a sugar island. How do they increase production when no two people on the island have the same goal?*

"Sangre Grande?"

"Somebody asked her to make somet'ing."

1808: 800 French, 250 Spaniards, 100 Brits, 5,000 free people of color, 20,000 Negro slaves, 22 Chinese, 1600 Amerindians. Too much difference in one country for self-governance.

Daddy leaned against the gate and crossed his arms. The sun lit the outer edges of a cloud, like gold trim, as it slipped behind it. "Your brudda home?"

"Sleeping." I moved toward the porch, leaving Daddy behind. *Brits make Trinidad a Crown Colony—all powers in Downing Street.*

"And Patsy?"

"Inside."

Still not enough labor. Chinese? 300 men are brought. Not fit for hard labor in the tropics. 40 return home.

"It's been tough on her, eh?"

I shoved the bowl into Daddy's stomach.

"Whya rolling those pretty li'l eyes for?" Daddy picked out a lime, rolled the wetness off onto his pants and began to slither it in and out of the spaces between each of his fingers, like a snake in a rodeo.

"It's been years since she failed that exam and you still feeling sorry for Patsy?" I took the lime from his hand and placed it back into the bowl.

"Of course. She worked hard, she studied. It's hard to fail like that."

"Studied the boys. That's what she studied," I said. "My exam is comin' and that's all that's on my mind."

Emancipation Bill of 1833 ends slavery. But not full emancipation. Slaves—now indentured servants—strike.

"What's she up to these days?" Daddy said, completely disinterested in the most important thing in *my* life.

"You t'ink she does tell me?"

Brits still want sugar production.

I took my shoes off at the door. Wesley was sleeping on his bed—a blue reclining chair some lady had given to Mammy in exchange for a wedding dress that could hold a big belly full of baby.

Daddy set the bowl on the table, then gave one good lash to Wesley's short legs. "Wake up, boy! No man should be resting in the daytime."

Wesley woke, startled, wiping the spit that had plunged down his left cheek. "Daddy? What you doing here?"

"You been sleeping so long, you forget I help pay the rent?"

I drained water from the semisoft split peas I had put to boil.

"I thought you were studying?" Daddy said.

"And what we gointa eat if I don't cook?"

Wesley stretched, then put on his socks. He liked to wear mismatched socks made from Mammy's fabric leftovers. Daddy had scolded him for it time and again. Told him only girls did such things. I caught Daddy studying the blue on the right foot, the purple on the left.

"I'm playing in the football game next week Saturday," Wesley said. "You should come."

"What about cricket?" Daddy fiddled with the limes on the table. "You playin' cricket these days?"

"Just football," Wesley said, buttoning his pants.

"Help your sista with dinner." Daddy walked to the front window and pushed aside one of the curtain panels. "You're almost twelve. You mustn't have her working like a slave, and you lying there sleeping."

I wished Daddy would tell Patsy that.

"I does help," Wesley said. The dimple in his chin was so deep it could've held a tiny pool of water. His whitish skin looked almost buffed. His Chinky eyes, like a stick figure's lips. "I'm the calming force in this house. If it wasn't for me, these ladies would be ripping each udda apart."

Daddy chuckled and grabbed Wesley's neck, tucking it under his arm. "Let's play cricket togedda soon," Daddy said. "You a batter or bowler?"

Wesley pushed him away. I wasn't sure it was in jest. "I never played."

If a boy Wesley's age, living in Trinidad, didn't know how to play cricket, it was his father's fault. We all knew that. Yet, Daddy said nothing before he moved toward the back of the house.

Wesley, smelling like a cigarette factory, came to the counter and began helping me roll the sticky split peas and flour into balls for *phoulorie.* I probably should've spent a few moments cheering him up, but if I wasn't able to study then I was surely not going to miss the action about to take place in the back of the house.

"Patsy!" Daddy's voice rang solidly between the walls. "Patsy?"

Daddy tapped on the wall beside the partition curtain. The radio news was blaring. Election campaigning was jumping off, but everyone knew Patsy didn't care about politics.

"Patsy!" Daddy yelled again.

Dust flitted like gnats in the bush when Daddy pushed aside the curtain.

Patsy's head popped up from under the sheet.

"What you doin' in here?" Daddy said. He pressed his palm high up on the wall and leaned into it with his feet crossed.

The boy's head inched up slowly, like a leatherback turtle on dry, heavy sand. I had seen his right leg when he'd climbed through the window an hour earlier. His leg was no different than the six or seven other legs I'd seen in the last month: skinny, eager, desperate, wiggling.

"Who're you?" Daddy said.

The boy scooted off the mattress and began tucking his shirttail into his pants. "A friend." His tone wasn't exactly respectful.

The radio announcer read an ad for Palmolive soap. "Well, 'friend,' "

Daddy said. "Next time I see you near my house or my daughter, your mudda gointa be making burial arrangements. Understand?"

The boy, not as ugly as Patsy usually liked them, slipped into his black loafers. To pass he needed Daddy to move out of the doorway. Daddy paused before letting him through.

Patsy's favorite baby-powder scent drifted out with the boy who nearly crashed into me, and then into Wesley. He sneered. We giggled.

"Go and do somet'ing with yourselves!" Daddy said, pointing to us both.

Wesley went back into the parlor, but I only pretended to do so.

Patsy turned off the radio. "This is what you does do with yourself all day?" Daddy said. He was drumming his fingers on the wall. "Listen, I came because I wanted to tell you that my brudda—your Uncle Abdul—can give you a job at the bank. You can stay home rolling around with your 'friend,' or you can work someplace decent."

He was offering her a job? I thought he would've given her a black eye.

"What does that shoulder t'ing mean?" he said.

"It means I not a charity case," Patsy said. "Did you tell your brudda your poor, stupid daughter couldn't pass the Common Entrance or you want me to go and embarrass myself when he asks?"

Daddy folded his fingers behind his back. Patsy had failed the one test needed to continue a free secondary education. Who could blame Daddy if he had been too ashamed to tell his brother?

"Funny how you can ask your brudda to help me, but when I beg you to help me get into police training school when I turn eighteen, all I get is a fat no," she said.

"Either you want it or not," Daddy said. "I'm trying."

"You does always try, Daddy. You does be always trying." Patsy spoke with more than a hint of sarcasm.

"I have more money since the promotion," Daddy went on. "Lemme pay and you can finish your studies. How 'bout that?"

"I have to go," she said, her feet shuffling past Daddy, toward the hallway.

"Where you going?"

"Down de road."

"Where to?"

"It's Carnival time, if you not noticing. People are out."

Patsy passed me headed for the front door. Her hips swayed under a pink, silk dress I had never seen before.

Daddy met me in the corridor. "Outside of givin' she some licks with my belt, I don't know what to do," he said. "Her life is turning into a complete disaster."

Mammy and Yvonne were sleeping when Patsy left through the window. Sometimes it hurt to see what was happening to Patsy. I still cared about her. I missed the girl she was before.

I tiptoed into the parlor.

"I need you to do me a favor?" Wesley was tossing about on his chair, his legs slung over the side. His head, held up only by muggy air.

"What?" he shouted.

"Shhh . . . you'll wake up Mammy and Yvonne."

"What's happenin'?" He reached blindly for the sheet, which had fallen to the floor.

"Get your shoes and meet me in the back of the house."

"I'm sleeping!"

"Shush! I'll let you sleep in the room tonight if you do what I say."

Patsy had stuffed clothes under the sheet on her side of the bed. I grabbed coins and ran to the back of the house, hoping the chickens wouldn't wake. "Go down the road and follow Patsy." Wesley was still rubbing the burn from his eyes. "Don't stay out long. You know how Mammy does like to come out in the nighttime and check up on us. Be smart. Take good notes in your head. I wanta know everyt'ing."

I pulled his cap onto his forehead and gave him the money. "Hurry and go!"

I stayed awake, waiting and studying. *Brits bring 150,000 East Indians as indentured servants. By 1894, Cuban cane and German beets dominate sugar market. Brits begin to buy sugar from outside the colonies. Trinidad flounders. Oil discovered in 1910. Indentured servitude abolished in 1916. WWI ignites political consciousness. Representation in government grows.*

I fell asleep. I would've slept 'til morning but for the scratching at the window.

I reached out my arms to pull Wesley up. He reeked of beer and Anchor cigarettes. "I ain't tell you to go and party."

He dusted his pants. "I followed her like you said." He sat down, breathing heavily. He'd glued a picture from one of the Carnival sponsors, Pan Am Air, to the wall across from us. Four American models under a palm tree on Maracas Bay beach. "She met up with some gals with half their li'l bamsees hanging out their dresses." He tapped my foot. "You gointa let me sleep in here?"

"Talk, nah-man!"

"Alright, alright." He pulled Patsy's sheets off the bed onto the floor. Her bundle of clothes fell in a soft ball. "They went inside this house to a party."

"What house?"

"Some house up on a hill," he said. "It wasn't a place for no pickneys, I tell you that. Big men with big money and big drinks." He slid off his shoes and unbuttoned his pants. "It's a good t'ing I had some extra change in my pocket because you didn't give me enough money." He climbed onto one sheet and covered himself with the second. "You know how tired I is?"

"What bus did you take? Where was the house?"

He pulled the thin sheet over his head. "You should be happy I didn't have to do none of that Bartitsu nonsense," he said. "I sure hope Patsy remembers how to."

FAROUK KARAM

"Take two bags this time," Marlock had said before I left the station. "Rogers'll be expecting you at midnight."

From across the parlor, I scoped out Rogers. Though it wasn't as festive or as crowded as it had been during Carnival week, it was a lively party for a Wednesday evening. He was sitting on the back of his couch, talking to a woman with albino-white hair. She seemed to be taking his drink order. His eyes found mine. He raised his chin.

Behind him, I walked to the corner room that had given me pause on my last visit. He left the door open.

The walls were a creamy tan. The plaster, smooth and flat. A carved wooden bust of an Egyptian pharaoh was perched on a narrow stand under a window that looked out onto the hilly backyard. A wide desk with a glass top spanned nearly the entire width of the room, making it hard for even skinny Rogers to squeeze behind it. To the right of the desk, in a corner, a double-door closet was secured with chains and a padlock.

"Gimme," Rogers muttered.

I moved forward and threw the bags into his arms.

Rogers reached underneath the desk into a drawer I couldn't see, gathering up handful after handful of loose cash. The bills were crisp and tumbled into the bags like feathers from a severed pillow. It was more money than I'd ever seen. Money that could've changed my life.

"Bloody police," he said.

On the white closet doors, dark red, almost brown specks, half the size of a peppercorn caught my eye.

"Take what's mine? Allyuh don't make shit. Allyuh don't build shit," he continued. "Allyuh not worth the ink on these focking dollars."

I hadn't gone there to hear Rogers whine about the deal he'd cut with the devil. I had my own deal to work out. "Just fill the bags, nah-man."

Rogers tipped his head to the right, then stopped. "You gointa tell me to fill the bags like dat?" he said. "Walkin' in like your shit not stinkin'. You's a good policeman just caught up in the mess? Eh-eh. You t'ink you betta than me?" He poked himself in his thin chest, like in some bad American Western. "You the worst kind. At least I does know what and who I am," he said.

Marlock had me meet him at a tucked-away snackette in Arima. The kind of place you could "buy" for the night if you ordered enough drinks.

When I arrived, no fewer than thirty policemen from various districts were mingling, playing cards, drinking Guinness stout and Carib. The burnt vanilla of Cuban cigars thickened the air. The Mighty Dougla's "Lazy Man," with its mellow horns, crackled from speakers hanging on nails on the walls. On the bar top was a basin of pork souse floating in a sea of cucumbers. There were six wooden-plank shelves stacked with double rows of spirits; the kind of expensive drinks those who had extra pocket change could afford.

"Eh, Karam, you wanta sit in on the next game?" Marlock called out.

"Can I speak to you?"

I could see Marlock's cards over his left shoulder: an ace of hearts, a queen of hearts, a king of diamonds, a jack of hearts, a ten of diamonds.

"Speak," he said through a half-smoked Punch.

"It's private."

"Nutting in here is private."

"It's private," I said again.

"These are your bruddas."

I watched Marlock, along with fellas I had known since my eighteenth birthday. I had taken such pride in the brotherhood.

"Inspector, I wanta talk to you now."

Marlock pulled a diamond-shaped glass ashtray away from the constable seated next to him and set down his cigar. "I'll be back," he said to the table of men. "Don't try nutting while I have my back turned, you hear?"

There was a nervous chuckle. Then the sets of eyes followed Marlock as he walked with me, across the clay-tiled floor. "Where the bags?" he asked.

"Outside."

"Outside? With who?"

"Don't worry. I hid them good enough."

"Man, you crazy or what?"

"I'm careful." I reached for the door handle. "You bringin' me to a crowded bar to exchange that much money and I not supposed to check the place out before I bring it in?"

He walked through the double-paned door.

"Listen, I don't know how to say this—"

"Don't trouble trouble until trouble troubles you. If a man don't know how to say somet'ing, it's best he don't say it," Marlock said, with searching eyes. "Where the bags?"

I led him to the far right of the snackette and pushed aside a flowering flame bush. Red petals had fallen in clumps to the soil.

Marlock searched the perimeter before he grabbed the bag handles.

"I need to talk," I said.

"After I do what I does need to do inside, we can talk. Alright?" He spoke slowly as if I was an annoying child.

"Eh-eh fellas, look what the cat dragged in!" he shouted. There was a muffled cheer from the other officers. Half-grins told a story of loss and greed. Marlock pointed to the owner of the snackette. He'd been pretending to wash glasses on the other side of the bar. "Go and have yourself a walk."

The owner rushed out the door before Marlock wiggled his petite hands inside the bags. "What the hell is this?"

The room grew quiet.

"Who t'rew this money in here like this?" Marlock tossed the bills around like confetti.

"Rogers," I said.

"You didn't see him do this?"

"Sure I saw him. What'd you expect?"

"Neat bundles. Like always." He sounded exasperated. "You managed to piss him off some more, eh?"

"Didn't say a word."

"How ya know how much you have in here?" Marlock wiped sweat from the top of his head.

"You didn't tell me how much I was supposed to have. That's between you and he."

"Come." Marlock pulled at my shirt with a hooked finger. I pushed it off. "Walters, count up that money and put it togedda for me to dole out," he shouted, as we walked back outside.

It'd been only a few minutes since we'd been on the porch. The lantern overhead had been dismantled.

"I'm not doing this no more," I said.

"What you mean by 'this'?" Marlock's hands sat easily in his pants pockets.

"You have two dozen men in there that'd be happy to do it. This isn't for me."

Marlock watched a motorcar speed by on the narrow road before us. "Alright." He shrugged. "Nobody's forcing you." The headlights from another passing motorcar brightened the porch and Marlock's face. "Your son," he said, smirking, "he's lookin' to be a policeman or a dressmaker?"

I tapped the tips of my fingers against each other in an easy motion. I didn't know what else to do with my hands. "What is it you're saying?"

He bent his knees as if to loosen them. "I'm saying you still need to keep your eye on Rogers. Every evening you should watch that house and let me know who does be going in and coming out. I have some eyes there, but I need somebody who'll know what they looking for."

I wanted to be done with Marlock and Rogers, and all of that mess, but it felt almost too easy; so within reach that it put me on edge.

"What am I supposed to be looking for?"

He yanked his hands from his pocket and reached for a shake. "You'll know."

MARCIA GARCIA

We sat on the porch, Jacqueline snugly tucked between my legs. I brushed out the tangles, parting her hair into small sections. I hadn't sat that way with any of the children in a long while. Feeling the softness of her hair in my hands, her head on my thighs, while I worked my fingertips between the strands, pulling them long before twining them around each other, was nice. She drank a glass of iced *mauby* I'd made early that morning. It only took an hour or so before she opened up, told me everything she knew about Patsy. Skipping work at the bakery. Sneaking out at night. The parties.

I had a good mind to go straight to Patsy and beat every last bit of crazy out of her. But I knew she would've made up some story, challenged me to prove she was a liar.

I needed to confront her in the act.

It was almost midnight. I was already wearing my wide-brimmed black hat when the footsteps moved toward the gate. Our street was quiet. The quarter moon was dim and the darkness felt rich, almost like walking through pudding. A pack of stray dogs met Patsy at the bottom of the hill, following her until she stopped in front of the shoe repair shop beneath the silvery overhang of a wide canopy date palm. She was wearing clothes I had never seen: a thigh-high charcoal-grey skirt and a white blouse that barely covered her chest. Men in cars slowed to put out offers I couldn't hear, but she waved off each of them, as if waiting for someone in particular.

I was on the opposite side of the road, leaning against a tall sign that read "Stop. Major Road Ahead," when the roaring engine of an approaching bus, jammed with passengers, noisied up the street. Patsy moved toward it. A slender Indian girl, with choppy copper-streaked hair and a face full of chalky makeup, got off the bus. They exchanged a few words before they turned back in my direction.

They crossed behind me, forcing me to walk farther ahead. There was a light tap of a car horn. I was sure it was the person Patsy had been waiting for.

"You need a ride?" The white car crept alongside me, keeping with my pace. The strange fella with ears like antennas waved. "Where you going?" he shouted.

I shook my head, trying hard not to move my neck.

"Come-nah, let me drop you," he pleaded.

I could no longer hear the girls' footsteps behind me. I turned back, walking maybe a hundred yards before Patsy and her friend strolled out of a still-open snackette. The Indian girl was holding a glass liquor bottle in a brown paper bag so thin, it looked like hosiery.

I stood on the walk before them. "You surprised to see me here?" I said.

Patsy's right hand was hoisted on her hip. The pose reminded me of the first time I had talked to her about babies. The day Farouk brought the stove. "No," she said. Her tone was sharper than it had been back then. "You t'ink that hat and them clothes you wearing foolin' me?"

The Indian girl glared at my fuchsia housedress, then walked closer to the road to wait for Patsy.

"You crazy or what? You running the streets in the middle of the night like this?" I pulled her by the wrist. "Come, let's go."

She snatched her hand away.

"You really wanta fight with me?"

A young man wearing a cap in a dark-colored motorcar slowed down to watch us. He gave a light two-tap to his horn. I grabbed Patsy's wrist again. She snatched it away a second time.

I moved nose to nose; eye to eye. She was a big girl now, about my height, with a solid build and a fierce scowl. "You comin' home with me right now, you hear me?"

"No."

"I'm not askin'."

"I'm not goin' home."

I dug my nails into the smooth skin of her forearm. "You don't tell me no."

She swung her arm outward, her elbow jamming into my chest. I slapped her cheek with the front of my hand, then a second time with the back of it. She held her open palm against her face. I had never hit her there.

"You want more?" I snatched her wrist, yanking her downward into the walk. The skinny friend moved toward me, eyeing me as if she would do something. "Miss Lady, you don't wanta piece of this," I said.

Black mascara ran down Patsy's full cheeks. But there was no sadness in the tears that fell. "Get off me!" she screamed, wrenching her arm away.

"You will do as I say."

"Why?" She stood, pushed her bosom against mine. "So I can go back home and hope some man will come and save me from a house fulla chil'ren?"

The knowing excitement in her eyes was almost unforgivable.

FAROUK KARAM

I watched Rogers's house for eight nights wondering how I'd gone from murder investigator to security guard. On the ninth night—the night I saw Patsy crossing the street to go into that house—I came to understand that I was neither.

I was a pawn.

I trotted toward the gate, hoping to cover the smell of anxiety and rage. "Allyuh gointa let me in?" I said.

"You jokin'?" was how the skinny, Spanish one answered. He had his back against the gate's opening.

"You know who I am."

"And we know we not lettin' you inside this gate."

"Man, I not interested in any rubbish with Rogers. I was across the street and saw a nice piece a tail. She just went in, wearing a black dress. Hair was t'ick t'ick and long down she back. Real pretty pretty, healt'y gal," I said.

"Oooh boy, she does be sweet," the pudgy, gold-toothed guard added. When he smiled his lips disappeared. "She used to be open, but she not for sale no more."

I tried to mask what I thought was the sound of the growing

lump in my throat. "Come on, man. I sure Rogers'll make an exception for me. I'm good for the money."

"He wouldn't let you in his house if it was burning and you was the only one with a bucket." The skinny one laughed. He leaned his baton against the gate.

"That gal . . . what's her name?" the pudgy guard said to the skinny one.

"Patty," the skinny one said. "Or Pat, I t'ink."

"Right right. She belongin' to Rogers now."

"She belongin' to Rogers?" I said. "That gal? She not his type."

"You askin' too many questions," the third guard, the Indian one, said. He'd been studying my eyes, my hand gestures, the sweat on my head. "You's police, right?"

"What's that mean? Policemen don't have needs?"

"She ain't got no interest in an old fella like you, so beat it," he said, with a hand-flick for emphasis.

From the corner of my eye, I saw someone step out of the bushes. The Spanish one instinctively reached for the baton. Then he quickly set it back down.

"Eh-eh, fellas, I hope allyuh ain't drink up all the—"

Wesley's reddened eyes popped as though they would fall out of his head.

"Eh-eh, that's the li'l fella who just picked my wallet!" I yelled.

I grabbed Wesley by the neck, pulling him toward me. Rogers's guards laughed at my sauced-up son. "Chupid li'l chap," the skinny one said. "Li'l pissant always comin' around bummin' smokes. T'row him in jail, Mistah Policeman!"

I spoke softly in Wesley's ear. "Don't say anudda word." His heartbeat was like a trapped rat's. I wanted to give him a good cut-ass, but I waited until we were at the bottom of the hill, out of the line of sight of the guards, before I slapped him across his back.

"Sorry, Daddy." He wiped his nose with his fist.

"Your mudda know you here?"

"No, Daddy."

"How long you been comin' here?"

"Jackie sent me."

"Jackie sent you here tonight?" I slapped him again. "Tell me the trut'."

"I followed Patsy here once. Then, I just started hangin' out at the gate with them fellas. Mostly during the day. Sometimes at night," he said.

"Them chupidee fellas you comin' out here to be with? Only fowls and fools does see shit and t'ink it's an egg, Wesley." I put his face into my hands and bent my head to look him in the eyes. I realized it was the first time I'd ever spoken to him in that way. "You're my son. You shouldn't be out here with these kinda men. You're a smart boy."

He pushed my hands from his face. "You don't t'ink that. The only t'ing I can do betta than the girls is sew. And you're ashamed of that."

I held his head against my chest. His hair smelled like cocoa butter and cigarettes. A baby and a man. There were no easy, truthful words I could say, so I gave him a few dollars and sent him home in a taxi with a promise that we'd soon talk.

I walked back across the road and waited at the bottom of Rogers's hill for Patsy to leave. Before the sun rose, all of Rogers's guests stumbled out, drunk, rowdy, shivering in the cool morning air. But Patsy wasn't in the crowd.

The next morning I couldn't go to work. I went to Curepe and met Jackie in the yard again.

Her lovely cane-rows were pinned up above her neck. Her high cheekbones were flushed from a morning full of outdoor chores, and she wore pants that fell above the ankles, which were all the rave for the youngsters.

"You lookin' tired," she said. The same was true of her. "You didn't shave?"

The tears stung the back of my throat. There was one grey cloud in the sky, leading a pack on an eastward journey. Focusing on their movements was all I could do to keep myself from breaking down.

"What's wrong?" Jackie set down a white enamel bowl of brown eggs and grabbed my arm, as if she needed to hold me up.

"I wanta talk to you," I said. "And I need you to be straight with me."

She knitted her brow like pinched dough.

"It's about Patsy," I said. "What's really going on with her?"

Jackie bit her bottom lip. "Why everybody always wanta talk about Patsy?"

"Shhh," I said. "You mudda will hear us."

"She not here."

It was strange that so early in the morning Marcia was already gone.

"Jackie," I said. "Please?"

She tightened her face. "Mammy doesn't want me to tell you. She said you'd blame her and it'd just cause a fight."

"I won't tell your mudda."

A neighborhood dog wandered over to Jackie. His left eye was bloodied and closed shut. His ribs were visible through his gold-colored fur. "Go on, Cowboy. It's too early. I don't have nutting for you." Jackie waited until the shabby dog limped out of the yard. "Mammy tole me she cuffed Patsy one good time across the face. Patsy doesn't stay here no more."

"You know where she's been?"

"No." Jackie bit the nail on her index finger. "Mammy's been out lookin' for her every day. Patsy does come when Mammy is out; she grabs up some clothes and makes us swear we won't tell Mammy. She leaves jewelry and does hide it in the room. Some real Indian gold bangles and necklaces, and all kindsa t'ings I ain't never seen her with before." She spit the fingernail she'd been chewing onto the ground. "I guess somebody does have to run wild to get attention around here, eh?"

"How long all this craziness been going on?"

She picked up her bowl again. "Mont's."

"Does your mudda know?"

There was a look of surprise, then she pushed the bowl into her waist. "Mammy knows she's staying out, but if Mammy knew about the boys in the house, the jewelry, the money . . . Patsy, along with any man she was with, would be long dead."

I watched Rogers's house for another week. Patsy came on a Saturday night.

I just wanted to talk to her. But by the time I got to the edge of the gate, she was already inside. Rogers's guards would never have let me through.

I trotted to the end of the dark road. A steep hill with several sloping homes was at the rear of Rogers's property. The lights inside his house flickered. His open windows dumped music onto the hillside.

I climbed a small fence and crossed within three feet of a sleeping dog. His nose twitched. He repositioned himself as I crossed the yard and hopped another fence, moving upward, toward the left, onto the next property. The air was a pungent rotted sweetness. Thick green mango leaves rustled in the breeze. Mosquitoes, big like cockroaches, swarmed my eyes, biting into the fleshy valleys of my skin, testing my will not to swat as I came to the last portion of the hill, panting and anxious.

An alert guard I'd never seen patrolled the back of Rogers's house. He carried a pistol, half-buried in his pants, on his left hip.

As I knelt in the dirt with the crest of the hill over my head, I wondered what I was doing there. Patsy wouldn't want to see me. She hadn't wanted to see or speak to me in so long it was hard to remember when it was good between us. No matter how hard I had tried, no matter how many promises I had kept, there was never any going back with her. So why, I had to ask myself, was I really there?

It was almost an hour of asking myself that question over and over, when the guard touched his crotch. He looked around, then walked to the edge of the yard to take a well-deserved piss through the iron bars. It was my one chance.

I leapt as high as I could, once, twice, three separate times, each time hoping to grip the thin, horizontal bar at the top. Each time, falling back onto the bald hill, a little further down the slope and seconds closer to being caught.

Desperate, I took off my shirt and knotted the cuffs together. I threw up the arched arms, hoping it'd catch one of the sharp rods.

The first throw failed. But the second time, the cuffs hooked. The guard's hissing stream had become a dribble. I pulled myself up, my feet braced flat against the bars. The guard, on the move, was headed straight to my side of the yard. I hadn't cleared the top. I had two, maybe three seconds left before the moonlight and the scarcity of tall trees would leave me exposed.

Then, quite unexpectedly, the pudgy guard from the front came around a side wall. "I got somet'ing." He held up a small paper bag. I had never been so happy to see the shine of gold teeth.

I remained in a push-up position. The metal spikes poked my stomach, my thighs, and the muscles in my arms and legs shook. The backyard guard snatched the bag from the pudgy fella and opened the wax paper. *Doubles.* Hot, spicy, thick curry *channa* sauce stuffed inside two soft, gold-colored *barra*. He devoured it.

"Go and get yourself a taste of that stout they have up front. I gointa wait here," the pudgy one said.

The backyard guard hesitated, but the idea of the fried flour barra and the fiery chickpeas washed down with a tart cold beer won out. He pulled up his pants and trotted away, leaving the pudgy fella singing the words to an old-time calypso. *"Arima tonight, Sangre Grande tomorrow night."* He forgot the lyrics and fell into an easy hum.

I jumped. But I wasn't quiet. The guard's hum died. He strained to hear more from the darkness. I held still, arched over a handful of small prickly bushes someone had planted strategically beneath the gate.

If I moved, either me or the pudgy fella would have to go.

He lifted his chin one last time in a listening pose, then he began an airy whistle. I rolled off the bushes into the tall grass and, bent at the waist, inched toward the base pillars. There, as I turned the bend, was the middle (the twenty-second step) of the long, unrailed staircase leading to the door. I was above the entry guards' eyeline. I attached myself, clad in my ripped white jersey vest, to the back of a small group that had just arrived.

Inside was less crowded than I had expected. If Rogers was anywhere near, he would spot me within seconds. I headed quickly to the back corridor, tucking my tee into my pants before approaching Anwar. He was standing in front of the room where I had seen the men with the cocaine.

"Hey, big fella," I said, holding out my hand for a shake.

He was wary, but shook my hand. "T'ought I heard you wasn't coming back."

"Rogers sent for me," I said. "Tole Marlock he wanted to see me tonight."

The big fella nodded. "I t'ink I heard somet'ing like that."

He moved aside. It was a dimly lit room. Quiet. I locked the door behind me. It took a moment for my eyes to grow accustomed to the darkness. When they finally did, I inspected the room. Five, maybe six writhing bodies on the couch to the right. Soft murmurs. To the left, two bodies. A man and a woman. I squinted.

I made out the shape of my firstborn child's head buried between Rogers's hairy legs.

I rushed to Patsy, yanking her thick, long ponytail, nearly throwing her half-dressed body across the room.

The three other couples scurried aside.

"What the fock?" Rogers's eyes quickly adjusted. His erect penis was wet. He reached for his pants. I stepped toward him, slamming my muddy left boot into his wrist, pinning it to the couch. "Don't blame me, nah-man." He worked himself into a forced chuckle.

"Marlock's the one who tell me about her. Your partner found me a beautiful gal. And I really really like her. Was gointa come and talk to you about my intentions."

I moved the tip of my left boot from his wrist, into his jaw. The *pfoof*, his flinging face, sounded like a blast of forced air.

I turned to the strangers. "Allyuh move or even groan and you gointa make me do what I don't wanta have to do." Patsy stood close to the door. "Put your clothes on!" I said.

Rogers spit out a palmful of dark, red blood and wiggled an incisor. "What you t'ink your fellas gointa do to you when they find out you messin' with their cash cow? And for a whore?"

Anwar twisted the knob.

Patsy was stepping into a short, red dress, her big dark eyes, wide and wet, smeared with makeup.

I grabbed a nearly empty Carib bottle and slammed its bottom into the maple. Glass pieces flew. Warm liquid ran down the hand that now held the bottle's sharp and ragged torso.

"Derrick!" the big fella yelled. "Everyt'ing alright?"

I slapped my left hand across Roger's sweaty forehead and held the sharp glass in the other, against his throat. The pulse in his neck throbbed. "Tell him everyt'ing is fine."

For the first time, I saw fear collecting in his eyes. "Yeah, yeah, man," he said to Anwar. His voice was sharp, but easy. "What now, Ka-ram? All this fat talk and you doin' what? You gointa kill me with these people in here watching you?"

"Patsy, come over here," I said. My eyes never left Rogers's face. "Look under the couch, look behind it, and find his gun."

I heard her tighten the straps on her sandals and move from the door. She patted her hands against the room's surfaces. She was quicker than I expected. The gun was behind the decorative pillow next to Rogers. If I had let him reach for his pants, I would have had a bullet in my chest.

I plotted our escape: We would take his gun, get past Anwar, blend in enough to make it to the door, and somehow get Marcia and the other children to leave home that night.

I smashed Rogers's head deeper into the back of the couch. Patsy, standing behind him, slowly turned the black pistol in her hand. She studied its hardness, its sleekness, with eager eyes. Her long fingers, much like her mother's, dipped under its weight. But instead of handing the revolver to me, Patsy shoved it between the fingers of the man she knew would kill me.

I jammed the jagged bottle into his jugular vein at the very moment Rogers pulled the "lemon-squeezer" safety.

It was a bloody mess. I took the pistol from his weakened fingers. "She's my chile," I said, pointing it to the six others. The words seemed more for me than for them. I pulled Patsy by her arm, hid the gun in the small of my back, under my jersey, and unlocked the door. In the dark corridor, the big fella, Anwar, seemed to be waiting for someone to explain something.

"I t'ink Rogers not feeling too well." I pulled the door closed. "He doesn't want anybody who does work for him to see him like that, but you betta not wait too long to check up on him."

Confused, the guard paused long enough to give Patsy and me a head start. I placed Patsy's arm underneath mine, pulling her toward the front door, rubbing blood from my hands onto my black pants. We ran down the forty-three steps and came to the gate. The backyard guard was just turning the corner, holding the shirt I'd left dangling on the fence. He stared. My ripped white jersey vest had blood splattered across its front.

"I ain't able with allyuh!" I yelled before he had a chance to speak. "You betta get inside. A fight breakin' out! What kinda party allyuh havin' in there? My shirt gettin' pulled off, my pants gettin' ripped up. The ruffians in Laventille betta than this!"

The guards, trained well enough not to think, dashed inside.

MARCIA GARCIA

Patsy's left cheek was bruised. She had fine scratches under her eye and on the tip of her nose, a crusted maroon scab. I brought her home from the lockup on a Monday, after weeks of searching for her every single day.

I pointed to the kitchen chair. She sat with her hands folded in her lap, like some schoolgirl. With a wet, clean cloth and a tube of antiseptic jelly, I tended to her face, placing a small bandage under her eye and giving her the cold rag to hold on the bruise. I nudged the middle of her head to let her know she could leave. I was too tired to fuss.

I could hardly believe what the police had told me about Patsy and the Derrick Rogers fella. The officer, when he spoke of it, couldn't look me in the eye. Meanwhile, Farouk was in confinement. No one could tell me anything of him.

I had to rest.

I could hear Patsy's radio from the other side of the house. I widened the crack in the bedroom window, hoping to drown the announcer with birdsongs. I took off my dress, my shoes, and sat at the edge of the bed. *Gawd, Patsy, what have you done?* The heels of my feet were cracked. I reached for the petroleum jelly. *Gawd, Farouk, what have you done?* The jelly was warm, thick on my chapped hands. I massaged my heels, then pulled a pair of Wesley's long cotton socks over my ankles, almost to my knees.

"Ooh boy." The cool sheets felt soothing to my warmed skin.

The moment my upper lashes met my lower ones, there was a knock at the door.

I tied on my housecoat. Anybody who knew me would've nudged the door open and called out my name. Whoever was on the other side was somebody I didn't want to see.

I put on my disgusted face. "Who you coming for?" I asked the policeman.

"Are you Marcia Garcia?"

"I'm the woman who just brought home she daughter from the police station and don't need some policeman standin' on my porch bringin' the neighbors outside again," I said. "That's who I is."

The man, whose angled eyes reminded me of two half-moons, smiled a little. He seemed to absorb me into two very deep-brown irises. His belly was round and though he was short, he carried himself with pride. He had a thick moustache, a slender button nose, and perfect white teeth, surrounded by a pleasant set of full lips.

"I not here to cause trouble, Miss Garcia," he said. "I just wanta talk to you for a few moments."

I let him pass through, pulling my robe tighter around my waist. "Excuse my clothes," I said. "I was just settling down."

"Sorry to bodder you," he said. "You must be very tired after the last few days."

"Would you like tea?"

"You havin' a cup?"

"I will." I offered him a seat and put on a pot of water. Wesley's socks swished like cotton mops.

"Boy, you does have plenty books," the policeman commented. "And plenty fabric." He sat in the chair facing the door, studying the place as if he hoped to find something specific.

I waited by the stove with two black tea mugs. If he had been a friend, I would've taken a seat, chatted, then gotten up again to make the tea. But I was in no particular rush to chat with the strange fella.

The water was beginning to bubble when the radio announcer was cut off in midsentence. Patsy walked in from the back. She had taken off the face bandages and put on a bit of concealing makeup. She was obviously hoping I would be resting in my room.

"Good day," he said to her. His tone wasn't exactly judgmental, but it wasn't pleasant either.

She looked at me, as if to ask what was going on. "Mind yourself," I whispered, as I threw water into the mugs. Her future wasn't yet decided by the investigators, or by me.

I had never seen her so nervous, and suddenly I felt quite sorry for her.

"Where you going?" I asked.

"Down the road."

"Nah, nah, nah, nah," I said, stirring in milk. "Go on up to Five Rivers to Aunty Baba's and sit with your sistas and your brudda until I come and collect allyuh."

She took a last glance at the policeman, then left.

I set down the teacups.

"Must be hard to have anudda grown woman in here," the policeman said.

"She not grown. Everybody does look at her, including her own self, and t'ink she's grown, but in that head of hers, she's a chile."

He traced his finger around the rim of the cup. "My name is Inspector Chung Marlock." He extended his hand for a weak shake, the kind of limp-fingered shake men often offered to women. "I'm a friend of Farouk's."

"A friend of Farouk's, eh?" I repeated. "I didn't know Farouk had any friends left."

He tilted his head. "You're his friend, no?"

I said nothing.

He snickered. "I guess that means you still t'inking about it, eh?"

It didn't matter what I said. The fella seemed to have his mind set. I took the seat across from him. "I usually don't let a strange man into my house for a cup of tea and ten minutes later I still don't know why he's here."

He sipped the warm, sweet, milky tea. "Is this honey in here?" He wrapped both hands around the cup, inhaling the scent.

"Yes."

"It's a lovely cup of tea." He took another sip, licking his lips like a little kitten. "Really lovely."

"T'ank you." I took a quick taste from my cup. I didn't know why he was making me so nervous. "Will we be able to see Farouk soon?"

"It's too early for that. There's plenty questions that need to be answered." He leaned across the table, his fists on both sides of his round face. "I'm here, Miss Garcia, because I'm told you're a very honest woman. A hardworking, decent woman, who happens to have a connection to two people involved in one of the worst criminal situations to face Trinidad in a very long time." He pinched his cheeks. It seemed like a nervous habit. "Yes, murders do happen. But this does beat all the cockfights put togedda. The murder of a well-renowned criminal by a police officer whose daughter might be caught up in the crime ring? Miss Garcia, Trinidad has rarely seen the likes of somet'ing like this."

He clasped his hands, the left into the right, and leaned forward.

I rubbed my neck. It had started to ache the moment I'd heard the police were after Farouk and Patsy. The policemen had come to my house first, pounding on the door, throwing things about, searching for a murderer.

"You tryin' to wine on me, Inspector Marlock?" I said. "You started with 'decent woman' and ended with an insult to my family. How you imagine that doesn't make the 'decent woman' part of your statement unimportant?"

He blew quick puffs of air from his nose, as though he were chuck-ling. But there was no smile. "You talk like an educated woman, Miss Garcia."

"It doesn't take an education to know that in Trinidad 'to wine on somebody' is not just to gyrate your hips. It does mean to take advan-tage, too. I'm not talking about being at no party, that's for sure."

"I never met a woman so quick like you," he said. "This is a real pleasure."

"I'm very happy for you." I pushed my cup toward the middle of the table.

"My company isn't bringing you pleasure?"

His tone made me uneasy. And excited. "Inspector Marlock, you still haven't tole me what you need with me."

He immediately sat up. "Nutting atall," he said. "I wanta make sure you're not holding somet'ing back from the police that'll come to haunt you later. The investigators are wondering how the wife and the mudda of the two people who remain alive in this story could know nutting. It strikes some people as strange. Because Farouk is my good friend, I wanted to warn you that people are asking ques-tions. And you mustn't keep information from the questioning offi-cers," he said. "It'd be especially bad for your udda chil'ren."

"I'm honestly fed up with people t'reatening my chil'ren." My voice was low. My words came out forcefully. "You doesn't bring up a woman's chil'ren if you meaning well."

His eyes grew big. "Nah, nah, nah. It wasn't a t'reat," he exclaimed, holding up both of his hands. "You mustn't take it that way. I felt you might need a friend down in Port-of-Spain, in case Patricia or Farouk tell you somet'ing you t'ink would be important for us to know."

"Inspector Marlock, if I'm in need of a friend, you not gointa be my first call," I said. "If you were *really* Farouk's friend, you would know he wouldn't tell me anyt'ing about anyt'ing. And since you were sittin' right here and you could see for yourself that I can hardly get a word outta that chile of mine, I'm sure you couldn't t'ink I knew she was carrying on the way she was, eh?"

I sensed he was digesting each of my words, pulling them apart, analyzing each letter. "So how did Patricia explain the jewelry, the extra money, and all the t'ings it appeared Rogers was giving her?"

"You see any jewelry and money here?" I stretched out my arms, and as I did, my robe burst open. My too-small brassiere, barely covering my too-large breasts, greeted him. I was embarrassed beyond belief. I clamored to pull myself together while Inspector Marlock, in a very decent way, turned his head.

When we faced each other again, his skin was flushed almost to pink. He blinked rapidly, as if he hadn't seen breasts since he'd been nursed.

"I'm very sorry to have boddered you, Miss Garcia." He stood, gently pushed his empty teacup next to mine. "I can see what a decent woman you are and I'm very sorry this all happened to your family," he said, walking to the door. "Farouk is a very lucky man."

I rose from the chair. "I'm sure Farouk, sitting in the jail, doesn't feel lucky atall."

"He should." Inspector Marlock pushed his cap down onto his head. "For many reasons."

After he left, I cleared the teacups. Jacqueline and Wesley had cleaned the house after the policemen had scattered our belongings. It was good of them to have helped so much. I held the damp dishcloth to my face. Fresh limes. Jacqueline had always disinfected the dishcloths in a bath of fresh limes. Warm tears fell. I dabbed them away. I had Patsy back home and Farouk had someone in the force looking out for him.

I changed into a simple lavender dress, patted my hair with a brush, and tried to clear the redness from my eyes. Two minutes from leaving for dinner at Aunty Baba's, another knock came at the door.

"Who's there?" I shouted from the bedroom.

The sun was beginning to dip, the shadows crisscrossing along the porch's boards, when I opened the door to find Inspector Marlock again.

He had his cap in hand and stood like a little boy, fidgeting. "I left without a proper t'ank-you for the tea."

"It's okay."

"You alright?" He touched my shoulder.

"I'm fine." I felt I would cry again. I turned quickly from the door.

He walked behind me, holding my arm, turning me into him. "No, you're not."

I folded myself into the strange man, breathing into his chest, as though it were my first breath in years. I felt the heat between us like bright sun on cut glass. He wiped my tears with his thumbs, letting them fall to my chin, tracing the outline of my shoulders until his fingers met between my collarbones. "I can stay if you want."

I couldn't take my eyes off Inspector Marlock's plush lips. "T'ank you," I said. "I'm fine."

His shoulders dropped. His smile opened. "I came back to say goodbye," he said. "But I didn't want it to be goodbye."

I put my finger to his lips. They were supple, smooth, like a perfectly ripened plum. "I don't t'ink this is a goodbye, Inspector Marlock."

Chapter 9

FAROUK KARAM

For twenty-two days, officers lined the corridors, waiting for their turn to crack me. For twenty-two days, all I could think of was what was happening to Marcia, to Patsy, to Wesley, Jackie, Yvonne.

On the twenty-third day, Duncan arrived. He walked with a limp, a downward left slant. The sewage hole in the cell floor, exposed and full, had been dug only steps from the cell's bars where we stood. The stench spoke of hundreds who had been there before me. Duncan spoke through a face of splayed fingers.

"Even your own daughter is willing to testify against you," he said. It was the first word I'd heard of Patsy. I was relieved. "She tells us you barged into Roger's home while he was havin' a private party and stabbed him to death because she wouldn't leave with you."

In the twenty-three days, I hadn't mentioned Marlock or the names of any of the officers involved with him. I hadn't said anything to anyone about how I thought I'd been set up. My freedom wasn't worth the risk.

I waited until Duncan turned to leave before I said anything. "Please mind my chil'ren." Those four words felt like smoking coals in my throat.

Duncan's sunken face, impossible to read, didn't leave me hopeful.

I was officially discharged from the police force on the twenty-fourth day. I hadn't been to court but had already lost the only job I'd ever had. The story went something like: Karam had masterminded Rogers's evasion of the police. Karam had sabotaged, many times over, Inspector Chung Marlock's case against Rogers. Karam had taken thousands of dollars in cash from Rogers. It is suspected that Karam used his parents and his brother, a Port-of-Spain bank manager, to funnel the money to his eldest brother, a doctor in Canada.

On the twenty-sixth day, they hosed me down, replaced my soiled uniform with a crisp white one, and led me to the visiting room.

"Farouk!" My mother covered her mouth and moaned. My hair wasn't brushed. My face hadn't seen a razor. My hand was bandaged in a fishy-smelling, blood-caked cloth. My eyes were swollen, and the wrapping around my broken ribs widened the appearance of my chest.

"Hello, Ma." I smiled as much as I could.

"My Gawd, what have you people done to my son?" She placed her index finger on the black-blue circles under my eyes. "Look what they did to you."

I hadn't slept more than three straight hours since my arrest. It had been difficult to turn off my thoughts. Everything—from the moment Marlock had demanded he accompany me to question Rogers to the second I ran with Patsy down St. John's Road—those thoughts didn't settle themselves into a peaceful slumber.

"I'm fine, Ma." I nudged her hand away from my eye. "They'll make you go if you keep this up."

I hadn't wanted to see her, but part of me was happy to see someone who wasn't there to destroy me.

"They not makin' me leave," she said quietly, sitting down. "They the ones who call me to come and see you."

"Tell me. What'd they say?"

She flapped her hands around her ears. "It hardly matters. I not here for them."

"It matters." I was desperate to know the inner workings of my case.

"You're my last-born chile and I'd die before I see you go on like this." She pressed her middle fingers into the inner corners of her large eyes. Black shimmery pools. Eyes like Jackie's. "If you don't help yourself what will become of you?"

I couldn't reassure my mother that all would be well; murder was punishable by hanging. I was trying to make peace with that fact every day.

"Farouk, you must tell them the girl did it," she said.

My mother had come without her jewelry. Her skin, without the glitter of gold, looked pallid. She was wearing one of her less expensive saris, a thin blue silk, which had an ill-fitting blouse. The *sindoor* powder in the middle of her forehead was slightly off center. She was still quite a beautiful woman, though the fattish pockets under her face had swallowed some of her chin. When I was a child, I used to wonder how my father, who was not a particularly good-looking man or from a wealthy family, had managed to attract her. How had he convinced my mother's family to allow her to become his wife? When I grew older, I saw that my mother's difficult personality had made it impossible for her parents to demand anything from a male suitor except that he take her away as quickly as possible.

"What girl?"

"The girl," she said, reaching for the comfort of her absent mob of bangles. "That Garcia woman's daughter."

I pressed my back into the wooden slatted chair.

"We can make it so the udda people who were in the room will say it's so. We can do that," she whispered with such excitement, it actually frightened me. "You'll tell the police you were just coverin' for the gal."

I dropped my head to my arms and stroked my wild hair forward. "You've gone mad, Ma."

She pulled my ears. "Me you callin' mad? You riskin' your life for that whore's whore and you callin' *me* mad?"

I was accustomed to my mother's angry, hurtful words. But this time the hurt wasn't the words. "She's my daughter, Ma. My firstborn daughter. What kinda man you t'ink I is?"

She scrunched her eyebrows with the tips of her fingers, the smudged sindoor looming like blood. "The kinda son I raised is not the kind who'd take money from a drug man, kill him off, and pretend it was because he wanted to help some gal who don't need to be saved by nobody udda than she own whore-of-a-mudda," she said.

"Ma—"

"Nah, nah, nah, nah, nah." She fanned her hands at me, as if she had had enough.

The guard, with his hand on a pistol, came over and gave my mother a stern warning. She batted her long eyelashes and said she was "so very sorry." Then, she turned back to me, her tone a midlevel whisper: "Me and your fadda are different people now. Last month, I wouldn't've been in a place like this. Not even in my worst nightmare, you hear what I tellin' you?" She was barely able to control the spittle forming along the edges of her mouth. "Your fadda has lost his standing. People does be comin' from all over Trinidad to be interviewed for the pandit job at the temple your fadda built himself. Because of this craziness with that woman we tole you not to tie up yourself with fifteen years ago, we're all havin' to suffer. What does hurt the eye does make the nose run!"

The guard seemed to have been waiting for another eruption. He gently pulled her up by the elbow.

"Please wait." She planted her pointy flat shoes firmly into the concrete floor and gently and maternally patted the guard's knuckles. "I need to kiss my son."

He released her. He looked at me. He wanted to let me know he was doing me a favor; I wanted to let him know he was free to drag her out.

My mother shuffled over. She pressed her pudgy body into mine. She smelled like honey. I had always loved her smell. She touched my head, pushing the hair back from my face, lightly scraping her nails along my aching scalp. "Your mudda just wants what's best for you," she said.

I thought about my mother plenty during the following days. About a day or two after she left, I realized she was just a mother, just a parent, like me, who'd do anything to keep her child from harm. She and I had been cut from the same cloth—impulsive, irrational, and neither praiseworthy nor courageous.

On the twenty-seventh day, I was left waiting in the visitors' room for almost an hour before they brought in Marcia.

"Hello, Farouk," she said.

"I've been worried about allyuh." My voice cracked.

"Patsy's home."

"T'anks for comin'."

She was wearing a pink-flowered dress. Not exactly a color of sorrow. And her hair was down and flowy. She looked like she was expecting to be photographed.

"How the rest of them chil'ren?"

"Everybody's alright." She looked over to the glass windowpanes layered with steel-rod curtains. "Jacqueline made sweetbread. They wouldn't let me bring it in."

"Tell her I said t'anks." I was sure the guards were already enjoying my favorite coconut and dried-fruit bread.

"What happened to your hand?" She pointed to the bloodstained bandage.

"Lost my pinky finger. Damn t'ing just popped right off. It was the best finger for scratchin' inside my ear, too." I forced a chuckle, but she stared down at her own fingers. They looked exactly as they had in Blanchisseuse.

Finally, she met my face. Her eyes were still a color I didn't know how to describe. "The deeper the darkness, the nearer the dawn, you hear?" Her bag slipped from the chair back. She placed it on her lap, then reached over and touched my arm. "I need to know somet'ing."

"I'm not talking about what happened."

"You still an ass, even in jail?" She gave me that disgusted, look-at-yourself face she was famous for.

"Sorry," I said, suddenly hoping she wouldn't leave.

"Are you?"

"You know I am."

For three weeks I had dreamt of speaking to her, dreamt of telling her how sorry I was. Now she was there, and I could only dance the same dance I'd always danced with her.

"Were you crooked like they're saying? That's the part that does bodder the chil'ren. Especially Wesley," she continued.

I scooted the chair back from the table and crossed one leg over the other thigh. She watched me carefully. "I went there because of Patsy."

"Not because of the money, like they're saying?"

"I never took one bit a money," I said. "You know who I am."

"I know who you used to be. *That* Farouk would've handled the situation with Patsy much betta."

"I'm the same Farouk. The very same one."

She placed the strap of her bag on her arm. The tone of her shoulders had softened some, rounded in the same way her face had, over the years.

"Both of we know that's not true," she said.

MARCIA GARCIA

Uncle Linton stood bent over stacks of white papers. They fluttered at a hint of breeze. I watched, from the door, his hands slapping the sheets, as if he were a bongo player, the jagged rhythm rattling my already-jittery nerves.

Waiting for permission to see Farouk, answering the children's questions about when he would be out, what he had done, why he had done it, had been hard. But not as hard as seeing him in the jail-house. Not as hard as taking the bus to Sangre Grande.

Uncle Linton took off his glasses, which he only wore on occasion. When I was a girl that very act would send Ginny and me into a panic. It meant he hadn't decided which one of us he would use up that day. Knowing that, if I was feeling brave, I would sometimes confront his flat stare and pretend there was more behind it than just evil, pretend he was a human being. Whenever I did this, he would choose Ginny.

He looked up from his papers with the same flat expression. I was suddenly reminded of the guilt I felt for having never shared that secret with Ginny.

"Some time ago, I tried to help him," Uncle Linton said. "I know his fadda a li'l, and we talked about what a fine policeman he was. I asked him to bring Farouk to see me. I wanted to give him some advice. But he never came." The top of Uncle Linton's bent, balding head was shiny with pills of sweat.

"That's when you t'ought he knew?"

He scribbled with a blue ballpoint pen. "Of course."

"He didn't know."

Uncle Linton put down the pen and leaned forward on his elbows. "Why wouldn't he come?"

"He couldn't understand how you could've left me to take care of two boys he t'ought were your nephews. He t'ought you were a selfish bastard. That's all he knew."

Uncle Linton took books from beneath his desk and placed them atop the windblown sheets. The air from the open window carried his minty cologne. He swiveled in his chair. The garden was lovely now. A scarlet ibis held its pose against the backdrop of the emerald-green lawn. The hedges were pruned to a boxed perfection. The stone Italian fountain spewed a clear stream from its unclogged center. The pink landscape roses were in bloom, with not a brown, withered leaf in sight. It was the yard, maybe, of a soon-to-be Prime Minister of Trinidad and Tobago.

"You told me he knew." Uncle Linton's voice was thin but firm.

"I did not," I said, though I had led him to believe it.

"You told me he knew," he said again.

The regret I was beginning to feel was unspeakable. "You did this?"

"He did this to himself, with your help, of course." He swung his chair back around, glancing at his watch long enough for me to take note. He unfastened the gold metal watchband with his curved fingernail. His hand had a slight tremor. "His arrest will certainly make it easier for me to argue that the current government is corrupt."

He was so satisfied with the outcome of what he had done.

"You're gointa get Farouk outta this mess." I pulled at my shirt-sleeves, pressing the French cuffs against my wrists.

He picked up his pen again, holding its tip upward. He seemed to be contemplating how best to explain to his ignorant niece what would not happen.

"You will," I said.

Uncle Linton rose from his seat and fiddled with his papers again, signaling that my time in his office was over. "Karam's a rogue officer and a murderer."

I reached across his desk and flipped over a sheet he was pretending to read. "Being the mudda of this man's chil'ren is getting me plenty of attention. I can get anybody to listen to me right now."

Uncle Linton eyed the deep parenthetical creases around my mouth. I had changed. I kept my palm pressed onto the paper. "You don't want me to start talking."

He curled his index finger around his top lip.

"What part do you t'ink they'll focus on most? Me being your niece? The part about me having chil'ren with Farouk? Or maybe that you took me like I was your woman when I was only eleven and then put two babies in my fourteen-year-old sista?"

Uncle Linton sat down, stretching out his legs beneath his desk.

"Because you like the Karam family and because Aamir Karam is a pillar of the community, you gointa call Farouk's fadda and tell him you'll make this t'ing go away," I said. "And when this is over, when we're all back on our feet again, whether you become Prime Minister or not, I'll take my chil'ren and leave this country."

"You will go right away," he said.

"I won't." I wanted Uncle Linton to understand this wasn't a negotiation. "I will see our lives return to normal and I'll not utter a word to anybody. When it's all done, we'll go to America and start a new life. You'll never have to worry."

Uncle Linton jiggled his legs. He wrote something on a yellow pad of paper that had been sitting beneath a copy of Marx's *Economic and Philosophic Manuscripts*. "A fella named Harlow will get in touch with you. He'll start your paperwork," he said. "But I can't promise anyt'ing and I can't make people forget what Karam's done. I'm not God."

I smacked my chair into his fine cherry desk. "You be as close to God as you can be. Make it 'all betta.' Isn't that what you said you'd do after Ma died?" I moved toward the door. "Unkept promises, like secrets, can't make it to the grave without effort."

A few days later, Uncle Linton was scheduled to speak near Five Rivers Junction. It would be a big day, full of speeches by all the candidates.

I packed a picnic lunch—cucumber sandwiches and a bag full of ripe *mammee apples*—for me and Yvonne. We ate quickly under a breadfruit tree and then I took her by the hand and pushed us through throngs of people until we were nearly in front of the bandstand.

Uncle Linton was reading his notes, perspiring through his starched buttoned shirt, fanning himself with a thick brochure.

"History is in the making here," I said to Yvonne. "December's general elections will be the last step to full self-governance. Trinidad is on its way, and its future depends on how great we are and how great our first elected leader will be."

Uncle Linton, the final candidate to speak, rose from his folding chair. His supporters roared. Many older Trinidadians believed Uncle Linton had protected them while the Brits ran the country; they felt they owed him the election.

Uncle Linton spoke of all the things Eric Williams had not done as Chief Minister. How Williams had failed to keep Jamaica interested in the West Indian Federation, how Williams had failed to get Venezuela to remove the 30 percent surtax on British goods shipped from Trinidad, how Williams had failed to make America live up to its agreement to provide development aid in exchange for its naval base being built in Chaguaramas. Uncle Linton talked of making Trinidad "a kinder place, like we had known before," "a place that would double the efforts and the positive results of a rapist-minded British Colonialism," "a place ready to lead the Caribbean into a post-war future, where it would align with America and use its greatest natural resource, oil, and its agriculture to supply the world."

When Uncle Linton's voice rose, the crowd's fervor grew and Yvonne bounced with excitement. A country was in the making. Even a child could feel the quickened pulse of its birth.

Uncle Linton waited for the hush of the crowd. In the forced quiet, I lightly tickled Yvonne's ears. She screamed, giggling with delight. When Uncle Linton looked up from his notes, searching the crowd to see where the laughter had come from, he saw Yvonne's beautiful face, with two new front teeth, and then he saw me, behind her, waving.

1962

"SPARROW COME BACK HOME"

BY THE MIGHTY SPARROW

Chapter 10

JACQUELINE KARAM

"Jacqueline!" That woman couldn't go one blasted day without calling my name. "Jacqueline!" The bloody neighborhood rooster wasn't even awake.

Mammy knocked a spoon against the cast-iron pot lip as a warning. Patsy was still sound asleep. I washed my face in the bowl next to the door, brushed my teeth with the last of the baking soda, and pushed open the curtain.

The kitchen smelled like hot grease.

"You didn't hear me callin' you the first two hundred times?" she said.

"I was tired."

"You t'ink you know what tired is?" Mammy was hustling crumbs through the open front door. "Chil'ren on they mudda's back don't know how tiring the road does be."

I set down my dirty washbowl and began to wipe the table with a damp cloth. Wesley, awake and dressed, swallowed the last of something. He placed the used cup next to me and tried to pass by Mammy. She blocked the door. "You see you?" she said to him, setting herself up to put the finishing touches on an earlier lecture that I had obviously slept through. "I took mont's of my time to teach you. Gave you

the only t'ing my mudda gave me. And the one t'ing I ask is for you
to help me every once in a while. You can't find no job, you not in
school. At thirteen, you takin' no responsibility for nutting." Mammy
moved away from the door, leaving Wesley unsure as to whether he
could leave. "You must grow up, Wesley. I won't be around to take
care of you forever."

Wesley slipped out when Mammy moved to the ironing board.
Wearing her housecoat and a red scarf in a knot at her forehead, she
pressed a blouse. "Patsy! I need you to go to the market this mornin'!"
Even if Patsy was willing, getting her to come back was a whole other
story.

"Somebody's comin'," Mammy said to me. She left her half-ironed
blouse on the board to empty the freshly fried channa from a now-
cooled iron skillet. Her movements were jerky, disorganized. She
sprinkled the warm chickpea balls with a heavy dose of iodized salt
and tossed them with a wooden spoon.

"It's Friday," I said, quietly to myself, as if I needed confirmation.
Having someone drop by to get measured, pick up a dress, or leave
clothes for repair, was part of the routine in our house. Saturday
through Thursday. On Fridays, Mammy worked. The rutted sounds
of the machine were near constant. It was the one day I didn't go to
work at the shirt factory. The one day she wanted me to handle everything that might come up at home.

I carried my bowl outside and on the lopsided wooden front step,
I inhaled the sweet thickness of the morning air. Even breathing took
energy nowadays. The last time I could remember feeling like myself
was the morning of my exam.

That morning Mammy asked me to drop off an outfit for Miss
Claire. Miss Claire lived in San Juan and Mammy surely knew I
risked being late if my travels didn't go smoothly. But she had insisted.
"You have plenty time," she had said.

The bus ride went as planned. Miss Claire answered the door, paid me, and even gave me a good luck tamarind ball. "You're a smart gal. You'll do fine."

I waited at the Quai d'Orsay Junction that morning, nibbling on the tangy, sugarcoated candy. I wasn't nervous. I went over my math, remembered important history dates. I watched post office customers move in and out of the door and food truck owners set up for the breakfast rush. I had spit out the last sticky tamarind seed onto the road when the bus rounded the corner. I would easily make it on time to the exam.

That's when I saw Daddy.

He had been in jail for almost a month and none of us, except Mammy, had seen him. It had taken everything to keep my mind on my studies with all that was going on with him. Suddenly, there he was, driving around, free as a bird, with a woman in the car next to him.

Instead of getting on the bus that had pulled up in front of me, I crossed the busy street.

Daddy was out of the car. I walked up behind him. His shoulders sagged, his hand was bandaged, and he had lost a good deal of weight. He wore a loose-fitting brown suit, a white shirt, and a blue-and-brown checkered tie. Gawd, I wanted to throw myself into his arms.

"Daddy?"

My voice startled him. "What you doin' here, girl? You got no sense?"

The smile fell from my face like a ton of concrete. "Mammy needed me to drop off a dress." I wanted to hug him, talk to him, let him know of the things that had taken place while he was away.

Instead, he said, "Isn't this mornin' your exam? Go and get outta here."

The woman stepped out from the passenger side. I had seen her face in a blotchy black-and-white photograph Daddy had in his home. She didn't look as old as I had imagined; her skin was browner than I thought it would be. She had eyebrows like bushy moustaches. She wore a tiny gold earring in her nose. She was only a few feet away. I could smell her honey-orange perfume.

"We're gointa be late," she muttered. She smoothed the fabric of her black and gold sari, and massaged her elbow. She never glanced in my direction.

"Go on," Daddy said, waving me off.

"Ajee?" I said to the woman.

Her head jerked, like I had hit her with a long, hard *louchet*. A breeze carried the odor of the breakfast carts' fried potatoes and onions.

"Farouk!" She jammed her black leather handbag up into her armpit. "What's happenin' here?"

I looked at Daddy. Maybe the woman wasn't my grandmother? But Daddy's tired eyes said it all.

"This is Jacqueline." He seemed to be struggling with the heaviness of his tongue. "Garcia."

The two little black balls in her eyes darted to Daddy, then to me. The resemblance between us was undeniable.

"She could be any half-coolie, half-nigga chile," she muttered. Then, she dragged her open-heeled shoes across the road and into a red-painted building.

A scarlet peacock butterfly flitted past the exam room window. I had been sitting at that desk for hours, hearing that woman's words over and over in my head. None of them made sense. Did she really believe I wasn't Daddy's child? Is that why my grand-parents didn't want to know me? When the bell rang, the only thing I had written inside the blue booklet was my name: *Jacqueline Karam*.

• • •

Patsy had left for the market. Mammy was taking out her pins and fluffing her hair, waiting for her "somebody," when I returned, red-eyed, from emptying the pot.

In Mammy's bedroom, Yvonne lay snoring, her narrow lips puffed out like a little fish's. Her hair, which I had combed the night before, was frizzy at the hairline, and her delicate hands, on the verge of no longer looking like a child's, were tucked squarely under her arm.

I lightly nudged her. She woke with a smile and a tight hug for me. "Come on," I said. "Mammy's in a state."

Yvonne had been attending Five Rivers Elementary School for six months, ever since we'd moved from Curepe. She had made plenty of friends and her studies were coming along nicely. Although the school was just down the road, I didn't mind walking her there. It got me away from my chores and also gave me a chance to linger in the schoolyard and watch Yvonne's teacher, Mr. Aldous, glide across the lawn to greet the girls. That man was a god, as blasphemous as that might sound—just watching him made me happy.

When I arrived back home, Mammy's "somebody" had parked his big, fancy motorcar by the gate. It was Australian. I had read about it in one of Wesley's magazines. "Hot Metal" it had read. There weren't many in Trinidad and probably none the color of a dandelion. The island sun made the yellow metal shimmer like pure gold. It had chrome handles, a white roof, brown padded seats, and two bulging headlights on a wide grill, headlights that reminded me of open arms.

I thought Mammy's "somebody" might be some rich fella from Port-of-Spain buying a dress for some poor razzy girl he was courting. But when he stood at our door with his car key swinging around his index finger, with this strange grin that reminded me of when some-one saw an ugly baby, I had this feeling he was there for something altogether different.

"Come in," Mammy said. The man was tall, with dark wavy hair. He used to be a *fatty booly*, I could tell by the way his clothes hung off him and the way his skin sagged under his neck. He wore round wire spectacles that kept falling onto his longish nose. He had a medium-brown complexion, like a coconut's, and pockmarked skin.

"Mornin'," he said.

I snuck in behind him, scurrying into Mammy's room, pretending to clean, but leaving the curtain slightly parted. He looked about the place, then sat across from Mammy. She was calmly drinking her cup of black tea with milk. Her back was to me.

"Missus Garcia," he started.

It was strange to hear him call her that. *Garcia*. I thought of Mammy as a Karam, like us. *Marcia Garcia*. There could be a calypso about her, the woman with the rhyming name, except no decent calypsonian, priding himself on important happenings and social criticisms, would've written a song about a seamstress with four children, no husband, and a half-buried smile.

"Tea?" Mammy said.

"No need." The "somebody" continued to twirl the car key. "Not here for long."

There was too much stretch in his words. The *ee* in the *need* and the *er* in *here* were longer than necessary. The *t* in the *not* had too much tongue. He sounded like a fake American.

"Look." Mammy pointed to the bowl in front of her. "I fry up some channa. Go and have some."

He set down his keys. "You cookin' up channa for a boy who ain't been home in awhile. That's a good sign."

Their behavior was odd. She clearly knew him, but how? And why was he in our home?

The crunch of the salty channa in his wide mouth rang out like growls. Mammy took another sip from her tin cup.

"How long you livin' in Five Rivers?" he said, breaking their silence.

"Not long."

I knew by the way she dropped her voice that she was embarrassed. We had moved to Five Rivers when Daddy ran out of money and when many of Mammy's clients stopped placing orders. It was a two-bedroom house, but compared to where we had lived in Curepe, it was more like a shack. Walking through the door put you directly in the kitchen. There was hardly enough room for the Primus or Wesley's recliner, let alone Mammy's fabrics or her books.

"So," Mammy said. "What them Yankees doin' up there?" She pointed upward toward the sheet metal roof as if America could be seen in the sky.

"Yankees does always be happy."

"Cold up there?" I was sure Mammy had finished drinking her tea. She pretended to take another sip.

The man reached for his key again, making it dance on his fingers. "Pretty powerful connection you have in Mr. Beatrice."

"Friend of my family's," she said.

Mammy knew Linton Beatrice?

"He's about to raise some hell now that he lost. He gointa try and kick up some dirt on Williams."

"I don't know nutting about that," Mammy said, even though she had been listening to and grunting at the radio for weeks.

"No? Apparently, Beatrice is planning to go to the Election Board and formally question the voting procedures *and* the Prime Minister's degree from Oxford. If Williams is a fraud—"

"It's not true. The Brits would've called Williams out a long time before now," Mammy said.

"Eh-eh. Even if it's not true, you betta believe Dr. Williams's camp will find somet'ing nice and good to t'row back at Beatrice," the "somebody" said.

Mammy sat back in her chair and crossed her arms. "I just tole you Beatrice was a friend of the family. Funny t'ings to be saying about somebody I know."

"Didn't seem to me that you cared too much for the fella, but . . .

forgive me anyway, Missus Garcia." He grabbed another handful of channa and chewed them halfway before speaking again. "Sometimes it's cold in America. But you get accustomed. The t'ing that's hard to get accustomed to is they don't understand a word of decent, British English. When you speakin', them Americans lookin' at you like you speaking Dutch." He laughed, covering his mouth with one end of a fist.

"You can get accustomed to that?"

"Missus Garcia." He swallowed the last bits of channa, sat up straight and pushed the empty bowl away. "You came to my office mont's ago, signed my papers, gave me your word," he said. "Mr. Beatrice's secretary tole me you were ready. I'm going back to America in a few weeks and my affairs are supposed to be in order. You can't leave me a message with the office gal saying you changin' your mind."

"Sure I can," Mammy said. "Nobody gointa tell me I have to go someplace I don't wanta go."

"You gave me your word," the man said again, shifting in his seat. "I have a family in Maryland. You know where that is? Not too far from that jungle, New York City. They does have a room in a nice house, on a farm, with horses and everyt'ing. They're decent people. They does have a fancy boutique in a li'l town and they need help making dresses. They'll pay you good money. You'll eat for free and save your cash," he said. "You makin' me look foolish if I have to tell them you changin' your mind."

Mammy cheupsed. "I can't worry myself about anybody's business in America. I have to t'ink about *my* business in Trinidad."

"I understand what the devil is going on here." The "somebody" tapped on Mammy's red starched tablecloth. "Getting away is the best t'ing you can do. Maybe meet a new fella who'll help take care of you. You must be scared of what that man of yours will do if you leave, but—"

Mammy held up her palms. "Mr. Harlow, you don't know me."

She pushed the tin cup. It swayed and landed next to the empty channa bowl. "My business is my business. I don't bodder with Farouk Karam and you don't bodder me with he."

The man's round, brown face seemed suspended in air. "Missus Garcia, what that crazy Indian man wanta make his business, he does make his business. I don't want no trouble atall with him." He placed Mammy's cup inside the channa bowl. "You stay in Trinidad. I'll have to understand."

"Who you talkin' to?" Mammy rose from her chair. "That man don't own me. I does put tea in my own cup. You understand that?"

If it were me in Mr. Harlow's seat, I would've been running. Instead, he challenged Mammy even more. "Missus Garcia, look around. Trinidad could be on the brink of disaster. Why place a bet on your chil'ren's future? Eric Williams can't get the crooks and the cliques, and make the indignities a woman must face here—even by her own husband—to disappear overnight. You want that for your girls? He might be a good man but even *Dr. Eric Williams* cannot do it all."

"Hmph," Mammy replied. It was the kind of "hmph" that meant she had been carefully listening. She sat back down in her chair, pursed her lips, and gave a short, not-very-convincing cheups. "Why you come here, Mr. Harlow?"

He rubbed his palms on the top of his flabby thighs. "I want you to reconsider," he said. "I made Mr. Beatrice's people a promise that I'd help you. Let me help you."

"I have chil'ren." Mammy rested her chin on her thumb, as if balancing the weight of her entire being there. "I know the criminals are here to stay. You want me to leave my chil'ren behind for who knows how long."

"Everybody must do that. West Indians are a transient people. If the need arises, we go."

Mammy bounced in her chair as if considering leaving her seat, then thought better of it. "You never miss the water 'til the well runs dry," she said. "Plenty people t'ink they'll be fine until the person they need does be gone."

Mr. Harlow nodded, as if no one could argue with Mammy. But he said, "Your chil'ren are big now. No more babies. The two big girls will watch the li'l one. And the boy, he'll manage the girls."

"Who gointa watch who?" she said, mockingly. "You ever seen that bigheaded boy I have? He can't watch his piss go straight into the big, wide ocean. No betta than he fadda." Mammy took Mr. Harlow's cup out of her bowl. "Jacqueline, come out from behind there!"

She knew I didn't like to be around strangers.

"Look at this chile." She lifted her chin toward me while I tugged at the hem of my skirt. "This is my second oldest. Almost fifteen. The best I have. And she does hardly talk."

"Hello, Jacqueline." Mr. Harlow's voice rose an octave, as if speaking to a baby.

"Good morning." I spoke loud enough for Mammy not to accuse me of a whisper.

"Your mammy's got a chance to make a betta life for allyuh. What you t'ink she should do?"

If I answered either way, Mammy would think me too grown for speaking my mind. So, I grinned like a li'l duncy-head.

"She can go to America in a few weeks and start a new life there. Then she can bring allyuh when she files for the papers," he said. "You must have *some* t'oughts?"

When have I ever had any control over Mammy?

My eyes darted between them. I was scared to stop at Mammy's face. She had this way of looking so disappointed when I was close by, as if she wondered how I could've come from her. "I don't."

The chair creaked on its way back from the table. "Involving chil'ren in grown people's business is not my style," Mammy said to Mr. Harlow. She stood and placed her index and middle fingers on my temple. "Go and leave," she said to me.

• • •

I hurried down the road, embarrassed, panicked, and, more than anything, confused. Mammy's conversation with Mr. Harlow—her thinking about going to America and him trying to convince her—she hadn't said a word about any of that to us.

It felt like forever to get to the main road. The narrow streets, children plowing into my knees—Five Rivers was a miserable little place, with dust, rocks, one big old *samaan* tree, and not a river to be found. The foul, yet familiar, smoky stench of burning trash was far behind me when a car idled at my backside.

"Jacqueline? Come, lemme talk to you for a minute."

Mr. Harlow was waving at me with his dumpling-shaped fingers. He pushed up his spectacles until the top rims were smashed against his forehead. The gesture made him seem harmless.

"Come, come," he said, urging me to move closer. "I not gointa bite."

I looked behind to see if Mammy was walking the streets in search of me, like she had done with Patsy.

"Your mammy t'rew me out." He smiled as if he didn't know what else to do. "Make sure you keep on her. America is the land of opportunity. You know that, right?"

I was sure poor in Trinidad and poor in America had to be pretty much the same, except in Trinidad there was at least a low-hanging fruit that could keep somebody from starving. I had heard that in America, they gave people powdered milk. I wasn't interested in powdered milk.

"Your mudda's a good woman, Jacqueline. Strange, yes. And hard, I know. But she means well. She wants the best for allyuh." He handed me five dollars. "You make sure you behave."

No one had ever told me they thought Mammy cared for us. Half of me believed no one had said it because it wasn't true. The other half of me hoped the first half was wrong.

• • •

For many people, Friday was the beginning of a weekend filled with possibility. For my father, Friday was a day to drown possibility in a bottle.

Although Daddy still lived in Tunapuna, he often left what little money he had burning up in a bottle of *caca poule* rum in Five Rivers. The snackette he frequented was a part-time rum shop, right off the Eastern Main Road, the busiest east–west street in Trinidad. It was just a few small tables with pole-legged chairs, watered-down bottles beneath the counter, misty drinking glasses, and some not-so-fresh curry the owners served to intoxicated patrons who wouldn't be able to distinguish drunken diarrhea from bad-curry diarrhea.

I'd been given a tongue-lashing more than once by Daddy about searching for him in places that served liquor. I waited next to the faded wooden rails of the snackette while the screened door creaked open and shut nearly a hundred times.

"Farouk," a strange male voice called out. "I t'ink it's your li'l *dougla* outside."

Daddy staggered to the door wearing blue slacks that dragged like heavy bags around his ankles. He squinted as if he hadn't realized the sun had risen.

"Hi, Daddy."

The wrinkled man before me looked nothing like the handsome fella I had once been happy to call "Daddy." Farouk, the taxi driver, was dirty, scraggly, and smelled like diesel fuel. He was missing a pinky finger, too.

"What you doin' here, Jackie?"

"Did you know Mammy was going to America?" The words from my mouth felt like vomit—sickly yet relieving.

He squinted harder. Car horns beeped and blared on the road behind us. "Marcia not goin' no place but right up de road."

"A man came today," I said.

Daddy leaned back into the wobbly, dusty porch rails and crossed his arms. "What man you talkin' 'bout?"

"A man in a big car. One of those fancy Australian cars. He had a li'l fake Yankee accent," I said, still unsure of how I felt about Mr. Harlow and if I should tell Daddy everything. "You probably know him."

"Probably." I watched his bottom lip grow fuller.

"I don't wanta go to America," I said. "He met me on the road, on the way here, and asked me to talk to Mammy."

Daddy walked to my side of the porch. The smell of the diesel was pungent. I was afraid a spark from a partially lit cigarette butt would blow him to pieces. "He give you somet'ing?"

"Like what?"

He watched me. "Men like to give pretty girls t'ings. He give you somet'ing?"

Every word between us since his arrest was colored by what Patsy had done. "Just a five dollar." I pulled the money from the purple-ribbon purse strapped across my shoulder.

"Come, give it to me." He held out his hand. "He take it from he wallet or he pocket?" Daddy touched it with two fingers only.

"I don't remember."

His breath smelled of tangy liquor. "Your mudda know I can get she some money." He placed the bill in his front shirt pocket and buttoned it closed. "She not goin' to America without checkin' with me. She not crazy."

Suddenly, a woman appeared at the snackette door. She was younger than Mammy, but older than I was. She wore heavy, off-color foundation on smooth evening-black skin, a cutoff cotton shirt, showing off at least six babies' worth of silvery stretch marks, and a pair of tight, grey-colored dungarees.

"Rouk," she said. "I waitin'."

"Woman, go on." Daddy waved her off.

The woman stepped back from the door, and bad-eyed me with

her strange, bluish eyeballs. I tried to ignore her. I batted away a
pesky gnat circling my ear. A car passed, blaring a calypso song I
liked. I snapped my fingers.

"Come," Daddy abruptly said to her.

I was embarrassed to see her walk onto the porch toward Daddy,
swaying her big hips and even bigger bottom. Yet, there was something that made it hard not to look at her.

Daddy handed her the bill, wiped his hands on his pants, then
whispered something in her ear. She started to walk back inside, but
instead she stopped and set those strange eyes on me again. Those
blue eyes. Like the old lady's in Tunapuna who had made Mammy
fall down.

"No wonder Mammy does hate you," I said.

"Your cunt of a mudda? She does hate my money?" Daddy put his
finger near my face. He didn't know I had been there that day with
Mammy, eight years earlier, at the obeah lady's house. He didn't know
I remembered his little girlfriend.

"What money? We takin' breadfruit and mangoes from Aunty
Baba's yard, eatin' dhal and rice every night," I said. "That's why
Mammy have anudda man!"

It seemed to be unconscious, the way Daddy gripped his stomach.
"Your mudda has nutting without me," he mumbled.

"No?" I said. "She has plenty."

MARCIA GARCIA

Patsy was the quickest, the smartest of my children, both with the books and with common sense. Sure, sure, she never properly applied herself, but nobody could tell me she didn't know what she was up to with that fella Rogers in that big house up on that hill. Patsy was no victim. We had to play that beat, to keep people from looking at her in disgust, to keep even her own sisters and brother from losing respect for her. We had to tell everybody Patsy fell in love with the Rogers fella, that he had tried to use her up like trash. We had to tell everybody she didn't know how to get herself out of the trouble once she was in it.

But a mother knows her child.

Patsy had always been a survivor. Just like me. But the difference between us was that Patsy wanted to be the biggest and brightest survivor of them all. She had this greedy, hungry, impatient urge churning inside her, and she didn't care who she had to climb over to get what she wanted. She didn't care who she had to swallow up to thrive.

Until Farouk ran into that place on the hill and pulled Patsy out, I had been losing her. And every mother knows when you lose one child, you risk losing the others too. So much of your energy is invested in saving one child, there's often nothing left for the rest. I had searched the streets for weeks, leaving behind everything and everyone, trying to figure out what was happening. Afterward, when I learned what she had been up to, I can't say I was surprised. I can only say that Farouk didn't just save Patsy the day he ran up into the hills of St. Augustine. He saved all my children. He saved me.

The elections were held in December and Uncle Linton's party lost. Although I had gone through all the motions Uncle Linton had laid out—meeting with Harlow in his office, filling out paperwork, traveling to the embassy for my interview—I had done every bit of it with no intention of leaving Trinidad.

The afternoon after Mr. Harlow's visit, I was as pleased as ever. I had told him to "kiss my bamsee" and to "never return." I sent Patsy to the market, I made Jacqueline take two dresses to Chaguanas, and I headed out, dressed and prettied up, for my weekly standing lunch with Chung Marlock.

Later that evening, I gathered the children at the table for a game of cards with a bowl of fresh corn kernels I had popped in the pit outside, along with five tall glasses of chilled, sweet sorrel. We laughed and played rummy until Yvonne fell asleep with her mouth full of popcorn. Wesley took her to my room while me, Jacqueline, and Patsy cleaned the table and collected the empty drinking glasses.

"Let's wash these in the morning," I said.

Jacqueline's eyes opened wide. "*You* sayin' we should leave dishes for the mornin'? No, no, no. Not you."

I swatted her behind with the dishcloth, laughing. "Shush your mout'. Go ahead and allyuh get some sleep."

I swept a few more crumbs out the front door, then went into my room. At the side of the bed I washed my face, and, for a few moments,

I watched Yvonne sleep. I thought too of the other three sleeping just past the threshold of my room. Thinking about how much my children meant to me was a luxury I didn't have. Maybe a luxury I hadn't wanted to have. I blew out the broad white candle and pulled the sheet to my thighs. "I love allyuh," I whispered.

JACQUELINE KARAM

A girl's got a right to dream.

There was a time when my only dream was for my parents to be together, and though that time had long passed, my crush on Mr. Aldous reminded me of then. My crush on Mr. Aldous made me wonder how Farouk Karam and Marcia Garcia ever got to hate each other. My crush on Mr. Aldous made me wonder if Farouk Karam and Marcia Garcia ever loved each other.

It was hard for me to imagine Mammy being young like me and eyeing up some boy. It was hard for me to imagine Daddy holding Mammy in his arms, telling her he loved her. What had happened to make them so different?

Part of me didn't want to know the answer, I wanted my life to be a whole other story. Courtship, love, marriage, a big happy family.

And Mr. Aldous was going to be my first step.

Yvonne had told me everything a girl could hope to know about the man she would marry:

He pressed the middle of his palm against his forehead when he wanted to calm himself. He deepened his voice when he spoke to the fathers who came to the schoolyard. He tied his shoelaces two times over and tucked the tips under the tongue of his well-polished dress shoes. He liked his morning tea, which he drank before class, with triple sugars and one-quarter milk. I knew that his favorite food was callaloo with pork and not crab, and that when he ate roti, he preferred cubed beef over still-on-the-bone chicken.

Yvonne even told me the bad things.

She told me that Mr. Aldous could be short-tempered, impatient, moody at times. She also told me that she suspected he had a strong liking for the trampy-looking new teacher, Miss Penny, who was from somewhere in Arouca, where apparently it was okay for women to wear miniskirts that rode the crack of their bamsees.

Why a man like Mr. Aldous would like a woman who would dress herself in that way, I would never know. But when I went to pick up Yvonne one drizzly afternoon, wearing a loose-fitting button-down shirt and a long pink skirt, and Mr. Aldous spoke to me for the first time, I had to look down to see if I had accidentally left the hem of my skirt tucked into my underpants.

"I see your mammy does have Yvonne reading *Wuthering Heights*. Ambitious for a nine-year-old, eh?" he said.

Mr. Aldous's voice was full like heavy brass. His narrow hip was against the schoolyard gatepost. His focus, squarely on me. I couldn't look at his face. If I could have, I probably would've told Mr. Aldous that Catherine and Heathcliff were easy for Yvonne—a story about love could hold almost any girl's interest. I would've told him that the real challenge was teaching Yvonne about life, about history, about her country. Even though there had been an oil boom after the war and even though we were moving toward a peaceful independence, things in Trinidad were hard. Especially for girls. I would've told him that what they didn't teach Yvonne in school was that without proper schooling, girls had no future in Trinidad, other than factory work, kitchen work, and babies. I would've said a girl had to fight to be a teacher, had to fight to be a policewoman, had to fight for work almost always against a more favored boy from Trinidad and from a half-dozen poorer islands. I would've told Mr. Aldous that I didn't want it to be too late by the time Yvonne understood Trinidad, like it had been for me.

But instead of telling him those things, I dropped my eyes to the puddles alongside the fence where the morning glories the girls had planted only a week earlier were flooded to their petals; my words stuck in the pit of my queasy stomach.

"Why didn't you tell him that you's my teacher too?" Yvonne asked on our way home through a veil of light raindrops. "You ask me everyt'ing about him and he finally speaks to you, and you don't say one word?"

I took a shirt from my bag and covered her head with it. "I didn't talk because I ate my favorite sandwich for lunch." I bent down and blew a puff of air into her dimple-cheeked face. "Onion and cheddar cheese!" Her laughter was like medicine.

I promised myself that if I had another chance, I would woo Mr. Aldous with my magnetic personality and the straight white teeth I had inherited from Mammy. I didn't see Mr. Aldous the following morning, but that afternoon I bounced from the shirt factory to the schoolyard and signaled to Yvonne that I would wait for her to finish chatting with her friends.

"Good afternoon," Mr. Aldous finally said.

I studied the way his long black sideburns reached down to tickle his sharp jawline. "Good afternoon," I said.

Mr. Aldous patted the top of his small, shapely bush. He seemed surprised by how confidently I spoke this time. "Today, Yvonne told me *you're* her teacher."

"Sometimes," I said. Sister Edwina had insisted that a proper girl should project humility. "Let another man praise thee, and not thine own mouth," is what she would say. I was ready to deflect Mr. Aldous's coming praise when he turned away.

"Eh-eh, come from there, Thomasine!" He pointed at a girl no bigger than a little sugarcane stalk. She'd been poking at a spiny gecko with a jagged stick when she heard Mr. Aldous's stern voice and began to cry. She ran back to the other girls.

"Sorry," Mr. Aldous said, pressing that palm against his forehead. "I was saying you must have a future as a teacher, eh?"

I lost my courage. The square-chinned little girl, Thomasine, was staring at Mr. Aldous and me from across the schoolyard. Staring in the same way I stared when he would speak to Miss Penny.

In a few years, that ridiculous lizard-chasing girl would probably snag Mr. Aldous. Her family would invite him over for tea to celebrate Thomasine's passing of the Common Entrance. Then, while her mother filled Mr. Aldous's cup with triple sugars and milk, Thomasine's father would offer Mr. Aldous his daughter's hand in marriage. Mr. Aldous would stop for a moment and maybe remember how he had once thought kindly about a girl named Jacqueline, a girl he would never be with because she had managed to gloriously flunk her exam.

I still couldn't believe it sometimes. It had taken me almost a half year to get used to the idea that I was no longer a student, that working at a shirt factory might be my future. The hopelessness could still grip me when I least expected it.

"Do you know her?" Mr. Aldous was standing so close I could smell his antiperspirant.

"No, no. I was wondering how come the school doesn't take care of the broken fence," I said.

He looked to the spot where the lizard struggled to crawl with its tail half-smashed. "Yes, I must go and jot that down." He moved his hand in half circles as if to speed us to the next topic. "How are you doing it? Yvonne knows t'ings a chile at this age shouldn't even understand."

I wanted to tell him that I too had been at the top of my class, but what was the point? "Yvonne is just bright," I said. She was only nine, but Yvonne was already halfway through Mammy's books.

"But smart chil'ren must be reached, no?"

I had passed my limit of comfort with Mr. Aldous. "Come go, Yvonne!" I shouted over the schoolyard noise. Yvonne was jumping rope with her friends. The older girls were singing their own calypso version of "Amazing Grace" behind us.

"Wait." Mr. Aldous lifted his hand from the post. "Come, let's talk more."

I felt things standing close to him—that big tall grown man. Things Sister Edwina would've slapped out of me with her yellow, priest-blessed yardstick.

"Mr. Aldous." It was the first time I had ever called his name. "I can't talk to you about teaching. I'm just a gal who works the presses at the shirt factory."

He moved his face so I would be forced to look at him. "I can learn from anybody. Where you work shouldn't matter to me or to you."

His was the response I had dreamed of.

"Tell me, what is it that you do with Yvonne?" he said.

"We play," I said, swinging my arms from side to side with clasped fingers. "I t'ink small chil'ren learn best t'rough play."

"You play at home and that does keep her mind focused?"

"Well, everywhere," I said. "If you mix the lesson of the day into the play, chil'ren learn without feeling they're working."

Mr. Aldous leaned back into the gate, as if really thinking about what I'd said.

"You Karam girls—" he started.

Then, his face changed.

I searched behind me. There was a blue car with a dented bumper on the road in the distance. I turned back to Mr. Aldous. He was glaring at me like I was the Sucouya witch—so horrible, so disgusting; he couldn't bear to look any longer. He quickly turned, leaving me by the white wooden gate with that pitiful lizard zigzagging toward me.

Chapter 11

MARCIA GARCIA

The day after we played cards, Uncle Linton announced his intention to contest the election.

By late morning, I'd received his note. *It will get personal. Honor your word.*

I was forced to cancel my lunch with Chung. I dropped off a warm coconut-and-raisin bread loaf for him. As I set the basket on his table, I uttered a few words about going to America and coming back to explain everything to him later. At his door, I left behind his confused face and a welcoming bed he'd sprinkled with red bougainvilleas.

Harlow's building smelled of fresh paint and plaster. The wood rail alongside the wall had been lacquered such that I could almost see my reflection. The gold-plated sign at the top of the stairs read "Harlow & Co." Who the "Co." was I never knew. I thought I would ask Harlow about it, but when I reached for the knob, I was stopped by the sound of sobbing women.

I gently opened the door. Two women, one I hadn't seen before, hovered over a round desk with beveled edges. It was covered with white file folders and wads of tissue.

"Good afternoon," I said, softly.

The tallest one, visibly startled, wiped her tears and straightened her long, formfitting dress. "Yes?" Her mascara marked her coffee-colored skin like streaks of tar.

"I'm here to see Harlow," I said. "My name is Marcia Garcia. I was speaking with him about going to America."

The tall one couldn't hold back her tears any longer. She unwrapped a few squares of tissue from a roll. The shorter one, the familiar-looking one, spoke in her place. "He's not here." She glanced back at the tall one. "Mr. Harlow is missing."

"Missing? He was just in Five Rivers a few days ago."

"They just now findin' his car," she said. "They t'ink he might've fallen from a cliff while fixing his tire."

"In the nighttime?"

She sighed, as if I had hit on something she too had been thinking. "In the daytime," she said. "He was here the morning before last. He usually comes back by five o'clock. Sometime between when he left here and five o'clock Wednesday, this happened."

The tall one blew her nose and shoved the roll into the shorter one's belly.

I pulled up my purse to leave. "So sorry," I said.

"You was here before, right?" the shorter one said. She had probably heard about the meeting with Harlow in my kitchen. How rude I'd been. "I t'ink he had your papers with him, but they didn't find anyt'ing in his car." Her shoulders drooped. "I don't t'ink we can help you."

I walked the narrow flight of stairs, wondering how long it would take for Uncle Linton to learn about Harlow. Wondering how long it would take him to remind me of our agreement and tell me to find my own way to America.

On the sunny streets of Port-of-Spain, the air had a slight curry and mango scent. Digging out coins from my bag for my ride home, I passed lunch carts serving the day's last customers and a boy selling his last few *Guardian* newspapers. Above a front-page picture of Uncle Linton and Dr. Eric Williams, the headline read: "BEATRICE ALLEGES VOTER FRAUD."

"You need a ride?" Port-of-Spain was full of unofficial taxi drivers, hoping to catch a few dollars on their way here or there. I paid the voice little mind.

"Marcia," the voice said. "You need a ride?"

Leaning on the front of a black-and-white Morris Oxford was Farouk, his arms crossed, his lips pinched. Since the visit to him in jail, I had seen him only once: the day he told me he couldn't help with the rent any longer. He had looked bad then, but now was worse—a crumpled, barely shaved mess of a man, waiting for me outside of Harlow's office, looking like he was up to no good.

"I'm in here cookin' because Jackie takin' so long to come home," Patsy yelled as we walked through the front door.

I untucked my blouse from my skirt and took off my shoes. There was a small puddle there where the floor sagged. Our roof had a hole that Daddy had promised to fix when we moved into the house.

"Jackie was talkin' to Mr. Aldous," Yvonne said, tossing her heavy books onto the wobbly, crumb-covered table.

"You tryin' to get back into primary school?" Patsy yanked off her apron and threw it at me. She had been treating me like shit for so long, it hardly mattered anymore. But that day I threw the apron back at her face.

"Everybody in here has to work now." Patsy lit the stove and drizzled oil into a tall scratched pot. She threw in chopped raw onions and held a sharpened knife in the air with one hand. "No more waitin' for Daddy to deliver us from starvation."

"It was you who made him lose everyt'ing," I said.

She dismissed me with a wave of her left hand. "Chil'ren should be seen and not heard." She moved a bowl to the table and began peeling cassava in her palm. The odor of the simmering onions filled the kitchen.

"How you t'ink you was gointa keep your nasty business a secret when your fadda was a police, eh?" My lip curled, as if I could smell the nasty on her. "You're such a cliché. Read any dime-store novel and you'll see: girl desperate for love finds it in all the wrong places and winds up being a whore."

Patsy moved at full speed, wiping her fingers, wet with raw cassava, on the white cotton apron, reaching back far and wide. I saw the smack coming, but was too slow to stop it. My face burned. The cassava slices she'd been holding rocked back and forth on the floor, their stringy insides like live wire.

I reached for Patsy's hair, yanking her thick wavy ringlets, shiny with oil, swinging her in a half circle.

That's when I felt the pop on the right side of my skull.

Through half-closed eyes, I saw Mammy's shadowy outline. Her hunched shoulders, her lips firmly pursed. "How could you?" She smacked my head with her long, hard fingers three times, as if checking the sweetness of a watermelon. Her face was bloated. Her crimson-colored eyes were damp.

How could she be so upset about a fight with Patsy?

"How many times I have to tell you my business is my business?" She jabbed her one finger so close to my eye I thought there were two. "Your fadda doesn't own me!"

My scalp was sweaty and throbbing. Patsy's onions were well past a simmer. There was a hint of burn in the air. Wesley had his arms around Yvonne, smushed in the corner of the recliner. Mammy beat her fist on the shaky table, as if it was the only way she could hold back her tears. "I had just one chance to get away from him. And the chile I does rely on the most go and mess it up!"

"Whatya tell him? Whatya say?" she said. Through the open window I could hear the crack of a stick and ball.

"Nutting, Mammy," I said. "Maybe that you might be goin' to America."

It was the first Patsy, Wesley, and Yvonne had heard of Mammy and America.

"You gointa try that beat on me? You lying! You tell him about Harlow?"

I took a few steps toward the door. "Yes, Mammy," I said. "But I didn't tell his name."

Her snarled lips quivered beneath her flared nostrils. "Your fadda was an investigator. You give him any li'l bit of information and he gointa find the story. And then he gointa take it to that damn obeah woman." Mammy leaned forward in the chair, rubbing her thighs as if she could calm herself by the act. "Your fadda been messin' with that obeah lady and her damn daughter for years. You knew that."

"No, Mammy, I didn't know."

Mammy came toward me. "You too chupid, chile!" She struck me on my left arm. "You need to t'ink!" She struck me on the right arm. Then, she covered her mouth and fell back into the kitchen chair. "I t'ink Harlow's dead. They found his car on the side of some road." She closed her eyes. "They didn't even bodder to talk about me going to America because the whole business was run by Harlow . . . and he's in a ditch somewhere. Right along with our chance to get outta this bloody country."

"Mammy, how you know it was Daddy's fault?" I said.

She looked at Patsy, then over to Wesley and Yvonne, to make sure they were watching me destroy myself. "He was right outside the man's office, waitin' for me against his stinkin' taxi. 'Allyuh t'ink you goin' somewhere?' he said. I know that man. Anyt'ing I ever try to do, anyt'ing I ever try to have without him, he gointa try and kill it." She placed her palms facedown on the arms of the chair. "Now, pack up your t'ings and go. I don't want you here no more."

MARCIA GARCIA

I had been pretty sure Jacqueline had seen Chung leaving the house one afternoon. She never said a word about it to me. Instead, she finds Farouk and tells him?

Jacqueline needed to learn. She was a child living in *my* house. If I had managed Patsy in the same way, she might never have gone astray. I didn't need another child showing me her backside. Jacqueline could stay with Farouk for a couple of weeks. Let him see what it's like to take care of a child; the body and the mind, day and night. It wouldn't be easy for him. He could barely take care of himself.

Gawd, he had looked awful. He appeared to have no pride left. Yet, even as that scraggly man pointed his finger at me in the middle of Port-of-Spain and gave me an earful about how I had been duped by Chung, there I was pulling a piece of loose thread from his ragged shirt.

If for nothing else, having to leave Trinidad might have saved me from my own foolish self.

Chung Marlock pecked me on the cheek. "So, you ready to talk now about this sudden need to move to America?" He was wearing a jersey vest and tan pants, readying himself for work. His house had the odor of thick black coffee.

I set my bag down on his kitchen stool. "First to begin, why you didn't tell me you were the one who set up Farouk and that whole Derrick Rogers mess?"

He touched the top of his balding head, the way he always did when he was nervous. "Who told you that?"

"Eh-eh? You didn't t'ink Farouk would ever tell me?"

He put on his shirt and fastened the buttons. "Slow down. I didn't do a t'ing to Karam."

He pulled two teacups from a shelf, filling one with coffee, the other with hot water. A red-winged blackbird sat on his windowsill near a feeder Chung had hung when we first started seeing each other. A man who feeds birds has to be a gentle soul, I had thought then. The bird held its wings away from its body, searching the yard for danger before nibbling. Each time, before dipping his beak he repeated the pattern.

"Draw a chair and let's have somet'ing warm to drink," Chung said.

"What's with you fellas and the damn tea? A woman doesn't wanta have tea when she's mad. She does wanta rip your t'roat out."

"Have the coffee, then," he said, switching cups.

"You t'ink this is funny?"

He tucked his shirt into his unbuttoned pants. "No, Marcia, I don't," he said. "But Farouk is not tellin' you the trut'."

"Oh no?"

"Sit down. We can't talk if you standing over me and I need to sit."

"I won't."

He adjusted his shirt cuffs. "I'm gointa be late for a meeting."

"You wanted me to sit and now you're telling me to go?" I wished I could've stopped my eyes from pleading not to be rejected.

"I wanted you to listen."

He pulled my arm. I felt myself melting, though I knew Farouk had told the truth. The bird on the sill looked left, then right, then flew off. "The operation I was working on for years was meant to trap crooked policemen. Farouk didn't take the money for himself, it's true. But he would have. Just like all the udda fellas I had been work-ing on getting out of my force." He sat and stretched a pair of brown socks, checking for holes. "Almost a hundred officers I had evidence against. Every one of them was involved somehow with Rogers. Farouk was no saint. Despite what you may believe."

"I don't need you to tell me what to t'ink about Farouk."

"Eh-eh. He tellin' you what to t'ink about me, right?" He pulled up his socks and loosened his thick shoelaces.

"I does speak of what I see."

"Farouk was crooked. And he messed up years of my work by kill-ing Rogers. Because he lost his temper?" He cheupsed. "I had nutting to do with Rogers and your daughter. I'm really sorry you had to go t'rough that, but if Farouk was a decent man and a good policeman, he would've never behaved like that. I don't care what he tole you. You're too smart of a woman to believe nonsense."

I picked up my bag.

"You runnin' away again?" he said. "I guess this is it?" Chung stood and tried to kiss me on the cheek.

"I don't belong here," I said.

"Maybe not." He handed me the basket I had brought the day before. The loaf of bread, uncut, was still inside. "But let me just say: No matter where you go, your problems will be the same. Marcia, you're the kind of woman who's always looking to find a way out and you'll soon realize that there's no place left to run."

I walked toward the door wondering if Chung wasn't right about me. For the last twenty years, I had been a jumble of confusion. Want-ing and not wanting Farouk. Wanting and not wanting Chung. Wanting and not wanting Trinidad. Until that moment in Chung's kitchen, I didn't know what I wanted.

Then suddenly I did.

I wanted Harlow not to be dead. I wanted Uncle Linton's threat to be an opportunity. I wanted to be somewhere where my children could be more than a failed exam and the offspring of shame and where I could be more than poor and pained.

Because I *had* been running, because I hadn't given myself a moment, I lost things I didn't know I wanted until wanting them was all I had left.

Chapter 12

JACQUELINE KARAM

Mammy threw me out on a mild, radiant afternoon. An afternoon meant for reading a book alone on a hushed riverbank, meant for letting the juice of a sweet *julie mango* dribble down your chin, not meant for walking the streets with a paper bag full of your belongings.

If I had had any friends remaining maybe it wouldn't have felt so bad. Maybe I could've stayed with one of them. But the few friends I did have had stopped dropping by once Daddy got into trouble and after I had failed the Common Entrance. "Rum done, money done, friend done," Mammy had said. "Dry weather friends" she had called them.

I thought for a moment to go to Daddy's. Maybe at some point, before all the mess, Daddy would've let me stay at his place. But bringing any of Marcia Garcia's children to live with him after all that had happened would have not only jeopardized whatever deal his family had probably cut to get him out of jail, but certainly would've sent the Karam clan into an even deeper tailspin.

I was on my own.

I wandered the streets for some time wondering what I had done to deserve such a severe punishment. Yes, Mammy had a right to be angry. I had taken her business to Daddy. But to have me out, alone, with the night coming?

I headed westward onto a street lined with drooping calabash branches. An airplane moaned overhead. Someone was approaching from behind.

"Where you t'ink you going?" I pretended not to hear Patsy. "I'm not here to ask you back. Mammy tole me to follow you. She wanta make sure you gointa Daddy's."

"Daddy?" I said. "Daddy wouldn't let me stay with him if he had the last house standing in Trinidad."

Patsy had gotten Daddy thrown in jail, destroyed Mammy's business, and *she* could still sleep at home.

She cheupsed. "You crazy? He would do anyt'ing for you."

"He's not laying his life on the line for me." I flicked my plait over my shoulder and continued walking.

"I know you tole Mammy I was leavin' the house at nights," she called at my back. "Maybe after this, you'll keep your mout' shut." I walked faster. "I'll tell Mammy you headin' to Tunapuna" was the last thing I heard Patsy say before coming to a market.

I hadn't eaten since morning, and the night sky was quickly moving in. The sellers, who'd already made their money for the day, sat on three-legged wooden stools reading papers and listening to battery-operated radios. The sight of wood crates piled high with semirotten fruits, bruised and spoiled vegetables, and slabs of fish with milk-colored eyes turned my stomach.

I was heading back to the street when my eyes landed on a familiar face.

"Miss Claire?" She was in work clothes: sheer hosiery beneath a short, black, billowing skirt. She was massaging two not-so-bright lemons, trying to convince the seller to give her two for the price of one.

She greeted me with her usual smile. Her armful of silver-braided bangles jingled sweetly. "You look like a li'l loopy-dog, chile." She handed six spotted lemons and a dollar to the freckle-faced seller. He shoved them in a bag and gave her back coins.

"I'm fine." My lip quivered. Miss Claire grabbed my hand.

When we arrived at her house she filled a flower-etched drinking glass with fresh ginger-flavored lemonade and set it down before me. The small round kitchen table was covered in a purple checked tablecloth. Its violet tint complemented the mauve roses in her wallpaper. Each of Miss Claire's chair legs was firmly attached to each seat: no wobble. Her forks and spoons, sitting rightside up in a short enamel mug atop a wall shelf, had the same oakleaf pattern as the plates stacked next to them.

"Tell me what's happenin'," Miss Claire said.

A small window above the counter let in the odor of fresh, salty bread from the bakery a few hundred yards down the road. I drank the juice. "Mammy sent me out," I said. "My fadda won't take me in. I have no place to go. We hardly have friends anymore."

Miss Claire reached out and placed her cool, moist hands on mine. Her fingernails were painted pink, shaped like daggers. She had a natural grey shadow on her upper eyelids, making her look both festive and sleepy. "What you mean your mammy sent you out?"

"She tole me never to come back."

"I don't know what you did or didn't do." She tapped my hand. "But I does find it strange that she could send *you* out into the streets and keep home the udda one."

I reached for the empty glass and rubbed my fingers along its scratchy surface. Miss Claire poured me more. "Your mammy is a tough lady to figure out."

The sun was setting. The dogs began their chorus of dusk-time yowls. "I'm working," I said. "Usually I does give the money to Mammy, but I can give it to you."

Miss Claire pulled at a tuft of hair at the base of her neck, separating the strands with her fingernails, stretching the rigid curls longer. "You know I does like women?" She blinked rapidly and poured herself lemonade in a glass that matched mine. At home, we had never had more than one of the same type of glass.

"What you mean by that?" I said.

Miss Claire sipped the juice and wiped her mouth with a folded cloth napkin that had been sitting in the middle of the table. "Have you ever been with a boy?"

I was embarrassed by the question. "No."

"Do you know about being with boys?"

How could I not? Patsy was my sister. I nodded.

"Well, I like to be with women like some women like to be with men." She stuck her index finger through the hole of her long, gold hoop earring. "You understand?"

Bloody hell! Daddy was a murderer. My sister had prostituted herself. Now I was sitting in the house of a "funny woman"?

"I can see you have a question." Miss Claire flicked the hoops toward me.

"Whya telling me this?" I said, as politely as I could manage.

"If you gointa stay here, you have to know my rules," Miss Claire said. "I have a private life that's nobody's business except mine. What happens here doesn't leave here, you understand? My nephew—he's very important to me—he does come and stay sometimes. If that bodders you, you should t'ink twice about staying." Miss Claire refolded the napkin and set it down between us. "I don't have chil'ren and don't need any. I expect you'll carry yourself and treat my house with respect. You alright with all that?"

She took the brown paper bag full of my belongings from my lap and set it atop the table. "Your mudda—I never cared much for her because she's a mean woman—but she can sew. She lost plenty customers after that t'ing with your fadda. Chupid women who t'ought they couldn't associate with her anymore," she said. "But I'm not them and I've always known you to be a good girl, so don't feel like you causin' me no trouble atall."

• • •

Miss Claire didn't spend much time away from home my first few days there. I was her pet project. Her topic was Lessons in Life: Sit properly at a table—elbows down, left hand in lap, feet together. Keep the soles of your feet soft and moist—a vigorous soap scrub followed by petroleum jelly and heavy cotton socks at night. Clip your *tatu* hair—neat, and very short, along your natural lines.

Miss Claire, when she spoke, was as animated as any person I'd ever met. Her eyes grew wild and bright, her hands swept broadly. When she laughed, she laughed hard; even her feet flew into the air at times. I'd never been around someone more happy with herself.

"A woman must always smell like flowers or fruit. Never like musk," she told me. "A woman must always have clean ears, clean nose, manicured eyebrows, and clean fingernails.

"A clean and presentable home is important, but not as important as a clean and presentable body. A woman can spend all day cleaning the house and never once stop to make sure she's fresh and beautiful. Then her man does come home and treat her like shit, and she wonderin' why, because the house is clean. Well, she not clean!

"You betta believe if I had any inclination toward a man," she said, "I'd have the best one there was to have, and he'd be properly trained. Just like a good dog." She threw her head back and laughed.

By my fifth day at Miss Claire's, I was getting homesick. I had thought to see Yvonne after school one day, but when I got there, I was too embarrassed to run into Mr. Aldous. I stayed at the bottom of the hill and waited almost an hour, but Yvonne never came down.

That same evening Miss Claire told me her nephew, Michael, was coming. "You two will get along," she said. "Two chil'ren like allyuh need each udda."

When Michael walked through Miss Claire's door, all I could think was, *Ewwwww*. He was skinny with ears like broccoli, sticking far and away from his long and crooked head. He had a pinched nose, like a bird's beak, and a cleft under his chin like a volcanic crater. He was definitely not a looker, but obviously no one had bothered to tell the poor boy, because he had entirely too much strut.

Miss Claire doted on Michael like he was the Mighty Sparrow himself. "How is your mudda, darling?" She cut him a huge slice of rum cake and put it next to his dinner plate. "She doin' alright?"

"His fadda . . . died," Miss Claire whispered to me, as if he couldn't hear her speaking.

I said, "Sorry," but then, as if I had chosen the wrong word, the kitchen grew quiet. Michael picked at the tan-colored rice lodged between skin folds of his fowl wing while Miss Claire pushed his food into a mound in the middle of his plate. I ate the last bit of the *pelau* I had prepared, trying to figure out how I could politely remove myself from the room.

"So," Michael said, pointing the end of his spoon at me. "How you come to be here?"

"Remember the lady who does sew my good clothes?" Miss Claire said. "This is her gal."

"You sew?" Michael asked, as if he wouldn't have believed me if I had said yes.

"Whya makin' the girl jump for?" Miss Claire tapped him on his cheek. "She's my company."

Michael backed down, but anyone with any sense should've known it wasn't over between him and me, which was why I was shocked when Miss Claire announced she was leaving. "Watch him," she said, rising from her seat. "I gointa run next door and get some *kuchela* for this good cook-up you made."

She hadn't released the doorknob before Michael cocked up his gym boots on the chair across from him. "You does like them old, eh?" He looked like a beaver. Bucked teeth. Unruly hair. I pushed back my chair and snatched my plate from the table.

"Don't pretend you doesn't know what I mean," he said. "Any girl takin' up with Aunty, not here to sew no clothes."

"Miss Claire's just being nice."

"Nice, eh? I does see how *nice* she can be with the gals who does come here."

I emptied the leftover pigeon peas into the pail, scraping the plate until the only things remaining were scratched oak leaves.

"I just foolin'," he said. "I didn't know you was so sensitive."

I washed my plate in the tub of soapy water.

"You not talkin'? What I gointa tell Aunty when she come back? She's hopin' we can be friends."

"Maybe you shoulda t'ink of that before you talked up in your behind." I dried my plate and set it back on the shelf.

Miss Claire came back holding a glass jar with a peeling white label. "I tell ya to watch him," she said, picking up on her joke, as if she'd never left.

I couldn't meet her eyes. "I watchin' him, alright."

Miss Claire stared at the both of us.

Michael suddenly didn't look so smug. "It was nutting, Aunty," he said. "I was just makin' joke."

"What kinda joke you makin'?" she said.

"Nutting, Aunty. Truly." He crossed himself, losing the Holy Ghost in the process.

Miss Claire wouldn't let it go. "What kinda joke he tellin' here?"

It wasn't hard to see that Michael was all she had left of her family. "I not feelin' well," I said. "Michael was chattin' me up and I was getting queasy. I couldn't make talk like he wanted."

Michael blew air from his worried cheeks. Miss Claire winked at me. I left them in the kitchen laughing and carrying on.

The room Miss Claire had offered me was spacious, with a burgundy and gold throw rug and a wooden headboard with carved angels on it. I decided to finally try and finish *Bleak House*. An hour passed before the knock came.

"Aunty tole me to tell you good night for her. She's goin' out. I t'ink 'cause I'm here she does feel alright leaving you." Michael stood with his hands behind his back. He seemed less angry, almost docile. "I'm sorry about what I said earlier."

I rested Mammy's book on my thighs. I couldn't remember if anyone had ever said sorry to me.

For three hours that night, he stood against the doorframe and chatted. By the third night of his stay, he had made his way into the room and to a seat on the frilled edge of the rug. We talked and laughed and told stories. The way we were with each other reminded me of how things were between me and Wesley and Yvonne. I missed them. With me gone, Wesley would have no one to notice his cowboy baths and no one to critique the clothes he made before he showed them to Mammy. With me gone, Yvonne wouldn't have anyone to properly comb her hair, to search for ticks, and to make sure her head was presentable for the next school day.

On the eleventh day of my stay with Miss Claire, the shirt factory was behind schedule on 150 tab-collar shirts and I wasn't able to leave on time. The machine jammed at noon, then again an hour and twenty minutes later, and then again, forty-three minutes after that. The factory owner never let the girls who ran the machines repair them, so we had to wait for some fella wearing too-small suspenders to hobble in from his cigarette break.

I arrived at Yvonne's school, breathless. Mr. Aldous was in his usual spot, seeing out the last of the children, chatting with Miss Penny. I had changed into my best dress—a sea-green, A-line number with ruffled sleeves—in case I ran into him.

"Were you comin' for Yvonne?" Mr. Aldous said.

I scrambled to get my story straight. I didn't want Mammy to know I had been there. "I guess my mudda already sent somebody for her," I said.

Mr. Aldous pushed his palm to his forehead. "Actually." He glanced over to Miss Penny. "Yvonne hasn't been here in some time."

I didn't know whether to be embarrassed first or shocked. Where was Yvonne? How come Mammy hadn't made Wesley walk her to school? Mr. Aldous and Miss Penny stood waiting.

"Oh," I said.

I kicked a shiny dove-grey pebble with my sandal. Red dust landed on my toes.

"When Yvonne was here last, I asked her what happened to you." Miss Penny inched closer.

Mr. Aldous peered down at me, with his hands folded. "Maybe you should t'ink about getting an honest profession, then your mammy won't be so vexed," he said.

Miss Penny tugged at the bottom of her smocked brown mini-skirt.

"Is that why you left me standing by the gate?" I said.

The haughtiness in his face said everything.

"Mr. Aldous." I looked up into his big, judgmental face. "I'm not the Karam girl you t'ink I am. You have me confused with my sista, Patricia, who was running with the wrong crowd. That's not somet'ing any of us are proud of, but I'm sure you can understand what it feels like to make a fool of yourself."

In my silly little head, Mr. Aldous was kind and humble, the sort of fella who'd make me feel better *despite* having Patsy for a sister. My Mr. Aldous—the one in my head—was nothing like the man I had left stuttering next to his nosy, simpleminded girlfriend.

That night while Miss Claire was out, Michael made his way home around seven o'clock. From the bedroom, I heard his shoes smacking Miss Claire's floorboards. He waited for some time before coming in to see me.

And when he did, it was strange.

He walked to where I was reading on the floor, and knelt next to me. His breath was weighty, urgent, sour.

"I was wondering—" I started to say.

He kissed me hard on the mouth with dry, cracked lips.

I nudged him away. The two top buttons of his shirt were unfastened. He had a fresh, low haircut, making his not-so-handsome facial features more prominent. If I'd been in a better mood, I might've laughed and turned the awkward moment into a joke. Instead, I wiped my mouth and watched him glower at me.

"Will you give it to me?" He said it so that it felt more like a command than a question.

I covered my stinging lips with my hand and sat with legs crossed. Had he discovered that I loved Mr. Aldous and suddenly flown into a maddening, jealous frenzy? Had he followed me to Five Rivers and seen the tears on my face as I walked downhill from Yvonne's school?

Until that evening, every moment between Michael and me had been simple and innocent. Had I missed something? Or was this how it was supposed to be when a boy and a girl decided to do it? One person asking the other and the other giving in, because saying yes was easier and less embarrassing than saying no?

As I sat before him, I wondered if maybe I owed "it" to Michael. He'd been with me when no one else in the world wanted me around. Maybe courtship, love, marriage, and all the things Sister Edwina used to say were important, weren't really? Maybe doing "it" wasn't such a big to-do? Maybe somebody wanting me was a compliment, even a blessing?

I made up my mind.

The room was dim. The bed, with its starched white sheets and stiff pillow, was made. I pushed down my underpants to just below my behind. My nakedness, my bare skin pressing the lumps in the mattress, made me question my decision. Michael, eager and smelling like three-day-old boy sweat, slid on top of me, as if trying to quash my doubts. I was a board, flat on my back, my legs lightly pinched, resisting Michael's prying palms. There was a poke or two here and a poke or two there. I started to feel like a poor dumb fowl moments before its neck is wrung—eyes popping, heat on its skin rising. Michael clumsily readjusted himself, hoping, I think, to take a better approach. His sharp elbows dug into my ribs. His bony knees pressed into my thighs. He frantically searched for where to put the bloody thing.

What boy couldn't figure that out?

He was giving me too much time to think. Too much time to feel the clamminess of his flesh against mine. Time enough to hear Sister Edwina's nunly man-voice and remember the picture of Jesus, tucked in a gold frame above Mammy's door—robed, dirty blond hair, outstretched arms. How determined I once had been to not let life happen to me. How sure I used to be that I wouldn't end up like Mammy.

"Stop!"

Michael hadn't actually started. He rolled off me and dug his knuckles into my shoulder.

"What's wrong with you?" I said.

"You askin' me what's wrong with *me*?"

"You actin' funny."

"You stoppin' me in the middle of this business here and *I'm* actin' funny?"

"What business?" I said. "You wandering down there like a lost soldier in the desert."

He threw his legs onto the floor. "You're a chupid girl."

"You're stupid too!"

He walked toward the door, buckling his mud-stained pants. His skinny brown ankle peeked out from under a folded pant leg. "The sad t'ing about you is that you're too chupid to know how chupid you really is."

I pushed the door closed, then scrubbed my lips and skin with a rag I kept in a wide-mouthed glass by the window. "Your li'l life is a disaster," I whispered.

At the front of the house, there was a loud crash and the rustling of paper. I had heard Michael leave. Was it Miss Claire? The click-cluck of high heels, shuffling feet, and then a voice. More than one. Two women.

Miss Claire had arrived home, and at her backside was her long-time seamstress.

The bus ride back home with Mammy was long.

The woman seated behind us clutched a large canvas bag and carried on a soft-spoken discussion with the older man seated across from me. The driver, while maneuvering the tight and bumpy roads, chatted with a young boy, not much older than Wesley. And Mammy, her back straight, her chest poked out, surveyed the passing trees, as if the girl sitting next to her was a leper.

On the short walk from the junction, Mammy marched nearly a yard ahead of me. We passed neighbors and other familiar faces. No one seemed to have realized I had been gone.

But for me, after that short time away, things in Five Rivers felt different, smelled different, appeared different. The leaves' many shades of green blended to make lush canopies. The blues and yellows and reds on the faces of the cozy homes signified pride rather than bad taste. The pebbles from waterless riverbeds seemed quaint and rustic. Five Rivers felt more like home than ever.

"I bringin' you back because you gointa mind Yvonne while I gone," Mammy said, striding on ahead. Her raspy voice hit me as a stranger's would. "What'd you go and tell that woman about me?"

"Nutting. I swear." I crossed myself with a flailing Holy Ghost. "Where you going?"

She cheupsed, long and hard. "They found Harlow. He took some trip to Venezuela and left his fancy car with a friend. The friend ditched the t'ing broken on the side of the road," she said. "I gointa America, next week Wednesday." I trotted to catch up with her. "You betta not tell your fadda or you gointa live on the streets for good. Next time I'm not comin' to fetch you."

• • •

The house was a complete disgrace. The floor hadn't been swept. Mammy's unfinished sewing projects had been thrown across chairs. The linens hadn't been changed. The kitchen was filled with dirty dishes. The yard was littered with Wesley's cigarette butts, and Yvonne was alone, sick, in Mammy's warm, sticky room.

"Yvonne?" She was sleeping under a thin, pink sheet. "Yvonne?" I gently rolled her shoulder. Sweat had soaked through her shirt. Her forehead was hot and damp.

In the kitchen, Mammy stood holding a jumper dress, looking around like it was the first time she'd actually seen the filth.

"Mammy, how long Yvonne been sick?"

She sighed, as though the very thought of Yvonne was too much. "A few days. Almost a week. She says it's her stomach." Mammy's face seemed older, as if she'd aged five years in the two weeks I'd been gone. "Gonjo said it would pass. He gave me some cod-liver oil, fever grass, and somet'ing else he mix up. I gave it to her. She went to the toilet and then fell straight to sleep."

It was a common belief that a person's home had to be organized, straightened up, thoroughly cleaned before they went on a long journey. If they left their place in disarray, old folks said they'd find a mess when they returned. So there was plenty to do before Mammy left for America. There were papers to gather and file, and laundry to wash and fold. A suitcase along with proper, closed-toe shoes had to be purchased and packed. From what I could tell, Mammy hadn't told anyone but us she would be leaving. Her few remaining clients spoke of future projects and fabric they'd ordered, as if nothing monumental was about to take place, which meant that there were clothing orders to complete and deliver, too. From the outside, life in our home continued just the same as it always had, until the day the woman fell by the schoolyard gate.

"Jackie!" Wesley screamed.

It was a lava-hot kind of day, the ground so hard and fiery I could've fried an egg on it. I was in the backyard, cleaning out the coop. I was beyond irritated.

"Jackie." Wesley was out of breath. "That woman Daddy does be messin' with—" He licked his parched lips. "She laying right up de road. And she dead."

I had been determined to ignore Wesley, but the word *dead* got my attention. I pulled my hand from the dark coop. "You been drinkin', boy?"

"I tellin' the trut'."

"The black black one with the bluish eyes?"

He threw his one hand on his hip and bent over at the waist.

I hustled around the dirty water bucket and into the long stretch of road. A tidal wave of women were rushing along the street, as if the news of something no one wanted to miss had been announced on a loudspeaker.

"That's her in the road?" I asked Wesley, who had come up behind me. "What was she doing up here?"

Wesley rubbed his sweaty hands on the front of his red shirt. "She and Mammy were quarreling. Somet'ing about Daddy."

Wesley and I fought our way into the circle. The talk between the neighbors was just beginning. "Isn't that Marcia's man's *coco lambie*?" somebody whispered.

I walked to the other side of the circle and peeked through the small gaps. Daddy's girlfriend was definitely dead. Her blue eyes and her large mouth were flung open like a giant goby fish's. She wore the same grey dungarees she had worn the day I saw her with Daddy at the snackette. Cars, blocked by the commotion, were beginning to turn around. Passengers hopped out to gawk at the spectacle, forming a larger gathering around the body.

Then suddenly, as if someone had turned down the dial, the talk grew quiet and the crowd parted.

I thought maybe the police had arrived and my mind began to swirl. How would my family get out of yet another scandal?

Wesley and I had been squeezed out. We walked to the other side of the circle. When we finally made it around the growing group of women, we realized they'd been making room, not for the police, but for Mammy.

I hustled next to her, with Wesley behind me.

Mammy was wearing a patch-quilt, multicolored housecoat that flared from her long arms like a disciple's robe. Her hair fell down below her broad shoulders and the skin on her full face appeared so smooth it reminded me of porcelain figurines of the baby Jesus. Her eyes were a golden brown and the light struck them in exactly the right way, so that they moved like calypso-dancing waters. Her feet were bare on the hot dirt road, her palms upturned toward the sky.

"Wesley," she said, touching him lightly on the head, "go and find your fadda. Make sure he comes back with you."

Wesley took off running. Mammy, with me by her side, moved slowly into the circle of women, women who had always been cautious in their admiration of her.

Mammy knelt beside the dead body. She placed her soft, long-fingered hand over the woman's face and closed the big, powdery-blue eyelids with a tender stroke. She bent down even further, her robe cascading across the woman's stilled chest, and whispered something into the dead woman's ear. I couldn't hear the words—no one could—but she spoke to that corpse as if she knew the woman was listening.

Then, grabbing my arm, she hoisted herself up, and turned to the women surrounding us. There was an expression in her eyes. An expression I've only seen shared among women—an expression of longing for understanding and compassion.

The women's eyes softened, as if no longer taken in by the spectacle of the cadaver, but rather by my mother's wordless plea. Mammy stretched out her arms, lightly nudging them back, and began to sing the Lord's Prayer.

Mammy was not what anyone would call religious. She rarely went to church. She never prayed before meals, only *after* and only *if* the food was really good. She wanted us to have God in our hearts, she would say. She and Daddy had sent us to Catholic school (until the money ran out), and she didn't mind when I went to Mass (if I finished my chores) or that I liked to carry my rosary tucked into my shirt. But religion didn't seem necessary to Mammy. At least not until that day.

Whatever had gone on between the two women, Mammy's behavior, as she stood over that body, left the impression that she was both sorrowful and innocent. By the time the policeman, who recognized Mammy, arrived, not one neighbor dared to mention that the woman and Mammy had been in a heated argument or that Mammy had cursed her so loudly and so forcefully from up the road, that it seemed the woman had dropped dead upon the words being uttered.

Daddy and Wesley arrived several hours after the body had been carried away. By Daddy's reddened, liquored-up face and his swollen eyes, it was clear he knew his girlfriend was dead.

"I'm leaving for America next week," Mammy said, as she lathered her hands in a bowl next to the stove.

"What's that you saying?" Daddy hadn't even had a moment to settle himself past the doorway.

"I'm leaving for America next week."

Daddy's face was covered with salt-and-peppery-colored hair. The dark circles under his eyes appeared permanently purple-black. "Whatya mean you leavin'?" Mammy pointed over to me and Wesley to let us know that we should be taking a quick peek at Yvonne, who was napping in the bedroom. We didn't move.

"Who gointa take care of your chil'ren, woman?"

"How you mean?" Mammy wiped her hands on a yellow dishcloth and turned toward him. "You will."

Mammy must've been joking, Daddy's smile seemed to say. He watched her pull out a tin of flour and throw some into a mixing bowl. "Who?"

With the open tin against her chest, Mammy stopped. "You, Farouk Karam, will take care of your own chil'ren." Hers wasn't the tone of a woman who was angry or tired or even resentful. It was the tone of a woman who had made up her mind.

Daddy sat at the table and held his head.

"You must come here and make sure Yvonne is okay," Mammy said. She threw water into the flour. "You must come here and remind Jacqueline of what she needs to do. You must come here and give them money if my money doesn't reach them on time. You must come here and make sure Patsy is treating herself and her family properly." She pressed her fingers into the moist dough. "Don't wait until the donkey's back breaks to take off the load. I have to take care of them in anudda way now."

Daddy's right leg shook uncontrollably beneath the table.

The day before Mammy was to leave for America, Yvonne cried most of the day, though she never let Mammy see. Patsy spent much of that morning in the bedroom with the radio blaring. She refused to do anything unless asked and whenever Mammy wasn't looking, she stared at Mammy's face, as if it would be the last she saw it. Wesley helped Mammy fold and pack, cracking jokes, pretending he was coughing when he was really crying, asking Mammy questions he already knew the answers to, as if getting her to talk would make her stay longer.

Mammy came to me in the yard where I was folding clothes from the line. "I haven't had a chance to talk to you." She gently pulled me close to her. "You know all I'm about to say, but I must tell it to you again," she said. "It's your responsibility to take care of Yvonne."

I was annoyed she felt she had to tell me.

"I know you know but listen anyway." Her nose flared a little. "You must keep t'ings going. I not sure your fadda can be here like allyuh need. Aunty Baba's getting too old to worry." She pulled a clothespin off a hanging sheet and stuck it into her dress pocket. "You listening?" She took two corners of the sheet and offered me the other end. "If you run into big big trouble, I mean, really big trouble, go to the Catholic Church in Toco. Ask them to tell you where a man they call Souse does live," she said. "When you find him, tell him your mudda's name and he'll help you. With anyt'ing." I wasn't sure I would be able to remember anything Mammy was saying. I was distracted by how different she seemed. "Promise me you'll never go and see him by yourself, you hear? And never leave your brudda or your sistas with him alone," she continued. "Take Wesley, take Patsy, take somebody, and go and get what you need, and then leave there."

She folded the sheet and pushed back a few strands of my hair, which had blown around my eye. It was a rare moment of affection and it scared me. And not just a little. Was it possible that a life without Mammy could be even more frightening than a life with her?

Chapter 13

FAROUK KARAM

The day Nicole was found dead was the day I made up my mind to let Marcia go. Better people had left Trinidad and had come right back home. America would be too much for her. Marcia didn't have it in her to stay long. She was a Trinidadian, through and through, like me.

Instead of fighting it, I would offer her a ride to the airport.

And a ride back, when she needed it.

It was still dark and a bit chilly outside. The children stood next to my motorcar, and Marcia hurriedly hugged and kissed each one. Of course, there were no tears. There were never tears between Marcia and those children. Theirs was a completely practical relationship: She provided for them because she was their mother, and they, in turn, showed a sensible appreciation.

As I drove Marcia away from Five Rivers toward Piarco International Airport, I had an urge to talk to her. Really talk to her. But I couldn't.

I couldn't allow myself to believe that a ride to the airport was all that was left between us.

Instead, she and I spoke of the things Trinidadians always chat about—music, politics, cricket, football.

"You remember that first football tour to England. What year was that?" she said. Her hands were between the pleats of her skirt. She had sewn pearl-colored buttons down the middle of her white shirt and with it, she wore a yellow scarf in a loose knot on the left side of her neck.

"You mad? Of course, I does remember. That was the same year Mighty Spoiler was king of the Monarch with 'Bedbug,'" I said. "Drove the crowd wild, singing about how he wanta come back in his next life to bite up all the ladies."

We laughed. "Only a Trinidadian does remember a year by a song," she said.

It was odd driving alongside her. We were strangers, yet we were not. We were lovers, yet we were not.

At the airport I parked the motorcar and escorted her inside. It was nice walking next to her again. I dragged her grip by its leather pull strap, managing to tip it over only six times or so. She giggled each time, making me want to do it more.

How sweet that sound could be.

"Well, goodbye, Marcia." I gave her a pat on the back.

"T'ank you very much." She moved toward the tarmac. "Keep well and keep your eye on them chil'ren, alright?"

It was the first time she had mentioned the children since leaving the house. I was surprised to see her eyes bubble up with water. I felt I had to say something. I said, "The land of the hummingbird will always be here."

MARCIA GARCIA

Oh Gaaawwwwddddd! The plane was just a metal and plastic box!

I was so dizzy. Even when I closed my eyes, the blackness under my lids spun. I needed to sleep, but I was trapped between two strange men, miles above land. How could anyone sleep under those conditions?

Mr. Harlow had told me my first plane ride would seem strange, but I hadn't expected to feel frightened. He had given me the phone number for the shop where I would be working, in case the Kole man didn't arrive at the airport on time. He had told me not to worry too much about the details of the work, because they would tell me what they needed when I got there. He had said to pack light—"much of what you'll need there, you won't have, but you'll get." I carried practical clothes—a housedress, a few skirts and tops, one pair of closed-toe shoes, a pair of pants, slippers, and a nightgown. I had given the children the post office box number Harlow had written on a slip of paper just before he handed me five U.S. dollars to "hold me over 'til my first pay." He had asked if I had any questions, but I didn't know what to say. America was a place so often spoken about in Trinidad that sometimes you felt you knew everything there was to know and if you didn't, you would never ask. Asking too many questions about America was the same as admitting you were uncultured, ignorant.

We landed with a soft thud. I stood when others stood and held my few belongings close to my chest, searching for clues about what to do next. Harlow hadn't given instructions on how to get out of the plane. I tightened the knot in my yellow scarf and followed closely behind one of the men who had been seated next to me. I waited to feel the cold American air, but when I got off the plane, I ended up in a narrow indoor passageway leading to a wide space full of people bustling about and waiting in long lines.

The man I had been following quickly broke for a door that read MEN. I waited.

America was big. Even in the airport. The men and the women were wider than most people back home, like they'd had more space to grow. They were varied, too, but not in the same way as Trinidadians. In Trinidad, people were many different races and of mixed races, but most people in Trinidad looked Trinidadian. As if bloodlines had crossed and recrossed so much on the island that everyone was related, if not to you, then to someone you knew.

In the airport in America, people were of different races and may have been of mixed races, too, but their tribal lines seemed more distinct. It was as if they had come to one place from every corner of the earth, but their paths might never cross.

The Americans moved, shoved, twisted around me, but one woman with whitish-yellow, coarse-textured hair, standing alone, stared. Her firm eyes made me uncomfortable. I looked away. When I did, I realized that the man I had been waiting for had left the washroom.

"Oh!" I shouted to no one in particular. I hoisted my bag onto my shoulder and rushed to catch him.

"Marsha?" someone said from behind.

The yellow-haired woman was jogging lightly behind me, reaching for my arm.

I had to keep moving. My eyes were fixed on the blue pants of the man. He was leaving me behind in the human maze.

"Marsha Garsha?"

I slowed. "Garcia?"

"Oh goodness," she said, tapping her forehead "Gar-see-a."

"Mah-see-a Gah-see-a?" I said.

"Mar-see-a Gar-see-a?"

"Yes," I said.

She threw her tall body into my arms. She smelled like a too-ripe banana and was very thin.

"I'm Suzanne," she said, slowly and loudly. She took my hand into hers and pumped it up and down. "Do you know who I am? Did Harlow tell you about me?"

He hadn't given me her name. I only knew the name Robert Kole.

"Do you understand what I'm saying? How is your English?" she said. "My Spanish is horrible. Well, actually, it's nonexistent. I don't speak a word of it. My sister lives out in Los Angeles and there's a whole bunch of native Spanish speakers there and half the time she's completely lost when she's around them, because she doesn't understand a word they're saying," she went on. "Mr. Harlow told me your name, but I never really thought about you being Spanish, being from the West Indias and all. But that's okay. Well, here I am, talking and talking and you probably don't understand a darn word I'm saying. I guess this is how it's just going to have to be. We're stuck together now," she said, hugging my shoulders.

I had read plenty of books before I had made it to sixteen. I could write in the Queen's English as well as anyone. I had even gone to an American movie once. But nothing had prepared me for the foreignness of her speech.

I followed her along the corridors of the airport. She walked briskly, cutting off people who were too slow for her liking. She wove in and out, and when we came to the line where everyone else seemed to be waiting to show their passports and papers, she hustled me through with barely a nod from a man in a blue uniform.

"Put your passport away, hon." She pushed my hands down.

I placed my Trinidad and Tobago passport back into my shoulder bag, not wanting to do anything wrong. When we arrived at the baggage area, which in America went round and round until you could snatch off your luggage, there was a giant, big-bellied man, holding my grip with a tag that read "MARCIA GARCIA. PORT-OF-SPAIN."

The ride with Suzanne and Robert was thick with quiet. We drove from the end of a partly sunny day to the beginning of a speckled-sky night, along a broad landscape of trees and open fields. America passed me by through a dog-licked window. Everything seemed larger than could be possible. The cars were big, and huge signs for advertisements, directions, and even public rest stops hung alongside the roads.

In Trinidad, when we said "American" we meant white. Every person in every car we passed was as "American" as I had ever seen. They were young, old, talking, singing, and sometimes just driving the expressways alone, men and even some women.

At some point along the way, I managed to fall asleep. It seemed to be a short nap, but when the car stopped I awoke to an empty-looking place.

I opened the car door and stepped out onto a gravelly road. The crunch of the pebbles sounded like Five Rivers, but there was a frigidness to the air I had never felt before. The coat Suzanne had brought for me had seemed sturdy enough inside the airport and in the car, but outdoors, the thin polyester was like a cheap cotton sheet. I shivered like a river's skim in a storm and searched for a light, a house, or anything that felt like home.

I wrote three letters to the address Mammy had given us. We heard nothing back.

Carnival passed without our notice. We had had no music, no ginger beer, no sorrel, no warm bake with butter, no *mas*, not even a little ash on the forehead.

I had wanted to make our home feel celebratory, but I didn't have enough money for radio batteries, my ginger beer had been too bitter, my sorrel too thick, and my roast bake had fallen before it began to roast.

We hadn't seen Daddy in two months. He had come by once a week for the first month but on his last visit, he and Patsy had exchanged some words about her not bringing home all the salary from the bakery and about him not leaving us with enough money.

"I'll see allyuh," he had said, pressing a few dollars into my palm.

After he was gone, I hid the money in a shoe behind the bed.

Maybe three minutes later, Patsy came out of the bedroom in a lightweight, pale-blue dress Mammy had made for her and which Patsy had shortened.

"Whya takin' our money?" I said.

She seemed surprised that I knew and even more surprised that I had spoken up. "It's *our* money. I can have it too," she said.

"It's for food. Not to run the streets with."

She reclipped her hair into a looser bun. "You don't know I'm not gointa the market."

"I'm in charge."

Her eyes grew wide and angry. It was a look I had seen cross her face many times; usually right before she pounced on me. "You in charge of this? Look at this pigsty," she said. "It's lookin' like allyuh takin' a shit inside here half the time."

"At least I does be trying," I said.

Patsy reached into her brassiere and threw the money to the floor.

The day before Easter, Yvonne, who had seemed to be recovering, seemed again unwell. She had another night sweat, more pain in her stomach, and didn't eat breakfast. I had taken additional hours at the shirt factory and had to leave her home with Wesley. After work, I stopped at the market to pick up some *eddoes* and yams for Easter Sunday, along with *châtaignes* to boil and peel for an Easter Eve snack. I was squeezing fresh guavas, wondering if I should tackle a cool lime-and-guava punch.

"Miss Karam?"

Mr. Aldous.

His big brown eyes nearly knocked me over. His moustache was gone, making him seem years younger, and instead of slacks and dress shoes, he wore short-pants that stretched to his knees, sandals, and a black cap, pulled down onto his forehead. He had nice, clean toes.

"Hello, Mr. Aldous," I said, quite formally.

"Is everyt'ing alright with allyuh?" he said. "I've been meaning to send a letter to your mammy. I haven't seen Yvonne in some time."

"She's been a li'l sick." I turned back to the guavas. I wanted him to know I had important things to do in my life.

"For mont's?" I hadn't realized until then that it *had* been months. "Allyuh take her to the doctor?"

Yvonne hadn't been to see anyone since Mammy took her to Gonjo, the bush doctor.

Mr. Aldous took the one guava in my hand and placed it back on the pile. He pressed his palm against his head. "Where's your mammy?" I felt like a child when he called my mother "mammy."

"She left for America a few mont's back," I said, even though I wasn't supposed to tell anybody.

He picked up, from the top of the pile, the same guava he had taken from me. He squeezed it a tad and rolled it between his fingers before handing it back. "Jacqueline, if you need somet'ing, anyt'ing, come by the school and let me know, alright? Don't t'ink you bodder-ing me, please."

For some reason, I wanted to cry. "T'ank you," I said.

He pulled up my chin a smidge with his fingers. "You still work-ing at the shirt factory?"

"Yes."

"Would you mind if I come by there sometime to check up on you?"

"No," I said. "I wouldn't."

Chapter 14

MARCIA GARCIA

An "unfinished guesthouse" they called it. It felt more like a barn. Drafty with the musky smell of long-dead animals, it had tiny, hazy, rectangular windows starting about fifteen feet above the doors. There was a mattress on the floorboards, its moldy condition hidden by fresh white sheets and a firm pillow. In the far-right corner, behind a filmy pink plastic curtain, were a rusty toilet with a broken flush string and a mildewy tiled shower. A glass-topped table, alongside the mattress, held an electric sewing machine; its cord, squished under one of two heavy wooden doors, connected to a longer cord that trailed outside and into the main house.

"Sorry. You'll have to work and sleep in here for a while. We're having the shop and your room inside our house repaired. The workers should be done soon. They'll tell you one month and before you know it, it's three months." She laughed.

I was actually all right with the sleeping arrangements. I preferred not being with Suzanne and Robert until I got to know them better. I found them a strange pair. Not strange like I had imagined Americans to be, but strange like people who didn't know how to behave around other people.

My first two days there, I worked on a few small projects: I hand-sewed a button on a shirt, made a long bed-skirt, using the electric sewing machine for the first time, and I tapered the ankles on a pair of pants, which I returned to Suzanne within an hour at the door of her house.

Her home was larger and sturdier than any house I had ever lived in. It was painted white, two stories tall, with a front porch needing four posts, not two. There were crisp black shutters on each window, two redbrick chimneys poking out from both the right and left sides of the roof, a small door next to the garage leading to the kitchen, and stairs, hidden underneath a trapdoor that seemed to unwind into a cellar.

I wasn't invited inside, but I peeked in when Suzanne cracked the door with her one knee poking out. Furniture with pink rectangular prints filled every corner.

"It's very dusty in here," she said. "I'm sure you wouldn't want to come in."

But everything, at least through the windows, appeared spotless. And the dog and the cat seemed to be breathing fine. I hadn't seen anyone but Suzanne and her husband at the house. No plumber, no electrician, no worker going in or coming out, but I kept quiet, did what I was asked, and otherwise mostly managed for myself.

Those first few weeks, I wrote a letter to the children every afternoon and after dinner I would walk the land. It was quiet out there, except for the occasional train in the distance. The foot of a band of mountains lay across the back of the barn. The hills, the Blue Ridge, reminded me of the Northern Range back home; the way they snuggled into the clouds and, at the same time, seemed to impose their will upon a less-than-threatening skyline. I stuck to the front of the house on those evenings, mostly because it was manure-free (the horses grazed only in the back). A gravel driveway was bordered on each side by a yellow tractor, then it emptied out onto a dark, treelined dirt road. Sometimes I walked a few hundred yards down that road, but I never saw another house, I never ran into another human being.

One late morning, after I'd had a night filled with walking and too little sleep, Suzanne brought in a dress pattern in a white envelope. An unsightly ankle-length dress in plaid was pictured on the cover. I had never sewn from a pattern, and if she had given me a chance, I was sure I could've made the thing by hand in three hours and it would've looked a whole lot smarter than the one the red-haired girl with pigtails wore in the picture. But "give the Americans what they want," Mr. Harlow had told me. And that's what I intended to do.

Suzanne stood next to the sewing machine as I studied the gathered cuffs along the red-haired girl's wrists. "What does your hair look like inside that little bun?" I could feel Suzanne's hot eyes on the top of my head, fighting the urge to touch it.

"Hair?" I said, never once looking up from the package, which was labeled "For Personal Use Only."

"I'm going to the salon today," she said. "Would you like to ride along with me?"

I never answered. I had realized from my first days there that pretending not to speak English had kept me from having to answer questions I didn't want to answer. Questions like how could you leave your children? Who's taking care of them? Don't you miss them? Are you married?

Yet, silence didn't always work in my favor; by three o'clock that afternoon, I was riding along with Suzanne in her big, rust-colored Chevrolet.

"I'm sorry we have to have you in there," she said again. "I can give you extra blankets if you need. The truth really is that Robert won't let anyone back into our house after the last gal we had from one of those countries down there in the tropics brought us some horrible virus. The three of us almost died. He said he was drawing the line with foreigners living in the house, and we didn't get to complete the barn the way we wanted. I hope you don't mind too much. In about a year, we'll have it all done.

"Oh, the girls at the salon are gonna love meeting you," she continued, taking a sharp curve with more authority than I had ever suspected she had. "They're all good people like me and Robert. I've never brought one of you with me before, but they're always asking me questions about what it's like to have you people working for us."

I assumed by "you people" she meant seamstresses. A car pulled up next to us. I heard through the window the same sweet melody that played from Suzanne's rasping radio. I began to hum.

"Do you know this song?" She pointed to the front dash of the car. "How do you know this song?"

I said, "Patsy Cline?"

"Yes!" she said. "How do you know Patsy Cline?"

We have radios in Trinidad, lady. I wanted to tell her that our radios played music from all over the world, not only American country-and-western songs, like the American radios seemed to. But by then, I knew Suzanne liked me better without words. To her, I was a project, not a person. By not talking, I had probably encouraged her attitude toward me, but it didn't seem important enough, just then, to change course.

Suzanne pulled onto a blacktop driveway, in front of a one-story grey house. To the left was a blue sign with a painted white-tailed rabbit and the words "Roberta's Hare" over its crooked, floppy ears.

"I just love this place," Suzanne said, excitedly. She bounced herself into the salon, leaving me trailing a few yards behind.

By the time I walked inside, many of the ladies were watching me, curious grins covering their shock. All of them, except for the Roberta woman, had yellow hair, bright reddish-hued lipstick, and brown sun-spotted skin. Roberta, who wore a jet-black beehive, tight red pants, and had a rabbit tattooed above her left breast, seemed happiest to see me.

"Oh, well hello!" she said, more slowly and more loudly than Suzanne had ever spoken. "It's nice to meet ya, hon."

Roberta turned to Suzanne, who smiled back at her like a proud mother.

"Yes," I said.

Roberta pulled me to a small sink. She sat me down, patted my shoulder to reassure me, then began unknotting my hair. "Good Lord!" she screamed. "Suzanne, do you know how much hair this one has under here? Good Lord!"

Suzanne rushed over. She ran her greedy fingers across my scalp. "It's so soft. I had no idea."

A woman wearing a wet towel around her head slammed it down on the counter. She shook her damp hair at Roberta and walked out.

"It's not 1950!" Roberta huffed and nudged my head into a hard white bowl.

I sat straight up.

"What is it, hon?" Roberta patted my shoulder again. "Suzanne thought it'd be nice to give you a treat. Relax. Relax."

She told me to close my eyes.

The water, warm and forceful, tickled my scalp. It felt wonderful. She pushed the nozzle against my roots, over and over until the squishy soapsuds were rinsed. She dried my hair with a short towel, then soaked my ends in a thick peach-scented lotion. "It's so curly now!"

Roberta rinsed out the dense cream and gently pulled me upright. I was more relaxed than I probably should have been.

"A little trim, Suzanne?"

Suzanne, who had tinfoil sticking out from her scalp, was across the salon, chatting with two other women. "Sure!" she said.

A few seconds later, Roberta began to clip my wet hair. I should've known better—cutting curly wet hair?—but part of me trusted she knew what she was doing. Dark brown clumps fell to the floor. "It's just hair. Just hair," I kept telling myself, still hoping for the best.

I didn't see the full extent of the trim until it was all over. By then the women had gathered. Roberta cursed, pulled, curled, recurled. "Damn it!" she finally said. "I'm sorry, Suzanne. I don't know what to do."

Suzanne helped me with my coat. She tried to keep me from passing in front of a mirror, but it was a wasted effort. My hair was a spiky, frizzy, uncontrollable disaster. I looked like a pygmy monkey.

"I'm sorry," Suzanne said, flinging back bright-yellow, conditioned tresses.

So was I. I had been such a fool.

After seeing my hair, Robert had a few choice words for Suzanne. I was taking my nightly walk past their open kitchen door. "Don't go spoiling that gal," he was saying. "She's a worker and she's too independent already. She can't be made to think she's the same as you." He shut the door with a loud whack.

Twenty minutes later, Suzanne came to the barn, her face full of dried tears. "I wanted to give you your pay and tell you how really sorry I am about your hair." She handed me a tray with dinner and a weighty sealed yellow envelope that clanged. I put the envelope on the sewing table. "I'll make it up to you, somehow."

She sat down on my mattress. I offered her the chair.

"No, no, I'm fine here," she said.

"Please." I pointed to the chair. "Please, here."

She finally moved to the chair while I pretended to be straightening the patterned dress I had finished.

"You did a wonderful job on that." She smiled. "But it's sure ugly."

Despite the dread I was beginning to feel in her presence, somehow a chuckle fell out.

"I guess 'ugly' is a universal word," she said through loud, hearty snorts.

After Suzanne left, I ripped open the envelope. There was $4.75, mostly in silver twenty-five-cent pieces. That was not at all what I had expected after weeks of working. Mr. Harlow had told me I was to be paid twenty dollars each week. I decided that I would talk to Suzanne in the morning, as I was too chilly and too tired to go knocking on her door then. I climbed onto the mattress, pulled the three wool blankets up to my neck and tried to sleep. But I couldn't. It wasn't the money, though it probably should have been. It was Robert. The way he had said "independent" real slow and "can't be made" with his teeth clamped.

I tossed about on the spindly mattress and fell into a deep doze maybe once, maybe twice, but I always woke to the same thoughts: Robert and his tone. Finally, in front of the wooden-framed television Robert had wired up, I finished the bland roast beef sandwich. I figured that between the beef and the television I would drop asleep for sure. But when that short fella on *The Tonight Show* went off the tube, I was still alert, still running my fingers through puffs of hair.

I always slept well after a walk. I had made a thick-hooded scarf from leftover fabric from the bed-skirt. It might not have been as warm as a wool coat, but it kept the icy wind from my neck. I fastened it under my chin. I put back on my one pair of pants, pulled the coat over my thin nightgown, and headed for the door. I wouldn't last long outside, I was easily chilled, but I only needed ten minutes to relax my mind.

The scraped wood on the double door felt prickly against my palms as I pushed. The strain of the bowing doors echoed beneath my right shoulder. The swinging padlock on the other side made a heavy, thick thud.

I fell to my knees. I wanted to pray. I really did. But I didn't think God was interested in hearing yet another pissed-off woman calling out his name.

Keep your head, Marcia. Just keep your head.

I watched the television screen until swarming black and white dots covered it. When the odd, dim light filled the barn, I thought about the manicou I had trapped and killed during the war. How he had waited through the chilly night, only to find me staring down at him the next morning with a hammer in my hand.

Sunlight spilled out between wooden slats. Suzanne and Robert began the process of unlocking the door not long afterward. I gathered they had come early, in the hopes that I would still be sleeping, but I was washed and dressed in a nicely pressed blouse and skirt, sitting calmly on the mattress with a butter knife under the pillow.

"Sorry we had to lock it." Suzanne smiled. She was wearing brown pants and a black knit sweater. Her face, fully made-up, her thin cheeks a deep pink, making her ivory skin gleam like plastic. Suzanne usually spoke to another person with barely a few centimeters between, but that morning she kept her distance. "We heard there's been a few robberies and we wanted to make sure you were okay in here."

I stood, flattening the pleats in my skirt. I wondered how long it would take them to realize that I wasn't buying what they were peddling.

"It was for your own good."

"Why you didn't say?" I said.

"What?" Robert seemed primed for confrontation. He was a tall, sturdy man with a full head of dark brown hair that swept over his wide forehead, making his pale skin even more pale in comparison.

Suzanne turned to him with very compassionate eyes. "Remember, hon, she's just learning English."

"Then, what's she speaking?"

"I was here." I said the words slowly, pointing to the floor. "Right here."

"We know you were here," Robert said. "That's why we did it!"

Suzanne pulled her hair into a loose ponytail, then crossed her arms, gripping her shoulders with her thin fingers. "We called out to you, but you must've been sleeping or using the potty. But I have to say, hon, your English isn't getting much better. We brought the television in here for you to start learning, okay?"

"Don't," I said, holding up my finger.

Robert understood me very well, then. Only four inches separated us. "You're not to leave here unless you have our permission." His hands were massive. He smelled like charred firewood and peppermint.

I tucked my blouse into the waist of my skirt and started toward the door. Robert yanked me by the arm. He shoved me into a wide-eyed Suzanne. "I said you're not to leave here. It's dangerous."

Suzanne asked me to sew place mats. During the next few weeks I sewed almost six hundred rectangles. Same color. Same pattern.

I worked into the nights and many times through to the next morning. By then all the good memories of the children had been used up and my mind wanted to go back, back to before Farouk, back to right after my mother had died, when my father would let Uncle Linton visit. The only thing keeping me from drowning in those thoughts was the loud *ch-ch-ch-ch-ch* of that machine.

After the place mats, Robert and Suzanne's demands became more varied. Some days there would be a pattern: "Make this dress like this," Suzanne would say; or sometimes just a picture: "Make these pants like that," Robert would say.

But they never came alone. Suzanne, usually behind Robert, watched the way I responded to him, watched how I kept my eyes down, my shoulders hunched, as he towered over me. I wanted her to see how I stifled my anger, became a shell of myself. I wanted her to see some part of herself in me and question why it was necessary to lock me up. I wanted her to doubt my strength, doubt her own judge of character.

It was a Saturday when, finally, Suzanne opened the door without Robert. "Why are you always dressed like you're expecting to go somewhere?"

I rubbed my hands along my sides, as if stretching my fingers, but I was feeling for my papers tucked into the sides of my underpants. I always kept them there.

"I'm gonna take you out with me today," she said proudly. By the way she lowered her voice, I was sure Robert didn't know. "Come on."

I moved slowly, making sure not to show eagerness. I picked up my coat, which was folded alongside the bottom of the mattress, and checked it for my money.

"I'm sorry we've had to keep the door locked. You've been working so hard, I thought it'd be good to get you out for a little while," she said, as we walked along the driveway.

"I wanta mail a few letters to my chil'ren," I said.

"Oh, that's in another direction. I'll mail it for you tomorrow."

I had no intention of giving her anything to mail.

We drove for some distance. In the quiet, I guessed that Suzanne had to be doubting her decision.

"How you learn that?" I pointed at the steering wheel.

"My daddy taught me." She fingered and named the dashboard gadgets. Her shoulders loosened. "The market I like is a bit of a ride but we're having guests tonight so I need to get things I can't get from the store here."

I nodded, although I wasn't planning on being there when her company arrived.

"Since there's two of us, this shouldn't take long," she said, as we walked inside.

I couldn't believe my eyes. That market, with doors that opened by themselves, didn't look anything like the markets in my world. Everything you could ever want was in that place: fruit, meat, fish, canned things, packaged things, wrapped things. *T'ings, t'ings, t'ings.* There were ten types of beans, four kinds of potato, three varieties of onion, six styles of tomato. There was already-squeezed orange juice, grape juice, cranberry juice. There was even prune juice to help alla those people move alla that food.

Suzanne filled her four-wheeled metal cart. How a few people at a house party could eat all those things, I wasn't sure.

"I don't get in here much." Her eyes darted guiltily. Did she know all I could think of was my children back in Trinidad, trying to scrape together a meal because she and her husband hadn't paid me much of anything?

I watched her place an order for several pounds of cut beef from the butcher and throw wrapped fish fillets into the cart I was pushing, before I spoke. "When I gointa get all my money?"

"What, hon?" I had distracted her from reading a box of dry cereal.

"Mon-ey," I said. "Harlow tole me I'd get twenty dollars a week."

She dropped the box into the cart, atop three loaves of already-sliced bread. "Oh." The corners of her striped mouth trembled, as they searched for a comfortable place to rest themselves on her tight face. "I can buy you anything you need, Marsha. Anything. Make a list." She pulled the cart from the front side. I took my hands off the handle, though I knew I had to be careful not to make her doubt herself again.

"You know, Robert is a really good man." She stopped in front of a box of something called Rice-A-Roni. "I know it didn't seem that way when he pushed you. I'm sorry about that. But he means well and he works really hard. He's just very passionate about making sure we keep what he's worked to build."

I listened to her ramble about how lucky she was to have Robert, and I realized that nothing I said, nothing I didn't say, nothing I did, nothing I didn't do, meant anything to Suzanne. She wasn't a friend. I had to get out of there while I had the chance.

We stood in the long line. I watched that mysterious door swing open, close shut, swing open, close shut. Suzanne added more and more items to her cart from shelves on both sides of us. She was wild-eyed, seemingly unable to stop herself from collecting more and more bits and pieces.

"Long line." She smiled and rolled her eyes at the woman behind us, who also had a cart piled high with food. The woman smiled stiffly.

"Such a big grocery day, I had to bring our housekeeper," Suzanne said.

Housekeeper?

I saw then that having me locked inside that cold place, feeding me lukewarm food, not properly paying me, were things they might have been ashamed for others to know. Things that might get them into trouble.

What if I told someone? What if I shamed them? What if I could find an ally, right there in the market? I couldn't go back to that barn and live like that for God only knew how long.

We were next in line. Suzanne greeted the young woman behind the register. "This is Marsha," she said to the auburn-haired girl. "She's working for us now."

I stared at the girl, searching for some connection, searching for some way to let her know that everything was all wrong. With her freckled face, the girl grinned, then squinted as if she noticed something odd. Maybe she saw my heart fiercely pumping through the walls of my chest? She turned away.

Suzanne chatted with the cashier about how great the world turned and how some fella Walter Kite would be replacing another fella on the news. After the food was bagged and put back into the cart, Suzanne pulled out a wad of grey-green cash from her purse and counted. The auburn-haired girl waited, seemingly disinterested, as if it was every day she saw that many American dollars flashed before her eyes.

"Thanks, hon," Suzanne said. "See you soon."

Suzanne readjusted her purse and I watched the door swing open for us and close shut behind me. What could I do? Go to the woman who had been in line behind us? What about the girl behind the counter? Could I trust anyone?

"Shucks! I forgot to pick up my beef from the butcher! That's my main course! I'll be right back!" She dashed back inside, leaving me with my hands gripping the metal cart filled with her food.

I released the cart. My pulse raced. Somehow I managed to move my feet. I got a few yards before I stopped. Where was I going? I didn't even know where in Maryland I was. I looked to the left. Parked cars, a hill, two women chatting, and a long, narrow road over the crest. I looked to the right. Flat and open, as far as I could see. Either way there was no easy place to hide. I moved left.

I ran across the road, making it to the end of the market's building, heading toward the hill that lay between me and freedom.

I had climbed a million hills in Blanchisseuse, but none covered in flakes of ice.

I pushed my left leg onto the ice-flaked grass, reaching for a small bush planted on the hillside. "Come on, Marcia. You're no old lady." If I could make it up that hill, the possibilities were wide open. I needed that bush to stay rooted in that soil.

"That's her!" a woman screamed. "She's got my purse!"

It was Suzanne. I couldn't make it over the hill. I scrambled back down, jetted the length of the parking lot, hoping she wouldn't be fast enough in her high-heeled boots to catch me.

I ran hard, pumping my legs, holding my papers in my elastic waistband with my right hand and my achy, flopping breasts with my left. I almost made it to the end, almost to the street where not a car was in sight, where only a patch of thick-trunked trees lay in the distance, but despite all that was in my favor, I had failed to account for the wiry, four-eyed grocery-store security guard who must've run track in primary school.

"Come here!" he grunted, grabbing me by the back of my coat collar, yanking me to the hard ground. My head hit the asphalt with a *cluck*. A sharp pain sprayed down my right leg.

"Didn't you hear me say stop?" He jammed his knee into my chest, slapping his sweaty palm against my perspiring forehead, pushing my aching scalp deep and hard into the ground.

"Why?" I mumbled beneath heavy pants.

Suzanne's heels were click-click-clicking across the parking lot. Horns blared. People in cars, who should've been on their way to their next destination, took their hands off their wheels, captivated by the pageant playing out before their eyes.

"Oh, Mr. Security, . . . sir," Suzanne spoke between rapid pants. "She must've dropped it when she saw us coming. I have it here." She held up her purse.

The security guard removed his knee from my chest. "It's still stealing, ma'am. I need to call it in."

"Oh, sir," she said. "She works for me and doesn't understand a word of English. When I told her I was running back inside to get my meat, I'm sure she got scared and tried to find her way to the car. You know how these foreigners can be sometimes."

He threw his hands into the air, as if disappointed. "No, lady, I don't know how they can be, because you'll never find one of them working for me." He dusted his pants. I had just mustered up enough strength to roll over and push myself to my feet. "She's your problem," he said to Suzanne.

He walked away, adjusting his glasses, motioning to the drivers in the parking lot to keep moving along.

Suzanne's hair was blown about her face, her lipstick was smudged. "If you say one word, I'll tell him my money is missing. You don't for one second think they'll believe you over me, do you? You'll see your kids in about three to four years. Right after you get out of prison."

She pulled me by the wrist and forced me to wait in the car, on the cold black vinyl, while she unloaded the groceries into the boot.

It was six thirty in the morning when the factory boss-man shouted over the loud press machine that I was to report to the front to see a visitor.

Mr. Aldous, with his back pressed into the blue concrete wall of the building, was smiling. He was wearing a white shirt with ebony buttons and black dress pants, perfectly cut to his lean frame.

"This place used to be a foundry," I said, pulling his arm. "It can get you good and dirty."

"Doesn't seem to have affected you."

I blushed, looking toward the almost-empty road before us. A vagrant with a green bag rummaged through street garbage. He seemed not to notice us there, both of us hoping the other would say something to relieve the pressure.

"Yvonne seems to be doing betta," Mr. Aldous said.

On Easter Sunday, Yvonne's fever had broken. It was only the second day of her return to school.

"She lost a lot of weight."

"That won't take long to fix." Mr. Aldous put his hand in his pocket and jingled coins between his fingers. "She tells me allyuh haven't heard from your mammy."

"My mudda knows we can take care of ourselves."

The vagrant sniffed a half-eaten nutcake and pushed it into his bag. He looked up when he heard the coins.

"No, I mean are you worried somet'ing has happened to her?"

The thought had never entered my mind. I had half-convinced myself that life in America was so good she'd simply forgotten us. "No," I said. "I suppose not."

Mr. Aldous couldn't have missed the worry in my eyes, but he seemed to understand that I wouldn't talk about Mammy. "We haven't had much of a chance to speak since the day I was with Miss Penny in the schoolyard," he said. "I'm very sorry if you were hurt." He reached for my hand and rubbed his thumb across the length of my index finger. The gesture felt forced. Not at all like I imagined it'd feel the first time he touched me. I pulled my hand away.

"Are you more sorry your girlfriend was there or that you said those t'ings?"

"Whoa." Mr. Aldous stepped back to the wall.

"I have a hard time understanding how you could've been so disrespectful."

"Yes," he said. "I admit it was disrespectful." His words tumbled like wet cement. "Again, I'm sorry if I hurt you."

"Is that why you're here? To apologize?"

"I wanted to talk to you about Yvonne."

I tightened my apron string, then extended my hand for a shake. "Mr. Aldous, I betta run back inside before I lose this job."

Mr. Aldous reached for my hand, but I could tell he was surprised by the chat's turn. He lingered with my hand in his. His touch felt more like it should have the first time. "Jacqueline, will you please call me Philip."

Once I said "Philip" we would never be able to get back to where we started.

"How many years do you have?" he said.

"Sixteen."

"You seem mature beyond your years, Miss Karam."

I released my hand, one finger at a time. "Maybe," I said. "But not in the way it's usually meant coming from an older man."

The lines in his face deepened. I had offended him, but I wasn't sorry. If there was one thing I had learned from my time with Michael, it was that boys would fill a girl's silence with their own thoughts. I didn't want Mr. Aldous ever to think I didn't have my own thoughts.

Mr. Aldous showed up every Monday and Thursday morning. He was respectful and kind. He was the one person, outside of Yvonne, who really talked to me. Our conversations moved from his classroom to modern-day politics, to his dreams of moving to England to be with his sister, and even, once, to how I had failed the Common Entrance.

"I feel bad that happened to you," he said, one unusually chilly morning, not seeming as though he felt bad at all. "But what happened with your father wasn't enough of a reason to t'row away your future."

I had shared the worst thing to ever happen to me and he tells me that I threw away my future?

"Figure out what's next." He glanced up at the factory building behind us. "Because this can't be it."

"I know that," I mumbled, though I'm not sure I knew it until that very moment.

Chapter 15

JACQUELINE KARAM

It was Sunday and I woke cheerful and light. One day more until I'd see Mr. Aldous again. I practically floated out from under the sheet. I washed my face, straightened the bed, and put on a pot of water for tea so I might sit with myself in the quiet of the morning.

Patsy hadn't come home the night before. Saturday nights she usually spent out. She didn't bother stuffing the sheets with clothes anymore. From the moment Mammy left, the angry Patsy had come right back as if she had been waiting for the chance to show her ugly face again.

There was no sign of Wesley that morning, either. Some mornings he was there; other mornings he would come just in time to get Yvonne ready for school. Yvonne and I had seen him walking around Victory Street with a Portuguese girl whose father owned a grocery. I assumed (more like hoped) he was spending much of his time with her.

I topped off my tea with a splash of milk. The pool of water by the door had evaporated overnight and I hoped Yvonne would be awake in time for a midmorning dip in Lopinot River.

With Patsy and Wesley gone much of the time, Yvonne was my one steady companion. One weekend morning when she was feeling all right, we took a bus into Port-of-Spain and walked the streets, peeking into the windows of shops filled with trinkets for tourists who rarely came. Another morning we picked zinnias in a light rain, our thick locks coiling with each drop. By the afternoons we were back home listening to the radio, singing loudly, preparing dinner on the Primus.

I stirred a spoonful of sugar into the cup and reached for a hard bread roll. "Yvonne, you sleeping long, gal," I said. Saving half for Yvonne, I dipped the corner of my piece of bread into my cup. Its soggy warmth was sweet, delightful.

If Mammy hadn't left, I wouldn't have had those quiet, joyful moments. I wouldn't have had the extra time with Mr. Aldous, either. I felt happy about the life I was making without her.

But as Mammy would sometimes say, "Around the corner from happiness, sadness is sitting on the porch."

From the second I pushed the bedroom curtain, hoping to gently wake Yvonne, I smelled something horribly wrong. Her wavy hair was matted on her colorless face, her body was shivering under the sheet, soaked in stale sweat. She was covered in her own thick vomit.

"Yvonne? Yvonne? Yvonne?" Her eyes remained shut. Her lips were set one on top of the other.

She'd been doing all right. Not too hungry. Not too active. She just needed to get her energy back.

I stroked her arm. "Yvonne?" The odor sickened me. The bedroom walls seemed taller, closer, somehow. Her eyes slid open, the lashes fluttering like injured black butterflies.

"Your stomach again?"

The butterflies stopped fluttering.

"Wesley!" I knew he wasn't there. But I needed to scream to some-body.

The neighbors were bustling about in their homes, preparing for service, when the second-oldest Karam girl shattered Sunday's peace.

"I need somebody to help!" I scampered from door to door, banging and stomping on wooden porches, hoping somebody would acknowledge my voice. "My sista! Is sick!"

Through the neighbor's window, three houses down, I heard a woman's voice. "The doctor don't wanta see nobody on a Sunday," she said. "You take her into town and she gointa rot 'til mornin'."

The woman didn't bother to come outside and meet my tearstained face. She sat on the other side of her windblown sheers.

"She's very sick. Come and see," I said. "They can't say no to her."

I left the woman's porch and ran to Aunty Baba's, half-expecting she would have left for service by then. "Aunty Baba! You here?"

There was a shuffle and then Aunty Baba, wearing a tilted hat and a dress with plump polka dots, rushed out the door.

After inhaling morning dew outdoors, the malignant odor in Mammy's room smacked me hard. Aunty Baba looked at Yvonne with a mixture of pity and horror. "How long she been like this?"

"After Mammy left, she got betta."

"You take her to Gonjo?" she asked.

"Gonjo touched her head, gave her Angostura bitters in tea, made her do all kindsa exercise t'ing, and sent us home. She went back to school for a few weeks. But when I wake up now, she was like this."

"Gawd, chile. We can't take her into town. They'll leave her there 'til Monday afternoon. Oh Gawd, let's t'ink. What we gointa do?" She held Yvonne in her arms, soiling her black and white dots.

"Yvonne?" Aunty Baba said. "You your mudda's last baby, and you was strong and fightin' when you come from she belly. You be strong." She rested Yvonne's head on the bed again.

"Who been takin' care of allyuh?"

"Me," I said. With Yvonne so ill, admitting I had been in charge was not a source of pride.

"Your mudda too damn independent for she own good," Aunty Baba cried. "How she gointa leave allyuh to fend for allyuhselves? You know how I heard she gone? Them people in Arima and in Tunapuna does speak ill of her because she left their clothing orders undone. They can't get ahold of her and that's when I realize she left for America."

"Wesley was to finish Mammy's orders," I said.

"I t'ought your fadda was here," she said. "You have anybody else to help you?"

I flipped through the names of two or three people Mammy would've called a friend. None of them seemed the answer. Then I remembered what Mammy had told me.

"Somebody in Toco," I said. "Mammy tole me if anyt'ing happened I couldn't handle, to go there."

"Chile, you know how far Toco is? You take this chile to Toco, she not gointa make it. Them hills and big holes in the road. And *if* you does get there, what you gointa do?" She cheupsed. "That's craziness."

Toco was my one thought. I needed to hold on to it until I had a better one. "I can't keep her here, Aunty Baba. There's no doctor who'll see her. You said so yourself."

"There's a doctor in Toco?" she said.

Before I could tell her that I didn't know, a car horn beeped. Car horns didn't beep much on Sunday mornings.

"Eh, Patsy!" a voice called out. "Patsy! Gal, come out here!"

I opened the door to get a good look at the fella. I had never seen him before. "She went out just now," I said. He was chubby, with wide hips and short fingers. He had tight beads of hair and heavy black eyebrows.

"Where she went?" He stood with one leg out of the motorcar, one hand on the wheel.

"I don't know."

"Tell her Tony come by to give her somet'ing and I wanta see she tonight." He sat back down in the driver's seat.

"If I let you keep your somet'ing and promise she'll be here tonight, you'll take me to Toco?" I said, leaning into his open window.

"Toco! You mad?"

"You wanta see Patsy again? If I tell her you couldn't give her two li'l sistas a lift up to Toco with your big shiny car, when you should be sitting in some church praying your sins away, what you t'ink she gointa say?"

He muttered something to himself and closed his door. "Alright, come nah." He tapped the steering wheel as if to time me. "It gointa take me all day to get up there and back. I not staying and waitin' for nobody. A drop there and I gone, you hear?"

"I hear," I said, running into the house.

Aunty Baba washed up Yvonne, changed her clothes, and put together a few pieces of crunchy and sweet *kurma* and a few balls of a molasses-heavy *toullum* in a bag for the ride. She set Yvonne into my arms. "I prayed over her, so she gointa make it there," Aunty Baba said, "but you gointa have to pray there to make sure she does make it back."

Patsy's friend Tony drove like a madman. We stopped only once to relieve ourselves in the bush and to clean out Yvonne's vomit from the backseat. Tony had shouted "damn" and "bloody hell," but when he saw, through the rearview mirror, that I was holding Yvonne against my chest, shielding her from his rage, he quieted down.

Yvonne's breath grew heavier, more guttural, during the ride. Then, about a half hour away from Toco, she began to groan. I didn't know anybody in Toco. Until the day before Mammy left, I didn't know she knew anybody there either. I should've tried to find Mr. Aldous. I should've searched harder for Daddy.

MARCIA GARCIA

When Suzanne came with Robert to give me instructions on the work I was no longer in a hurry to do, she had the look of someone who had been betrayed. As if she couldn't understand why I had wanted to leave.

We never spoke of what happened. She for sure hadn't told Robert, though I had no idea how she explained her changing attitude toward me. Her hostility showed mostly in the quality of the food she was now sending with him on the tin tray. No more half-cooked roast beef. Instead, thinly sliced cold meats between thick cuts of stale bread. I ate what little I could stomach, and when the darkness came I began tucking the loose waistbands of my clothes into hidden interior pockets, hopeful that one day I could let them out again.

During those weeks alone in the barn, my desire to read almost made me weep. I had nothing for words but small tags on blankets— "Dry Clean Only" and "Wash in Warm Water with Like Colors"— and memorized passages from Nelson's *West Indian Reader*: "What can he do? He walks. I can walk. He eats. I can eat. He rides. I can ride. He lies in bed. I lie. He creeps. I creep."

Between the blanket tags and recited passages about doing, walking, and eating, I was losing hope.

Sewing—once my very lifeline—was becoming intolerable. The fabric between my fingers, weighty. The pedal beneath my foot, oppressive. The thought of someone else wearing my labor, cutting. But worse than anything, sewing reminded me of my children. I didn't want to think about the children.

When I bit the thread, I remembered how small Wesley's teeth had been when I had first taught him to twist and pull it. When I stitched the hem of a skirt, I couldn't help but think of Patsy, who pretended she hadn't learned sewing basics, but whose secret hemline stitches were no worse than mine.

When Suzanne and Robert piled high their demands, my fingers and wrists numb and my eyes burning, I would stretch out my legs, toss my neck back onto my shoulders, and thoughts of Yvonne would come. How she would seize my restful moments, jumping into my lap.

And when I put the final touches—the cuff on a shirt or the buttons down its front—I thought of Jacqueline. The child who always seemed to be there at the end. "It's lovely, Mammy," she would say, her words making me feel a piece of clothing had been worth the time.

My nose ran like a faucet. I couldn't stop myself from shivering. Suzanne stood by the door, her hair still in curlers, while Robert gave me instructions and then tried to find flaws in the clothes I had finished and hung on a rack.

"Look," I whispered to Suzanne, holding up a dress. "Pretty?"

Suzanne looked over at Robert, who was busy admiring the lining of a burgundy smoking jacket. She took the dress I held and spread it with shaky hands. "It's beautiful."

A black wool dress with a cinched, belted waist. Its pleated hem fell a hair below the knee. The wrist cuffs flared from the hand, revealing a slit almost to the forearm. The bodice, with a one-inch, satin-trimmed strip down its center, extended from the modest neckline to the top of the middle pleat.

"You do really lovely work."

I wiped my nose with a handkerchief sewn from the bedskirt fabric of those first few days. My chest, my teeth—everything ached. "You should have it." She seemed surprised by my words. "You took before."

Her eyes swept to Robert, who directed a suspicious glance at us. He took down four pieces—my first completed collection, each with sari-inspired draping and textured layers in soft neutral tones—and hurried Suzanne out.

By the afternoon, Suzanne was back with worry on her face and thirteen dollars in a sealed envelope. I counted the money twice. "What allyuh took earlier was some of my best work," I said, shoving the ripped envelope into my brassiere.

"I'll give you more when I can. Robert can't know about it," she said. "If you tell him, I'll tell him about the market."

"You t'ink he gointa be upset with me or with you about that?" I coughed up a mouthful of phlegm and went to the toilet to spit. The walk there gave me time to think. "Look," I said upon my return. "Every woman does have secrets. A li'l somet'ing like a nice dress is nutting. We all have wants. I does want a good meal. A friend. Somebody who understands how I feel. Women all want the same t'ings, right?"

She placed her hands to her bosom and brought her shoulders close to her chin. A move so practiced it seemed almost natural. "I was just very angry with you. You could've gotten . . ." She stopped herself, seemingly unable to finish the thought. "Let's start again. We'll start again," she said.

I nodded, forced myself to smile. She held her arms open and walked toward me. "Let's start again. Okay?"

· · ·

That evening Suzanne brought me roasted chicken and two ears of boiled sweet corn on her heaviest tin tray. I ate until my belly hurt, then offered her a seat on my bed.

"I had been wrong to try and leave before," I told her. "I was just very lonely."

Two days later she came with a slice of fresh apple pie. I offered her a chartreuse hobble skirt I had made with fabric I had hidden from Robert. "For you," I said.

Nearly every one of her teeth showed. "It's wonderful."

Each day she came, I pulled her in with garment goodies and made-up stories of a terrifying life in Trinidad where even being locked in a Maryland barn seemed a better choice.

On Holy Saturday, I woke sick as a dog. I had been fighting the illness for weeks, but that morning I could barely move. The congestion in my chest, my nose, my throat, was thick and plentiful. When I coughed my lungs ached to the very core. It had been days since I had completed any work. Robert was growing anxious.

"Those people don't have good constitutions," he told Suzanne. They were standing outside the barn door while I pretended to sleep.

"Let's take her to the doctor. She can't work if she's sick."

"Are you nuts? What if she talks?"

"She won't," Suzanne said. "She has nothing else." They wrapped the chain between the door handles. The metal rang hollow against the door's solid oak.

"We'll give it a few more days."

"You said their constitutions are bad," she said. "They have clinics for those people downtown."

"Baltimore?"

"I can take her."

"Shut up," he said. "I don't wanna hear another word about it."

I pushed myself to get dressed. I knew Suzanne wouldn't leave me alone. I managed to be sitting at the sewing table, slumped over yards of fabric, when she returned.

She grabbed my shoulders. "Why aren't you in bed?"

"I have to work," I said, gingerly lifting myself upright. "I can't sleep the days away."

"That's how you'll get better."

I gently nudged her. "I'll be fine." One of my coughing fits began. The crackling phlegm echoed through the barn.

"Do you wanna take a ride?" Suzanne asked. "I'll make one stop, then we'll drive to Baltimore to a clinic."

"I don't want to." I coughed.

"I can't tie the chain up again after I spent all that time untying it," she said. "They'll give you something to get rid of this thing, and the fresh air will make you feel better."

I slowly reached for my coat. "Please let me run to the toilet first?"

The pink plastic curtain rustled. I flushed and quietly reached behind the tank, sticking my papers and the cash I'd hidden into my waistband.

We were side by side when I touched Suzanne's shoulder to let her know how thankful I was.

"It's not a problem," she said.

We sat for several minutes warming up the car, listening to the American music. I couldn't stop shivering. "Still a little chilly, huh?" Suzanne said. I sniffled and coughed again. I had left my dirty handkerchief in the barn. Suzanne handed me another. "Got this from Robert's drawer for you." She grinned. "I have some letters I picked up from the post office. From your children," she continued. "I'll give them to you when we get back." She put on her black gloves. "They write in such perfect English. My sister, the one who lives out in California who I was telling you about, she tells me it's possible to learn to read English but not speak it very well. I mean, I just had to call her and tell her about the flawless penmanship of your daughter . . .

um . . . Jacqueline? How lovely she seems through her letters. They do seem to miss you. I know you must want them with you. I've told you before if you stick with the plan, they'll be here in about three or four years. Wouldn't that be great?" She shifted the car into gear and pulled out of the driveway.

Suzanne drove into the narrow parking lot for a small strip of short buildings—a gas station, a snackette and a store with the name JILL'S in red letters—bordered by cornfields.

"Robert's brother-in-law is pretty crotchety, so ignore him," Suzanne said. "He's horse people, like us. We bought this boutique for Robert's sister Jill to run. Robert will do anything to keep her happy. She wanted to be a fashion designer but came back from New York with her tail between her legs." Suzanne turned off the car and placed her gloves in the space between us. "Some people think they can pick up one day and just move to New York." She stepped out of the car. "Come on in. I have to get a few things from the storeroom. It'll be nice for you to see the place you help keep in business."

I walked beside Suzanne, taking in the icy blue sky, the white speckles of frost dissolving into the walkway. The afternoons had recently become warm. I didn't understand how the temperature could swing so widely from morning to afternoon. My first weeks in America, the lack of sunlight, the lack of outside odors, had frightened me. There had been nothing to smell but coldness. No scent of freshly washed clothes on the line, not even the wicked scent of pig dung left by the gate. But now, even through my stuffed nose, I was beginning to smell life. Hints of musky tree leaf buds and moss.

"Marsha, make sure you make nice. They're my family and I know you're not well, but the most important thing you can do with Americans is to smile. Americans smile, even if we're not happy."

Suzanne was smiling when she pulled open the glass door. Bells rang overhead. The place was warm, bright. It was the kind of place

Harlow told me I'd be coming to. The kind of place I could've spent my days sewing with the radio playing softly behind me, a proper cup of black tea by my side. There were colorful cotton fabrics, silks, satins, and wools lining the walls. Yards of cloth, folded with pointed corners, beautifully shelved, waiting for someone like me to transform them into something radiant.

"Hello?" Suzanne called out.

An older man, with a half-spent cigarette dangling from the left side of his mouth, walked through two floral-printed curtains. He dried his wet hands on his khaki-colored pants. He didn't smile. "Robert didn't tell us you were coming," he said. "You're supposed to let us know before you just show up."

"Oh, really, he didn't?" Suzanne said. "Well, I'm here." She flipped her hands outward as if to present herself. "I'm gonna grab the fabric Jill told me had come in. Is it easy enough for me to carry or will I need your big strong hands?" She winked at him.

The old fella tapped the end of his cigarette into a tin ashtray already overflowing. "You don't need me."

"I'll yell if I do," she said, still smiling. "Oh!" She touched my shoulder. "Let me introduce you to the gal who's been working on those projects."

"Jill's in the back," he said.

I reached for my handkerchief and blew my nose. Suzanne touched my arm. "Are you all right?"

With my eyes, I pleaded for her not to think of me.

"I'll be right back," she said, placing her coat and purse on the counter.

The old fella twisted the butt of his cigarette into the pile. Ashes fell over the sides. He rubbed his fingers on his shirt and stole a quick glance of me before picking up the *Baltimore Sun*.

I had my focus on those lovely folded textiles until I noticed, in the far-left corner, a circular rack with a sign that read "New York Fashion" in the same red script as the sign over the front door. The rack was perched under a window. Sunrays brightened the woven threads, highlighting the flawless stitchwork of every dress, pants, skirt, and blouse. I had made them all. I caressed the garments and brought a taupe sleeve to my face, inhaling the faint scent of my own odor. I pulled at the white tags pinned to the shirt collars and pants pockets with bright yellow yarn. "Halston," "Yves St. Laurent," "Pierre Cardin." The prices: "$369," "$423," "$184."

I had been paid forty-two dollars.

Out of the corner of my eye I could see the man watching me. I faked a sneeze and wiped my nose with Robert's handkerchief. The string of bells on the door jingled. A woman wearing a red peacoat and pink pearl earrings the size of marbles stepped inside.

"Hello, Dick." She leveled her eyes at me and ran them back over to the old fella.

"She's not buying here," he said.

The woman walked toward the rack. Next to me she pushed the clothes aside as if looking for something specific. She smelled of cake batter and vegetable oil. "You marked down this black dress?" she said to him, trying to hide her delight. She held the dress close to her chest.

It was my black wool dress. The one with the cinched waist and pleated hem. The one I had given to Suzanne.

I coughed into the crook of my elbow. The crackling in my chest shook my entire body. The woman smashed her hand over her face. She placed the dress back on the rack. "I'll come back later."

The old fella waited until the door closed before he slammed his newspaper to the counter. "Suzanne needs to get you outta this store." He rose from the stool, nearly knocking over his ashtray, stomping to the back.

My heart pounded like a *tassa* drum at an Indian wedding. That was my chance. I snatched Suzanne's purse from the counter. Three silver bells rang at the back of my pulsating head as I burst from the store.

To the left I saw the woman in the red peacoat unlocking her car door. I dashed to the right. The cornstalks had been chopped to half their size, the sheaths were brown, wet. Mucous lodged in my throat, blocked my airway. I knelt in the mud and coughed, then peeked through the curtain of stalks to see the woman staring into the fields, directly where I crouched.

Move Marcia, move.

My lumbering body swished and swayed the old stalks. Snot from my nose dripped to my lip. My panic, my searching eyes, my heavy chest, all too familiar. "Gawd, help me. Help me."

I was too weak. My body too weighted, too sore. I fell down into the melting, muddy earth.

Suzanne screamed for *Marsha*. If it hadn't been for the supermarket incident, I would've never thought to take her bag. If she caught me, I knew I would rot in an American jail. I yanked her cash from her wallet. I threw the purse into the soil.

Get up, Marcia. Get up. There had been many days I had wanted to give up and didn't. I had to convince myself not to let that day become the first.

Mass had ended. Three women, each rounder and firmer than the last, stood chatting outside, just in front of the church's portico. I ran from the car to ask them about Souse. They searched my unfamiliar face. Toco was big, but not that big. Who did I belong to?

They pointed to the next road and said, "Around the bend and behind the bush."

Patsy's friend Tony drove us as far as the bend. He helped me lay Yvonne near a water-filled drainage channel. The mud from his wheels left splatter marks on my nose.

"I have to go and get some help," I whispered to Yvonne, kissing her soured, soft cheek. "I comin' right back. I promise."

I wanted hustle, bustle, people walking in the road, but there was no one. The hum of crickets and the lone cry of a sparrow made me feel more alone than ever.

I glanced back. I could see the top of Yvonne's head until I passed the clump of bushes the ladies at the church had spoken of. Yvonne's shiny black waves disappeared.

The small house was painted mostly white. Built on wooden legs, it had a sturdy-looking fishing boat tucked between them. The door was salmon colored. The wooden knocker felt glassy between my fingers.

"Good morning?" I called out. Two Demerara top-hinged lou-vered windows were on either side of the door. Tall potted plants rested in front of the windows. I scooted one pot over and peeked inside. The back of a standing book, a Bible maybe, was pressed against the sill. The house was quiet.

"Hello?"

I heard a faint noise. The sound of bare feet across uneven wood. A man's voice. "Who's that?"

"I looking for Souse. He livin' here?" I said.

Gardening tools were stacked in the grass. A *crapaud* leapt out from behind the wooden handle of a hoe. I waited a few more seconds, then peeped through the window again. Two eyes in deep folds, one over the other, met mine.

"Whoya want?"

"Souse," I said.

"Nobody by that name does be livin' here." The eyes disappeared.

"Please, mistah." I tapped the siding, trying to force him to meet my face again. "Can you tell me where I can find Souse? Some ladies at the church tell me it's here."

"I don't know no Souse," he grumbled. "Go and leave."

I stepped off the porch, into the muddy yard. A flock of chickens came around a corner in a flurry. I fanned them away, furiously. Blinkin' chickens! Blasted chickens! Bloody chickens!

I ran back toward the ditch. How quiet Toco remained. It was a Sunday afternoon and other than those three ladies, and a pair of old eyes attached to some crazy man who wouldn't open the door for a desperate child, I hadn't seen one other person.

Yvonne's head felt like wildfire on my fingertips. I couldn't leave her again. "I'm back. You see? I tole you I was comin' right back," I said.

I didn't know which way to go. I didn't know how far we would get, but I had to believe God would help me find somebody. I gently dragged Yvonne onto the flat surface of the road. The vegetation around us was covered in sunlight-filled droplets of water. I bent my knees and scooped my hands under the pits of her arms, slinging her over my shoulder, trying not to press her body too hard against mine.

I had walked about a hundred yards in the direction of the church when the old man caught up to me.

"That was you knockin' my door just now?"

I was panting, scared to put Yvonne down for fear I wouldn't be able to lift her again. "Yes," I said.

"What's goin' on with that chile?"

"I dunno. I dunno," I said. "I'm trying to find that fella Souse."

"How you know Souse?"

Damn man wasn't asking if I needed a hand with the seventy-pound child over my back!

"My mudda tole me to come here and look for somebody named Souse if I needed help."

Yvonne's weight was sinking me into the road. I stumbled to the right and placed her against the trunk of a weeping tree.

The man bent his creased neck to keep the sun from his eyes. The top of his head was the color of brown sugar in white milk. It was shiny, with a thin strip of silver at its edges. His long face, covered in a white shag, was younger looking than his crunchy, tanned arms and bare chest. His mouth, slim and tight, was pursed like a man who hadn't had his teeth since the First World War. He had "an honorable face and dishonorable eyes," Mammy would've said.

"Who's your mudda, chile?" He peeked at Yvonne. Her eyes were closed but her face was not at rest.

"You know Souse? I'm tired, mistah."

"That's how your people does teach you to speak?" The muscles in his face hardened. He picked at his nose with the knuckle of his index finger.

"No," I said. I wasn't frightened. He wasn't the kind of old fella who could frighten anyone, but he did seem the kind to leave if he got mad enough.

"Souse ain't a chap who does wanta be boddered with no li'l gals."

I moved back toward the tree. "I'll find somebody who can help me find him."

"What you need him for?" he said, as if not wanting me to leave before he knew.

"Can't you see?"

And without warning, I began to cry.

"A'right, a'right, a'right." He held up his palms, like he had had enough experience with crying children. "*My* name is Souse," he said. "Now, you gointa tell me who the mudda is?"

I wiped my tears with the back of my hand. "Marcia Garcia is my mudda," I said. "I'm Jacqueline Karam. That's my sista, Yvonne."

The old man lost much of his color. "Marcy is your mummy?"

I'd never heard anyone call Mammy "Marcy" before. "She left for America. I can't get ahold of her and my sista's sick. I can't find my fadda. The bush doctor in Five Rivers keep telling me it's nutting, but she's too sick for it to be nutting."

He peered over at Yvonne, as if to confirm the extent of her sickness. "Come, let's take her back to the house." He walked to Yvonne, lifted her into his weathered arms, holding her across his body with ease. She was like a baby, so light in his hands; her white shoes dangling like bells.

From the moment we walked inside I knew Souse didn't live alone.

Tongueless shoes bigger than Souse's feet sat by the door. A shirt twice the size of his smallish frame hung on a nail in the corner. Three unwashed breakfast plates were near a tub of water.

Three men lived there. No signs of a woman.

Souse placed Yvonne on a small bed with a plain wooden headboard in a room off the kitchen. It was sunlit and smelled like candle wax and vinegar. He positioned her on a square pillow and carefully inched up her shirt. She hadn't begun to grow breast buds, I reminded myself. He kneaded his aged fingers along her small body, searching for what, I didn't know. He moved them the length of Yvonne's chest and stomach, pressing down harder at certain points, easing up at others. When he got to the lower-right portion of her stomach he pushed hard against her sweaty flesh. Her scream pierced the quiet room.

I reached for her curled fingers. "Eh-eh, what you doing?"

"How long?" he asked.

I resisted the urge to take her from him. "Mont's, I t'ink. It came, it went, and now it's back."

"It came and it went?" He moved his finger to the left on "came," to the right on "went."

"I t'ink so. Some weeks without much pain, then she was sick again," I said.

"I need to fix her up." He rushed to close the bedroom curtains and moved a one-legged table next to the bed. "You go and come back in a few days."

Remembering Mammy's warning, I said, "I'll stay. She'll need to see me."

He angled his elbow toward the corner, signaling me to move out of the way. "Dog don't make cat," he muttered. "You just like your mudda."

Souse made concoction after concoction. Leaves, bark, roots, weeds. Anything from the house and yard that could be crushed, pummeled, mixed for salve. Anything that could be milled, boiled, ingested for tea. Everything he could think of to break the veil of fever covering Yvonne.

Nothing worked.

"Let we go," he mumbled.

He picked up Yvonne, whose complexion had deepened, and we walked downhill, toward the sea. People passed us but they kept their eyes on the road before them. I could hear the water, loud and vengeful.

By the time our feet hit the sand, Yvonne was no longer moving. I wanted to put my head to her chest, to hear and feel her life, but Souse held her tightly, and waded into the water.

He pushed her body against the breaking waves. It was violent and forceful. The foam collected at the soft baby hair framing her face. I could hear him praying. Prayer—the one thing I had forgotten to do.

Whipped and knocked around by the currents, I recited every prayer Sister Edwina had drilled into my skull. I was picking myself up from the seafloor when Yvonne began to cough.

"Jackie." Her cry was weak. She opened her eyes. She seemed shocked to find herself in the arms of a wet and ancient man. "Jackie!"

I took her hand and Souse carried her back toward shore. She coughed again. Her chest rattled. The pain seemed to shoot through her like hot swords.

"Jackie."

Souse stumbled onto the floury sand. Yvonne's hair collected grains like a magnet.

"You alright?" I said into her dripping ear.

"I don't feel good. I want Mammy."

I wanted nothing more than to give Mammy to Yvonne.

Souse prepared a hot and salty chicken broth with white rice while I sat next to Yvonne's bed. She slurped two spoonfuls, then slept. Her breathing was sluggish, but she seemed more at ease.

"T'ank you," I said. He had wiped the kitchen table clean of the leaves and bark and placed a tin bowl in front of me. He offered a dash of pepper sauce.

"I t'ink she's on the mend," I said.

He sat across from me, humming.

I touched the bowl to my lips and blew. "Don't you t'ink?"

"I not a doctor," he said.

"You actin' like one."

A black Bible, the same book I had seen that morning against the window, lay between us. He pulled it to him and flipped through the pages. "You does talk too much. Chil'ren should be seen and not heard."

"Am I livin' like a chile?"

My tone was improper and he wouldn't justify it with a response.

"Tell me," I said, while he searched the verses. "Who are you to my mudda?"

He dragged his finger along the words in a careful motion. "You don't know I is your grandfadda?"

Mammy had told us many times over that her father had left her alone in Blanchisseuse after the deaths of her sister and her mother. Mammy had learned later that he had died. She was an orphan. Living by herself until she met Daddy.

"That's not true."

He stood and opened the lid of the coal pot as if considering whether he should eat. "You t'ink your mudda does tell you everyt'ing? I tell ya already, you just a chile," he said. "Your mudda run away." His eye twitched. I wouldn't have noticed the eye except Daddy had a rhyme: "A twitching eye means a big fat lie." And I was sure, right then, that Daddy's little rhyme was right. "I looked for her a long time until I give up and move here," he said.

I didn't want to eat. I sipped only a bit of the broth from the lip of the bowl. It was salty and lemony.

"She was a strong gal," Souse continued. " 'Wild meat,' I used to call her. You couldn't hold she back. Now look. She make it all them years on her own. Even in America? She does make me proud."

He sat across from me again, taking stock of my bowl as if he wanted to finish my soup.

I thought of Mammy. She had been left by her father. Then left by my father. I thought of the time she fell down at the obeah lady's house and how distant I had felt from her then, how small she had seemed, how ashamed of her I was. Sitting across from that man who called himself my grandfather, I realized that it was *not* knowing Mammy that had made me think of her in that way.

I'd fallen asleep in the small chair by Yvonne's bedside. There was the heavy dragging of feet on the other side of the drawn curtain. "Eh-eh?" Souse whispered. "Allyuh supposed to be gone 'til tomorrow. I have a sick gal in the bed there."

I decided to be thirsty.

Two men were removing their extra-large boots next to the table. Their eyes were flat, almost empty; their faces, round, exactly the same as each other's, and slow to react.

"Good night," I said.

They looked up. Souse ladled soup into their bowls. They hovered over their dishes, protecting them with bent arms.

"Say somet'ing, you dummies," Souse said. Then he barked at me. "Go back in the room and mind your sista."

"Are they your sons?"

He pounded his fist into the table. Soup sprung from the men's bowls. "That's my business, chile. Where you go, asking a man questions like that?"

"I just wanta know if they're my family, too."

"Hmph" was all he said.

I returned to the bedroom and wanted to sleep but instead I sat trying to figure out how I could get word to Patsy and Wesley that I needed help getting Yvonne home.

The front door squeaked. There were light taps across the porch. The night was too black and I could see nothing from the bedroom window. I listened to the footsteps mellow. Had Souse left? Or had it been one of the other men? I thought to tiptoe into the kitchen again, but Yvonne began to twist and turn.

She moaned worse than a birthing woman. Even my gentle touch pained her.

I ran to find my grandfather, whose God-given name I didn't even know. "Souse! Granddaddy!" There was no answer, no stirrings. I stumbled over something cushy on the floor. "Souse!" Down the gravel path, and around the bushes, into the road. "Souse!"

Upon my return, I reached for the lamp. I begged Yvonne to hold on. The light shone on the three empty pallets and Souse's Bible, all on the floor. Yvonne was calling my name. Yvonne was calling for Mammy.

Chapter 16

MARCIA GARCIA

The truck driver I had flagged down let me off at the bus depot in Baltimore. "Best place for new beginnings ain't here," he had said. "Get yourself to New York. It'll be hard but worth it." He stuffed the five-dollar bill I had given him into the pocket of his blue dungarees.

I slept in the station, upright on a hard seat, shivering, my head against a white-tiled wall. I pretended to wait for the next bus and then the next, until finally the first morning bus to New York City was announced.

"You shakin' like somethin' awful." The woman seated next to me was my age, flat-chested with a folding stomach. She smelled of talcum powder. "Where you going?"

"New York."

"We on the bus to New York, so I know that," she said.

I tried to remember the names of places people had tossed around back home. "Kings," I said.

She scrunched her face in polite confusion. "You mean King's County Hospital in Brooklyn?"

"Yes."

"Oh, I thought I noticed one of them Jamaican accents. Got lots of Jamaicans livin' in Brooklyn."

I told her I was from Trinidad. She shrugged as if she'd never heard of it. "Don't matter. Only thing people care about here is whether you black or white, and what you can do for them," she said.

I don't remember falling asleep.

"You better get up or they gonna be taking you back to Baltimore." My seatmate hoisted her bag onto her shoulder. "Good luck."

I was the last person off the bus. The driver wrung his hands outside the door. "Lady, I got a line fulla people waitin' to come through."

A neighboring bus hissed. The air smelled of fuel. I opened a glass door and passed the line of people waiting at gate number sixteen to board my now-empty bus. The crowd thinned as I moved toward three sets of double doors at the end of the hall. Two sets of stairs, one on each side, curved around opposite-facing walls. On the right, on the second step, a heavyset Negro man bent over his knees. On the fifth step, a dark-haired American woman, in short-pants, sat foggy-eyed.

The sign over the doors read NINTH AVENUE EXIT. They opened onto a narrow street filled with idling buses, inching in a line that seemed never to end. Trash bins, piled high, stood to my left. Two men in jumpsuits stuffed down debris with yellow-gloved hands.

I walked back inside. The Negro man on the step watched me. His pants, rolled to his knees, his legs, shiny, swollen, hefty, like a wet elephant's.

Back at wall number sixteen my chest ached terribly. The uncertainty about where I was, how I would get out of there, started to crawl up into my throat. At the other end of the passageway a crowd grew. A woman with three small children set down bags. A teenager, against a wall, held an uncreased, white book with the words "Agony" and "Ecstasy" on its cover. An old man in a heavy coat stared upward, stargazing into ripped ceiling tiles. There were no nods, no whispers of "good day," no eye contact. Not one recognizable face as I approached the steps.

The staircase was tall, broken in halves, formed from chunks of hard stone. A man in a plaid sports coat with a bad limp lugged an oversize suitcase in front of me. He pulled the strap with one hand, bracing himself on the almost thread-thin, brass handrail with the other. At the top he moved down a ramp to the left. I stopped at a blocky pillar. There was a boisterous rattle underfoot. I held the tiled pillar with both hands while the earth shook. People darted in every direction, yet there was no panic in their expressions.

The rumbling stopped.

A young woman carrying a baby adjusted the child in her arms. "Sorry?" I said softly. She pulled down her sweater and straightened the child's pink and white bonnet. The baby had cheeks like clementines. "Sorry." I tapped her shoulder. Terror blanketed her face. "Sorry." I held up my hands. "How do I get to the street?"

"What?"

"The street," I said. "Which way I does need to get outside?"

She plopped the child back onto her hip. "Upstairs." She nodded toward a staircase across from us. Another traffic jam of human beings. I wanted to scream out to her, to ask her if there was another way, but she moved quickly through a finger-smudged set of doors where a sign overhead read SUBWAY.

Subway. The train. I had heard plenty about it, but feeling it rumbling beneath me was far different than how it'd been explained to me back home.

I squeezed into the ascending crowd. The mingling of bouquet-scented perfumes and of not-so-fresh bodies was making me nauseous. My insides felt like bubbling sugar. I stopped on the top step to catch my breath.

"Lady, you can't just stop in the middle of the fucking stairs!"

There were ways of living in New York—rules—different from back home.

Home.

I had this intense longing for it. I had a strong sense that if I could get back there, I could make everything right, better than ever before.

• • •

On the corner of Eighth Avenue and Fortieth Street, thirty feet from the front door of the bus terminal, I couldn't move, My chest walls felt inflamed, my muscles ached, my ears were clogged, my skin, like ice.

Before she died, my sister Ginny and I would spend hours walking into the bush of Blanchisseuse. Hours surrounded by vegetation so lush and heavy, even sunlight had difficulty finding its way through. When it got too cold, too quiet, Ginny, who was older and had a better sense of direction, would lead us out. Walking behind her I never felt lost, I never felt confused. I never felt the fear of being alone. And I never thought to meet that bush without her until now.

New York City was like the deepest deepness of Blanchisseuse. A city-bush, where people, rather than animals, slithered and lurked, where people, rather than trees, smashed and bumped. In the city-bush, like in the bush of Blanchisseuse, there was barely a sky. Barricaded by metal structures, left behind were only rectangular and square swaths of blueness. In the city-bush, people lived with the disturbing echoes of bus squeaks, engine rumblings, flicking cigarette lighters, the click-cluck of heels against concrete walks, the awful cries of those with disturbed minds and maimed bodies, shuffling, encroaching. Ambulances, fire trucks, and police cars busied the streets, their occupants pretending to know what kind of war they could wage against it. But no one knew. I could sense, as I watched them—all of them—behaving repressively wild, with fear and dread built up behind the whites of their eyes, that none of them knew how to get out either.

On the edge of the city-bush, awash in what seemed to be an unbreakable fear, I decided that like the rest of them I didn't have to know. I pried my feet from the concrete and moved from the corner of Fortieth Street toward Forty-First, thinking of Yvonne and Wesley and Patsy and Jacqueline, who waited and trusted that I would somehow figure it out.

Chapter 17

FAROUK KARAM

There was a motorcar parked at the white picket gate. A palm-size *lingam-yoni* hung from its rearview mirror.

A man was in the house.

I slammed the door behind me. It smelled like wretched sickness inside.

I lit the lamp. Wesley's chair: empty. The front bedroom bed: stripped. Filmy cold water in a bowl under Marcia's bedroom window. Footsteps and hushed whispers coming from Jackie and Patsy's room.

Marcia had left me one, maybe even two whores to manage while she went traipsing around America.

I set down the lamp on the floor next to me and listened. "I already know what you doing! I'll give you ten seconds before I come in and make some bloody hell!"

A boy stepped out, his hands in the air. He was chubby, with coiled hair and unzipped pants.

I threw him against the wall, holding his neck. "Who you here with?"

Patsy, in Marcia's pink housedress, eyed me like she paid the damn rent.

"It's t'ree o'clock in the morning. I'm coming from the airport, and the only ones I findin' here is you and him? Where your brudda and sistas?"

I pushed the fattish boy toward her. I could see the hatred for me in her eyes. Eyes the same misty brown as Marcia's. "Whatya want me to say?" she said.

I had never before put my hands on any of my children. "What I want you to say?" I grabbed Patsy by the long braid hanging over her right shoulder and twisted the plait around my wrist. She pushed at me, tripping over the boy's feet. "You li'l cunt!" I slammed her against the wall. "What use are you?"

Her smirk made me want to kill her.

"I took them to Toco this morning," the boy spoke up. He had a slight mouth tick at the upper-left corner. "The li'l one was sick. The big one was trying to find somebody named Souse. To help her."

I held on to Patsy, Marcia's housecoat crumpling in my hand. "What craziness he sayin'? Yvonne is sick?"

Patsy, relaxed and loose beneath my grip, raised her eyebrows as if mocking me. "If you were here, you woulda known that."

Schoolchildren were waking up when I pulled into Toco-proper. Though I had little reputation left, I knew a few of the younger constables in Toco. One of them gave me the name and address of the man people knew as Souse.

"Souse" had been an unfamiliar name when the boy with Patsy had said it. But "Clifford Garcia" was a familiar name, indeed.

I knocked on the door for five long minutes. Finally, a red-skinned old man opened up. His eyes were wet and inflamed.

"You Souse?"

"Who's askin'?"

The resemblance between him and Patsy was jarring. It made me angry.

"I'm Farouk Karam. I'm looking for my daughters."

The old man opened the door wider. He seemed unsure about his decision to let me in.

It was moist and dark inside. I stood by an ebony-colored table surrounded by three chairs. A cup of milky coffee and a Bible sat on the tabletop. A medicinal odor, like burnt grasses and mint, blanketed the room.

"Are they here?" I looked around for any signs of the girls.

"I put the big one on a bus. She headin' home," he said.

"And the li'l one? In the hospital?"

He hung his head, as if dangling it from a short rope. "I just now meetin' them. My grandchil'ren," he said. "It was nighttime when I figured out it was a burst appendix. Already rotting. Closest doctor was too far. She wouldn't've made it." He gripped his head in his two weather-beaten hands. "They was sleeping when I left. By the time me and the doctor reached back, she was already gone. The big one wailing and holdin' on to that baby's stiff body."

I replayed his words. *Appendix. Stiff. Body.*

Then I vomited on my black lace-up shoes.

I had killed a man. Seen men dead on the street. Lived through heartache. Nothing had prepared me for that kind of wretchedness. The nausea, the heavy chest . . . I crumpled, layer after layer into the floor, my knees in my stomach, my teeth breaking the skin on my knuckles.

I never really knew you, Yvonne. I had been running from those children. And the mother. And the whole damn situation. I unfurled my legs and rolled to my side. The wood floor clawed at my shirt threads. I had been too scared to love the only woman I ever loved.

"Come. Sit down, young man," Marcia's father said.

God, what would I say to Marcia? I had never understood how she felt. How much pain you could be in and how numb you could be all at the same time.

After those boys disappeared she was never the same.

And I had taken advantage. I had used her pain to get what I wanted. When I learned things weren't what they seemed, I had cast her aside.

Marcia's father's toes nearly grazed my cheek. He pulled me up by the elbow. He was embarrassed for me, I could tell, but I wasn't ashamed.

"I can let you take the body home. We had a small burial up here, me and the big one. But if you need to take her, you can."

"Nah, nah, nah, nah, nah." Drive home with my lifeless child in the backseat? Was he mad?

Clifford Garcia began to clean up my vomit. The way he fussed over the floor, mopping it over and over, upset me more.

I gazed out of his open windows, at the trees, listening to the distant echo of rough sea waters, letting my mind go to the day when Marcia threw that cup at my head. I hadn't wanted to hold the baby.

"Go and take her," Aunty Baba had commanded.

Reluctant, I took Yvonne in my arms. I didn't want to feel it: the magic I had felt when Patsy and Jackie and Wesley had been born. I was so angry. So prideful. Maybe even scared. And for what? What if I had just stayed? What if I had let it all go and decided to love them?

Clifford Garcia's door swung open. I was thinking back to how Marcia's eyes had watered when she realized I didn't want to see our child. Two big men who moved like boys took off their boots. Through my foggy mind, I heard Garcia speaking to them. He was angry—not in the way a man got angry with another man, but with a child. Like I had done to Wesley the day of Yvonne's birth. I had called him a *buller*. I had told him to behave like a man.

The two big men rose to wash their hands in the rinse bucket. Their motions, sloppy and uncoordinated, their mouths downturned, their eyes blank, their hair frizzy, their brows heavy, their faces the same.

My Gawd.

I sat with my legs spread, my head thumping between my hands. "Why'd you take them from her?"

Marcia had never stopped searching the faces of strange young boys.

Clifford Garcia, standing across from me with a teacup in hand, turned slowly. He was like a little house woman—the mopping, the tea making—not at all like I knew him to be. "Me? I didn't take them."

"That's not a propa answer."

"What kinda answer you want?"

"Don't upset me more," I said. "I want the trut'."

"The trut' does be too many years and too many lives ago for me to remember." He set down a spoon and a cup of what looked to be coffee before me. My stomach was sour. The grounds smelled singed. He pushed the sugar toward me.

"They're yours," I said. "You should know when they came here."

"Yes, they're my grandchil'ren, but it doesn't mean an old fella like me does remember the years like that."

A side glance. That was how I knew he understood exactly what I meant.

The two men left the kitchen, unaware, it seemed, we were speaking of them.

"Must get confusing keepin' your lies straight, eh?" I knew from experience how lies were built on shifting sands. "Or maybe chil'ren and grandchil'ren for you is the same, right?"

He pulled the cup back, as if he thought not having it would've hurt me. "What you saying?"

"You shoulda take them chil'ren with you when you left Blanchisseuse. You left Marcia to raise your sons? She lived with shame hanging over her," I said. "I t'ought for years how I wished you were alive, so I could . . ." The thought was indeed murderous, but speaking of death reminded me of why I was there.

Garcia yanked his mop from the wall again. "You don't know nutting, boy."

"I don't know nutting?" My knees hit the underside of the table. "When I first went to Blanchisseuse, them neighbors didn't even speak to her. They'd pass her by without so much as a 'good night' or a 'good day,' " I said. "You did that to her."

"It was them same people who ran me off. Made me go and leave her and them boys there alone."

"It's no wonder—"

"No wonder what?" He dug the mop into the floor. "You makin' like you know somet'ing you don't know a damn t'ing about!"

The twins returned. Garcia shooed them back outside.

"If I hear anyt'ing from Jackie about you even t'inking about looking at her the wrong way, I'll drive here and put you in the ground underneath my own chile," I said. "I swear I will."

Garcia held on tight to the handle with both hands. "Listen here." The spittle gathered at the tip of his thick tongue. "You betta get outta my house. You spreading falsities," he said. "Maybe I wasn't perfect, but I did what I could do with what I had. And what I had was them two girls. I never touched them like that!"

His breathing was heavy, his eyes danced like sheets of paper in wind. It wasn't the expression of a lying man. I knew that expression. I knew the sound of a lie. I was sure he wasn't completely innocent, and I knew he wasn't the father of those two boys.

"When they bring them boys up here, they tell me she was getting married and that the boy she was marrying would give her a good life." It seemed as if he was happy to finally be getting his moment. "They tell me she needed to have them boys gone so she could move on with t'ings."

"She would've never sent them away," I said.

"That's why they were taken. She wouldn't have let them chil'ren go. Not even for you."

"Who did it?"

He grinned. Happy that I'd been so predictable. Then his face grew bitter. "It doesn't matter. It was the right t'ing to do. It was the only t'ing I could do."

He hung the mop back on the rusty nail. "You betta go," he said. "I can't have no man disrespecting me the way you doin'."

I wasn't sorry. All my "sorries," all my regrets, were used up.

Chapter 18

MARCIA GARCIA

Find work. That was all I could think. But I was too nervous to venture off Eighth Avenue. I walked slowly, taking in bug-eyed, square-topped yellow taxis that spun half-circles in the road. I read from a discarded paper: "Macaroni takes Caroline for a ride." And snatched bits of a conversation: "Knicks ain't gettin' over Chamberlain's one-hundredth." There were trinket shops, tattoo parlors, rowdy gentlemen's clubs. Corners packed with wisecracking men, who smoked, drank, laughed.

A tavern around Forty-Fourth Street with black-painted trim and a red door was the first place I came to with no pictures of naked women in its windows. The door swung inward. A fiddle played from the light-dancing jukebox. Men with reddened faces and booming voices sat along a wood-topped bar. The joke seemed to be on a yellow-haired fella with feathery whiskers and a bulbous nose. I thought to clear my throat to get someone's attention, but I didn't have to.

"Who do-ya want?" shouted a short, curly-haired man from behind the bar.

"I lookin' for a job," I said, pulling my coat over my chest.

The men stopped and turned. One of them, with a thick, reddish-brown moustache, dropped his head to the bar-top in a fit of laughter.

The other men chuckled. The barman set down the drinking glass he'd been cleaning and leaned in my direction. Before he could speak, the moustache-man raised his head. "They don't hire no Puerto Ricans in here."

"I'm not Puerto Rican," I said, softly.

"They don't hire gals who even remind them of a Puerto Rican," he shot back.

The barman put up his hand to hush the fella. "Wha's ya name, girl?"

I should've turned on my heels and left just then. "I'm from Trinidad and Tobago," I said, not as proudly as I should have. "My name is Marcia . . . Garcia."

The men flew into uproarious laughter.

When I walked outside the sky had become a deep purple-grey. I'd lived my whole life watching the changing hues of clouds and I couldn't risk getting wet when I was already unwell. I crossed the road a little further up Eighth Avenue. An unexpected draft of air swirled my uncombed hair. A man scurried into a restaurant with a picture of a red pie in its window. Inside, the storm seemed the topic of conversation. I searched the place for a seat. Most of the booths and two-seater tables were filled. The man who had come in before me was ordering food from a selection on the other side of a scratched wooden counter. Pies like steering wheels, covered with tomatoes, pressed meats, and diced vegetables, seemed to be the only food offered.

"Whaddya havin'?" A man in a stained apron had his fists balled into his waist.

"Good afternoon."

"Whaddya havin'?" he said, again.

"Cheapest t'ing you have and a cup of water, please?"

He closed his eyes as though praying. "Lady, just order something."

I leaned over the counter, close enough to his face that I could smell the raw dough on his neck, and I drew out my words: "Cheap-est-t'ing-on-de-men-u."

"One slice and a water!" he shouted to a man beside him.

He pointed toward the end of the counter where I, discreetly, removed my money and then, growing warm, took off my coat. Gawd, I needed to bathe. I immediately put it back on. Back home, a woman who had ripened like I had would've been thrown out of a place.

With paper plate in hand and my arms close to my body, I searched for a seat. The only unoccupied chair and table was next to a trash pail. Somehow it felt wrong to have garbage sitting where a person was expected to eat, but my stomach rumbled with hollow displeasure, and I sat down.

Hot cheese, tomatoes, and warm baked dough could probably make anyone feel better. The bite was a moment's joy in a tiring two-day misadventure. I leaned back against the wall and closed my eyes for what felt like only a few moments, when someone bumped my chair.

"You finished?"

The cheese on the tomato slice had gone firm. The other tables were now empty.

"No," I said to a woman cleaning tables. I wiped my eyes and bit into the cold triangle. "Sorry."

"Tired?" she said.

I smiled. She nodded and wiped the table next to me with a greying rag.

"Do they need help in here? I lookin' for a job," I said.

She kept wiping. "Hey, Donny! Got a gal over here who wants a job!"

My throat had dried. I drank a sip of water. The fella who had taken my money wiped his hands on his apron and stepped out from behind the counter. *Gawd, let it be my good fortune to find a job on my first day in this city.*

My throat tickled. I faced the wall and coughed. My chest rattled. I coughed again and then again.

"Is this her?" the Donny fella asked the woman.

Water streamed from my eyes. The cough wouldn't let go. I took a few deep breaths, but the cough begat another cough and another.

"I don't have time for this shit," the Donny fella said.

The woman stopped wiping tables. "Geez, she's just coughing."

The man, with beefy eyebrows and a hook nose, shouted over my coughing. "Let me give you some advice." He pointed out the window of the restaurant. "You need to go down to the pharmacy, get yourself some Coldene and rest. After that, you *might* find a job. Nobody's gonna hire you if you're coughing all over the goddamn place." He turned back to the woman. "If you wanna help her, get her some damn tea."

The rain had tapered, though the breeze had not. More rain would come. I left the pie place with hot, tasteless tea swirling in my half-empty belly. The warmth of it had stopped my cough long enough for the table-cleaning lady to tell me I could find a pharmacy if I made a left at Forty-Third Street.

Outside the pharmacy door, I stuffed toothpaste, a toothbrush, a bar of soap, and one pair of too-small panties I had purchased into my coat pocket. I poured four capfuls of syrup down my throat and pinned my hopes on the American people's remedy.

Another bloody rain cloud followed me down Eighth Avenue. It had positioned itself over my head and opened up just as I yanked the door to the bus terminal. I had hoped it would be quieter inside, now that the morning rush was over, but instead, the sounds of irritated, rain-soaked people bounced against brick walls.

Back down the steps, past door sixteen, I curled up on the staircase where I had seen the elephant-legged man. I listened to children laugh and whine. A boy with droopy eyes ran from his mother to stare at my reflection in the glass doors.

The late day became early night, and the rain fell in white sheets. Perhaps it was the medicine or maybe just fatigue, but I felt I would sleep. I moved back to the busier, passenger-loading area where it felt safer and, surprisingly, found an empty bench on the backside of another, occupied by a sleeping man with long pink earlobes. I stretched out the same as he had, yet despite my exhaustion, it wasn't easy to sleep. The lights flickered, the passengers yapped. I had to send my mind to my warm, roti-filled island, with its morning cocks and quiet nights, before I dozed.

My heart leapt from the hard tap on my leg. "Get up!"

The white man with the pink earlobes who was on the bench behind me was the man leering down at me now. White, spiky hairs sprang from his mostly bald head. His face was clean-shaven and he smelled like he had been scrubbed in bleach. He wore unpressed black pants and a well-fitted brown coat. "If you wanna get arrested for vagrancy, you keep laying there!" he said.

A bus to Chicago was being announced. I watched the old fella's eyes lock on two uniformed police officers at the end of the corridor. They were staring at us.

I stood, tidied the loose wisps of my hair and wiped my dry mouth. The old man moved to my right and looped his arm into mine.

For a moment, I couldn't even think. His touch, his smell, the closeness of that man pretending to be my lover while we tried to avoid the police . . . Whose life was this? I wanted to go home. I didn't care about Trinidad being an ending and not a beginning. I didn't care about surviving the city-bush. I wanted to be safe. I wanted to know what would happen day after day, week after week.

I trembled as we walked, the tapping feet of the law on our backsides, up the first flight of steps and past the pillar where I had once leaned. The old fella kept my hesitant feet moving through doors and under the sign that read SUBWAY, where the girl with the clementine-cheek baby had walked.

We hustled down a dark, chilly-aired ramp, past a booth housing a uniformed man and out of sight of the police officers. The old fella let go of my arm, pulled something from his pocket, and pushed himself through a metal gate.

I stepped back to the ramp. The bus terminal was just through the doors on the other side of the massive building . . . past the policemen who had their backs to a rail, their eyes on me. I couldn't go back. But where would I go?

The man in the booth picked at his ears. The clock over his head had a green face and red numbers. It was five minutes after one o'clock. The last time I'd been awake at that time back home was the night I had chased Patsy into the streets. I hadn't been frightened then.

On the wall next to the booth was a paper longer than the longest Port-of-Spain street sign. "New York City Subway" it read. Colored lines crisscrossed the poster. It was a map, I was pretty sure. But there was no compass, no scale. It was like none I'd ever seen.

The air curled. The odor of human urine bounced between my stuffed nostrils. Sheets of paper lifted slightly from poles. The ground beneath me shook again, the rattle even more jarring than the first time. A train could make such noise? A train could move the earth?

The rumbling stopped.

A young woman, no older than Patsy, came down the ramp across from me. She wore short, scuffed, white boots and two silver bracelets that squeezed her chubby wrist. How sure of herself she seemed when she walked up to the booth.

What was he giving to her?

She moved to the twisted metal gate, did something with her fingers, then strolled through. Within minutes two other people, not bothering to stop at the booth, pulled something from their pockets, and pushed the gate with their legs.

I decided to try. Walking past the booth man, who hadn't once taken note of me, I pushed the gate. It didn't budge. There was no give. No thud of a lock. Nothing.

I watched a young Spanish fella mumble something to the booth man. He put his hand to the window. Something clinked-clinked as he moved. His fingers fell below his waist. Then, he opened the metal gate with his short legs.

The uniformed man yawned when I approached. He had silver molars. "How—how do I get in there?" I said, pointing to the gate.

"What?"

"I wanta go where those udda people went," I said.

"What?"

Through the doors at the top of the ramp, the policemen were still there, explaining something to a bearded man in a red turban.

"The people who went t'rough that t'ing . . . ," I tried again, pointing to the gate.

"I don't know where they're going, lady. You wanna buy some tokens or what?"

"Tokens? Yes. Tokens."

I ran to catch up with the Spanish man who I only then noticed had a slight gimpy leg. His thick, shiny black hair glistened under the yellow-tinted lights. His lumbering footsteps echoed to the beat of mine. The tiled sign, with an arrow pointing in the direction we were walking, read UPTOWN. Were we downtown? The young man cranked himself around twice to watch me. Each time he seemed to try and put more distance between us, but each time I raced closer to his heels. At the bottom of the staircase, he moved quickly to the right. I was too frightened of his wariness to follow him again. I stood alone on trash-littered concrete. Cement caves were on both sides. The walls were covered in yellowed paper, the ceiling over the platform, peeling paint. It was a blackened, grimy dungeon.

Another mild gust of urine-tainted wind stroked my face. To my left, the pink-eared fella walked from behind a pillar to the edge of the concrete. I was surprised to see him again. I moved toward him—a known in an unknown world. Another whirl of wind, stronger this time, blew. The old fella stared down the mouth of the cave, past me, while I studied his darting eyes, his jiggling feet, his motionless hands.

Something roared past my face.

A train. It seemed as big and as powerful as an airplane. It slowed and hissed. EIGHTH AVENUE EXPRESS, the sign on its side in white letters read. Two doors split apart, leaving a wide opening. The old fella stepped through the opening, onto the train. And so did I.

The doors were watertight, and the clunk-clunk of the train's wheels startled me. The old fella walked to the other end of the almost-empty car. Another man, in black rain shoes, stood against the door. Where had the girl with the boots and the Spanish fella with the shiny hair gone? I was alone with two men on the wrong side of closed train doors. Panic crept again into the pit of my belly. The old man stretched out his legs on the seat next to him, and closed his eyes.

For some reason, the thought of him resting there calmed me.

Above me, a man smoking a Chesterfield cigarette wore bright yellow. His ad was next to one for a fiery red Ford Thunderbird. Beneath the two ads, pressed under a scratched piece of glass, was a smaller version of the map I had seen earlier. I stood up. The train jerked and bobbed. I fell back down into my seat. The man with the rain shoes glanced and quickly cast his eyes back toward his notepad. I stood up again, this time holding a long metal pole bolted to the floor. I put one foot in front of the other and crossed over to the seat in front of the map. I began to study it. The old fella slept soundly as the train stopped at most, though not all, of the places written under my fingertips. Somewhere after the 186th Street stop, after I had studied much of the "8AV" and "7AV" lines, and after the rain-shoe fella had hurried off the train, I fell asleep.

"You need to get off this train." A man wearing a uniform towered over me.

"Sorry," I said, pinching my coat's narrow lapels. "I fell asleep."

"Obviously." The train was empty. "Don't *ever* fall asleep that hard on these trains, lady. You'll get yourself hurt."

I nodded.

"Where you going, anyway?" he said.

I didn't know how or if I should answer. He stared at me for a few moments. Then, a flash of compassion lit his face. "Don't make this a habit, you hear? Go up the stairs and go down on the other side of these tracks. That train is leaving for downtown in three minutes. So move fast."

The old fella was seated in the last train car when I boarded. He saw me, got up, and walked into the next car. I didn't want to make him angry, but I was too frightened not to follow him. I kept my distance, sitting on the other end of the train car from him. The train inched forward. He closed his eyes again.

I tried to convince myself I wouldn't oversleep, that no one on the slightly more crowded train would rifle my resting body, but I couldn't rest. A woman boarded, holding a blue-tinted baby. She snuggled against a hard metal corner and closed her eyes, unafraid it seemed, of the night-walking strangers, unafraid a deep slumber would loosen her fingers from the child. I didn't think my worried mind would ever settle, until I awoke to find the old fella standing in front of the train door at "Jay Street–Borough Hall."

I scrambled to follow him. The small cast of strangers stared as I squeezed my body through the almost-closed doors. The old fella looked back, seeming both angry and amused. I panted and ached. I hadn't moved that fast since I'd been in the cornfields watching the truck approach in the distance.

I followed my human compass through those dark morning hours onto the Sixth Avenue subway line, headed uptown. I took a seat in front of another enclosed subway map and watched how Sixth Avenue met Eighth Avenue until it split off toward a place called Queens. I woke. I slept. I woke. When we got to Queens, I followed the old fella up and down to another platform. To his dismay, I christened a dark corner and then quietly waited behind him for the downtown train.

I dreamt of Yvonne on that next train. She came as vivid and as bright as a Trinidad sun, smiling and blowing kisses as she fought the lashing surf. I waved to her, then woke, yearning for her breath against my back.

People, some freshly bathed, some with glossy hair, began to fill the train. I lost sight of the old fella behind a man who stood with a serpent-headed cane. The pulse of the train felt more vivid in that first full morning in New York City—Stop, Start, Lights off, Lights on. "What the hell?" a man screamed out to another who stepped on his foot. The doors opened and the sound of a trumpet and a bass drum penetrated the car. A fat man breathed heavily across from me. The train stopped. In a black tunnel, bodies fidgeted. The train moved again. People sat back. A beggar with saggy pants and an outstretched paper cup recited a dirty poem about "liking my body when it is with your body." A gal with a partial updo and curly bangs adjusted a white corsage to cover a stain on her tight black sweater.

The cold syrup had thickened, but I swallowed two more doses before signaling to the old fella with a wave of my hand that I wouldn't see him again. I mouthed a soft "t'ank you" and returned to the bus terminal. I washed myself in the washroom down the hall from door number sixteen and, though my chest remained heavy and my wind still rattled, I knew I would make it through another day.

I knocked. I begged. I pleaded in my heavy Trini tongue for one chance, a few hours of work, but not one shopkeeper could meet my eye when he told me "No thanks," "Don't need anybody," "Not looking for help."

Remembering the routine of the previous night, I moved from Manhattan to Brooklyn to Queens in the rigid darkness of the underground. The next morning my slumped body, smothered once again by purpose-filled morning commuters, headed back into Manhattan.

I awoke to an Oriental boy seated next to me, cradling a pastry and a Coca-Cola. An Ovaltine-colored man with baby-smooth skin gripped the metal loop bolted to the ceiling overhead. The two of them poked, knocked, prodded my legs with theirs, to the rhythm of the rocking train. I hadn't eaten the previous day (which is possible in a place where fruit trees aren't abundant) and my Coldene-filled belly sloshed and jerked. I tried to keep my focus on the Oriental boy's red-and-white-striped shirt; the way the lines crossed along his hunched back, the way the white cuffs were ripped, as if it had been chewed. I thought of its structure, its firmness, the broad cut of the shoulder, all so that I could ignore my stomach's sway. But then he licked his powdered-sugar-covered fingers and the sight of his tongue, ridged and white and wanting, made me all the more nauseated.

The doors opened at Van Siclen. The finger-licking boy got off and the Negro fella moved into his seat. The smell of diesel fuel rushed through the open train doors. I held my stomach. I hadn't noticed the map just behind the Negro fella's head. It had become comforting to pore over it. The blue outline of the Harlem River ran along the top left, linking into the Long Island Sound at the upper right, both meeting at the East River, which didn't seem very far east on the map.

The queasiness subsided enough that I planned to hop off at the next stop and cover new territory. Someplace in New York had to be hiring.

The lights went off, followed by a child's gasp and the usual sighs of annoyance. The man seated next to me began to sing quietly, almost inaudibly, yet in the rhythm and the bass of his voice, I could hear the Spanish-flavored trumpets, the horns playing on the little radio back home. I felt I might be dreaming.

I strained to hear his feathery words. I leaned back into the seat. The Mighty Sparrow's sweet baritone against the calypso beat. It seemed only yesterday I'd first listened to "Royal Jail" over the radio. Jacqueline had turned up the volume and she had sung those words, memorized so quickly, swaying, shaking her pretend tambourine.

And I had softly hummed along:

Dit dit dah dit dit dah dit dit dah dit dit ti.

"You's a Trini?" The fella had the most excited eyes when he spoke. "Yes," I said.

We chatted about Sparrow—his antics, his lyrics, and then the fella began to pepper me with questions: Where in Trinidad you from? What's your family name? Do you know such and such? Do you know so-and-so? He told me his name was Leroy and that he was on his way home from a nighttime construction job. He was younger than me, by maybe ten years, and had an innocent face, like a loved puppy. As we rode alongside each other I peeled back the layers of some of my story, but I was wary of telling too much. He felt my guardedness, and he grew careful with his questions. We were almost to the Kingston-Throop stop when Leroy tapped my wrist and said, "Come."

I glanced at the map. "You want me to come with you?"

"Come see Brooklyn," he said, smiling.

I pushed myself up from the seat. *Whatya doing, Marcia? You don't know this fella.* I stepped out of the train, following Leroy up a narrow concrete staircase.

Brooklyn. I had only ever passed below its roads. It welcomed me with the odor of fresh, buttery bread. FULTON STREET, a sign read. The ground beneath us trembled.

Leroy went left on Fulton. West Indian tongues prattled as the Negro American men's "boom-bop" caught the music waves blaring from windows. But a right turn down a side street, oddly enough named Marcy Avenue, was what stopped me.

What if it's a trap? What if this Leroy fella means you harm? What if he steals the li'l money you have left?

In Manhattan, my sun-soaked skin, my uncombed hair, my wrinkled clothing, my something, my everything, had all been too unfamiliar. But in this place, the smell of Caribbean curry and burnt sugar hung deep behind the air; even the fruits packed in boxes on sidewalks, outside storefronts, seemed to have been sent straight from my island. I didn't need a Leroy. I didn't need to follow him into some dungeon or alley and have my throat ripped out after everything I had been through. I could make it alone in Brooklyn.

Leroy, finally noticing I was no longer beside him, stopped. "What's wrong?"

I don't trust you was too hard to say.

"Don't worry. I not doin' you no harm, my friend," he said, walking back toward me. "Nobody from home should live the way you been livin'. It's not right. If anybody find out I left you to fend for yourself, they'd hang me on Fulton Street. We can't leave each udda to fall down in the streets. It's too hard. Come. I live with my mudda. She won't mind letting you have a plate of food and someplace to rest your head. Come with me, nah. Don't lemme have to beg."

Leroy's mother hid her annoyance behind semi-kind words, while Leroy showered off soot. Clad in a fluffy robe and house slippers, his mother offered me a spoonful of sardines stewed with onions and tomatoes, and a slice of buttered toast. I accepted her offer, not sure when my next meal would come, but she watched my every bite as if wishing she could snatch it from my mouth.

After eating, I asked Leroy's mother if I could use the toilet. She stammered through an "alright" and I went into her washroom. It was still foggy. The steamy air soothed my dry face. Fluffy pink rugs, a plastic pink shower curtain, and even a pink toilet. It felt luxurious.

I mercilessly scrubbed my skin and relieved myself after days of a cramping stomach. I slicked down my hair with a mixture of water and some kind of blue grease Leroy had left on the sink. I washed out my underclothes, brushed my teeth three times, and reappeared in the parlor almost an hour later, only to be met by Leroy's mother's agitated eyes.

"I used my own soap," I said, apologetically.

She cheupsed. "That's not the problem." She put her hand to her hip. "I'm wondering when the bill come, where Leroy gointa get the money to pay for all that water you wasted."

Leroy shifted uncomfortably in the chair, continuing to stare at the television.

"Oh Gawd, I'm sorry," I said. "Back home, *if* you have water, it does be free. I didn't know you had to pay for rainwater here."

I felt more than guilty. I was embarrassed. She had allowed me into her home, fed me, and now she thought I had taken advantage of her kindness, when, in fact, I hadn't given any thought to her. I had been completely selfish during that hour in her washroom, thinking of nothing but how good it felt to be somewhere safe with clean water to bathe.

"Please let me help you with somet'ing to make it up. I'm a pretty good seamstress. If you have somet'ing ripped or torn, maybe I can mend it for you? Or maybe I can clean the dishes?" I said, moving to the sink.

Leroy's mother cheupsed again, picking at her teeth with a wooden toothpick. "How much water you gointa use doing that?" she said.

Leroy was pretending to sleep on a recliner not much different than the one Wesley slept on back home.

"I'm sorry again," I said, quietly.

"Let me ask you somet'ing?" Leroy's mother leaned over her metal-legged, two-seater table while I stood. Her hands were pressed together under her chin. "You come to America not knowing one person here?

Not one udda Trini you know does live in this country? I find that
hard to believe." The broken blood vessels beneath her eyes were like
spider legs. A ring of white patchy skin outlined what surely used to
be a nice set of lips. She had once been a good-looking woman, I could
see. But she was tired. In a different way than my tired, but still tired.
"Your story just don't seem to add up and I wonderin' what kinda
game you runnin' on my son," she continued.

"Ma!" Leroy threw down his legs and sat upright. "Leave her,
nah."

His mother tightened her lips. The dryness spread like a long-
waiting risen dough. She crossed her arms and eased back into her
green vinyl chair.

"That's not who I am," I said.

She shook her head in disgust at both me and her naïve son.

I thanked her for the plate of food, pulled out a dollar from my
bra, and set it down on the table. "This is all I have to give," I said. "I
hope I'll be able to repay you later for your kindness."

It had begun to drizzle. The chilly raindrops felt like an icy cutlass on
my skin. The sky was an ashen grey, the air had taken on a distinct,
salty odor. I walked away from the relative quiet of Halsey Street with
a loose plan to head back to Fulton and look for work.

I was still upset about the exchange with Leroy's mother. Being
alone in the world with no minute-to-minute purpose, no day-to-day
direction left me with too much bloody time to think. There had
been a time when I would've turned down her insincere offer of food
and told her to kiss my behind. Not anymore. And I had to learn to
live with that. I had to learn to move on from insult, from injury,
because I didn't have any additional room on my back; the burden of
carrying myself and my children was enough.

At Fulton Street, Brooklyn grew louder. Women with umbrellas and plastic bags fastened around hot-combed hair filled the streets, screaming behind scattering children.

"Hey!" Leroy's white sneakers bounced bright against the damp grey sidewalk. He was wearing a jersey vest and a pair of half-buttoned dungarees.

"Sorry about my mudda," he said, panting and buttoning his trousers.

"No problem atall. I very much appreciate what you did for me."

"It's not right what she did."

"No need to apologize for your mudda. She raised a nice boy," I said. "You betta get yourself back there or you gointa catch deat' from this cole rain."

"My fadda died six mont's ago." Leroy dug his hands into his pockets. His shoulders touched his small ears. "I had to move in with her. She's been t'rough a lot." A handwritten flyer, with a sketch of a saxophone, for a show at someplace called the Blue Coronet had been nailed to a pole next to me. "Listen, lemme help you," he continued. "I know a fella, Mr. Harry, who does own the li'l bakery up the street on Fulton. I'm sure if I talk to him, he'll let you clean up around the place. Pay you a li'l somet'ing. Maybe not much, but it's betta than nutting, right?"

Part of me wanted to tell him I was all right by myself. That I didn't need his help. That I wanted no more favors. Instead I said, "A li'l somet'ing is always betta than a li'l nutting."

I began washing the heavy metal mixing bowls and the black-bottomed baking pans in the kitchen of the bakery minutes after Leroy introduced me to Mr. Harry, an older Grenadian man with a thick, spongy Afro and long sideburns. Mr. Harry wasn't outwardly friendly by any means. He seemed the type to use his voice sparingly. He didn't seem concerned about where I had come from or where I was going, so I kept my head down, scrubbed what needed to be scrubbed and removed whatever needed to be removed from the few tables in the bakery.

Although I was thrilled to finally have work, after the lunch rush, I started to wonder where I would sleep that night. The thought of another night on the train filled me with dread. The Jamaican girl behind the register, who hadn't said more than two words to me, seemed to know many of the customers who had come in.

"You know somebody who might have a room to rent?" I asked her.

She dug her elbow into the lime-green wood counter and leaned into her fist. The midday sun streaming through the large glass window at the front made the red glitter in her hair sparkle. "For you?"

"I just got here," I said.

She examined my clothes, still stained with Maryland mud, and my hair, glistening, not like glitter, but like a grease pit, and then said, "Nah."

I asked the same question of the old woman baker and the late-afternoon register girl. "No," they each said.

The first wave of Manhattan workers was flooding back into Brooklyn when I got up enough courage to ask Mr. Harry. I hadn't wanted him to think of me as a problem, but the day was quickly running to meet the long night. Mr. Harry, who was counting the day's take, grunted and walked away with a pile of cash in hand. I mopped the kitchen floor one last time, resigning myself to sleeping another night on the trains.

I was rinsing soap from the last muffin pan when Mr. Harry handed me a slip of paper. "Go and call on her now. She should just be getting home. Come back to help me close up when you done."

The name "Theresa" was in blue ink, "Pacific Street" in black.

The walk took longer than I expected. The sun was only slightly visible when I found myself in front of a bloodred brick building with a white marble entrance and the name "Cecil Court" over the door.

There was a wide concrete patio, enclosed by a black metal gate. Up the steps, through a set of unlocked double doors, the walls inside were tiled up to the tall, peeling ceiling. Another set of double doors—glass interior doors—with sheer curtain panels, attempted to hide a foyer. Its brass knobs were more successful. A pad of buzzers rested on the left. I read Mr. Harry's paper again—"4D"—and rang the bell.

Perhaps she hadn't come home yet? I rang again and then again.

After some time, I went back outside. A six-pane window creaked open above my head. A woman, the color of red clay, with pink rollers pinned to her scalp, looked down. "Who you looking for?"

"Theresa."

"Who?"

"Theresa," I said louder. "Mr. Harry sent me here."

"Who?"

"Harry."

"Grenada Harry or Jamaica Harry?" From a blue tin she threw out stale coffee grounds into the soil beneath the window. A little grit blew into my eye.

"Grenada Harry," I said, rubbing my face.

"Who you to him?"

"I'm working at his place."

She touched a loose roller, winding it back to her scalp. "Theresa's in 4-B. You know her?"

"Uh . . . well . . . no."

She tipped her head to the side. The rollers swayed a moment later. "Your shit don't sound right," she said. "Go on away from here, girl. Tell Harry he better know somebody before he send them over here."

"But wait!" I couldn't hide my desperation. "I really need to see Theresa. Mr. Harry said she might have a room. Can you get her for me, please?"

"Hmph," she said. "I ain't makin' no promises, but I'll go and talk to her."

She shut the window before I could say thank you. I waited on the floor of the blue and brown triangular-tiled lobby for a buzzer that never buzzed.

About a half hour later, the woman from the window, her hair out of rollers and down around the ball of her cheeks, came bursting through the double glass doors. She was shocked to find me on the floor in front of her. "Theresa ain't buzz you in yet? You island people is too much," she said.

She gestured for me to follow her. A ripped burgundy rug lay through the middle of the interior lobby. Narrow doors on each side led to bottom-floor apartments. A leaf-patterned crown molding was nailed low, into the dusty, concrete ceiling. A patch of brass mail-boxes, their doors ajar, sat to the left of the stairs.

The woman began briskly up the steps. I tried to follow, but my lungs couldn't keep with her pace. She stopped halfway up the next staircase. "What's wrong with you?" she shouted. "You sick?"

I hung my head. I wasn't as sick as I had been, I wanted to say, but I was bone-tired.

"You got three more flights to go," she said. "I ain't got all day."

I made it to the top floor, exhausted, sweaty, but thankful. The hallway smelled of baked ham. My stomach howled. I hadn't eaten since the morning at Leroy's. Before that, one slice of pizza pie. I had been too afraid to nibble at Mr. Harry's burnt pan bottoms for fear of being fired on my first day.

"Good luck." The woman knocked. "Theresa! Theresa! That girl up here to see you."

Within seconds, the door flung open. A woman, tall as any I had ever seen, stood on the other side. She had a dark-brown complexion and bushy hair that stood a foot higher than her frame. It was dyed a vivid bronze. Her teeth, though crooked like the string on a wet tea bag, were white as bleached rice. Her nose, long and slender, her full lips like two wet cotton balls lying one on top of the other. She was probably the most striking woman I'd ever seen.

"Wha' ya want?"

"Mr. Harry sent me. Tole me you need somebody to rent a room."

She checked me over, then shook her head, emphatically. "Nah."

I was tired. I didn't even have enough energy to beg, yet I knew I had to say something. "I know I not lookin' right," I said. "I just now gettin' to New York after runnin' from some crazy people in Maryland. I left my chil'ren back home in Trinidad mont's ago. I started with Mr. Harry at the bakery and I been workin' there all day. If you let me stay I promise when I get my first set-a-money, it's yours."

She looked me over again, while I searched for a glimmer of compassion. "You got no deposit money, then you not stayin' here. Nah," she said, closing the door.

I slept on the trains again. It was harder than the previous nights. My uterus began to cramp around three in the morning, forcing me to find a toilet at a diner near the end of the Third Avenue line. The blood had stained my panties and the crotch of my already-filthy pants. I wrapped toilet paper into a firm mattress, tucking it between my legs, hoping the padding would suffice until I returned to the bakery and could figure out how to turn my last few dollars into enough money for a sanitary belt. I wanted nothing more than to bathe. My mind sprinted to hot sprays of water, a pink toilet, fluffy pink rugs.

I hated the idea of waiting on Fulton Street, moving from the corner of Brooklyn Avenue back toward Marcy, again and again, in search of him.

Twenty minutes later than I expected, Leroy rounded the corner. I cast my eye downward, kept in a straight line, and walked so close to him he couldn't have missed me.

"It's you!" He grabbed hold of my shoulders.

I looked up into his innocent face with fake surprise. "Hello," I said.

"Where'd you sleep last night?"

I refused to answer, making him want more. There was sadness in his expression.

"What time is it?" I said, tightening my shoulders.

He showed me his watch, which had given his beautiful brown wrist an Irish-green tint.

"I'm late!" I wrung my hands. "I should already be at the bakery."

Leroy held my arm. "Come, come," he said. "Come with me. Use the bat'room and brush your teet' before you show up at Mr. Harry's like that," he said. "It'll only take a few minutes to get yourself togedda."

I protested lightly enough for it to be overlooked. When we arrived at his mother's basement apartment, it was quiet. Leroy opened a pot lid, then flipped the empty pot over. "My mudda must be sleepin'." He seemed to be in shock. "Probably betta this way. Go and get yourself togedda."

I gently touched his arm, then walked into the washroom. Yes, I felt guilty. Desperation was not a good enough excuse for manipulation. Yet, there I was, stealing his mother's feminine products, stuffing them into my coat, hoping not to run into her on my way out.

The morning rush at the bakery required all hands up-front. I wrote down orders, cleared plates, wiped tables, anything and everything to get people moving before they missed their trains into Manhattan. It was after seven o'clock when the woman, Theresa, came in to order coffee and a pastry. She seemed to be a regular customer. Mr. Harry greeted her kindly and smiled into her oval face. They whispered to each other over the counter. Lime green reflected onto her fresh white blouse, while I was wearing the same clothes I had worn at her door. Theresa sipped her tea and bit into Mr. Harry's famous currant roll with the perfect flaked crust.

"Come again this night and we'll work somet'ing out," she said, brushing crumbs from her blouse.

I gripped the broom to my chest. "T'ank you," I said. "T'anks very much."

Chapter 19

MARCIA GARCIA

A poor landlady from Grenada with an even poorer tenant from Trinidad. It's true what they say: "When rain does fall, sheep and goat does have to mix!"

After helping Mr. Harry prepare the bakery for the next morning, I returned to Theresa's. She greeted me with a pat to the shoulder, then showed me around. Her place was smaller than I expected, and dim. At the entrance was a tiny oval table holding up a vase filled with fresh white tulips. To the left was the kitchen, maybe three paces long, with a square cut in the wall overlooking the living area: an old sofa, a wooden rocking chair, and a television atop a metal stand. A tiny window facing out onto the street was the only source of sunlight in the room. In the bedroom, Theresa had hung a baby-blue sheet from the ceiling down the middle of the room. A box spring with a soft quilt on the side with the window, a bouncy mattress on the side of the room with the toilet.

After the brief tour, she offered me a cup of tea. It was the first cup of decent tea—three lumps of brown sugar and plenty of milk—I'd had since leaving Trinidad. We sat together at her table, and with great humor and openness, we traded stories. I was in my thirties, Theresa was in her twenties. I had four children, she had five. I had had

Farouk, she had had Edward. I had come to America with proper papers, she had come for a two-week visit four years earlier, when Harry, who had known her from back home, introduced her to an American man who promised to marry her.

"Don't matter that I'm already married in Grenada." She laughed. "I just need Clive to marry me and help me bring up my chil'ren. I can't even go back to see them if my papers not straight. You know how hard it is to be away for four years?"

I couldn't imagine.

"You know you not bringin' your chil'ren to America on the money cheapskate Harry givin' you. You need to find a betta job," she said. "He talked me into lettin' you stay here, so he can be a good fella sometimes, but Harry can also be a real shyster."

"He tole me I can start work earlier and leave by t'ree o'clock. My plan is to leave there each day and knock on every door I can find."

"You have papers, right?" she said, as if reminding herself of what I'd told her earlier. "Lemme give you the name of this place. The jobs does still be under-the-table 'cause the white people wanta pay in cash and pretend like they ain't usin' you up. And they'll work you like a dog, but they'll pay more than Harry."

That night, after Theresa had gone to her side of the room, I sat and wrote a short letter to the children:

Hello All,

I'm dropping a line to let you know I'm keeping well. I left Maryland and have since moved to New York. I'm very busy with work. Hope all is well at home and that all of you are behaving yourselves while I'm away. Please let your father know I've written. I'll write again soon when I have a few more minutes to spare. I promise to send money in the next letter. The number at the bottom of this letter is to reach me only at nights. Please take as many coins as you can spare and go down to Port-of-Spain and call me so I can hear your voices. Continue to keep well. Love, Mammy.

The next afternoon, after I cleaned the bakery's kitchen, I found my way to the corner of Twenty-Third Street and Eleventh Avenue. Red and blue cargo ships filled the river. The smell of decaying fish saturated the air. Through the open lobby door of a hotel on the corner, two women showed half-moon bosoms and laughed with ship workers in rubber boots. Just next door was a short building with broken walls and cracked windows. I glanced down at the address to confirm that, indeed, that was the place.

A sheet of white paper with the word "jObS" written in black ink was taped to the wall next to the inside staircase. One flight up, four long lines of women waited in the stuffy corridor.

I stood at the back of the first line I came to. A beige-colored woman ahead of me, wearing bright orange lipstick and a ponytail on one side of her head, checked me out. "If you got paper, you go there," she said, pointing to a slightly shorter line at the other end of the building.

I thanked her and moved up the narrow corridor, and waited for another hour.

"Papers?" A young Negro woman was seated behind a wobbly folding table. The room where she sat was cooler than the corridor. The lights were yellow, the window cracked like a nest of spiders.

"You need to see them?"

"What you think?" She stuck a wad of chewing gum from her mouth onto the back of her hand, then stared down at stacks of paper on the table, while I dug into my waistband.

"This is a plane ticket stub and a letter. Where's your papers?" she said, shoving the loose pages back into the envelope and handing it over to me. She slurped the gum back into her mouth, then waved to the woman behind me, who had a grain of rice from her early dinner stuck to the collar of her shirt.

I held up my hand. "Wait." From my waist, I pulled out a second envelope, one I had taken from Mr. Harry's office when the first began to rip. "I got them mixed up."

The young woman flipped open my passport and read through my crumpled stack. "This is better. But this ain't get stamped. How'd you get outta the airport?"

"What?" I reached over the table and took the papers, searching the pages of my passport and the documents that both the embassy and Mr. Harlow had given me. Then, I remembered—Suzanne walking me through the line, waving me past the officials, making sure I could never leave and that no one could ever find me.

I pushed the papers back to the young woman and tried to remember all of the good things that had happened in the last few days: the old fella, Leroy, Mr. Harry, Theresa. "Please, let me have a minute to explain." And I began telling my story.

She listened, straining to understand the anxiety-induced deepening of my accent, telling me to slow down so she could get the facts straight, and when I got to the part where I had been locked in a Maryland barn, she stopped snapping her gum.

"You people got some stories." She opened to the picture page of my passport again, checking it and rechecking it against my face. "Look, you gonna need to go to that line down the hall. They *might* take pity on you, but with no references, I doubt it. We can help without good papers but not without references. White people in this country ain't interested in having nobody work for them, unless they checked out first," she said. "If that line don't work out, I'mma give you the name of somebody who can help you get your papers in order. Especially since they were filed. He ain't no Jesus Christ and he ain't cheap, but if you get your papers straight, you can find a real job." She handed me a card with an address, a phone number, and the name "Klein, Esq." written in large letters.

Mr. Klein's office was on the top floor of a yellow concrete building close to the corner of Twentieth Street and Ninth Avenue. There was a butcher on the first floor. The entire building smelled of rancid beef.

I rang a buzzer that crackled with static. I was sure that a thousand women before me had pushed that same button and that whoever was on the other side had taken their money, giving only a promise to do his best in return.

But I didn't know what other choice I had.

"I'll do my best," Mr. Klein said after I told him my story. While I had been speaking, his wolf-grey eyes had floated from the floor to the wall, reminding me that my story was probably no different than the thousand others.

"Your best?"

"Yes, Miss Garcia from Trinidad and Tobago, I'll do my best," he said. "Fixing a situation like this won't be easy. I'll have to write letters and explain how you slipped past immigration. Maybe find the people you say you were employed by in Maryland. I'll do my best."

Mr. Klein held the door open. I slipped off my coat and remained seated in his saggy-cushioned chair. He walked back to face me from behind his desk. He was wearing a battered pair of wing-tips and off-the-rack brown pants, which sat below a very round and very firm stomach. His beard was V-shaped, his glasses thick and a bit foggy.

He picked up a can of cola and watched my breasts as he drank.

"I don't pay until you find the best within you, right?" I said.

He smiled a little, but not enough to cover his annoyance. "How long did you say you've been here?"

"Long enough," I said.

He placed the cola can back on top of a two-inch heap of papers and twirled a pencil between three fingers. His eyes rose from my chest. "Long enough for what?"

"Long enough to know the people's ways not much different here than back home. To you I might only be a seamstress, but I'm no fool."

He placed his hands in his already-stretched blazer pockets. "Let me give you a bit of advice, Miss Garcia from Trinidad and Tobago. Without legal papers, you can be sent back home to your beloved country in ten seconds flat. Anybody can be your enemy. So the best thing you can do for yourself is to keep your mouth shut, lay very low, and come back with some money when I call you. If you want any chance of turning your luck around, it's gonna take real discipline on your part."

I received our first letter from Mammy on a rainy, windy Tuesday. I was soaked through to my panties, but didn't bother to change into dry clothes before I ripped open the envelope. I read each word over and over as if I would find something new buried behind the letters. I wanted the note to say that life in America had been terrible and that she would soon be on her way home.

But it didn't.

She mentioned moving about America, from Maryland to New York, like some great adventurer.

How could I write her back? How could we call her and crush her with the news?

Yvonne was the soft spot on her underbelly.

After I came back from Toco, neither Wesley nor Patsy said anything for days. It was pretty clear that both of them believed Yvonne's death was my fault. Of course, they were right. I knew, days before I put her into that boy's car, that if she got worse, the responsibility would fall on me.

Daddy had moved in two weeks after he returned from Toco. Although he didn't bring peace, he did bring stability. He was there every morning and every night. There was more money for food, there were rules, and there was somebody else who understood how grief felt, burning its way, like acid, through chest walls. I showed Mammy's letter to Daddy a few days after I got it. "Gawd," he said, reading the cheerful words written in blank ink. "I was hoping she'd never write to us," he said.

"Me too."

We both chuckled a little. "I have to tell her," he said. The seriousness of the coming act cut off our chuckle at its knees. "She won't wanta talk to allyuh until she can get herself togedda." He read the letter again, walking to the stove with it. "Your Aja and Ajee have a telephone. I'll call from there."

Daddy had never mentioned his family. By his rapid blinking, I could see it made him uncomfortable. "You know your Uncle Khalil went to school in America. He's a doctor now. Real smart. Like Yvonne was." His voice trailed off.

We both reached for the teapot. His hand touched mine and he squeezed it, just a bit.

MARCIA GARCIA

Mr. Harry paid me half of what I was owed for three weeks' worth of work. Fifty-two dollars. He told me he knew I had been taking loaves of bread at the end of the night. "Somebody betta pay for it," he had said. "Or alla you girls gointa be out of a job." Of course, I wanted to tell Mr. Harry to go to bloody hell, but I needed the money, and I also needed to stay in his favor because of his friendship with Theresa.

That Monday evening, after I left Mr. Harry, so angry I could've spit fire, I went back to Theresa's apartment. I had been searching for a second job every minute I wasn't sleeping or working and had found nothing but a one-dress job for an overweight woman who lived off Atlantic Avenue. I had mailed that job's eleven dollars to the children, but as I sat at Theresa's table, counting my stack of one-dollar bills, I had to wonder how in God's name I was going to bring four children to America with so little money.

"Fifty-two dollars he's givin' me? I owe you twenty," I said to Theresa, who hadn't seen a dime of rent from me. "What's left for the chil'ren? I tole them to call me and now I'm dreading it."

Theresa, who was preparing to leave for her second job at a salon, touched my back. "Just give me ten dollars for now. But if you can do me a favor and talk to that lawyer fella you met? I need some help with my papers."

"Sure. T'anks, Theresa," I said.

I smoothed George Washington's face with my fingers. "Mr. Klein's not gointa wanta hear from me again if I don't get him some money. If I could just sew, get a few clients, I could make a li'l extra—I know I can."

Theresa and I had often spoken about how much things had changed. How people preferred to buy clothes from shops, how the art of homemade clothing had died, especially in the States, and how I had come all the way to America for an old woman's hobby. "I have to run." Theresa put on her jacket. "I'll speak to my docta lady, Mrs. Silverman, about you. I sent her four people for a job already and she don't like none a them. Four hardworkin' women and there's somet'ing wrong with each one? She don't wanta hire nobody to help with that sick husband 'cause she feel guilty."

Theresa smeared on red lipstick, lining it below her actual top lip. "You no betta than the udda four, but you never know who she knows," she said. "Plan to go there tomorrow night, unless I tell you different, alright? Here's the address." She scribbled it down on a napkin. "I'll let her know you comin'. And please don't forget to call that lawyer for me."

After Theresa left, I placed the money into my bag, left a message with a woman in Mr. Klein's office, then I washed out my second pair of panties, hoping they'd be dry enough to wear by morning. I was taking out cockroach spray from under the kitchen cabinet when a draft of air blew onto my backside.

"You forgot somet'ing?" I called out to Theresa.

"Oh." It was a man's voice, then the click of the closing door. "You must be the girl Theresa was talking about."

Theresa hadn't told me anyone else had a key to the place. "And you are?" My words were steady, though the can bowed under the tightening of my fingers.

"I'm Clive," he said, tossing his brown plaid hat onto the table.

Theresa had told me about Clive. How he had helped her, how he had looked out for her in her times of need, how she had hoped he would someday keep his word and marry her. The memories of her kind words about him kept me rooted in place, despite the uneasy feeling in the pit of my stomach.

"Where's Theresa?" He peered toward the bedroom, though I suspected he would've been more surprised to have found Theresa there.

"At work. You want me to tell her you stopped by?"

He rubbed his nose with the front side of his hand. "Nah, I'mma stay here and wait 'til she comes back."

"Every bread does have a cheese," people back home liked to say. Though Clive wasn't a bad-looking man, he wasn't a good-looking one, either. He certainly didn't look like he belonged with Theresa. He was wide in the hips, thick in the midsection, about a foot shorter than her with cratered skin, small recessed eyes, short arms like a kangaroo, and jowls so broad they seemed swollen. He sat down on the rocking chair and put his feet atop the coffee table. I spied him through the cutout in the kitchen wall.

"I was about to spray. The smell might be strong. You wanta come back later?"

"Nah, I'm used to it," he said, waving his hand.

I shook the can and began to spray along the floorboards, the corners, behind the stove, wondering how quickly I could get myself out of there.

Then over the *shhhh* of the spray, Clive said, "He told me you were good-looking, but he ain't tell me you were this fine."

I threw the empty can into the trash.

"Yes, yes, yes, you are," he added.

The bag and the sweater I had borrowed from Theresa were on top of the television. Next to the rocker. All my money, my papers, everything important to me was in that bag.

"Did you hear what I said?"

I washed my hands in the sink under the cutout. The top of his lip vibrated. "Eh-eh, you said somet'ing? I didn't hear you over the spray," I said.

He searched my face hard. I forced a grin and began the walk toward the television with outstretched arms. Reaching for my bag, I listened for every whisper of movement, every breath besides my own. There was nothing. I clutched the sweater and bag with a trembling hand and moved toward the door.

"Where you going?" he said, bolting from the rocking chair. He latched his finger into the belt loop of my pants. I smacked his hand, which only made him grip harder. His arms were solid. He spun me around, yanked me into him.

"I have to get to work," I said. "Please get your hands off me."

"You ain't got another job." His breath smelled like currants.

He shoved his left hand down the front of my pants and I punched him. The *thmpf!* to his wide chest echoed. I scratched his face, then he snatched my hair and muttered something. Something I couldn't hear over my hectic breaths, something I couldn't hear over the sounds of my panic. I was weakening and he knew it.

He pushed me to the floor and straddled me. My lungs caved as he slapped his hand over my mouth and nose. I couldn't catch my breath. My head felt airy, the setting sun sent blue slivers of light through the window. *Are you willing to die here?* I was angry with myself—so angry with myself—for not fighting harder. *Did you come all the way to America to be raped by yet anudda bastard?* Inside my head, I screamed.

My mind raced back and forth between Trinidad and America, between my children and myself. I remembered how disappointed I had been when I learned I had given birth to each of my girls. I remembered how frightened I had been when I thought of some man—a man like Clive—putting his hands on them, making them feel as I had felt as a child, as I was feeling again. I was failing them. Even if I couldn't fight for myself, how could I not fight for my children?

"Get off!" I finally screamed into his muffling, sweaty hand.

I rocked my body from side to side, side to side, side to side and gnawed at the skin of his palms with my teeth. As I struggled beneath Clive, I felt my body loosen and my newfound outrage began to thrash beneath the surface of my scalding skin. I bucked up then down, up then down, up then down, trying to throw him off. He held on strong, pulling away at my shirt, pulling away at my bra, becoming more angry as he sensed my growing rage. He smashed my head into the foot of Theresa's rocking chair. The breath I had left, escaped. I was losing myself.

I was back with the children. I had so wanted to protect them. I had so wanted to make sure they would be all right. I had thrown all the books to the floor in search of magazine pages that would teach me how to teach them.

"Disturb the balance. Strain the neck, shoulder, elbow, wrist, back or ankle, so they can't resist you." I had made the children repeat those sentences over and over.

I pushed up my middle finger and jabbed Clive in the left eye. He screamed out, grabbing for his face, releasing his thigh-grip just enough for me to throw him off. I scrambled up from the floor, holding my blouse together with my hand and slamming the tip of my shoe into the side of his fleshy neck.

"Bitch!" he yelled.

I jammed my heel into his head and again reached for the borrowed sweater and bag. I ran as fast as I could.

I slept on the trains again that night. I knew the routine. I wasn't afraid.

The next morning I met Mr. Harry, before the other employees arrived. I must've looked like hell. "How could you tell that man to come and look for me?"

The sun was coming up, bright and strong over Brooklyn. It was garbage day; the vermin had ripped through the thin plastic bags, the streets and sidewalks were littered with bones and badly soiled cloth diapers. Mr. Harry unlocked the door, denying everything without uttering a word.

"You cheat me out of my money then you send that Clive to pull off my clothes and t'row me to the floor?"

Mr. Harry twisted the door handle and hurried me in. He seemed shocked.

"He tole me you tole him how I looked, when I worked, all kindsa t'ings that would pique a man's interest. Why?"

He fussed with the register. "I didn't mean you harm. I was just talkin'."

I went into his office. He had a needle and thread, I knew from one of the other girls, in a cabinet drawer. I sewed my shirt and washed up in the employee washroom. I met Mr. Harry waiting for me outside the door.

"I found out who was stealing the bread." He handed me ten dollars.

I wanted to ask him when I would get the rest, but he was already shamed and I still needed the job. The day turned out to be long and, before I knew it, I was starting late into Manhattan. I took the Eighth Avenue train and suprisingly arrived at West Seventy-Second with time to spare.

Trees were in bloom. Pink and white petals were wind-scattered along the pavement. Horse-drawn carriages plucked straight from a fairy tale and shiny red bicycles with spinning wheels headed toward crowded ice-cream stands. Lovers walked arm in arm and carefree children played games while their mothers hung behind them, pushing prams filled with napping babies. I hadn't stopped almost since I had arrived in New York City. Being there, on that street, made me feel hopeful, as if having good luck and a good life was contagious.

The Ruxton Towers, a redbrick building with brass-framed double doors and slabs of stone around the archway, didn't appear that different than some buildings in Brooklyn. Until I walked inside.

The lobby's brown marble floors were white-veined and spotless; the leaf-patterned ceiling molding was backlit by amber-bulb brass chandeliers. The large mahogany desk to the left was rich in detail and even richer with an attendant behind it. "May I help you?" The man straightened his uniform jacket.

I handed him the napkin and explained that I was Theresa's friend.

"The Silvermans don't like for me to call up anymore. Please, go up and knock on the door quietly. Mrs. Silverman is there."

I got off the elevator at the fifth floor. I grew anxious as I moved down the pale green runner toward the end of the hall, searching the brass numbers.

A short white woman with thinning ginger-colored hair and a chest twice the size of mine, opened the door. She had tender brown eyes, though they fell sharply at the outer edges. "Yes?"

"Hello. I'm Marcia."

The woman narrowed the crack between us. Her pupils grew small in concentration.

"Theresa's friend," I said.

She sighed, then shook her head. "Theresa didn't tell me she was sending yet another friend."

My heart raced. "She tole me you were lookin' for somebody to help with your husband. She tole me to come and meet you today."

Mrs. Silverman paused, reading my face. She widened the crack. "What's your name again?"

"Marcia."

"How do you spell that?"

"M-a-r-c-i-a."

"Like Mar-sha, but pronounced with a see-a?"

"Sure," I said.

She rubbed her open palms along the door. "You're already here . . ."

Mrs. Silverman shuffled in stockinged feet along her wood floor. Colored blocks covered the hallway and papers were piled atop a six-seat, formal dining table to the right. There was a parlor to the left, with canary-yellow furniture topped with thick, clear plastic and at least two weeks of unfolded laundry in wicker baskets on the floor.

"How do you know Theresa?" Mrs. Silverman asked.

The wall, just above a wooden-framed television, had a family picture, in which Mr. and Mrs. Silverman and their children smiled.

"We share a place," I said.

Mrs. Silverman's brows crumpled. She pointed to a chair at her kitchen table. "Would you like some coffee? I was just going to pour myself another cup."

"No t'anks," I said.

She threw black coffee into a mug, then sat down across from me. "You probably know my husband has cancer and that I'm a physician," she said. "There isn't time between work, children, his business, and his illness to teach someone about what we need." She chopped hard clumps of white sugar with the end of her spoon. "My dream once was to wake up one morning and feel like I've slept. To have someone who can manage his meals, his doctor visits and who can sleep in the room some nights and attend to him, while I nap. But I've given up trying to have that." The cling of her spoon reminded me of home. "I've conveyed all this to Theresa but she keeps sending you people, who keep coming because each one of you is trying to take care of your families. But I can't help you or anyone, any more than I can help *my* family." She took a deep breath. "I'm sorry you wasted your time."

"I understand." And I did. Mrs. Silverman hadn't gotten to that point yet where she could accept help. Nobody could rush a woman to that place.

I turned to leave when a tall thin man wearing red flannel pajamas blocked the doorway. "Honey, I was calling you." Mr. Silverman had a coin-size bump at the top of his nose and wore thick, circular glasses that covered much of his ghost-white face. His teeth were sharp and seemed to elbow one another for space in his mouth.

"Sorry. This is Theresa's friend." Mrs. Silverman put on a big, tired smile.

Mr. Silverman leaned against the threshold of the door, as if he needed it to hold him up. "Hello there." He smiled warmly but continued to block my path while he carried on a gentle-voiced conversation with his wife, who had moved to the other side of the kitchen to find a missing bottle of medicine.

"She needs help. She's just too overwhelmed to know it," he whispered. "But good luck to you."

I left Manhattan feeling beaten, only to arrive back at Theresa's to find her seated at her table, next to a bouquet of fresh red roses and a bag filled with my belongings.

"Theresa . . ."

She held up her hand. "You can't stay here no more."

"Theresa . . ."

"I didn't know he was gointa come here. His face was bruised-up and the place was a mess. You musta done somet'ing to make Clive act crazy. I know how you does like to walk around the place." She shifted herself away from me, not wanting me to see she didn't believe her own words. "This apartment is in Clive's name and he helps pay the rent. That's why I didn't have to bodder you about getting me that twenty dollars. Clive does help. Clive is the reason my chil'ren not starving back home. And Clive is the only way I'll get them here." Theresa reached for a rose petal, lifting it slightly, stroking it gently. "Even if sometimes he's not so nice, I does have to do right by Clive."

"I understand," I said, pushing the brown bag under my arm. "Be well. And t'ank you."

The sky had blackened by the time I stepped off the concrete patio. A window creaked open above my head. "Did you ever talk to that lawyer fella for me?" Theresa yelled down.

"Left a message for him to call me back."

"Alright." She paused as if considering if she should say the next thing on her mind. "Somebody from back home called for you. He called a few times. I didn't know if you were coming back so I tole him you probably wouldn't be living here anymore. Sorry," she said. "When you find a place and get a number, let me know and if he calls again, I'll give it to him."

"Was it one of my chil'ren?" I asked, staring up into the black outline of her bushy head.

"No," she said. "It was a man."

In Blanchisseuse, the old people used to say, "Every day is fishing day but not every day is catching day."

I gave the same story and Theresa's note to the evening doorman. He seemed too afraid of Mrs. Silverman to call up. He rang for the elevator but warned me of his impending wrath if I was telling an untruth.

It was almost ten o'clock when I knocked on Mrs. Silverman's door again. She was well beyond angry. She bit her lip while she spoke. "Excuse me? Why are you here? Again. Who let you upstairs? I will call the front desk and have you removed if you don't leave right this minute."

She was wearing a white robe that had a fresh coffee stain on the front. She hadn't been sleeping. She didn't sleep. She was one of those women who stayed awake while everyone else in her life slept.

I held up my hands. "I'm sorry," I said, trying to force her to meet my eyes. "I was t'inking about what you said. About being tired. And your dreams." I was taking the biggest risk of my life as I stood on the other side of a very thick, unwelcoming door. "I won't tell you a sad story because my story isn't sad. It's just a story. Like yours. I came back here because I was once a girl who helped my mudda fight a disease that no one in my country knew was cancer until she was already dead. I took care of a fadda whose legs just stopped working one day and I had to mind my sista's sick chil'ren after she died in chilebirt'. I've had to take care of sick people I love, Mrs. Silverman. I know what that does do to you. It does kill you from the inside out while everybody's watching you, t'inking how brave you are, t'inking how well you're keeping it togedda. Let me help you," I said. "Yes, I need the money. But I also need a day-to-day reminder to keep me fighting this fight. I will help you if you can just give me a reason to keep being here."

Mrs. Silverman's eyes filled with tears. She led me once again into her kitchen, where we whispered underneath her soft striplights, between her whitewashed walls, atop her bright red rugs filled with cracker crumbs, about a woman's life lost between death and sacrifice. I took her empty coffee cup from the table and quietly replaced it with a cup of warm milky tea with sugar. She fell asleep on the kitchen chair while I slept on the floor outside Mr. Silverman's bedroom door, listening for the call of need; a call that a woman, to be a woman, must grow accustomed to listening for.

The next day during Mr. Silverman's nap, Theresa brought the Silverman children home from school. "I don't know how you did it," she said, "but I'm happy you're here." Helping the Silverman daughter unpack her schoolbooks, she added, "I spoke to Mr. Klein. He said he could probably help me. If you does need a place to stay on the weekends, you can come by me. And if that fella calls again, I'll give him this number to call, alright?"

Day after day I waited for Theresa to tell me that the man, who I was sure was Farouk, had called again. But as the days passed I had to put aside my longing and focus, instead, on keeping Mr. Silverman, who seemed to be getting sicker, out of those dark places. We watched television, we laughed, chatted, and after lunch, when he napped, I would sit next to him and get to do the kind of slow, thoughtful sewing I enjoyed most. The kind of intricate hand-sewing—backstitches, chain stitches, slip stitches—that made the hard times with Mr. Silverman more purposeful, the kind of slow and wistful sewing that made waiting for another call almost bearable.

Mrs. Silverman said she would pay me at the end of every week. My plan was to put most of the money into the *susu* that me and Theresa had joined. The collection hand would be equal to half the money needed to buy a ticket for one of the children to join me. I hoped by the time it was my turn to receive it, Mr. Klein, who I planned to pay regularly, would have my paperwork straight.

From Saturday morning to Sunday at noon, I was free to do as I pleased. My first Saturday off, I shopped for food, then, after Theresa swore that Clive was home with his wife and children, I went back to her place and listened to eight-tracks of calypso and reggae music she had bought from a guy near Nostrand Avenue, praying the whole time that the phone would ring for me.

The next Tuesday, before Theresa left the Silvermans' apartment for the day, we crossed paths in their narrow hallway. She was planning a party. Clive wasn't coming.

"This Saturday?" I said.

"Come and have a li'l fun."

"I betta go up to Fifth Avenue and get my good dress off the layaway." I laughed. "I'll pick up some t'ings on my way there."

I was at Theresa's by noon. She filled me in on the party details. It seemed she had invited every West Indian immigrant she had met since arriving in America.

"By the way," she continued, "that fella called again earlier. I didn't know what time you were coming today. I gave him Mrs. Silverman's number and he tole me to tell you he'd call on you tomorrow."

"Why you didn't tell me that first?" I said.

"Knowing ten minutes earlier wasn't gointa make him call back today," she said.

I wanted to run back into Manhattan and wait by the phone, but I knew Theresa was right. I had to put the phone call out of mind and try to enjoy the evening.

Theresa and I squeezed ourselves up in her kitchen and cooked well into the night. She made a pot of rice and peas, mushier and saltier than mine, along with a tasty, spicy chicken that reddened my ears with one bite. After she was finished with the two burners, I prepared stewed beef in a thick soy sauce I had found in a Filipino market, and fried shark I got from the fish store on Fulton. For dessert, I put together a quick quick version of a rum cake and two pans of *cassava pone*, sweet enough and burnt enough, on the bottom and edges, to make anyone who knew what was right, happy.

By eleven o'clock the people were flowing between rooms and neighbors' apartments. Theresa's breakfast table had been turned into a card table; the rocking chair and couch, now in the bedroom, were piled high with spring jackets and sweaters. We had lined up a dozen folding chairs along the perimeter of the walls, creating a dance floor big enough for Theresa to run from a big-bellied man with a head that topped off at her bosom, who wanted nothing more than to commence a good grind.

Of course, nobody showed up empty-handed. Our stomachs were full full from the extra food, our heads were light from liquor. Half the people who poured in hadn't been invited. As neighbors walked the street below, they heard the roar of the crowd through the open windows and welcomed themselves inside, hoping to get warmth from the somewhat chilly night, hoping to feel a bit of what they had missed about being home. Even Leroy passed through, hugging me and eating a plate of food I had dished out for him while we chatted. "I'm happy t'ings are alright with you," he said.

After Leroy left, I got on the floor with some fella, following his steps, trying to keep up with his moves, trying to let the music seep in, and after some time, I got the hang of it again.

Chapter 20

FAROUK KARAM

"What you doing here, Farouk?"

My eldest brother, Abdul, the banker, was the most successful of the Karam clan, the child who made my parents the proudest. He was tall, though not very handsome, had married a quiet Hindu girl, ran his life with integrity, and managed to keep up with everybody in the family, except, of course, me.

"I need to use the phone."

"You calling overseas?" he said, moving into my mother's kitchen behind me.

I had been there four times and had called and called and called the number Marcia had written in the letter and, still, I hadn't reached her. I had finally gotten the correct number and had returned to Valsayn to call her again.

"I need to speak to my chil'ren's mudda."

Abdul crossed his arms and stood before the phone. "Ma and Daddy are in Tobago."

I was sure he knew I already knew that. "And?"

"And you should seek permission before you come into their home and run up the bill. I shouldn't have to tell you this."

I cheupsed and reached around him for the phone.

My brother grabbed my hand.

"Release your hand, brudda," I said. I was stronger and angrier than Abdul could ever hope to be, but I didn't want to fight him. "It's important that I speak to her."

"I know you been here already. What's so important it can't wait until Ma and Daddy come home?"

I smacked his hand, knocking the receiver onto the floor with a loud crash. "My chile is dead, Abdul! My chile is dead! Is that enough of a reason?"

Suddenly, I began to weep. I was angry with myself for not being able to keep it inside. My big brother took me into his thick arms and held me tight like he had when I was a child. "I'm sorry," he whispered.

"The mudda left to take a job in the States," I sobbed. "I went prospecting. Got word of where I could gather up a li'l gold in B.G. to make some fast money for them chil'ren's care. Made a li'l change too. But when I got back, I find out Yvonne had taken ill. I been trying to reach the mudda, but I haven't talked to her yet."

Abdul had never met my children. Or Marcia. Never even seen their faces in a picture. He rubbed the back of my head. "Come, let's call her, togedda," he said. "She needs to come home for the *daan sanskara* and settle the chile's spirit."

"Yvonne's already buried, Abdul. She was buried before I got back to Trinidad. My second oldest, Jackie, was by herself and it was the best she could do. I don't wanta make her feel like she did somet'ing wrong."

He nodded, pulled the phone's cord and dialed the number I had written on the back of a cigarette box. The phone was moist from Abdul's sweaty ear. The crackle from the connection was achingly loud. It rang and rang, and I feared that again I wouldn't reach her.

"Good afternoon," the voice on the other end finally said.

"Marcia?"

"Farouk?" Her voice sounded different across so many miles. It was tight and it vibrated as though she already suspected that something was wrong. "Where are the chil'ren? Are they there? Can you put them on the phone?"

"Marcia," I said, softly. It'd been years since I said her name in that way. "I'm so sorry."

"They couldn't come with you this time to call? It's okay. Let's make anudda time. I'm dying to talk to them."

"Marcia," I whispered. "No, it's not that."

She readjusted the phone. There was silence between the rustling. "Farouk? What's going on there?" Her tone was hard and forceful.

"Gawd, I hate calling you like this."

"Which one?"

"Marcia." I struggled to get my child's name to fall from my tongue. Struggled with how best to tell her mother. "Yvonne."

There was more static on the line as if it knew that we each needed the extra moment. "Yvonne, what?" she asked. "In the hospital?"

I knew she already knew.

"Farouk, don't break on me. You tell me what's happenin' there."

I shut my eyes, as though the coming words didn't want to be seen. "I'm here. I just . . . don't know how to tell you Yvonne is gone. She's not in the hospital."

The short whiffs of air on the other end were like the first breaths of a newborn. Furious and desperate.

"She died in Toco, with your fadda and Jackie there." I pushed through the pockets of air on the other end. "By the time I got back, she was already gone."

Marcia chewed on every word. "By-the-time-you-got-back?" she repeated.

"I was in B.G., prospecting. Trying to make some money. Jackie had already taken her to Toco." Even to me, my words, which were all true, sounded untruthful.

There was more static and faint words. Someone was speaking to her.

"Marcia? You there?"

I heard her say "alright"; then she said, "Yes. I'm here."

"I know you hate me," I started again. "But you must know I loved that chile too. I love alla them," I said.

"She was in so much pain," she whispered. "Why did I leave?"

"Marcia—"

"I *knew* she hadn't been feeling well. I *knew* it was serious and I kept trying to tell myself it was nutting. Nutting too serious. What kind of mudda am I?" I could feel something shift in her voice. "I didn't learn this lesson before, so God had to teach me again."

Her words trailed off as if they were following miles behind her mind.

"Listen to me," I said. "Don't do this. You're the best mudda. You've given your entire life for alla your chil'ren. All you ever wanted was to give them a betta life. Look at what you did with that chile. She was brilliant and beautiful and kind. Chil'ren aren't born that way. They must be made into them t'ings."

She bawled into the phone. "Why is He taking my chil'ren?"

I clawed around in what seemed like a vast desert for some gem to give her. "I didn't wanta tell you this now," I said. "But I feel you must know."

"Oh Gawd. What? Somet'ing wrong with one of the uddas?"

"No, they're all fine. They're crushed, especially Jackie, but they gointa be alright."

"Jacqueline," she said. "Oh Gawd, that chile must be dying." Marcia's breathing remained uneven. I wondered how much more she could take.

"Jackie has been t'rough a lot, but I'm here. I'm makin' sure alla them get t'rough."

I wanted her to say "t'ank you" or "I know," but her silence spoke volumes.

"When I went to Toco, I saw the boys there. With your fadda," I said. "They been living with him the whole time since they disappeared."

Abdul looked over at me, as if the one side of the conversation he could hear was now too confusing for him to follow.

"What boys?" she asked.

I paused, trying to remember their names, but my mind was a blank.

"Your boys," I said.

The phone crackled again.

"With my fadda?"

"Somebody took them from Blanchisseuse that night and brought them to Toco. Tole your fadda you needed them gone so that . . . so that . . . you could be free to marry me."

"Whatya saying?"

"They're alive. And well. I saw them with my own two eyes."

"My uncle," she said.

The static ate the rest of her words. "Marcia?"

I sat across from my brother, waiting to hear Marcia respond, but the line on the other end of the string, hundreds of miles away, had gone empty.

MARCIA GARCIA

After the phone call with Farouk, I dried my eyes and went back into the room to check on Mr. Silverman. I tried to keep my mind off of Yvonne, but it was as if her spirit had been waiting for me to hear the news before she came. I could do nothing else without feeling her around me, blowing into my ear, giggling in the folds of my neck, laughing at the dimples in my bamsee cheeks. I could feel her in my arms, the softness of her hair on my shoulder, I could smell the coconut oil of her skin, I could see her eyes flicker as she slept in the sunlight. She broke into a happy skip as we walked to the market. She tossed her long black braid behind her shoulder as she poured over her studies. I could see the fold of her toes, the length of each finger, the size of her earlobes, the crimp of each eyelash.

I was scared that I might stop remembering. I was scared of being crushed by remembering.

I wanted to get on the first plane and properly bury my child. Make sure her grave was marked. Make sure that even as she lay beneath hot soil, she was under a tree and could hear the ocean.

But home would've paralyzed me, killed me with an unbearable guilt—mothers are never forgiven. I had to find a way, other than going home, to close that hole in me. Some other way to live so the grief didn't gnaw at me day and night.

The old me, the real Marcia, had been all but destroyed when those boys disappeared. In her place stood a monster—the Sucouya witch, I sometimes called her. She was angry, bitter, loveless. She was how I had protected the little bit of me that was left. She was how I had gotten out of bed after the boys had been gone for months. She was the reason I was able to sit at my Singer and work into the night after Farouk left me with a new baby. She was how I had raised four children alone. She was what kept me alive on the streets of New York. She wanted to survive.

After Farouk's call, I sat quietly next to Mr. Silverman's bed, watching his chest rise and fall, listening to the quiet hum of his humidifier, wondering why the patterns in my life repeated themselves. Who was responsible for all that damn misery? Had the Sucouya given me strength? Or was she fear, dressed up like a witch, pushing anything and everyone I had ever loved away? What kind of weak, pathetic, crumbling human being would I have been without her? Walking the streets open, exposed, waiting to be somebody's victim again. But if she was supposed to protect me, why did I still feel the pain she was supposed to protect me from?

"That man been comin' here almost every day," one of the factory girls whispered during a break. I knew she wanted that news to uplift me, but knowing that Mr. Aldous hadn't forgotten me only made me more miserable.

I worked late—until after five o'clock—forcing myself to think of nothing but the hum of the heavy, hot machinery beneath my hands. When I stepped outside, the sky had taken on a pink-orange hue that threw me right back into grief's arms. Yvonne would call it "the papaya sky." And once I had told her how I wished I could have lipstick the color of that sky.

"I'll buy that for you," she had said.

Gawd, why did it all have to hurt so much? Why did every pair of skinny legs and long feet remind me of her?

Mammy told me that I was never to say I was tired, because a child who hadn't walked in her shoes couldn't understand tired. But that day, as I walked home, I could've told Mammy for certain that I understood tired.

I turned the curve onto my road, relieved not to see Wesley smoking cigarettes with a bunch of good-for-nothing boys and frustrated to see the outline of the basket of wet clothes I had asked him to hang early that morning. *I'll leave his clothes right in there,* I was thinking, when I spotted a shadowy figure in the road. An odd remnant of sunlight blocked the man's face, but his forceful glide in my direction was familiar. The dogs and chickens gave sound behind him. I had missed that part of the day when children ran wild after school and mothers rushed home to clean and cook before settling into their evenings of loose laughter and more work, and panic swept across me. Extra hours on the machine had meant work at home left undone. As the man strode toward me with unwavering strides, the only thoughts I had were of the chores that lay past him.

The papaya sky had transformed into a midnight blue. The intensity of the man's stare, the whites that seemed to grow as big as the harvest moon, fed a longing for life buried deep, deep within me. Mr. Aldous stretched out his long arms and pulled me tenderly into him.

1964
"MAMA DIS IS MAS"
BY LORD KITCHENER

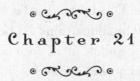

Chapter 21

JACQUELINE KARAM

For eight months, Mr. Aldous and I met almost every weeknight, sometimes for just a few moments, sometimes for hours. We didn't plan for our meetings to be a secret, but secrecy was easier, as we tiptoed back and forth between friendship and love, between forbidden and permissible.

In those eight months, Mr. Aldous became my confidant, my teacher, my companion, and my love. He was the only one who remembered my birthday and the only one who acknowledged Yvonne's. For me, a bouquet of wildflowers in yellows and blues. For Yvonne, a quiet birthday song, while the sun rose over the Northern Range.

"You ever been to a proper fête?" he asked one Friday morning, at the gate of the schoolyard.

"I never been to a fête, proper or improper," I said.

"What kinda Trinidadian are you, gal?"

That night, I stole from Patsy's dress box a pretty sleeveless purple dress with a simple A-line and ruffles along the neck. I had Mammy's white pumps hidden behind my back.

"Where you going?" Daddy said.

"To my friend Angela's house. A few gals from the primary school getting togedda for a lime-'n'-t'ing."

"Oh yeah?" Daddy put down his newspaper to read my face. "Watch yourself. Your name represents you. And remember, if bad guys can knock off the President of the United States, they can surely get you, too."

I didn't know where Daddy thought I'd be that night, but in a million years I knew he wouldn't think I'd be with Mr. Aldous at a steel band festival in the middle of an open field, with the star-filled black sky hanging over my sweating body.

The *ting-ting* of the pans, the four-five rhythms of the panmen, the *cling-cling* of the fellas in the crowd tapping to the beat on glass bottles with whatever metal objects they could pull from their shallow pockets. "A Trini fête," Mr. Aldous said. The people wined and jumped and jumped and wined. *Jump up, Trinidad! Jump up!* Hundreds of Trinidadians poured in from as far south as Fyzabad and from as far north as Matelot, packing themselves against one another in untainted joy. It wasn't Carnival. There were no tourists, no lines at the airport, no new road pavings. It was just Trinidad. Trinis in all their colorful splendor, gathered to enjoy the beauty of the music and the life we, the descendants of African slaves, Indian indentureds, defeated Spaniards, French farmers, robbed Amerindians, Chinese plantation workers, and British plantation owners, had created.

Mr. Aldous held me long and hard. We wined up the place until our knees were sore. We sang lyrics to songs we had once listened to on home radios. We laughed and drank rum 'n' coconut water. We ate warm roti stuffed with curried chickpeas, potatoes, and tender chicken straight from a hot pot lit by fire.

"You alright?" Mr. Aldous said as we stood next to the food tent, the burn of pepper sauce stinging our lips.

"Very alright," I said.

He kissed me in a cloud of thick white smoke. His lips were soft like flower petals, his tongue light like the air.

· · ·

I smiled through Saturday and well into Sunday. I kneaded dough on the wooden *chouke* for Daddy's Sunday roti and boiled callaloo bush in coconut milk. I smiled right up until the moment Philip Aldous showed up at the door.

Daddy glanced up from the newspaper. "You expectin' somebody?"

Patsy had been working regularly and wasn't home much. Wesley had won back some of Mammy's clients and stayed busy picking up and dropping off clothes. So, I knew, before I saw the face, that whoever was standing outside was a story that would unfold around either Daddy or me.

"Who you looking for?" Daddy said to Mr. Aldous. Daddy was wearing his navy-blue pajama bottoms and a white cotton jersey-vest.

"Are you Mistah Farouk Karam?" Mr. Aldous said.

My hands shook. I could see only a portion of Mr. Aldous's face. It was taut, and his voice, though deepened, vibrated.

"And you is?"

"My name is Philip Aldous. I was your daughter Yvonne's teacher."

"Oh, I see," Daddy said, seeming none too pleased. "Well, come t'rough."

Mr. Aldous stepped inside, and I moved about the kitchen, wearing Mammy's apron, pretending his presence meant nothing to me.

"Jackie, say hello to Yvonne's teacher," Daddy said.

"Good afternoon," I said, lowering my eyes.

"Good afternoon," Mr. Aldous answered. "It's nice to see you again, Jacqueline."

It was something about the way he said my name or maybe the way he said "again" that made Daddy's neck flinch. Daddy held out his hand to offer Mr. Aldous the good chair—the recliner. Mr. Aldous sat on a kitchen chair. "You'd like some mauby, a li'l ginger beer or some Scotch, maybe?"

Mr. Aldous rubbed his palms together and smiled. If he had known Daddy was testing him, he wouldn't have been smiling so wide. "Sure, sure, a glass of mauby would be very nice, t'ank you."

Daddy sat in Wesley's recliner and slowly folded his newspapers in quarters.

I hurried to our new icebox to pull out the small pitcher of boiled-bark drink Daddy had been saving for his dinner. He had offered it and I had no choice but to give it to Mr. Aldous.

"T'ank you." Mr. Aldous placed his fingers around the tall glass, making sure not to touch my hand.

I walked back to my chouke, picked up my pin, and rolled out the now crusty-topped dough. I pushed hard against the white mound. Had Mr. Aldous lost his mind sometime between Friday night and dawn on Sunday? Had he come to declare his intentions? If he had had any sense, he would've talked to me first. I could've told him not to bother Daddy on a Sunday before dinner. And not to bother Daddy at any time on a Monday or a Tuesday, a Wednesday, Thursday, Friday, or even a Saturday, with any nonsense having to do with me and some man—any man—even a decent man, like himself.

After a few moments of chatting about the weather and cricket, Daddy asked the burning question: "So, what can I do for you, sir?"

Mr. Aldous scooted up to the edge of his chair and reached into his shirt pocket. He took out several sheets of folded paper.

"Well, I comin' for a few t'ings," he said. "I've been meaning to come here for quite a while, but the timing hasn't been ideal."

Daddy rolled the corners of his paper in his fingers. "The timing hasn't been ideal" was what Daddy would tell us every time he missed a week or two or three of seeing us. "The timing hasn't been ideal" in my family meant you weren't quite important enough to cause someone to break away from all that was *really* important. If Mr. Aldous had talked to me first, I could've told him that too.

"I have here in my hand, a li'l project Yvonne had been working on at school before she . . . when she stopped coming," he said. "She loved to write very much and she wrote a few beautiful pieces for her two sistas, you, her mudda, and her brudda. She didn't finish the one for the brudda, but she gave it a good start. I t'ought you might wanta have it."

He stood and placed the papers in Daddy's four-fingered hand. I caught Mr. Aldous staring at the missing digit.

"I wanta say how very sorry I am for your loss," he said to Daddy. "She was the brightest, sweetest chile I'd ever met in my life. I'm just not saying this. She held a very special place in my heart and the hearts of many at the school. We want you to know how much we cared for her there."

Daddy's jaw tightened. He squeezed the papers in his hand. "You held on to this for so long?" The meaning was clear to me. "T'ank you," Daddy quickly added. "This will mean a lot to alla us."

Mr. Aldous bowed his head and scooted back in the chair, as if making himself more at home. "Mr. Karam, I've also come here to talk to you about anudda matter."

"Excuse me, Daddy," I said. "I'm almost finished and I need to run to Aunty Baba's for somet'ing, quick quick."

"Jacqueline." Mr. Aldous stood up from the chair. "I'd like for you to stay while I speak to your fadda."

Daddy pulled his neck out of the comfy little hole where it'd been resting and settled his gaze on Mr. Aldous's face.

"Go on," he said to Mr. Aldous, signaling with his hand that I was to keep put.

I waited next to the stove. If only Mr. Aldous would've done me the courtesy of asking how I wanted the nail to be inserted into my coffin. "Straight and t'rough the heart," I would've said.

"Well, as I said, I should've come sooner, but my feelings . . . well, my feelings weren't even known to me any earlier than these past few mont's." Mr. Aldous folded his hands between his open legs. "I no longer feel it proper to carry on as I've been without being clear to you, the fadda, about my intentions."

Daddy's forehead creased. He did not look away from Mr. Aldous.

"Let me say, as simply as possible, I have fallen very hard for your

second-oldest daughter, Jacqueline. She's a lovely girl and I greatly
enjoy her company. As I sit here with you I don't know where this'll
lead, but I can assure you that I have her best interest at heart."

Daddy unfolded his paper, resting it facedown on his lap. "Whatya
want from me now?"

"Your blessing, Mr. Karam. That's all."

Daddy flipped his thumbs over and under each other. He sat back
into the recliner, pretending to consider Mr. Aldous's request. "So, let
me get somet'ing straight," Daddy said, in that tone I knew all too
well. "You sittin' in my house tellin' me my daughter is your woman
and you just now comin' to ask me if this is alright?" Daddy's voice
was not much above a whisper. "I have a good mind to cut ya right
here, eh? She got to be ten years younger than you, man." He could've
stopped there, except he wanted Mr. Aldous to have a bellyful of bad
news. "She got no idea about the world, about men, about nutting.
And you want me to trust you? A man who does be sneaking off with
my daughter *before* and sometimes *after* work? A man who does drop
her off at the junction *before* Five Rivers so as not to have to run into
me? You t'ink I didn't know? You crazy or what?"

I leaned against Mammy's Primus. What in Gawd's name had
Mr. Aldous been thinking? Had he forgotten that Daddy had killed
a man?

Mr. Aldous rose slowly from the kitchen chair. Daddy returned to
reading his newspaper. Mr. Aldous had worn his best dress pants and
his shiniest black shoes for the occasion. "Sir, let me say that I apologize if I offended you," he said. "I simply needed to take us out of the
dark, now that my feelings—our feelings—are clear. I meant no harm
to Jacqueline, and I intend, t'rough my actions, to show you as much."

Daddy studied the international cricket headlines. "If that's true,
then I'll expect she'll never see you again," he said.

FAROUK KARAM

That teacher fella shouldn't have had to knock on my door to tell me about my own daughter's feelings. If Jackie was big-woman enough to have those feelings, she should've been big-woman enough to come and talk to me herself.

But Jackie wasn't a big woman. She was still a child.

I headed to Port-of-Spain to use the public phones outside the phone company building.

"Good afternoon, the Silverman residence," Marcia answered.

Since I had broken the news about Yvonne, we had had two brief conversations. Once *before* she had spoken to Jackie, Patsy, and Wesley. And once *after* the conversation with them when I had to tell her how emotional they had been after speaking to her and that it might be best to communicate through letters.

"It's Farouk," I said. "Nice to have a phone in the house, eh?"

"Very," she said.

It was the height of rush hour. The lines for the phones were getting long behind me. I had to wait for a bus to pass before speaking again. "Some man—some ole-man teacher of Yvonne's just finished knockin' the door. Come to tell me he loves Jackie. What kind of foolishness you does let happen in this house, Marcia?"

When Marcia spoke again, it was in a calm tone, a tone I had learned not to expect from her. "Fuck you, Farouk," she said. "You can't handle one li'l situation? Jacqueline's nearing eighteen and you pretendin' like she's ten? Them chil'ren need somebody to guide them, not somebody to t'reaten people to prove a point."

I wiped the phone on my pant leg. I had left my hat in the front seat of the motorcar and the sun was beating my head. "Eh-eh, you knew about this all along?"

"Knew Jacqueline had a crush on the man? I knew that. She does run her mout' too much, but she's lovely and smart. What man wouldn't want to get to know her?" she said. "Unless he's an ignorant jackass like you."

"Alright, alright," I said.

She tapped her nails on the backside of the receiver. "Farouk, he's a schoolteacher. And this is Jacqueline we talkin' about. It's not the same as before."

She knew me well.

"The man lookin' like he was worried I had a cutlass behind my back."

"No one can call him stupid." She chuckled. "But no matter. My susu hand is comin' around soon and I bringin' Jacqueline here first."

I wasn't sure what to say. "She doesn't need to come there. America is a tough place. Jackie's not made for that kinda life."

"Jacqueline first. Wesley a few mont's later. I gettin' the first susu hand the next time." It was like she didn't hear me.

"And Wesley's as fragile as a moth." I inserted another coin into the phone. The lady waiting behind me cheupsed. "Marcia, you hearin' me?" She drummed the receiver again with her nails. "And what about Patsy?"

"All that mess in the papers. Just one person at the embassy puts two and two togedda . . . It's already hard enough to get your grownup chil'ren into this place," she said.

"You leavin' her behind? That's what you doing?" I was angry that she was giving my opinion no weight. I was the father.

"If she doesn't come now, she'll come soon," she said. "I wouldn't *ever* leave and forget my chil'ren, Farouk."

1965

"PORTRAIT OF TRINIDAD"

BY SNIPER

Chapter 22

FAROUK KARAM

Marcia sent letters every week. Jackie worked every day and hoped to get a job at the airport, tagging baggage. Patsy worked at the Five Rivers' snackette, where she cooked a better batch of curry than the owner's wife and mixed up a mean rum punch. Wesley had taken a real interest in his mother's business and had even gotten a few male clients. Meanwhile, I drove my taxi and did my best to manage the home.

Ours wasn't a lovefest, but they came to understand that I was through with leaving.

I had driven a ten-hour shift and hadn't slept in over twenty hours when I arrived back to Five Rivers one late Saturday morning to find the children at home milling about in the kitchen. It wasn't often I had them all there like that.

"Come, let's gather up some uddas and get us a cricket match going," I said. I clapped my hands with excitement. Jackie, at the stove, kept her back turned. Patsy was blowing puffs of air onto purple fingernails. "Come, nah," I said. "Let we go."

They walked a few paces behind me, partly embarrassed and partly excited, while their father knocked on every door along the street searching for willing cricketers.

Within seventeen minutes we had twenty-two players. Eleven people on the Karam team and eleven people on the Marshall team, named after a family of seven boys who lived down the road with four uncles and a thick-legged mother who blew kisses at me every time she saw me coming.

"Back in 1953, at the Test Cricket match between India and the West Indies, every Indian in this country, even from way up in the bush, brought themselves into Port-of-Spain to Queens Park Oval," I said, as we walked to the field. "It was the first time India came to play in Trinidad. And you know who Indians were supporting?"

"The West Indies?" Wesley said.

"Nope." I looked behind to make sure our pickup team was all together. "India."

"You too, Daddy?" Jackie asked.

"You crazy? I'm a true 'n' true Trinidadian. As Trinidadian as a *guabine* fish." I bent over to pick up a shiny black pebble I had almost pressed back into the road. "I went with a whole buncha fellas from work, and back then, I was one of the few Indian boys on the force. Man, they gave me a hard time. Said I was gointa turn my back on the Trini players and any minute start cheering for my homeland.

"What was so great about that match was not the game, but how much fun we had that first day. The sky was like this one. Blue and clear, with not a cloud. Even the dry breeze felt the same. Everybody was drinkin' and eatin' and picnicking in the Oval. There was music and laughing, just a good good time. The bigwigs from Port-of-Spain were out in their fancy clothes. And people who couldn't afford tickets had climbed into the trees on the backside of Queens Park.

"What I trying to tell allyuh," I went on, "is that it's all in the fun, right?"

The Five Rivers field had a rough-sketched oval marked in the dirt, a makeshift wicket with three wooden stumps placed in a not-so-straight line, and a rectangular section of ripped grass for the pitch. The Marshall family, with their botched haircuts and gangly legs, moved toward us with lashing fingers to signal the impending cut-ass they would deliver.

The children and I had a brief chat with the seven neighborhood boys who had thrown in their lot with us that day.

"Wesley, I'm gointa make you the bowler, alright?"

Wesley had the expression of a frightened three-year-old child. I demonstrated a few times before handing him the ball. "Run up as hard as you can for as long as you need and t'row the ball over your head, fast and hard. Make that ball hit the wicket behind one of them Marshall boys, and don't let them touch it, alright?"

"I never bowled the ball before," Wesley said. "I can't do it."

"It's supposed to be fun." I gently pressed my fingers into his shoulders. "Just give it a shot."

Wesley turned to face the Marshall family. They were swinging their bats hard and fast over their shoulders.

We didn't win any trophies that day, but we did have plenty fun. Wesley was a terrible bowler. But he was a solid batsman. He had a helluva hook and a helluva pull.

Patsy was a wicked wicketkeeper. Without gloves or pads, she fielded like a tried-and-true cricket-playing man. And by the end of the game, Jackie, my bowler, could "toss one up." Her ball was slow, but tricky to hit.

We got back to the house full of stories from the day. I was tired as all hell and the last to go and wash up. I bathed quickly, planning to sleep until the middle of the next morning, but back inside I found Aunty Baba in the kitchen, talking to the children.

"Good night," she said. She pointed to me. "Can I have a minute?"

Marcia had been the only seamstress who could make real handsome clothes for a woman of Aunty Baba's size, and the prospect of living on her street in Five Rivers was the only reason Marcia hadn't given me more hell when I told her I needed to move the family. But Aunty Baba had never much liked me.

"What is it?" I said.

The children scattered.

"I know this is your place and the lady of the house does give you permission to run it as you see fit," Aunty Baba said. "But I gointa stick my nose in, whenever I does see them chil'ren in harm's way."

"Whatya saying?" She was two seconds from having me push her out with the heel of my foot.

"I saying, whatever stupidness you got into with that bat down in Tunapuna and she daughter is still in this house. You bring that darkness here, so you must take it out." Aunty Baba planted her oversize index finger into the tabletop. "Every time I set my foot here," she continued, "I does feel the coldness shoot straight t'rough my bones. Whatever you packed in your bag when you come, you need to pelt it into the fire, pelt it into the sea, pelt it somewhere, but get rid of it. Then you need to take a good bush bath. Until you do that, nutting but trouble will come, and them chil'ren been t'rough too much already."

She started to walk toward the door, but thought better of it. "I'm a God-fearing woman. And I does know evil when I see it. You, Farouk Karam, is still fulla that evil you went seeking. If you want your life to change, purge yourself. Purge your body, purge your soul! I tellin' you what you must do. This day." She pointed to the floor, like it would move to meet her, and then she waited for my response.

Aunty Baba watched me until she was tired of the quiet.

Damn roosters in Trinidad should all be shot! They does make you want to run outside and bash them between the eyes. I grabbed the bedpan from under the bed and relieved myself. Trying to sleep again was useless.

It was Saturday morning. I half-expected Jacqueline would be outside collecting the eggs. Instead, all I heard was quiet. A kind of quiet that made me think too damn much.

"Jackie, the sun gointa beat you to the day."

She stirred in the same mellow way she had as a little girl. "Everyt'ing okay?" she asked, through a long stretch and sleep-soaked voice.

"Get your sista up. I need everybody dressed."

By six thirty, the children were at the front of the house.

"Make sure you take your bath clothes. Then let's get in the motorcar," I said.

"I have plans," Patsy said, with folded arms.

"Your freedom papers burned. Come go."

I drove the three of them in a thick, unrepentant silence up the winding, mountainous North Coast Road, surrounded on all sides by hummingbirds, oil birds, and a scarlet ibis or two, against a backdrop of vivid greens. Every now and then, I caught Jackie's eyes, burning with curiosity, in the rearview mirror. Wesley, who was wide awake and seated next to me, stuck his head out of the motorcar and peered down to the sea below us. Patsy slept with the brightness of the morning sun toasting her face.

The roads to Blanchisseuse were far better than they had been twenty years earlier. We passed the rough waters of Maracas Bay, its fearless morning swimmers trampling the breaking waves. I couldn't remember the last time I had taken a swim in the coolness of the sea. And suddenly I longed for it. I longed to see Las Cuevas beach and its calm surf, and longed to touch the golden-flowered *poui trees* that covered the landscape. I longed to inhale the thick and sweet country air of Blanchisseuse and feel it welcome me back.

"Come, leave your belongings in the vehicle. Let's walk."

The children, having no memory of the place, walked cautiously.

Along the curvy main road I had strolled maybe a thousand times before, the sky threatened a light rain with its lackluster blue. The children straggled behind, picking their way along the broken road's terrain.

Marcia had given the house to me to manage many years earlier. And years after we'd separated, she had asked why I bothered taking care of the place. As I stood there with one less child, I knew the answer. Their story began in Blanchisseuse.

The latch on the gate was rusty. "Hello!" I yelled. "Good morning!"

I had long stopped collecting rent from the old man who lived there. The small bit of money hadn't been worth the trouble of hunting him down.

"You bring us all the way to Blanchisseuse for this?" Patsy cheupsed.

We strolled to the unstable front door. There wasn't a curtain in the window.

"Hello!" I said again.

I pushed open the door.

A strong gust of Marcia slapped me across the cheek. The cool temperature of the room. The table where she sewed. Every moment. Every second with her in that house. Patsy's first breath. Jackie's conception. The nights we spent holding each other. I had been there many times without her, but I had never felt her in that place in quite the same way I felt it that day, with my children's breath on my neck.

"Whose house is this?" Jackie asked.

"Ours," I said.

None of the children had ever heard their story. By the time they were old enough to wonder, they knew better than to ask Marcia anything about her life with me.

I started from the beginning. The Duncans' home, the bus, the stay with a cousin I barely knew.

For some reason, while they listened, they stayed close to the door.

"Why you didn't marry her if you loved her so much? You gave her your chil'ren but couldn't make her your wife?" Jackie asked. The accusation burned.

"We *were* married," I said. Hearing me say those words made me feel such pity. Such shame.

"You were married? All those years you were married?" Jackie straightened her clothes—something Marcia did when she was upset too. "Why didn't she tell us?"

"She hated me. I was an idiot."

"Not hard to believe," Patsy said.

"We all does act like fools sometimes," I said.

Patsy's bottom lip trembled only for a second. But in that second I recognized my child again.

"Look, I gointa take a li'l walk to the sea. If you wanta stay by the motorcar, I won't be too too long," I said, closing the door behind us.

"I'll go," Jackie said, and the two others followed.

It was a nice stroll. We passed by the warped wooden shack on the right of the road where they sold warm colas, beer, and end-of-the-week pastries. A few fellas had gathered on the wide steps, keeping loose eyes on bare-chested, shoeless children who scurried around them, all of them—men and children—looking more alike than not.

A chain and a Morris Minor blocked the pathway to the beach. I had heard an American or South African or some other foreigner had purchased acres of Blanchisseuse land to build a bed-and-breakfast, but I never thought the somebody would take ownership of the beautiful stretch of sand that bordered the village. I told the children to duck under the chain, and we proceeded downward.

"Where you headin'?" a deep voice called out.

I kept walking, but the children stopped.

A hard-faced white man, about my age, shirtless and covered in tattoos, stood next to the motorcar. "Semper Fidelis," the blue ink across his red-hued chest read.

"Always Faithful?" I pointed to the tattoo. "Does that mean somet'ing to you?"

"It's on my chest."

Wesley took one step off the path, into the surrounding clump of bushes.

"I'm sure you understand that trying to keep Trinidadians off a path we been using for generations is not only against the law, but it's not faithful to anyt'ing that's the true meaning of being a Trinidadian."

The man walked toward me, his back straight, his hands in slack fists. "Hooligans come and ruin this path every single day. I'm being faithful to the land by protecting it."

"It's not your land, mistah."

"Oh, it's purchased through and through by me," he said. "You need to remove yourself."

I couldn't take that fella seriously. I gathered the children in my arms. "I'm not taking my family off this path. We gointa go where we intend to go, and if you wanta settle this, meet me down there and we can settle it." I nudged the children. "Come go."

The man disappeared behind us as we walked down the slope blanketed with crushed pebbles. We were followed by two black-and-brown-spotted dogs, and surrounded on both sides by bamboo trees and overgrown red-berry bushes. The path was less steep than I had remembered but the sound of the water's spray was just as lovely as it had always been. The sight of the Marianne River, with only a narrow strip of white sand between it and the sea—nearly in a kiss—almost broke me.

The stray pups lapped up the cool, sure-to-be-a-bit-salty river water and splashed around on the banks while the children, each walking by themselves along the stretch of blue, took in their mother's land. Did they think of her, as I did?

I sat down on the warm sand. My feet sank into the powdery grains and I threw a few handfuls over my ankles. The cloth bag in my lap was heavy and as I rummaged through it the weight seemed greater, as if the contents had firmly rooted, deciding not to leave.

Tinfoil squares of tea leaves, nearly a hundred, each the size of a tea bag, were nestled at the bottom of a torn, brown paper bag that Tanty Gertrude had given me more than twenty years earlier. Tanty Gertrude had promised me that Marcia would never love another the way she would love me, and I had wanted that more than anything. Marcia had thought the tea leaves a kind gesture by a young man in love.

I opened the packets, one by one, until I had collected a mound of dark-red leaves. I stirred them, letting them roll between my hard calluses, feeling nothing but brittleness. Into the sand next to my hip I pressed the leaves deep into a cool hole and covered them.

I reached back into my bag and pulled out a small glass jar with a metal pinpricked top. It was a thick, oil-based brew Tanty Gertrude had given to me when I'd been feverish with pneumonia. I had rubbed it all over, under my arms, under my scrotum, behind my ears, just as Tanty Gertrude had instructed, and two days later I was back to work, after having been sick for more than two weeks. The day after I returned to the station, Nicole, who was by then all grown up, had offered herself to me.

I scooped out the mixture with a tree branch and buried it alongside the tea leaves.

The last item was a rancid-smelling, vinegar-based concoction in a glass jar no larger than a tin of sardines. Tanty Gertrude had given it to me to drink after I killed Rogers, promising me that I would never be convicted of murder.

Tanty Gertrude had served her purpose in my life. But Aunty Baba was right. For my children's sake, I needed to do away with that rubbish once and for all.

My bag blew down the shore as I headed into the ocean. The water to my knees, I gripped the open jar and poured the liquid into the lashing salt water. *OM Gam Ganapataye Namah.* I needed, I wanted, a new beginning. *Vakratunda Mahaakaaya Suryakotee Samaa Prabha Nirvighnam Kurume Deva Sarva Kaaryeshu Sarvada.* "O Lord Ganesh, with the brilliance of a million suns, please make all my work free of obstacles, always." I hadn't prayed in many years. Could God, in all His many forms and manifestations, have taken better care of me, my worries, my desires?

I turned back to the shore. My three beautiful children stood side by side, the water lapping at their ankles.

Jackie took the first step forward. She touched my shoulder. The touch was feathery, but with such lightness she lifted the weight of the world from me. Wesley and Patsy moved next. They reached out to hold their father for the first time since they were babies and I cried into the soft creases of their shoulders.

The ride back from Blanchisseuse was quiet. We arrived home in the dark of night.

"I'll see allyuh tomorrow," I said.

"You doing your shift?" Jackie said. The three of them stood outside the driver's window.

"Eh-eh, who you t'ink gointa feed you if I don't go and work?"

"You crazy," Patsy said. "Look at your eyes."

"I'm fine," I said, shooing them away.

JACQUELINE KARAM

There was a *boom-boom-boom* at the door.

"Patsy, you hear that?" Patsy smashed the pillow over her ear. "Patsy!"

I left the bedroom and walked, almost drunkenly, toward the front of the house. I hoped to see Daddy there, thirsty, recovering from a little knock into something. Instead, there was another *boom-boom-boom* and a troublesome light through the window.

I reached through the darkness for Wesley's warm body.

"Wesley." The chair was empty. We had all been so tired. Where could he have gone?

The two policemen were walking back to their car when I opened the door. "Hello?" The night air was cool. The sky so black the stars were like glitter sprinkled on ebony paper. The policemen turned and stared. I was in my pajamas and a head scarf.

"Are you Karam's daughter?" The officer spoke with a lisp.

"Yes."

"Your mudda home?"

"You can talk to me," I said.

"Your fadda's been in an accident. He's not doin' so good."

Wesley had fallen asleep in the latrine, dealing with a case of gripes. Patsy dressed quickly. The policemen drove us to the hospital.

In the bright lights, Daddy had lost all of his color, except for the bloody gash down the middle of his face. He looked frail. Not at all like the man who had been with us in Blanchisseuse, challenging a U.S. Marine to a duel on the beach.

"What's happening to him?" Patsy asked the doctor.

"We don't know yet. Most of your fadda's injuries are inside. We don't have the ability to see inside," he said. "But we know it isn't good."

Daddy wasn't able to talk. The hospital staff warned us that when he had tried to do so, dark blood had poured from his mouth.

"Daddy went to his mudda's house when he needed to reach Mammy, right?" Wesley said.

"His mudda and his fadda need to know too," Patsy said, never taking her eyes from Daddy's face.

"There has to be anudda place we can call from," I said.

"Go on, Jackie," Wesley said. "You're the only one who's seen any of them."

I took Daddy's wallet, where he had Mammy's phone number written on the inside of a ripped cigarette box, folded into quarters. With the money he had made that evening, I took a taxi to Valsayn.

It was two hours of searching until, finally, a few late-night partiers pointed me in the direction of the Karams'. "You knockin' them ole people's door this time of de mornin', chile?" They giggled in various stages of drunkenness. "Ole' man Karam's son'll cut ya good if he hear you stealin' from he fadda."

It was almost four in the morning. The night air was brisk and the clouds had slipped over the glitter, making the sky look patchy. Before we left home, I had changed into a long white skirt, but I was still wearing my pajama top and my blue cotton scarf was wrapped tight around my head. I wandered up the walkway to the very door I hadn't been invited to walk through my entire life. There was a small lamp lit in a front window. The kind of lamp old people believed kept burglars away while they slept.

I heard a man's voice. "Who's that knockin' at this time in the night?"

Someone pushed aside the white sheers covering the two windows. Our eyes connected. The sheers were refastened.

"Who you coming for at this time in the night, chile?" the man asked.

"The Karam family."

"Who?" he said. "Speak up! Is this some kinda game?"

"No," I said. "No, sir, it isn't. My name is Jacqueline. Karam. I'm Farouk's daughter."

There was a stretch of silence before the doorknob began to rotate. A tall man in a *kurta*—I presumed he was my grandfather—stood before me. He had a full head of glossy grey hair, heavy, hunched shoulders, and my brother, Wesley's, long-drawn nose. His eyes were a bleak brown, almost black, and surrounded by shadowy circles that hung like jack-spaniard nests almost to his cheeks.

"Who'd you say you were here for, chile?"

"For you, sir, Aja," I answered. My throat was dry. "I'm your son Farouk's second-oldest daughter."

"I don't have a son by that name," he said, with extraordinary certainty.

For a moment I doubted myself. Then there was the flash in his eyes. The flash that questioned whether the gal on his front porch was stupid enough to buy his lie.

"You're Karam, no?"

"I am."

"And you are my fadda's fadda, right?"

"Chile, I don't have a son by that name," he repeated.

The woman, my grandmother, called out to him, "Aamir, who you speaking to for so long at the door?"

That shrill voice was too unique to be forgotten.

"The chile has the wrong house," he said. "Go back in the room and rest yourself."

Her slippers scraped the floor, the sound moving further and further away. "You must go," he said. "My wife's not feeling well, and I ain't able with this nonsense." He began to close the door. I pushed my foot into the threshold.

"My fadda's in the hospital. He may die tonight." I thought I would choke on the words. The door gaped an inch or so more. "I have to call my mudda. She's in America and I have to tell her," I said.

My grandfather, my Aja, helped me dial the number. I had never used a telephone. He placed the receiver to my ear and whispered when it was time to speak.

The second Mammy heard my voice she wondered which one of her remaining children had perished.

"Me and Wesley and Patsy are all alright, Mammy. Daddy's not so good. I'm not sure what's gointa happen."

"He'll be fine," she said. "Calm yourself."

The doctors couldn't even find all of Daddy's injuries, but suddenly she was making me feel stupid for being worried.

"Don't let too many people know. It'll bring too much wrong attention and could mess up allyuh paperwork. I can't have you stuck in Trinidad because your fadda can't handle his affairs," she said.

"Daddy didn't do anyt'ing wrong." My grandfather sat across from me, his hands folded on the table. "Somebody ran into him on the road. He was working. Didn't you hear me say that?"

My grandfather watched me push the phone into my face when I couldn't get a word out between hers.

"Don't stay in them people's house," Mammy said. "I can't believe you went to them. Didn't I teach you anyt'ing?"

I didn't want to cry. But as I walked toward the door, with its drab, peach-colored paint and peeling brass knob, I couldn't help it. My Aja paced himself behind me, unsure of what to say to the whimpering granddaughter he had never met.

He pulled the door open. Then he slowly closed it, leaving me on the other side with dawn breaking over my chilly shoulders.

The doctors operated on Daddy two separate times. The first time to his spleen, which was a success. The second time to his liver, the success of which remained to be seen.

The hospital room stayed noisy. Waves of conversations from the families of the three other men who shared the room with Daddy swept over our thoughts. Patsy, Wesley, and I took turns going home to prepare food for ourselves.

For eight days we watched Daddy go in and out of consciousness. The lines around his eyes deepened, the skin on his cheeks slackened. A strange man came once to ask about him—a big, older Negro man with a crooked face and a slight limp. He didn't say much. He took a long look at Daddy sleeping, then he left.

One evening, while trying to play a game of All Fours with only three players, tired of being with one another but too scared not to be, we heard the click-click of heels. We always turned to see who was coming and going. That night we were hoping it would be the men coming to fix the hole in the ceiling that dripped-dripped-dripped brown droplets of water between our seats and Daddy's bed. But when we turned, it wasn't the maintenance men, another visitor, a nurse, or even a doctor.

"Allyuh playing cards or takin' care of your fadda?" Mammy's smile was as broad as the heavens. Her eyelids were heavy, but her skin glowed. She had the look of an American woman—"casual elegance," they called it in the magazines I'd seen tossed around in Port-of-Spain.

I ran to her first, and held her thickish body in my arms. She smelled like she'd been washed in a tub of cherries.

Wesley waited patiently, then hugged her long and hard, like a boy who'd gotten a second chance at his first love. He pulled at her blouse and smiled, as if to indicate that she'd done a good job with it.

Patsy's breaths were deep and I could see how much she wanted to throw herself into Mammy as we had. Mammy grabbed Patsy's hand and stroked the back of it. Then, she ran her eyes over to Daddy.

I hated how she stared at him. As if he was all done. "We didn't know you were coming," I said.

Mammy seemed to think better of what it was she wanted to say first, then she said, "How is he?"

"They come in, look him over, but they don't tell us much," Patsy said. Mammy was still holding her hand.

"Is he eating?"

"He wakes up only a few minutes during the day," I said.

Mammy walked over to the bed and rolled Daddy on his side. "Anybody making sure he does be clean and dry?" she asked. "Wesley, come over here and help me."

She touched Daddy's bottom and grabbed Wesley's hand. "Feel here." She pressed Wesley's hand into a wet spot. "You want your fadda to lie in his own piss? He wouldn't want Jacqueline and Patsy doing this. You must make sure to keep him clean."

Wesley immediately began to tend to Daddy.

"Allyuh speaking to him?" Mammy said.

What could we say to someone who wasn't going to talk back?

"Jacqueline, you must talk to your fadda every minute. Use your big voice," she said. "If you in here, speak to him. Get a book and read it out loud. The man is alive. And if I know him, he wants to stay that way."

Mammy rolled up her sleeves. "Patsy, come here," she said. "You need to make sure to bring him broth every day. Make a different one every two days and bring it for him with a straw. Lots of provisions and other vegetables and make sure you boil it and grind it down real real good so he doesn't have to chew it, you hear? Even if you're boiling all night, when the morning come, your fadda must have somet'ing to eat."

Mammy, dressed in flat brown shoes and a white cotton dress with cap sleeves, went back to the hospital the next morning. After that, she rarely left Daddy's bedside. I don't know what she did there all day with him, but by the fourth day, the leaking ceiling had been patched, the doctors were coming in three times a day, and the nurses were checking up on Daddy and changing his bandages. Daddy had opened his eyes each day she was there, but it wasn't until the sixth day that he realized it was her.

His thick eyelashes were crusty, his skin ashen. He squinted and pushed the words out from his lead tongue. "You here?"

"Where am I supposed to be? I'm here with my chil'ren who, for some strange reason, does feel the need to take care of you."

"Listen to the freshwater Yankee." Daddy eyed Mammy with what looked to be deep satisfaction and went back to sleep.

Mammy looked exhausted.

"Go and rest," I said. Daddy had had some good days. Mammy had helped him sit up and take his first gulps of water. He had listened intently whenever Mammy was reading to him. But the night before, he hadn't slept well and Mammy had been arguing with the doctors. "I'll stay with Daddy," I said.

Mammy was picking up her bag filled with books and fabric from the floor when Mr. Philip Aldous approached the edge of Daddy's drawn curtain.

"Good morning," he said.

"Good morning," Mammy said.

Since Daddy had been hospitalized, I had seen Mr. Aldous only once. We had arranged to meet at the market on my way home one evening. It had been a short visit, one warm embrace.

"I take it you're not here to have anudda discussion with her fadda about your intentions, right?" Mammy smiled.

"I might have a better go of it with him in a hospital bed." Mr. Aldous peered down at Daddy. "I hope you're not in here too much longer."

Finally, he looked over at me. He had this way of winking, so that no one but me could see it.

"When will you go back to America, Miss Garcia?" he said.

"We're leaving next week." Mammy adjusted her books in the bag. "I've already been here longer than I t'ought I would be."

"Who's we?" I said.

"You know you and Wesley comin' back with me."

"We can't," I said. "Daddy's here."

"Your fadda's doing betta. Patsy will mind him. If the t'ree of us go back, we can work and send money so Patsy can take care of your fadda until he's ready to get back to driving his taxi. He'll be a driver with lots of action stories to tell now."

Daddy reached for Mammy's hand.

"They belong with their mudda, Farouk." She fanned her hand. "You knew I was comin' back to get these chil'ren."

"Mammy, please." I moved next to Daddy, taking his fingers in mine. "What are we gointa do there? Wipe behinds?"

Mr. Aldous moved closer, as if hoping he could protect me from Mammy's wrath.

"Eh-eh. Getting you outta Trinidad is the best t'ing I can do for allyuh and that's what I'm gointa do," she said.

Mammy squeezed past Mr. Aldous and myself, and left the room.

Daddy looked toward the finger-smudged window. He watched the rain fall like standpipe water from the roof.

"Jacqueline, let's take a walk," Mr. Aldous said.

The rain slowed almost as soon as we walked onto the outdoor staircase. The sun seemed to be dueling with the clouds. "Your mudda is right. It's betta she take allyuh and go."

My mind was in a million places and I had little patience for nonsense. "I hate when you make like your nine years means you know so much more," I said. "I'm not a chile." Raindrops glistened on his forehead and gathered at the top of his thick-piled hair.

"You can't stay here, doing nutting with your life, working at the shirt factory, taking care of your fadda," he said. "That's no life."

I closed my eyes, not wanting to see into his. "What about us?"

"I'll come and see you," he said.

"Truly?"

There was naughtiness in his eye. "It's probably the only way I can get you to stop calling me Mr. Aldous."

Wesley was at the Singer when I arrived home. He had been on the machine almost every minute since Mammy had come back, trying to finish all the work he had taken on. The Singer felt like his now—his chair, his materials, his work.

"You alright?" he said, with his back turned.

I told him yes and began to make dinner. Patsy came home from work before the batch of curry potato was finished. We told her Mammy's plans. "Somebody's gotta stay here," she said. "It's alright." Then, almost to herself, she said, "You t'ink they let foreigners join the police in America?"

The three of us ate a late dinner together and listened to the radio news. Prime Minister Dr. Eric Williams was looking forward. "We have been passive agents of a history made and written for us by other people," he said. "We are determined now to write our own history."

It was almost midnight when Mammy walked through the door. She was bright and wired, as if it were morning.

"Which one of allyuh can drive your fadda's car?" she said.

"Mammy, the car is all smashed up. Jackie barely got it here," Wesley said.

"If the engine works, it's drivable." Mammy walked over to the stove and lifted the lid off the pot of curry. "This smells good." She picked at a mushed piece of yellow-curry potato and sucked it. Then she looked past the curtain, into her room, at the bed she hadn't slept in once since she'd arrived.

Chapter 23

MARCIA GARCIA

When I was a little girl my father's mother lived in Toco. My father would take me and Ginny there on the weekends. It was a magical place. Like a fairyland. My grandmother would shower us with cookies, cakes, fresh bread. She would take us to the sea and sit for hours watching us bathe, feeding us snacks from her hand as if we were fragile chicks. She would cross her feet, the left on top of the right, brace her body's weight against her hands, which were buried in the sand, and jiggle her toes with delight, as she watched Ginny and me play with the turtles and dive headfirst into the water, hoping to catch a fish in our mouths.

On a piece of paper found in her bedroom, my grandmother willed her house to me and Ginny. When we had to leave Blanchisseuse to save Daddy from the embarrassment of Ginny's pregnancy, we went to Toco. We pretended we were two grown-up women on holiday, living in that house alone, waiting to learn about how to birth a baby.

We spoke to no one, until the night Ginny woke up screaming and peeing all over the floor. My father had given us only one instruction: "When the time comes, go and find a woman and tell her you need help."

I knocked on four doors before I found a woman willing to leave her bed.

"I'm Tanty Rose's grandchile!" I screamed. "My sista's having a baby!"

The strange woman's face flushed with embarrassment when we arrived back to my grandmother's house to find Ginny there crying, her belly so big she looked like just one pinprick would send her sailing away.

"Who sent you here?" the woman asked me.

"My fadda," I said, though she didn't seem to hear me.

I wanted to tell her that Ginny wasn't a bad girl. She was only sad because my Uncle Linton brought food for us now that Daddy couldn't walk. I wanted to tell the strange woman that me and Ginny had been the smartest girls in our classes, yet we didn't know how that baby got in her belly.

But Daddy had sworn us to secrecy.

"Run down de road until you see a li'l green house on de right and knock on de door. Ask for Mildred and if you tell her Miss Julie send you, she'll come," she said, pushing my backside.

I ran screaming Miss Mildred's name. It didn't take long before almost everyone in Toco knew what was happening.

When me and Miss Mildred got back to my grandmother's house, I knew something was wrong. There was pink water on the floor.

"Mildred, I t'ink it's two in there!" Miss Julie screamed from the bedroom.

Miss Mildred kicked off her slippers at the front door and ran into the bedroom, which had been my grandmother's. "This chile is having a baby?" I heard her ask.

It seemed like hours before I saw any of them again. I paced the floor, nervously excited. Until we had left Blanchisseuse with a bag of food and a few dollars from Daddy, Ginny and I hadn't been allowed to leave the village without Mammy or Daddy. Being in Toco for a month, without an adult, having a baby by ourselves, had been scary and lonely, but it had also felt like a grand adventure.

Until the quiet came.

Miss Mildred came out of the room. Her hair was frizzy, tight, crunchy from sweat. "Who sent allyuh here?" she demanded to know. She braced herself against the table and watched me.

I wanted to bend around her to see inside the room. I wanted to see Ginny. "My fadda," I said.

She pulled up my chin. Her lips were cracked. She had had nothing to drink and the house was baking. "Who's your fadda, chile?"

"Clifford Garcia. This is my grandmudda's house."

Her mouth parted, just enough to slip something the size of a slice of orange through it. "You them two li'l ones that does belong to Tanty's boy?" she asked. "The two who used to come and visit she?"

"Yes."

She wiped her eyes. "Tanty would be sad. She talked about allyuh 'til her last breath."

"Did somet'ing happen to the baby?"

"There's two babies. They're not well, you hear? Don't tell your sista. She's very weak. Don't talk for long." She held my head between her hands and nudged me into the room.

The other woman, Miss Julie, was holding the two quiet, light-brown babies near the window. Dark red blood was on almost everything. My big sister, my Ginny, my best friend in the world, was covered in a blanket that seemed to be growing a larger bloodstain with every second that I stood there.

"Marcy, I don't feel good." Her voice was hoarse.

"Don't worry." I rubbed her hand, but couldn't keep my eyes off the blood crawling closer and closer to her chest.

"The babies alright?" she asked. "I don't hear them."

"Fine," I said, though I didn't know what "fine" looked like in two tiny babies.

"I don't feel so good," she said again. She cried loud tears, if there could be such a thing, and put her hand lightly on her belly. "Take care of them, alright? Keep them like they is your own."

I touched her soft, wet hair and watched the bloodstain crawl up to Ginny's chin and swallow her up like a wild river.

I can't remember whether it was Miss Julie or Miss Mildred who took the bus ride back to Blanchisseuse with me and the babies. What I do remember is hearing the beginning of the conversation between the woman from Toco and the women of Blanchisseuse. I held the two limp babies in my arms and walked into my father's house.

It wasn't long before there was a knock on the door.

My father hadn't moved from his chair since I showed him the twins and told him Ginny had died.

"Garcia, come out here!"

There were maybe a dozen women screaming at him. *Murderer. Rapist. Immoral. Cheater. Liar.* Some true things. Some not.

"Leave today!" they said. "And leave them chil'ren here!"

My father put up a fight, yelling about it being his damn house and his damn property. Then the men, who had been watching from the road, moved toward the door. "Garcia, you don't want us to have to take this any furder. We can't have you livin' here no more."

My father limped back inside. "They're making me leave, Marcy. It won't be for long. But you mustn't talk, you hear me? Even if you know it's a lie, leave it that way," he had said.

No one, not even the few cousins we had in Blanchisseuse, ever set foot in that house to help me. I was a nasty little secret everybody wanted to forget. My own father never wrote a letter, never sent money. I would have died happily never seeing his face again.

• • •

When Farouk's car would go no more, a taxi picked us up. My father was standing in the yard when the taxi pulled up to the house. He stared at the strange car. He looked stronger than I remembered, but had the same face I knew as a child.

I stepped onto the road.

He strained to make out my face. When he saw Jacqueline, a look of recognition crossed over him. "Marcy?" He moved forward with indecision before each step. He stood inches from me. "You lookin' good," he said.

"Jacqueline tells me allyuh put Yvonne into the ground here," I said. "Can you show me where?"

"You gointa take her?" he said, as if it wasn't my right to do so.

"I'm her mudda."

"I paid to have her next to your grandmudda and Ginny. I been keeping her grave tidy."

We walked for nearly half a mile. I kept glancing behind, hoping the taxi driver wouldn't leave while Jacqueline listened to my father tell stories of the times he would bring me and Ginny to Toco. He spoke as though they had been some of the best times of his life.

The air was unusually mild. We stood high up on a hill overlooking the sea. It was a place Ginny and I had once climbed, racing to see which of us could get there faster. We had laughed so hard after we got to the top. We fell onto the grass and giggled until our breath was nearly gone.

Who would've thought her small body would be there without me next to her?

I crawled over to the dark soil piled next to Ginny's marker.

Yvonne and Ginny were probably the same height.

"Yvonne . . ." My voice cracked. "It's Mammy."

My fingernails gripped the soil, the burn in my nostrils and my eyes felt like hot oil. I bent my neck and buried my forehead into the cool soil, right where I imagined Yvonne's little stomach would be, and I cried so hard I thought I would bind myself up into that earth and die right there. "Yvonne," I sobbed. "I'm sorry Mammy wasn't here with you."

Tears and dirt smoked my face.

After a long time, I gathered myself and pushed my aching body up from the ground. My father stood against a tree. Jacqueline sat in the tall grass behind me, looking out over the cliff.

I didn't want to leave. Ever. I would've buried myself in the chilled dirt right next to Yvonne and closed my eyes for a deep eternal sleep. But I had three living children.

As we walked back to the taxi, I could feel the heat from Jacqueline's arm on mine.

"I'm so sorry," she said.

"For what?"

Tears poured down her face.

I grabbed her by the shoulders, turning her to me. "You didn't let her die. Don't ever t'ink that."

As we walked back toward my grandmother's house, I suddenly, desperately, wanted to leave Toco. But I couldn't.

I walked at a measured pace. Slowly. Hoping not to scare the two men tilling the soil at the outskirts of my grandmother's yard. Tall. Handsome. Their hands, large and wide, their skin, the perfect color of wet sand, their unruly hair high atop their oval heads. They worked in the dirt, in earnest, side by side, as they had done when they were children.

My father stayed behind me, but Jacqueline didn't lose step.

They looked up.

"Ainsley? Franklin?" I had given them formal names. I had wanted their lives to be lives of distinction. "It's your aunty."

Their eyes moved across my face, then down to my hands, but nothing registered.

I walked closer. I had thought I would feel overjoyed, overwhelmed, unbelievably delighted if I ever saw them again. All I felt was a quiet relief.

• • •

It's strange how I can think, for so long, that I'll feel a certain way when something happens and then when it happens, I behave completely different.

I thought I would feel horrible—guilty and sad—for leaving Patsy, for leaving Farouk in a hospital bed unsure if he'd ever get out. But when I boarded that plane with Jacqueline's and Wesley's fingers gripping mine, headed to our new lives, I was as close to happy as I had ever been.

ACKNOWLEDGMENTS

I am grateful first to my parents for reading every page again and again: Jennifer DeGannes Francis, one of the seven wonders of my world, who loves me as a mother was meant to love—because of you sharing *your* stories, I could envision *this* story; and Leonard "Terry" Francis, who answered the phone when I most needed it, enthusiastically offered wonderful stories and insight, and who, by example, showed me how this is done. I love you both forever and forever.

To my grandmother, Jane, for her courage. So many questions left unanswered. Writing this story helped me understand better.

To my husband, Anand, my best friend. Thank you for your wisdom, enormous heart, and for giving me the space. You are the true love of my life. To my children, Sage and Ava, whose zaniness gave me fortitude, whose presence in my life made Marcia a possibility. Without you two, this book does not exist. To my sister, Halcyon, who said yes to watching the children during this story's birth. You were the key to this journey. I am extremely proud of you and I will always love you.

To my dear friends, Dr. Tricia Bent-Goodley, a woman whom I admire endlessly and who never let me forget HIS plan, and Tanisha Lyon Brown, for the belly laughs, for letting me cry, and for believing from the beginning. Love you both so much! Much love to Tebogo Skwambane and Raqiba Sealy Bourne for your friendship and love, to Amanda Bastien, a great friend, who helped me see the meaning behind every setback, to William Cameron for your endless encouragement, to Alexa Dupigny Samuels for always checking in, and to her father, Michael "Bunny" Dupigny, for a wonderful chat about coming to America. To the members of my original writing group: Fataima Ahmad-Warner, Jonathan Roth, Lois Berge, Toby Perkins, and Donna Sokol. You beat me down, then lifted me up. Thank you. To my in-laws, Anita Sharma and Khemraj Sharma, who fed me delicious food and kept me in prayer. I love you both. To my cousin, Neal Charles, for your patient explanations and who, without fail, always found the answers. To all those who, along with the grandmothers, took care of and loved my children when "Mommy" couldn't be there: Patricia Williams, Teresa Leite, Mona Francis, Nadia Raphael, and Donna Raphael. It takes a village, indeed! To my agent, Victoria Sanders, the woman who has made me smile from the moment I met her—you ARE the best. Also to Bernadette Baker-Baughman, who kept things moving with great humor. To Benee Knauer, my first real fan—New York is alive and well because of you! To my wonderful editor, Barbara Jones, classy, smart, witty, and fierce—the perfect answer—thank you for being such a champion. To Maggie Richards at Holt for such unbridled enthusiasm. To Steve Rubin, Pat Eisemann, Melanie Denardo, Joanna Levine, and the entire team at Holt for all your support and encouragement. To the memory of Dr. F. Elaine DeLancey, who in her professorial brilliance taught me how to see. I hope I make you proud. To Morgan, my original muse—I miss you very much. To Karin Focke and Susan Lynn Martin, who saw it and then made me believe it. To Jane Wu Adams, for your healing hands. To my friends and family who kept me in their thoughts during this process. Thank you! And most importantly to God, who never let me forget that I had a dream that needed attention. Thank YOU.

SOURCES

Mendes, John. *Cote ci Cote la*. Trinidad, West Indies: New Millenium First Edition, 1986.

Watkinson, Freya. *Nelson's New West Indian Readers*. Nelson Thornes Ltd. Educational, 1978.

Williams, Eric. *Capitalism and Slavery*. London, England: Andre Deutsch Limited, 1964.

———. *History of the People of Trinidad and Tobago*. New York: A&B Publishers Group, 1942.

'TIL THE WELL RUNS DRY

by Lauren Francis-Sharma

*A
Reading
Group Gold
Selection*

For more reading group suggestions
visit www.readinggroupgold.com.

PICADOR

picadorusa.com

LAUREN FRANCIS-SHARMA, a child of Trinidadian immigrants, was born in New York City and raised in Baltimore, Maryland. She holds a bachelor's degree in English literature with a minor in African-American Studies from the University of Pennsylvania and a J.D. from the University of Michigan Law School. A former corporate lawyer, she lives in Kensington, Maryland, with her husband and two children. *'Til the Well Runs Dry* is her first novel.

"I thought about how I had never asked her questions about herself. I had never asked about her life, about her journey to America from Trinidad, about why she left home."

Credit: Sonia Suter

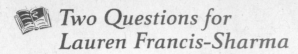 ## Two Questions for
Lauren Francis-Sharma

What was your inspiration for writing 'Til the Well Runs Dry?

'Til the Well Runs Dry is a story that comes out of one small moment in a hospital room. When I was still nursing my youngest daughter, my grandmother had a stroke. With the baby asleep in the car seat, we drove into the night from Baltimore to Brooklyn to see her. As I was sitting next to my grandmother's hospital bed, I thought about how I had never asked her questions about herself. I had never asked about her life, about her journey to America from Trinidad, about why she left home. There were so many questions and I felt such an immense sense of loss.

Nearly six months after my grandmother had that stroke, my paternal grandfather passed away. My parents, my sister, and I had to travel to Trinidad for the funeral. While we were there, we were in a pretty reflective mood, and we took a trip up the North Coast Road to the village where my grandmother was born, Blanchisseuse, which is also the place in Trinidad where the novel opens. We took a walk along the beach, and I sat down in the sand. I felt very connected to the place. It's a lovely, quaint town, and I imagined it felt much like it would have seventy years ago. I thought about my grandmother being a young woman there, and when I rose from the sand, I realized I had to write a story about a girl from this place. That girl became Marcia Garcia, the protagonist of 'Til the Well Runs Dry.

Before writing 'Til the Well Runs Dry, you had a distinguished career as a lawyer. What made you decide to become a writer?

I think I had always imagined myself as a writer. I had invested so much into being a lawyer, though I was not always a happy lawyer. I knew from pretty early on after law school that lawyering was not the thing that would make me most happy. I was a second-year associate at a firm in New York City, and had one of those moments that a lot of lawyers have, where you are just shaken to your core by some incident that takes place. Usually, those happen in a law firm [laughs]—sorry, law firms!

Nonetheless, I was working on a deal for a client, and we were logging very long hours for several weeks, in fact, pulling all-nighters. It was football playoff season, and the senior associate on my deal wanted to have a party at his home to support the New York Giants. We needed to prep for closing, and he asked me if I could handle it, and I said I could, because, indeed, we both thought I could. He told the client that he was going to leave me in charge of closing prep. The client lost his temper, and told him that he would not be leaving his deal "with the [expletive] coat-check girl." I think that was probably the moment when I realized that practicing was not going to be fulfilling enough, and definitely not worth *that*.

I left the office immediately, and walked to the local bookstore, which was one of my favorite places. I cried a little bit, and strolled around, looking at the books there, pulling myself together. After a half hour or so, I walked down the steps, and who was standing there just outside the bookstore? One of my favorite authors: Stephen King. It was a really amazing moment for me. I was obviously at a fork in the road of my life. Law practice or . . . something else. And there was Stephen King. I walked up to him, and I said, right to his face, "I love you!" And of course, he looked at me oddly. Rightfully so! But for me, that moment was simply joyous. To see him reminded me of how much I loved reading, and how much I love to write. And how much I had wanted to be like him. That moment stayed with me through those many dark times as an unhappy lawyer and a closet writer trying to get published.

"I walked down the steps, and who was standing there just outside the bookstore? One of my favorite authors: Stephen King."

Discussion Questions

1. Each chapter in *'Til the Well Runs Dry* is told from the perspective of one of three characters. Why do you think the author chooses three characters to tell the story? How do you think this choice enhances the storytelling?

2. Why does Marcia choose to keep the story of the twin boys a secret from Farouk?

3. Tanty Gertrude is known to dabble in obeah or the "darker arts," as the author suggests. Do you think Farouk understands the inherent risks when seeking help from Tanty Gertrude?

4. Tanty Gertrude tells Marcia that her relationship with Farouk did not work out because Marcia has too much pride. Marcia, however, feels that Tanty Gertrude sabotaged her relationship with Farouk for her own benefit. Who do you think is correct? And why?

5. Why do you think Marcia is so firm with Jacqueline?

6. Freedom vs. commitment are important themes in this book. How does a desire for freedom inform each character's story? What role does commitment play in limiting the characters' desire for freedom?

7. There has been a lot of discussion in literary circles about the likeability of characters, particularly female characters. Do you feel you have to "like" or "identify" with a character to enjoy a novel? Do you like or identify with Marcia?

8. In telling the story of Marcia Garcia and her children, the author paints a memorable picture of Trinidad's natural beauty, particularly of the northern coastal village of Blanchisseuse. In the earlier parts of the novel, Farouk wishes to take Marcia away from Blanchisseuse, yet close to the end of the novel, he takes a day trip there with the children. Why do you think it is important for him to return?

> "I had been there many times without her, but I had never felt her in that place in quite the same way I felt that day, with my children's breath on my neck."

9. How is Farouk's character revealed over the course of the novel?

10. What do you think is the reason behind Patsy's rebellion?

11. Inspector Chung Marlock tells Marcia that she is the kind of woman "who's always looking to find a way out." Do you think this is true of Marcia? What impact do these words have on Marcia?

12. For Marcia, New York City symbolizes risk. How does going to New York change her?

13. Were you surprised at the end of the novel when you found out about the twin boys? How do you think Marcia's life would have been different if they had not been taken away from her?

14. This novel sheds light on many of the challenges immigrants face in America. Why, after all the mistreatment she suffers, does Marcia still feel as if bringing her children to America is the best decision? Do you feel more informed about recent immigration history after reading this book?

 ## A Deleted Scene

*In this deleted scene, Marcia and the children are
in the hospital with Farouk when his family pays
him a visit. Ultimately, I decided this scene was more
for me than for my characters. As much as I wanted
Marcia to have a moment like this, she did not need
this melodrama to move on from her past.*

Farouk's father turned and smiled politely at Wesley
and Patsy. He stared at Jacqueline a moment longer
and I was reminded that she had gone to their home
to call me while I was in New York. Farouk's mother,
not surprisingly, refused to acknowledge my children.

I picked up my bag from the chair. I would not be a
part of that charade.

"Marcia," Farouk said. "Don't go."

"Let she go!" his mother said.

"Ma . . ." Farouk said to her.

"Ma, what?" She turned to Farouk. "She's the
reason we're all here in this filthy place looking at you
half-dead." She turned from him to Farouk's brother.

"Abdul, take me home. I knew we shouldn't have
come here."

Abdul stood motionless for a moment before
turning to Farouk, then to the children, and finally
to me. "My parents have been ruined because of the
shame you and your children have put upon our
family."

The first words that man, my brother-in-law, had
ever spoken to me were those?

"Let us go," I said to the children.

Wesley, Jackie, and Patsy seemed too stunned to
move. I reached out for Patsy's arm, while Farouk's
mother suddenly rushed to put herself in front of me.
"You're not going anywhere until I have a few words
with you."

I looked over at Patsy whose eyes were wide, filled
with trepidation. I hated that someone else could
make my children feel small. They had no reason to
feel small in front of those people.

"Miss Lady," I said turning to Farouk's mother.
"Please remove yourself from in front of me and my

chil'ren before I does really get angry."

I looked over at Farouk's brother. I hoped he would
have the good sense to interfere. But all Abdul Karam
did was sigh. He could not control his mother any
more than Farouk.

I exhaled. Then, I braced myself and shoved
Farouk's mother aside. I had been waiting for years to
put my hands on that woman.

She gasped for breath and stumbled into
Jacqueline.

"Who you t'ink you is?" Abdul bellowed out from
his brother's bedside.

I didn't bother to look at Farouk's expression. It
didn't much matter. I was watching his mother. She
had shoved off Jackie's helpful hand and moved
herself back to the bed to stand next to her two sons
and her husband.

I turned my back on them. I was leaving. Farouk
and his family could all go to hell. I had been through
too much to stand in that hospital room and have any
one of them judge me. What had I done other than
to fall in love with a man who had brought nothing
to my life but children to take care of and a whole set
of misery? I moved toward the door. The patient with
whom Farouk shared the room, a man with his left
hand bandaged and his right arm in a sling, watched
me as I walked past his bed. I could feel him urging
me to stay and fight. And as I watched him, a perfect
stranger cheering me on, it occurred to me that the
shame that I felt, the fear that I felt, the humiliation
that I felt, was more about the past than about the
present. It was more about breathing new life into an
old history and giving the past a new lease because I
had chosen to keep it in the darkness. I had nothing,
absolutely nothing to be ashamed of, to fear, to be
humiliated about. Nothing.

I stormed back to Farouk's side of the hospital
room, practically spitting fire.

"Who I does t'ink I am?" I shouted. "You know who
I am? I'm the mudda of your grandchil'ren." I pointed

to Mr. and Mrs. Karam. "The grandchil'ren you've never seen until now, never loved and never cared to be with. That's who I am. I raised four chil'ren who have allyuh's blood running t'rough them and allyuh have been nutting but evil."

"You, having babies for my brudda, does not a family make," Farouk's brother said.

"Abdul, you have no right," Farouk said. I raised my hand to Farouk. Nothing he said twenty years after the fact could right the many wrongs.

"Please don't give us your sad story," Farouk's mother added. "You were a fast woman who already had two boys and you tried to trap my son. You didn't, and still don't deserve, anyt'ing from this family."

My children looked from Farouk's mother back to me. They had never even heard such an accusation leveled at me. They wanted it not to be true. I could see it in their eyes. Two boys they never knew about?

"What did you know about me?" I said, jabbing myself in the chest with my finger. "What did you know?"

I thought about leaving again. I did not want my children to hear about my life in that way. They didn't deserve that, did they? Then I realized that what they deserved, what I owed them, was to speak the truth.

"Did allyuh know them two boys left in my care were my sista's chil'ren? Did allyuh know that as she gave birth to them and died in my arms, she made me promise I'd raise them and take care of them as my own? What did allyuh really know?" Farouk's father lifted his eyes from the floor. He looked at me, really looked at me, for the first time in his life. "Did allyuh know that if I told people that they belonged to her, they woulda known my sister had been raped by my own uncle and them boys would've been taken from me? Did you know anyt'ing about me? You spread lies to your son about a woman who loved him. Who really loved him. And you made him hate me and resent his own chil'ren," I said, more sure of myself than I had ever been.

Farouk's mother cheupsed. "And we should believe you now?"

"Who you t'ink is responsible for getting your son outta that jail?"

"My husband!" she screamed. "His fadda. At great sacrifice."

"Lady, you don't know about sacrifice. Sacrifice is telling my uncle, Linton Beatrice, to get Farouk outta that jail in exchange for leaving my chil'ren in Trinidad to fend for themselves. That's sacrifice. My uncle is the same man you believe helped you to set your son free. You did nutting for your son. Nutting," I said, shooing her with my hand. "I've always done right by Farouk Karam."

The air felt different the moment the last word fell from my lips. There were questions in the eyes of Farouk and the children and answers yet to come, but I had finally made my peace with the truth.

A Snapshot of Lauren's Writing Process

Here's a photograph of a hand-edited page from the part of the book I read aloud to audiences most often.

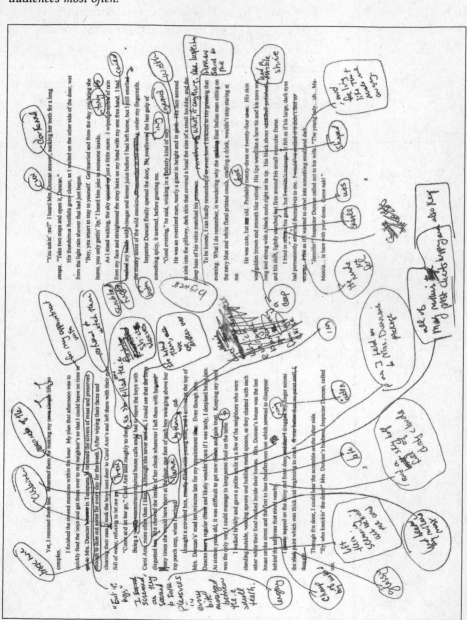

 *Recipes*

With a distinctive blend of African, Indian, Chinese, and indigenous influences, the cuisine of Trinidad infuses the sensual environment of *'Til the Well Runs Dry* with its resplendent sights, smoky aromas, and rich flavors. From the stewed chicken that Marcia ladles into her children's bowls at dinner, to the rum punch that Patsy mixes at the Five Rivers' snackette, here are three of Lauren Francis-Sharma's favorite recipes—no opossums involved.

CURRIED POTATO AND CHANNA (CHICKPEA)

1 cup of chickpeas soaked overnight

2 tbsp vegetable or canola oil

2 tsp minced garlic

1 cup diced onion

1¼ cups of water

2 tbsp curry powder (taste will vary depending on variety and freshness)

1 tsp ground cumin (optional)

2 cups of sliced or cubed potatoes

2 tsp salt

1 tsp black pepper and/or Caribbean pepper sauce, to taste

A curry that has time to cook a bit before the addition of meats or vegetables has a more full-bodied flavor.

Directions:

1. Boil chickpeas until tender and drain.

2. In large pot, heat oil over medium heat. Add garlic and onion. Sautée.

3. Heat 1 cup water and set aside.

4. In separate bowl, mix curry powder (and ground cumin, if desired) with ¼ cup water. Add curry/water mixture to pot and stir constantly. Add potato, ensuring that all pieces are coated with curry. Add the cup of heated water, salt, pepper, and/or pepper sauce.

5. Cover and cook for approximately ten minutes.

6. Stir in chickpeas (careful not to break peas). Cook until gravy is thicker and potatoes are tender. Add water for additional gravy.

7. Adjust for taste with salt.

8. Serve with rice.

*Reflecting
on the Food*

STEWED CHICKEN (TRINIDAD STYLE)

6–8 small pieces of chicken OR 3 lbs sliced or cubed (dark, light or both)

2 tsp garlic powder or minced garlic

2 tsp lemon juice

1 tbsp salt

1 tsp black pepper

1 tbsp vegetable or canola oil

3 tbsp sugar (preferably brown) OR thick soy sauce

½ cup chopped onions

¼ cup chopped tomatoes

1½ cups water

Directions:

1. Toss rinsed chicken pieces with garlic, lemon juice, salt, black pepper. Let sit for five minutes.

2. Heat oil in large pot, add sugar (or thick soy sauce) to middle of pot and allow it to brown and bubble. Add chicken, onion, tomatoes, water. Cover pot and cook on medium heat (stirring occasionally) until chicken is tender and gravy thickens to desired consistency.

3. Add a little more water for additional gravy and adjust to taste with salt.

4. Serve with rice.

Rum has a long history in the Caribbean and the rums of each island have distinct flavors. This recipe requires the rich flavor of dark rum, preferably from Trinidad, which is harder to find in the U.S.; if you must substitute, try another dark West Indian rum.

RUM PUNCH

2 cups sugar

1½ cups of water

4 tbsp lemon juice

¼ tbsp Angostura bitters

6 tbsp dark rum

½ tsp very fine nutmeg (dust)

*Reflecting
on the Food*

Directions:

1. Boil sugar and 1 cup of water in small pot for five minutes until syrupy.

2. In a small pitcher, combine sugar/water mixture with lemon juice, Angostura bitters, rum, ½ cup of water. Stir well. Sprinkle with nutmeg.

3. Allow to sit overnight (in direct sunlight when possible).

4. Serves two over ice.